At what price a cure? At what cost a miracle?

The Healing Powder

Lynne Martin

My favorite of the three.

LYNNE MARTIN

CLB.

iUniverse, Inc.
Bloomington

The Healing Powder
At What Price a Cure? At What Cost a Miracle?

iUniverse books may be ordered through booksellers or by contacting:

iUniverse
1663 Liberty Drive
Bloomington, IN 47403
www.iuniverse.com
1-800-Authors (1-800-288-4677)

ISBN: 978-1-4759-2311-7 (sc)
ISBN: 978-1-4759-2310-0 (hc)
ISBN:978-1-4759-2309-4 (e)

Library of Congress Control Number: 2012907909

Printed in the United States of America

iUniverse rev. date: 6/15/2012

DEDICATION:

I dedicate this work of fiction not only to my husband, and my family, but also to my teachers. Those special individuals who struggled to instill a love for Shakespeare and a deeper understanding of calculus with limited resources and fluctuating attendance during harvest.

I grew up in a small rural community in Western Canada. In later years, many post secondary classmates have argued whether a school in such a community can provide an adequate education. Both schools I attended had dated equipment and sometimes more than one grade in the classroom. However, I believe my education was superior to what I could have received in a crowded city school

The latest in software and first-rate chemistry equipment cannot compete with the hands-on encouragement and personal attention lavished on each child. When your teachers know your grandparents, and routinely share coffee with your mom and dad at the local hockey rink, you become part of an extended family in a small town. In such a family, everyone is looking out for your best interests.

The annual Christmas concerts and sport teams in our small town were only possible because of the untold volunteer hours of our homeroom teachers working hand-in-hand with our parents. With this kind of personal attention, I would never consider my education as second-rate.

With the consolidation of many communities, Canada's rural schools are slowly disappearing. I believe this is a loss for the children. I wish that the youngsters of my community could experience that special care and attention that my generation was so very fortunate to receive.

To those teachers who have retired, or passed on...your contributions are greatly appreciated, and I will never forget your extra efforts. A special thank-you to my English and Drama teachers: G.F., L.C., K.W., M.C., P.F., and of course, a special thank-you to H.M. Without your love of the written word and your continual encouragement, I would not have the skills or the perseverance to write today, and I definitely would not be able to comprehend and even enjoy Chaucer's *Canterbury Tales.*

Lynne Martin / CLB
www.lynnemartinbooks.com

The Healing Powder

A Novel by

Lynne Martin

CHAPTER ONE

"Women need a reason to have sex, men just need a place."

—City Slickers, 1991

The coconut rum was almost 40 percent alcohol, but with the inherent sweetness effectively coating her taste buds, Camille barely registered its potency. Stopping for yet another swig from the half-empty bottle, she continued to stagger down the hill toward the communal fire pit, her skimpy tank top, and form-fitted jeans already soiled from previous falls.

At least a hundred kids had congregated at the party, so with the music blaring from the portable speakers mounted in the back of a Jeep, very little could be heard over the general thumping of the bass.

Camille nearly fell flat on her face for a second time, and grabbed an unknown shoulder as she stumbled by, barely able to right herself until the very last second. When she finally reached the outer rings of the bonfire, she continued to trip over the empties and collected deadwood, literally bouncing off the dancing bodies as she searched for any familiar face. She'd come with her boyfriend Todd, and his buddies, Ramon, and Grizzy, but no matter how many trips Camille made around the fire, she still couldn't spot them. Tonight was the first summer party after high school graduation, and she was pissed off that she seemed to be spending most of the night alone.

She flopped onto the trampled grass, and dropped her shoulders in defeat, fixating on the rum bottle cradled between her knees. The reflection of the fire dancing off the walls of glass caught her attention, briefly blinding her to the two sets of legs circling her.

"Camille, where the fuck you been?" Ramon laughed, the first to drop down onto his butt, nearly knocking her over with the gentle nudge of his massive shoulder.

"Where's Todd?" she slurred, continually blinking her eyes as she attempted to focus on their darkened faces.

"Give me a shot," Grizzy demanded, reaching into the inner circle of Camille's legs, roughly brushing one of her denim-covered thighs as he snatched the rum bottle from her clutches.

"Damn girl, this shit's straight," he said, shaking his head. "But still good," he admitted, throwing back the bottle for another long pull.

"Give it back, it's mine," she barked, reaching up and ripping the rum out of Grizzy's dangling hand.

"I think you've have enough," Ramon interceded, inadvertently knocking the liquor bottle out of Camille's wobbly grasp.

"Fuck, there goes my rum," she mumbled. She clasped Ramon's shoulder in an awkward attempt to right herself, struggling to rise to her feet. "Todd has more booze in the car," she announced, struggling to turn and make her way back up the hill.

"I'll help you," Grizzy announced, moving to follow her back toward the parked cars winding along the gravel road.

"Wait for me," Ramon yelled out. "No way are you guys going

to leave me here like last time—no booze, no smoke, and no ride home."

Camille accepted Ramon's helping hand, and allowed him to drag her up the hill, nearly falling twice when she lost her footing on the steep incline. "Where's Todd?" she asked for the hundredth time, still bothered by the fact that she hadn't seen her boyfriend for the better part of an hour.

When they finally reached the road, Ramon suddenly turned to shove his right elbow into Grizzy's ribs, motioning toward the two partially clothed bodies thrashing around in the back seat of Todd's car.

"Todd?" Camille called out in disbelief, lunging forward and yanking open the passenger's rear door.

"Oh fuck," her boyfriend groaned as he rolled off the naked girl laying in the backseat of his car, his rock hard cock popping out from between her legs during his dismount.

"You bastard!" Camille screamed, slamming the door shut before turning to escape into the darkness of the gravel road.

Todd scrambled to pull up his pants, finally jumped out of his own car, and shouted, "Camille!"

"She's long gone," Ramon shook his head.

"Find her," Todd barked at Grizzy, turning back to face the disapproving stare of his other friend.

Grizzy turned to follow orders, and began trotting down the gravel road, calling out Camille's name, peeking into car windows and open SUVs.

"Leave me alone," a familiar voice cried out in the night.

As he moved toward Camille's voice, Grizzy stopped to watch another inebriated partier try to entice her to join the private party in his car.

"I said piss off!" she shouted, leaving no doubt about her lack of interest.

"Camille," Grizzy called out. "Are you alright?"

When she turned, oncoming headlights suddenly illuminated her face. Camille began to sob, the tears rolling down her face and falling into the shadows at her feet.

"Come on, let's go," Grizzy sighed, throwing his arms around her shoulders and leading her back down the road.

"He was fucking her, wasn't he?" she wailed, stopping dead in her tracks as they began to near Todd's car. "I don't want to see him. I hate his guts, he's a scumbag loser… and… and he was fucking her," she muttered again through her tears.

After checking over his shoulder to see if anyone was watching, Grizzy quickly leaned in a pick-up window and snatched two beers from an open cooler, before gently guiding Camille off the road toward a grassy field, away from all the commotion. "Let's take a walk," he offered, linking the muscular fingers of his left hand through the petite fingers of her right.

Camille allowed him to lead her into the darkness, stumbling along at Grizzy's side. She tried to shake off the fog that threatened to descend down over her consciousness.

"Sit with me," he encouraged her, turning and dropping down to the soft clover of the farmer's hay field. Not so much out of interest as out of necessity, Camille joined him on the ground.

"Beer?"

"Why not." She shrugged her shoulders, accepting the can and downing a large quantity of the chilled liquid.

"So, you gonna be fine?"

"He's such a jerk," she began to whimper again, her emotions raw from the fresh betrayal and over-consumption of coconut rum.

"It's alright, baby," Grizzy attempted to comfort her, slipping her right arm around her shoulder and pulling her firmly toward his side. "You deserve better. I've always thought you were too hot for a guy like Todd."

"Really?"

"Really," he nodded, his left hand reaching up and turning Camille's face in toward his own. "You could have any guy you want. You're gorgeous."

She laughed, and blinked, trying to focus on Grizzy's features when he moved in toward her face. When she felt Grizzy's lips pressed up against her neck, Camille dropped her head back and allowed him to continue nuzzling her skin.

"You're so hot, baby," he growled, his right hand sliding down the small of her back toward the gapping space between her denim jeans and her bare ass.

"Thanks," Camille dropped her chin, attempting to pull her head and body away from Grizzy's affections.

"What's the matter? We're just starting to have some fun."

"We should go back," Camille suggested, picking up her beer and downing another slug.

"Alright," Grizzy agreed. "But, can I have one kiss first?

Camille turned back toward her ex-boyfriend's lacrosse teammate, and was about to launch into a speech about how she wasn't ready to jump into another relationship, when Grizzy took the lead and pushed her back down toward the grass.

"I know you want me just as bad as I want you," he growled in her ear, as he held her down with his two-hundred-ten pound frame. "I'll never fuck around on you," he promised, while his left hand rushed up under her tank top, and cupped her naked breast.

"Please don't," Camille begged. "Don't touch me." She began to thrash underneath his oppressive weight, fighting to free her face from his slobbering kisses as her own long hair began to hamper her movements.

"What's the matter?" Grizzy continued with his attempted seduction. "We're both adults, and maybe what's good for the goose is good for the gander." His muscular legs pinned her lower torso to the ground.

"Grizzy! Get the fuck off me," Camille shouted, releasing the hold on her beer to reach up and push against the weight of his crushing chest.

"Shut up!" he barked back, pushing down his face to try to match his lips with hers.

When she suddenly felt Grizzy's massive hands pin her wrists to the ground, Camille fought with all her might to wriggle out from under his oppressive weight. It was a futile attempt.

In response to her struggles, Grizzy transferred both her wrists to his left hand, freeing his right to reach down and roam freely up the length of her entire body. He finally settled on the roundness of her left breast, roughly massaging the tender tissue with the brute strength of his entire palm. Grizzy finally pulled his mouth off her bruised lips.

"Help!" she shrieked, her muffled screams instantly drowned out by the pulsating music and vehicle engines.

"Don't worry, baby," he hissed in her ear. "This is gonna feel real good. I promise," Grizzy vowed, moving his hand down to the front pocket of his jeans.

"I don't want to have sex," Camille shouted up into his face; her emphatic statement just bounced off his glazed eyes and fell uselessly down past his ears.

"You've been waving your ass in my face all night," he reasoned, ripping open the condom with his teeth as he dropped his hand down to his own crotch to free his cock.

She was now fighting for more than just her personal comfort. She violently twisted her head back and forth, and spit in Grizzy's face, attempting to bite any soft tissue she might be able to reach with her teeth.

Grizzy responded by yanking up her multi-layered tank tops,

freeing her naked breasts before forcing his hand down between their bodies toward the button on her low-rider jeans.

A wave of panic suddenly washed over Camille. The huge body of the athletic male pinning down her one-hundred and twenty-pound frame was real. And unless someone showed up immediately to rescue her, the impending rape would be very real, too.

Todd had been by his ex-girlfriend's house at least twice a week for the last month and a half. But Camille wouldn't relent. She didn't speak to him again after that awful night, or the morning after the party, and try as he might to apologize, she just wouldn't have anything to do with him.

"Please?" he begged the family's housekeeper. "I know she's out back by the pool, cuz I saw her sitting up on the diving board when I drove past. I just want to speak to her for five minutes. Then I'll go. I promise," he solemnly vowed.

After she finally admitted the young man into the foyer, the housekeeper went out to alert Camille.

Camille agreed that she might as well get it over with. She rose from her lounge chair and wrapped a towel around her slender waist as the housekeeper left to retrieve her guest.

"I'm so sorry," Todd blurted out the minute he was within earshot. "I don't know what the fuck I was thinking. I don't even know that chick's name."

"Whatever." Camille turned her face away as if staring off toward the pool house before returning to her chair.

"Do you think we have a chance?" Todd begged, reaching across the table to pick up her hand.

Camille turned to stare right back into his eyes, leveling a gaze that could have stopped a clock. "No!" she said.

"Well, I just wanted to let you know how sorry I was," he explained, pulling his hand back from her clammy fingers. "It's been kind of lonely. Ramon is working full-time at his dad's store and Grizzy is taking summer classes at his college."

Camille took a deep breath to calm the nausea rising in her throat. "Actually, I do need to talk to you about that night."

"I know. I was so blitzed, I shouldn't have been such an asshole, I should…"

"Listen," Camille interrupted his rambling apology. "I'm pregnant, and I want to have an abortion."

They'd only been dating for two months prior to the bush party, and had only had sex twice during their entire relationship. Frankly, Todd was a little surprised that she would name him as the father. "I thought we were careful. I thought…"

"I know," Camille cut him off again. "I'm not even sure you are the father," she blurted out just before the housekeeper arrived with a pitcher of kiwi-strawberry juice and two tumblers filled with ice.

As he reached for the pitcher's handle, Todd poured himself a shot, and downed the liquid while he scrambled to make sense of the conversation.

"Grizzy raped me that night in the grass field, while you were too busy banging that cunt you'd hooked up with. You didn't even care where I was," she began to cry, dropping her face back down into her hands.

"What?"

"You heard me," Camille shouted back. "He pinned me to the ground and shoved his cock inside me while I screamed for help."

"Why didn't you tell me when you got back to the car?" Todd demanded.

"I don't know," she ripped a tissue from a box on the patio table before suddenly standing. "I was so mad at you, and hurt by Grizzy, that I just wanted to go home and get away from everybody. I just wanted to hide."

"Did you call the cops?"

"Yes," she quietly admitted, her back turned, shoulders still shaking as the tears silently rolled down her cheeks. "But they said I'd have to come in and fill out a full statement of complaint to make the charges. I couldn't do it anonymously. But I can't go public," Camille stopped to blow her nose. "My dad would freak."

Nodding his head, Todd rose from his chair and stepped around the table to face Camille. "Do you want me to go with you to the cops today?"

"No, I just want to get rid of it." She dropped her gaze to the tiled patio, sneaking a peek at the flatness of her stomach on the way down. "It costs about $900 at Planned Parenthood, but I don't want to go there. They have protestors and reporters outside. No one can know about this. I want to go to a normal hospital, and it costs about $2,000. Can you help me out?"

"Yes, sure, you know I will," Todd continued to stumble. "But Grizzy, he brags about being the *King of Rubber*. You know, he always has condoms in his car, his locker, his gym bag."

"I guess it ripped when he was struggling or something. I don't know," she cried again. "All I know is that I'm pregnant, and unless someone helps me raise the two grand, I'm really fucked."

"I'll get it," Todd promised, not exactly sure how, but confident that he'd be able to find a way.

The drive had only been three hours long, but the cramp in Todd's neck and lower back made him feel as if he'd been on the road for days. Following the handwritten instructions scrawled on the map from Grizzy's mom, Todd made his way up the two flights of stairs and stood outside the door of his buddy's dorm room.

"Looking for me?" Grizzy called out, strolling down the hall with a girl in tow.

"Yes," Todd simply stated.

"I'll stop by later," Grizzy whispered to his companion, patting her on the ass as she turned and made her way down the opposing hall.

"Why didn't you call me and let me know you were coming down? You could have brought up a shitload of stuff I forgot," he casually chided his childhood friend, before turning to open the door to his room.

"I hadn't really planned this," Todd mumbled, following Grizzy into his messy quarters. "I just needed to talk to you."

"Forgot how to punch a number in your cell?" he teased.

"Listen," Todd started in, unwilling to continue with the casual banter. "Did you have sex with Camille at the bush party back in June?"

"Why?"

"Grizz, don't fuck around. Just answer the goddamn question!" Todd demanded, kicking a pile of dirty clothes out of his path.

"Well, we were both really drunk."

"Did you get a little rough, maybe force yourself on her?"

Grizzy leaned down and grabbed two cans of soda from his mini-fridge, throwing one in Todd's general direction, without even asking if he was thirsty. "Look man, I didn't do anything illegal. And if she says different, she's messing with your head."

"Save it," Todd barked. "She's not going to the cops, but she's pregnant and wants an abortion."

"Fuck me," Grizzy moaned, dropping onto his bed. "I can't be the father, I used a rubber," he argued in his own defense.

"So did I," Todd added. "But it's either you or me, so I figure we're each going to cough up half. That's a thousand bucks a piece."

"Like shit I'm going to blow a grand when there's a fifty-fifty chance I'm not even the father," Grizzy argued back, rising from his bed to open up his can.

"Fine," Todd conceded. "Camille can let the cops decide who's responsible. They can do a little DNA testing for paternity, and…"

"A check okay? Cuz I don't keep that much cash around in a place like this."

"A check will do," Todd nodded, as Grizzy yanked his wallet from his desk drawer and began to scribble an amount on the blank check.

CHAPTER TWO

"Sometimes the things you want the most don't happen and what you least expect happens."

—Love & Other Drugs, 2010

Olga Heinz turned the dial on her stove, and set the oven to three-hundred and twenty-five degrees, just the desired temperature for baking cookies. She loved to be in the kitchen, developing and testing new recipes, but unfortunately living alone, no one was home to share in her creations. So every couple of days, Olga boxed up her newest offerings and carted them off to the hospital staff lounge, leaving them out for whoever was interested. Nursing, cleaning, and general hospital staff alike all partook of her goodies; everyone but the doctors who were intentionally sequestered in their own private lounge. Tomorrow morning, everyone would be treated to peanut butter cookies, assuming they first passed Olga's own taste test.

After digging through her cupboards and refrigerator, she began assembling all the ingredients; even before cracking open the first egg. Satisfied that she had everything she needed, Olga turned on her kitchen radio and began to bake. Starting with a large plastic bowl, she dumped in half a cup of room-temperature crunchy peanut butter, one cup of soft, spreadable margarine, and one cup of a white sugar mixture instead of the usual brown sugar. Then Olga took a deep breath and began to make her adjustments.

She'd been working on writing *An Everyday Cookbook* for years. She wasn't a young woman, so before her retirement from the hospital, Olga planned to finish her pet-project. Over the years, she had tirelessly compiled a collection of recipes for lower-income families who might not have many of the usual ingredients listed in all the generally accepted cookbooks. Olga knew that cooking from scratch was much cheaper than buying many prepared foods, but if you had to spend extra money on special ingredients, then there would be no savings.

There were two different ways to replace a cup of brown sugar in baking recipes. With a previous batch of cookies, she had tried the first method, using one cup of white sugar with a teaspoon of molasses on top. This time she substituted a quarter cup of pancake syrup and three quarters of a cup of white sugar instead of the more costly brown sugar. With a table fork, she began beating the margarine, and brown sugar substitute. Satisfied that she had mixed it thoroughly; she added two eggs, one teaspoon of salt, and one teaspoon of vanilla extract and began mixing again.

She set the bowl aside, and dumped in two-and-a-half cups of flour. She stopped to make a note that a standard fourteen-ounce can of pork and beans washed out and dried was a decent two-cup measuring unit. Measuring a teaspoon of vanilla extract, and one-and-a-half teaspoons of baking powder, mindful not to heap the teaspoons, but always shaving off the top with a knife, and she was ready to do the final mixing. She always employed the small techniques she had learned from her grandmother when she was a young woman, almost forty years before.

Olga clanged her fork on the edge of the bowl to clean it, and then picked up a large wooden spoon. She began to stir the concoction, careful not to send clouds of flour swirling onto her kitchen counters. Looking back over her recipe, she checked to make sure that she'd noted the fact that most dollar stores now carried vanilla extract, baking powder, and baking soda for very reasonable prices. The ingredients were cheap and the recipe easily yielded two to three dozen cookies. It looked like she'd found another winner for her files.

With her fingers, she scraped the clinging cookie dough off the spoon and began to knead it with her bare hands. Olga rolled balls of the dough about the size of a small meatball, and dropped them into a small bowl of white sugar. Then, she placed them a couple inches apart on an un-greased cookie sheet. When the sheet was full, she picked up a fork, and pressed down to flatten the balls until they were only half an inch thick, leaving the fork marks visibly patterned across the top. After sliding the first tray into the oven and setting the timer for twelve minutes, she turned back to the second cookie sheet. She began rolling another twelve balls of cookie dough, mindful to brush a small wisp of brown hair from her cheek with the back of her hand.

She pulled the first tray out of the oven when the cookies had spread out and turned golden brown. Then Olga attempted to use her newest gadget, a homemade metal cookie spatula. When she had previously opened a large can of tomato juice, she'd kept the circular top. She had previously bent one quarter or the circle upwards at a ninety-degree angle. She grasped the short side, shoved the remaining three quarters of the metal circle underneath the hot cookies, and slid them onto her counter to cool. Satisfied with her ability to make the transfer without having to purchase a spatula, she couldn't help but smile at her own ingenuity.

When she was finished with her baking, Olga cleaned up her mess, before sitting down at her kitchen table with a cup of freshly brewed tea for a taste test and a chance to record a few handwritten notes. With her stocking feet up on the vacant chair beside the kitchen table, she couldn't help but notice the varicose veins crisscrossing her lower calves.

When she'd been a young girl, she'd had a decent set of *gams*, more than one doctor commenting on her figure with a wink and a subtle smile. But now, pushing sixty, time had definitely taken its toll, not to mention the forty-four hour weeks spent on her feet for the past thirty-four years.

As she finished the last cookie on her plate, Olga turned and looked at the kitchen clock. It was just about nine thirty p.m., so she'd have to hurry if she wanted to be ready for the ten o'clock movie, a remake of the Billy Wilder classic that had stared Audrey Hepburn, Gregory Peck, and Humphrey Bogart. She's heard that the *Sabrina* of the nineties, starring Julia Ormond and Harrison Ford was supposedly just as good, but as with all things in life, she'd reserve judgment until after she had a chance to form her own opinion.

After boxing up the remaining cookies in an old chocolate tin, Olga wiped up the counters and quickly lifted her cookie sheets off the drying rack, setting them down on the corner of the stove while she bent down to open the oven's bottom drawer. Without realizing it, she had precariously balanced the two metal trays on top of an old heavy-handled paring knife, and when she reached up her hand to pull the trays off the top of the stove, Olga accidentally dragged the knife to the edge of the stove and sent it plummeting downward toward her leg.

As the finely honed blade sliced downward through the air,

picking up speed and continuing on its vertical path, the point hit home. The knife stabbed directly into the soft flesh padding the bone, just inches above Olga's kneecap.

Olga's gaze dropped to her wounded leg and followed the blood as it began to run in fresh rivulets down her calf, and drop with tiny little splatter marks at the base of her heel.

The seasoned nurse shook off the shock of the moment, and grabbed a dishtowel. She pressed down on the wound with her left hand at the same moment she pulled out the knife with her right hand.

The gash was deep; the blood was beginning to pour out at an alarming rate. By the time Olga had wrapped the towel around her leg and applied the appropriate pressure, she had a puddle on the kitchen floor the size of a dinner plate. She hobbled over to the kitchen table, and dropped down onto the first available chair, winded from the simple act of hopping across her floor. Maybe she needed stitches? There was only one way to tell, she'd have to pull off the towel and take a peek.

"Here we go," she mumbled, carefully peeling off her impromptu bandage and gazing down at her bleeding wound.

The slash wasn't more than an inch and a half long, running vertically down her leg just inches above her right kneecap, but the depth of the wound was Olga's ultimate concern. The knife had landed point first, stabbing her deep tissue before continuing on its path toward her kneecap. Stitches wouldn't be a bad idea, but with stitches and an open wound came the obvious hospital report and the mandatory time off. No, she wasn't interested in logging a medical leave into her personnel record with the promotional reviews only a month away. Hell, she was a professional nurse. She'd take care of herself and she'd be fine. After all, she was scheduled in post-op, which translated into hours of observation and a good chance to rest her leg and take it easy.

Camille Greenway grabbed her overnight bag and her tennis racket before strolling into the family dining room. She had purposely made a production of announcing her plans to spend the weekend at Mindy's house to enjoy a pool party and the tennis pro the family had graciously hired for the weekend.

Nobody bothered to question her plans; it was the summer before college, she was expected to have fun and be ready to settle down to her studies in September. After all, she'd be leaving for school in just one week.

Camille was certain that no one at the breakfast table would imagine that she, the youngest member of the Greenway clan, was on her way to a private clinic to terminate an unwanted pregnancy. But then, why would they? She was only a bubbly, seventeen year old, cheerleader. Why would they have guessed that she was about to hand a stranger two thousand dollars to reach up into her uterus and yank out an unwanted fetus?

She passed on breakfast, since the clinic's receptionist had instructed her to ingest nothing but water twelve hours prior to the procedure. An unnecessary warning, since she couldn't have swallowed a bite of food if her life depended on it. "Good bye." Camille forced herself to wave, stoically turning to leave the comfort of her home.

Todd waited silently in his car, watching the front of the house, nervously strumming his fingers on the steering wheel. Clearing his throat as he watched her step out the door and rush toward his car, he reached across the seat to grab the inside handle and push open the car door for her entry.

"Let's go," she announced, discarding her tennis racket by throwing it into the back seat before turning forward to clutch her monogrammed bag.

"I drained my account," Todd offered Camille a stuffed white envelope. "I was able to come up with eleven hundred and forty bucks, but I can't get Grizzy's check to clear. The bank has to get a hold of his dad, since it's over five hundred dollars, and he won't be back into town until next Friday."

"What?" she screeched. "I'll be away at school by next Friday. What did Grizzy say?" Camille shouted directly at her ex-boyfriend's face, his chiseled good looks suddenly melting into worry.

"I've tried him a hundred times, but he won't take my calls."

"I'm so screwed," she wailed, no longer feeling concerned that someone might walk out of her house and see her crying in the front driveway.

"I have an idea," Todd confided, "but you're going to have to lie about your identity."

Camille's neck seemed to snap as her head suddenly spun back toward Todd's face, already nodding her agreement, not the least bit concerned with any of the details, as long as the ultimate goal was achieved.

"Miss Ramirez," the nurse called out.

Todd gave Camille's hand a quick squeeze, prompting her to rise from the waiting room's chair and make her way toward the beckoning nurse.

"I'm Maria Ramirez," Camille confirmed, turning and solemnly nodding back at Todd before she disappeared behind the door.

Lying back on the table, with her feet secured in the stirrups, Camille nervously waited for the doctor to come into the room and take care of her problem. To complete the procedure... deal with her concern… or whatever other terminology the County hospital wanted to assign to her abortion.

"How are you doing?" Olga Heinz asked the young woman as she checked her vitals and continued to prepare for the doctor's arrival.

"I'm fine," Camille mumbled, turning her head away from the nurse in an attempt to hide her tears.

"This won't take long, dear," she attempted to comfort the patient. "You have arranged for a ride home? Right, honey?"

"Yes. My boyfriend's in the waiting room," she only half lied. Todd wasn't her boyfriend anymore, but he was waiting for her. "He'll drive me straight home as soon as I'm done," Camille confirmed their intended plans just as the examination room's door swung open.

"Good morning," the doctor smiled upon entering the room. "My name is Dr. Hood, and I'll be performing your procedure."

Camille slowly nodded her head as she fiddled with the hair-tie now adorning her wrist, unsure what she was expected to say to a man about to kill her baby.

"Has Nurse Heinz fully explained the procedure to you?" he routinely inquired, turning to scrub his hands thoroughly before donning a fresh set of gloves.

"Yes," Camille forced out the one syllable reply, not bothering to waste empty words on a conversation soon to be erased from anywhere in her memory banks.

"Thank you, nurse," the doctor turned, accepting the towel from Olga's hand. "Well, well, I didn't know you were scheduled back in day surgery this month?"

"I was in post-op, but you know staffing—transferred at the last minute."

The doctor assumed his position at the foot of the bed. "Nurse Heinz and I have worked together for years, longer than I believe you've even been alive." He nodded, lifting the sheet to assess his patient before beginning the procedure.

Camille winced at the doctor's initial touch, and then turned her face away, wishing she was anywhere in the world but here. She prayed that it would be over within a minute; hoping that she'd blink and wake up in her own bed. The young girl screwed her eyes shut and unconsciously began to hold her breath.

"I'm going to turn on the suction," the doctor explained. "Please don't be alarmed by the noise." He nodded at Olga, signaling her to take her position at the patient's side, where she usually held the girl's hand in a gesture of comfort.

The noise wasn't terribly loud. It actually allowed Camille to focus on something other than the dull ache in her lower abdomen as the doctor moved some sort of instrument up inside her uterus and began moving it around. The shot that the nurse had given her earlier had dulled her senses and numbed a degree of the pain, but she was still aware that some kind of evasive procedure was taking place up inside her lower body cavity.

"Almost done," Olga stroked Camille's left hand as the young girl's fingers suddenly twitched in a nervous response.

"We're finished," the doctor announced, standing up from his sitting position and snapping off his rubber gloves. "Do you have any questions?" he gently asked his patient.

"No."

"Well then, you take care, and please remember to come in for your follow up examination. It's very important for your long term health."

Camille nodded as the doctor left the room and the nurse moved to the foot of the bed to clean her up before the orderly came to wheel her into the recovery area.

"Just close your eyes and rest," Olga instructed her, confident that if the patient really allowed the sedative to take hold, she might actually be able to nod off and catch a few minutes of sleep in recovery. Quietly swabbing the young girls inner thighs and pubic area, Olga then moved the patient's legs up and out of the stirrups, placing them gently back down on the table as she secured a leakage pad between Camille's closed limbs, suddenly aware that the patient had indeed succumbed to the medication and finally nodded off to sleep.

After she held the door open for the orderly to wheel the snoozing patient carefully out of the room, Olga took a deep breath and leaned back against the sink. She carefully raised her own pant leg to check on the wrapping just above her knee. The blood had soaked through the gauze pad and first layer of bandaging, and was now threatening to stain her uniform. Gingerly unwrapping her dressing, Olga prepared to re-bandage her wound just as the door suddenly swung back open.

"Nurse Heinz," the orderly interrupted her, looking for further instructions.

Spinning to hide her own wound, Olga accidentally knocked the canister of aborted fetal tissue from its position on the suction machine. The lid popped open upon impact with the floor, sending the liquid splashing up her legs, where it soiled her shoes, both pant legs of her uniform, and saturated the area of her open wound.

"Oh, I'm sorry," the orderly began to apologize. He immediately stepped forward and tried to help with the clean up.

"It's fine," Olga assured him, as she reached for a towel to blot her soiled uniform. "Go call housekeeping." She shook her head as the blood and liquefied tissue continued to spread through the weave of her cotton and polyester uniform. "I'm going to the locker room to change into clean scrubs and wash up."

The orderly nodded his head in agreement. "I'm so sorry," he added once again, "Let me pay for your cleaning or buy you a new pair?"

"No, it's okay, just go call housekeeping." After she dismissed the worried young orderly, whom Olga was positive made less than a third of her salary, she hurried down the halls toward the back stairs and made her way straight to the women's locker room.

"What happened to you?" another member of the staff asked. She had a startled expression at the amount of blood running down Olga's right leg and dripping directly into the white leather of her shoe. "Did you get cut?"

"No, I was just caught in the cross fire," Olga assured her fellow nurse. "Just going to clean up and change my uniform," she explained, turning away before dropping the scrub pants and exposing her concealed wound.

Washed, changed, and re-bandaged, Olga moved toward the nursing station. Reaching for the last patient's file, she immediately scanned the recorded history for any mention of AIDS, Hepatitis C, or any other blood borne diseases. Luckily, she found nothing on the patient's file. She hoped that the girl had been telling the truth, especially since the patient's fresh blood and tissue had invaded the perimeters of her open wound.

CHAPTER THREE

"I don't blame people for their mistakes, but I do ask that they pay for them."

—Jurassic Park, 1993

A twelve-hour shift was a long time to be on your feet, especially for a fifty-nine year old woman, but nurse Olga Heinz held her own and never complained. Not a single person would ever know that she'd shown up to work with a wound that would have sent most people rushing in to the emergency room. Olga was not soft, and a cup of blood wasn't about to derail her day-to-day plans. She may be graying, but she still had the stamina to match any twenty-five year old nurse on her floor.

"Paper or plastic?" the grocery boy repeated for the second time as Olga stood in line and scanning her additional shopping list.

"Oh, paper is fine," she finally acknowledged, nodding toward the pile of recycled bags piled in the corner of the cashier's stand.

She followed the grocery boy as he pushed the cart across the asphalt parking lot toward her car. Olga was surprised to find that her leg wasn't bothering her any longer; the painkillers obviously were numbing her receptors, as they walked silently through the darkened lot.

"You want your bags in your backseat or the trunk?"

"The backseat," she smiled, unlocking the door and stepping out of the way as her groceries were loaded inside. Tipping the young boy two dollars, she slid into her driver's seat and took a moment to check her to-do list before heading out of the parking lot toward the pharmacy and dry-cleaners.

Two more stops and she was finally home. Unbelievably, her leg still wasn't throbbing at all. So, even before she took the time to change the dressing, Olga decided that she'd unload the groceries and put away her supplies.

"Knock, knock," a female voice shouted from her backdoor.

"I'm inside," Olga called out to her neighbor. "Watch the bags. I'm still putting my groceries away."

After she dragged in the recently purchased twenty-pound bag of flour, Helen dropped the heavy load down onto the kitchen counter. "You're the only woman I know who buys flour on a weekly basis. Maybe you should just dial up and order a bulk truck that delivers flour to the bakeries? You know; the ones that carry about thirty thousand pounds at a time."

"Why don't you put on the kettle," Olga shook her head, stowing the remainder of her groceries before taking a break to make a couple of sandwiches. "Ham or salami?" she asked, holding up both deli-wrapped bags.

"Either," Helen answered, reaching into the fridge to grab the butter and mustard. "You want some gherkins with the sandwiches?"

"Sure thing. I'll be right back," Olga excused herself, grabbed the fresh bandaging supplies from the pharmacy, and headed off to the bathroom. Not even bothering to close the door completely, she quickly undressed before turning and pulling the tape and gauze padding out of the bag before taking a seat on the edge of the bathtub to check her wound.

"Good," she nodded to herself. The seepage had obviously abated, and the top layer of bandaging was not the least bit soiled or stained. Olga carefully slid the scissors up under the gauze and began to snip. Without warning, the pad she'd placed atop the open wound slid right off her leg, only a few droplets of dried blood evident on the cotton as it fluttered down to the bathroom floor.

Staring down at the cotton dressing and then back up at her leg, Olga almost lost her balance and slid back off the edge of the tub.

"It's… it's all healed," she mumbled in amazement, setting down the scissors and leaning in to inspect the wound's location further. Suddenly changing her mind and rising to her feet, Olga wet a face cloth and began carefully dabbing at the line of dried blood, her mouth dropping open as the brown, scabby-like clots also fell off her leg and ended up on the floor.

"Sandwiches are ready," Helen called out from the other side of the bathroom door.

Olga never answered; she was too absorbed in her personal investigation even to notice that Helen had gently pushed open the bathroom door.

"What you doing?" Helen asked, walking over, careful not to step on any of the discarded bandages.

"I was changing my dressing, but… but it's all healed."

"Well that's lucky. So, let's have our supper. I bought a new movie, and I thought we might be able to watch it later. It's all about a hockey team from the 1980 Olympics in Lake Placid. It's got that yummy little actor Kurt Russell in it."

Olga raised her face and just stared at Helen, not having heard a single word she'd just said. "You don't understand. It's all healed up… without even a scar."

"I heard you," Helen argued back. "And I'm no doctor, but isn't that a good thing?"

Olga bent to the floor, and began throwing the discarded bandages into her wastebasket. "Yes it's good, and I've always been a fast healer, but this is quite extraordinary."

"Maybe it wasn't as bad as you first thought."

"Well, I never had it stitched, but it was really deep. It took me at least half an hour to clean all the blood off the kitchen floor last night."

"You cut yourself last night?"

Olga threw her new cache of unused supplies into the medicine chest and squeezed right past her neighbor. She pulled the boiling kettle off her stove, and began making a pot of tea to enjoy with the sandwiches, while Helen settled herself on the other side of the breakfast nook.

"You telling me that you cut yourself yesterday, bled all over the kitchen floor; and tonight you're all healed?"

"I know it sounds crazy, but that's essentially what happened," Olga admitted.

After picking up the two plates of sandwiches, complete with pickles and potato chips, Helen followed Olga as she led the way to the living room, carrying two steaming mugs of Earl Grey tea. "Did anyone look at the cut besides you?"

"No."

"Well, then it probably wasn't as bad as you thought. Probably more of a scratch than a cut. Must have just sealed itself up."

Olga sipped her tea, balancing her lunch plate on her lap as she sat back and watched Helen feed the DVD into the machine. "But it was really bleeding last night."

"Shh," Helen shushed her. "I love the previews. It's like watching a handful of movies for free."

Both women began to munch on their late night supper, each lost in the depths of her own thoughts.

The entire movie had run past Olga's eyes without her even registering a solitary scene. Helen had laughed at the characters, cheered the non-stop action, and cried at the conclusion—three of the qualities necessary for good entertainment. But Olga just hadn't been able to get her mind around the story. She'd been too busy replaying the last twenty-four hours of her life.

"Well, thanks for watching the movie with me," Helen abruptly rose from her seat. "I gotta run. I have to open the shop tomorrow and the first wash and set is coming in at eight."

Olga bid her guest goodnight and locked up the back door, strolling through her house and flicking off the lights as she made her way into the bedroom.

Undressed, sitting on the edge of her bed in her nightgown, Olga couldn't help herself from inspecting her leg one last time. There was nothing. No mark, no scratch, no trace of a healed wound… just smooth skin.

She yanked open her nightstand drawer, reached in, and grabbed the magnifying glass she used for her petit point, determined to examine every inch of skin above her right knee. Still, there was no evidence of a wound anywhere. She couldn't find any sign of a laceration—neither fresh, nor healed, or anything else in between.

She put away the magnifying glass, pulled her feet up onto the bed, and threw the thin summer covers over her legs. As she switched off the lamp and lay back against her pillows, she couldn't help but picture the pool of blood on her kitchen floor. There was no way in hell she'd imagined that.

CHAPTER FOUR

"Life's simple, you make choices and you don't look back."

—The Fast and the Furious: Tokyo Drift, 2006

When she woke and began to dress for her shift at the hospital, Olga suddenly froze. Something was obviously different with her leg, and she needed to take a much closer look. Padding into the kitchen in her bare feet, she set her foot up on the kitchen chair and examined her own right leg under the bright morning sunshine.

"Oh my god," she whispered, suddenly glancing around the empty kitchen to see if anyone was peeking through her windows.

The patch of skin over her original wound site was not only healed, but the skin appeared perfect, just like that of a newborn child. There was no dryness, no pigmentation, and no signs of aging at all. It was if she'd had a palm-sized patch of brand new tissue grafted directly onto her leg in place of her own fifty-nine-year-old skin. This was unexplainable.

She noticed the time on her kitchen clock, and rushed back

to her bedroom, finished dressing, and made her way over to the hospital. Still scheduled in day surgery, she checked the roster to see which physicians were on the floor for morning rounds. Unfortunately, Doctor Hood wasn't back today, and personally, there was probably no other physician she trusted enough to even mention her concerns.

"Morning Olga," a third-year nursing student called out as she took up her position at the desk.

"Morning Clair. How many scheduled for today?"

Claire grabbed the roster, and began running down the list. We have six first-trimester vacuum aspirations, and two second-trimester dilations and subsequent evacuations after that. I don't see any saline infusions, or hysterectomies listed for our department."

Olga made a few abbreviated notes on her personal pad, smiling to herself, amused with Claire's textbook announcement of the morning's surgery schedule. As she continued to reorganize all the patient charts that the resident doctors had pulled for their morning rounds, the senior nurse quickly set her station into working order.

"Can I ask you a question?" Claire whispered just under her breath.

"Sure."

"Well, I was just wondering. Why don't these women use the RU-486 prescription pill? It's good for the first fifty days of conception. Then they wouldn't have to go through any of these procedures," she pointed to her clipboards running list.

"Many reasons," Olga began to explain. "First off, the drug wasn't even tested in the US until after 1993, secondly, we always have to consider the cost of medications."

"But these procedures," the student argued back. "They're invasive, they can be painful, and if performed too late in the pregnancy, the women run the risk of infection, cervical injury, perforation of the uterus, hemorrhaging..."

"I know," Olga placed her hand on Clair's upper arm, gently steering her past the nursing desk and into an empty patient room. "Every woman who comes in here arrives for her own personal reasons, dealing with her own set of worries and fears. To be a good nurse, you must not judge them for the choices they have made, just help them through the procedure, and offer them counseling if you deem it necessary."

"But some are so young. Some girls are just fourteen or fifteen."

"Yes, but you and I both know that even late abortions place teenage patients at less risk than full-term deliveries."

"Did you know that one of the girls in here yesterday with her mom and dad actually had an eighth grade math book sticking out of her backpack? I couldn't believe it. Grade eight?"

Olga sat down on a stool and folded her hands in her lap, beckoning Claire to do the same. "If you're going to nurse these patients in judgment, they're better off with no nurse at all. And besides, what gives you the right to judge them? Do you really believe a young girl in eighth grade should have a baby? Should a forty-something mother, with four or five children, be forced to add another child to her brood that late in life? How about a rape victim, should she be forced to carry the child of her attacker to term?"

"Those are pretty deep moral issues," Claire reminded Olga. "I'm just talking about better choices. What about birth control? Abstinence? Wouldn't it make more sense to offer education, instead of abortions? What about the rights of the unborn fetus?"

The idealistic dreams of the young—Olga nodded to herself. She couldn't help but remember her first year on the floor. She'd silently cried every time a woman lay down and waited for her abortion, cursing every doctor who flicked on a vacuum pump and then picked up a metal curette. The first year had been the roughest, and for many young floor nurses, it was almost an unfortunate rite of passage.

Still, as the years passed, Olga had come to realize that terminating a pregnancy was a personal choice, and no two cases were exactly alike. She had long since forgiven the women who filled the patient rooms, and she had come to terms with doctors who performed the procedures. This would be a very difficult year for Claire, as it was for any student nurse. All Olga could hope was that Claire would come out the other side with some sense of compassion.

After picking the clipboard up off Claire's lap, Olga ran her finger down the list. "We have two minors, four patients in their twenties, one over thirty, and one over forty. This is a wide range of women, from all different backgrounds and levels of education. But I can guarantee you one thing. They're all going to be frightened and very nervous, and many will remember today as one of the most traumatic events of their life."

"So, what can I do to help?" Claire relented.

"You have a choice. Either, you can help ease them past the physical discomfort, the fear, and the embarrassment—or you can stand by and be hard as a rock. These women have made their decisions. Whether it is right or wrong is not for you to say. You can be a good nurse and take care of them while they are under your care, or you can stand in judgment and turn a cold shoulder. Ultimately, the choice is yours, and *you will* draw a paycheck, no matter what you decide."

Claire nodded as Olga rose to make her way back to the desk. The remainder of the morning passed without incident, but the afternoon, unfortunately, was not the same.

"Nurse! Nurse!" shouted the resident rushing past the desk. "Where's the orderly? I've been calling for ten minutes. I need the patients moved from rooms three and four to recovery, and no one's come by to do it."

"Then let's do it," Olga encouraged, setting down her bandaging tray to lead the way.

"Me? You want me to push the gurneys to recovery? I'm a resident doctor. I don't push gurneys," he firmly reiterated.

"And I'm a senior duty nurse," Olga instructed her resident in training. "So, doctor, do you want some help, or do you want to push them both yourself?"

He threw his hands in the air, turned, and stormed off down the hall, clocking a good twenty feet before turning to look back at Olga. "Can you please help me?" he asked through gritted teeth.

Olga walked up to his side and offered her most accommodating smile.

God, how she hated to deal with the new batch of resident doctors. They were all like little puppies—either barking and snapping to assert their presence; or whining and crying, in search of help. They needed to be continually reassured that they weren't abandoned and left on their own, and they were always looking for someone to tell them exactly what to do.

It had been an extremely long shift, and Olga was dead on her feet. The young orderly named Steven had never shown up, and she'd spent most of her shift covering his absence. Claire had told her twice to call down and request a replacement, but some little voice inside had warned her against it. She had a strange feeling that the young man might be going through a little personal crisis, and she wasn't ready to blow the whistle on him quite yet.

When she walked over to the floor's supply room, Olga slowly pushed open the door, but met with a slight resistance, so she turned to lean her shoulder into the effort. "Steven?" she called out, noticing the pant leg of his white uniform.

"I'm on… I'm on a break," he slurred. "I'll be right there."

"It's nearly supper time," Olga answered back, wriggling past the half open door into the darkened room.

"I'm not hungry," the orderly answered.

"Steven, what's the matter?" Olga demanded, reaching for the light switch to illuminate the room.

"I'm on a…" his explanation was cut short by the blinding overhead light.

Dropping to her knees, Olga picked up the empty gin bottle lying beside the young man's leg. "Did you drink all this?" she demanded. "You're on shift, you should be working."

"Leave me alone," Steven snarled. "I'm on a… a break."

"You better go home before someone sees you. You could lose your job for this. And drinking at the hospital? There's no alcohol allowed up here," she began to shout. "You better sober up and get out of here before one of the residents spots you, and writes you up."

Although he attempted to stand, Steven's rubbery legs proved unable to support his weight, his entire body sliding back down onto the floor. "I don't have a home," he mumbled, his tears mixing with his own salvia as they both ran down his lips toward his chin.

"You've been evicted?"

"Fire," he simply stated, pointing to a scorched bag in the corner of the storage room. "Everything I owned was in my trailer, and last night," he sobbed, "it burned to the ground."

Olga dropped the empty gin bottle inside a trash cart and stepped over to the water stained duffle bag. Peeking inside, she spotted some clothes, a few ceramic mugs, and an old thirty-five millimeter camera. "Is this everything you own?"

"That's it," Steven shook his head. "I don't even have a clean uniform," he began to sob into his own hands. "Everything's gone."

After peeking out into the hallway, Olga made sure no one was looking before she scooted out of the room and hurried toward the vending machines. She returned with two cups of black coffee, and managed to sneak back into the storage room unnoticed.

As they sat together on the supply room floor, she kept encouraging Steven to drink the instant brew. Eventually, after ingesting the second cup, she noticed a little more clarity in his speech.

"I'm sorry," Steven bowed his head in shame. "I didn't plan on this, but I've lost everything I owned."

"You still have your job," she said, and smiled at the young man. "Well, you'll have your job until someone on the night shift notices that all the patient rooms haven't been fixed up after today's procedures."

He took a deep breath, and struggled to rise to his feet. "I've gotta finish my shift. I can't lose my job now."

Olga stood up and patted him on the back. She swung open the door and led the way as Steven sheepishly followed her back onto the floor. "I'll help you," she offered, "and between the two of us, I'm sure we'll be done before the seven o'clock shift hits the desk."

"I owe you," Steven whispered toward Olga's ear.

"Let's start in room eight," she answered, pushing open the first patient room door. Watching Steven begin his work, Olga was surprised at how efficiently he moved back and forth across the room. First, he stripped the cotton sheet off the table and tossed it into an open hamper. Then he grabbed the disinfectant bottle, wiped down the entire table, and the mounted stirrups. When that was completed, he collected all the errant trash, and tied up the main bag.

"Can I help with anything?"

"You can take all the instruments off the tray. Clean or dirty, they gotta be collected for sterilization."

Olga followed his instructions and gathered up everything, excluding the small flexible cannula tubes, and dumped them into the sterilization box.

Steven sighed and gently removed the canister from the suction machine. He gingerly carried it over to the medical waste receptacle. Unfortunately, the plastic receptacle was already full of other canisters, and there wasn't room for another one. "Damn," Steven cursed. "This is all my fault. I should have changed out this receptacle right after lunch. Now I'm really up shit creek. What am I going to do?" Steven began to nervously pace back and forth across the room, running his hands through his jet-black hair. "I've still got all the patient rooms to tidy up before the cleaning staff hits at seven o'clock, and if this one's full in this room, then I'll bet some of the others are, too. What am I going to do with this?" Steven waved the sloshing canister full of aborted fetal tissue.

"Let's just box it up, and we'll worry about it after. Right now, I suggest that we just keep moving and clean up the rooms."

"Well, I can't just toss it in the garbage. It's medical waste. If somebody finds it, I'll definitely lose my job, and the hospital… well," he nervously shook his head. "They'd be in really big shit."

"I'm aware of that," Olga snapped back, wondering just what she'd gotten herself into. "I'll go out and find an empty box, and you finish up with the other rooms."

After returning with a cardboard file box, Olga followed Steven from room to room and collected the extra canisters. The load becoming heavier with each stop as the box neared capacity, stacked full of sloshing tissue. With the box threatening to drop its load right through the straining flaps of its glued bottom, the pair finally made their exit out of the last procedure room.

Olga swallowed hard as she imagined the disaster it would be if the box she was carrying inadvertently tumbled out of her arms and crashed down onto the unforgiving floor. She remembered the bloody disaster that had run down her pants legs from just one canister, a couple nights before. She couldn't imagine what a dozen would…

Olga stopped dead in her tracks; her heart pounding what felt like a thousand beats a minute.

CHAPTER FIVE

"So you see, Miss Ventura, sometimes... when life shuts one door, it opens a window."

—Maid in Manhattan, 2002

Olga and Steven leaned against the counter at the nursing station; taking deep breaths and watching the seven o'clock shift descend on the unit. Steven was grateful that they'd completed their tasks just in time.

Looking down at the box at their feet and then up at his new co-conspirator, he subtly nudged Olga in the side. "What about those?" he whispered, as he casually set his duffle bag down on the top of the box.

"Carry it to my car," Olga whispered back out of the corner of her mouth.

"But if I'm caught, I'm dead."

"If you don't, you're still dead," she reminded him, raising her eyebrows to accentuate her point. "Besides, I have an idea, and no one will think twice about it, since they're used to me carrying baking in and out of here, all the time. You see, I'll take the canisters home tonight, and bring them back tomorrow. Then we'll slowly feed them into the waste receptacles, one by one, throughout the dayshift."

"You're the cookie lady?"

"Yes, but don't worry about that right now. Let's just move."

"Sure thing," Steven confirmed, suddenly confidant that their plan had a slight chance of actually working out.

"Let's move it," Olga ordered. She picked up Steven's bag and she led their getaway out of the hospital's doors.

"I can't thank you enough," Steven repeated once he'd carefully set the box down into Olga's trunk. "I don't know how to repay you," he rambled on, rubbing his temples as his hangover effectively began to set in. "I'd sure like to know how I can make this up to you."

"Let's just get this problem fixed up before we worry about any kind of payback."

"Thanks again," Steven smiled, waving his hand as Olga slid into her car and prepared to drive away. As he turned to go to the bus stop, he suddenly stopped dead in his tracks—he realized that he actually had nowhere to go.

Back in her car, with the motor running and her gearshift in drive, Olga looked over at Steven as he came to a standstill in the middle of the hospital parking lot. His shoulders slumped, his duffle bag hanging loosely in the fingers of his right hand, Steven stood motionless as if frozen in time.

"Steven," Olga called out. "Can I give you a lift to a friend's house? Maybe a relative or someone else you know?"

"That'd be great," he turned and smiled, jogging up to the nurse's passenger door and hopping right inside, unconsciously cradling all his worldly possessions.

"So where are you heading?" she inquired, backing up her older model sedan.

"Don't matter, any direction is fine."

"That's what I thought," Olga shook her head. "We're heading east. I live two blocks off Maple, and I have a spare room if you need it. I'll trade you some yard work and a few house chores for a couple weeks of room and board. That'll give you a little time to get back on your feet. Deal?"

Steven just nodded, damn grateful that a little luck had finally landed in his lap.

It was their first date, a set-up between her parents and one of her dad's friends from the golf club. Normally, Camille would have run so fast from a parental set-up that she'd have just left dust, but she was bored to tears, and it was a night out.

"Would you like a little wine?" Alberto had asked, still sipping his club soda and lime.

"No, soda is fine," she smiled, somewhat relaxed to see that her date wasn't drinking any alcohol either.

"I was thinking about chateaubriand for two, with shrimp cocktail as an appetizer. What do you think?"

"Sounds fine," Camille nodded, noticing the appreciative glances Alberto was receiving from many of the passing waitresses.

"I usually don't eat quite this heavy, but I'm on a protein diet to drop a few more pounds of fat and maybe build a little more muscle mass before competition in September."

Camille looked at her dinner date, and honestly couldn't imagine where this extra fat would be hiding on his frame. "How long have you been competitively wrestling?"

"Started training in seventh grade, but I really never got serious about competing until high school, especially in my senior year when the scouts started sniffing around. Now going to college, I really want to give it my all. It's about time the University of New York got their money's worth for their full ride."

"I like that," Camille smiled just as the waiter neared their table.

"Like what?"

"A man willing to take responsibility for his actions."

Alberto smiled, turning toward the waiter to order on behalf of his date.

They both opted to pass on desert, and Alberto suggested that a movie might not be a bad idea.

"Okay, so what have you been dying to see?" Camille inquired.

"Lady's choice," Alberto instantly offered back.

"No, you don't understand," she explained. "My older brother downloads all the new releases from some kind of contact on the internet. He knows a guy who gets bootleg copies of everything out there. I'm telling you, I've seen it all."

"How's that possible?"

"I'm not totally sure. It has something to do with kids in Hong Kong sneaking digital camcorders into the theaters, and then posting the copies on the net."

"That's wicked cool," Alberto laughed. "How's the quality?"

"Bootleg," Camille shrugged her shoulders. "But I saw the new *Mission Impossible* before anyone else."

"Isn't that just another installment in the Tom Cruise franchise?"

"Yup," Camille agreed. "But it's still good, no matter what you think of sequels."

"Well, I haven't even seen it yet."

"We have a winner. *Mission Impossible* it is," she confirmed the plans as they both stood and made their way toward the restaurant's parking lot.

"Wanna ride with me?" Alberto casually offered, motioning to both their cars as they sat side by side in the lot at the five-star restaurant.

"Sure, why not."

Settled in the movie theater, with the action well under way, Camille finally felt herself relax. It had only been two days since her abortion, but her physical health seemed fine, and her mental health must have been healing just as well. Or so she thought.

As he reached across Camille's lap for no less than the fifth time, Alberto innocently missed the medium-sized popcorn bag, and his fingers landed directly onto the top of her right thigh.

"Sorry," he laughed, the second she jumped up from her seat.

"I… I have… I have to go to the bathroom," Camille stuttered, pushing her way past Alberto's knees and rushing up the theater's aisle. Alone in an empty bathroom stall, she fought to catch her breath. What the fuck was the matter? Why was her heart threatening to pound right through the walls of her chest? She dug into her shoulder bag, and pulled out the half bottle of Valium she had stolen from her mother's medicine chest. She popped one into her mouth before debating whether she felt good enough to return to her seat.

Parked in her garage, with her house unlocked, Olga stood guard while Steven unloaded his duffle bag and the box of medical waste.

"Where do you want them?" he asked, unsure where to turn.

"Put them in the utility room, off to the left. Just set them on top of the dryer and I'll take it from there."

Steven did as he was told, and then returned to the kitchen. Olga reappeared from her bedroom, wearing a flowery summer dress and a pair of house slippers. "Your room is the one on the right with the blue bedspread. Go ahead and get settled. I'm going to put a little supper on. Feel free to grab some towels and washcloths from the hall closet. And help yourself to the television in the living room. I rarely watch it; so don't be surprised that I don't have satellite or cable. Just good old peasant view," she joked.

While Steven busied himself settling in, Olga threw together a quick supper. After opening a can of tuna and draining it, she dumped it into a fry pan with a tablespoon of margarine. Stirring the tuna until it had broken down and heated throughout, she added three cups of water, a box of macaroni and cheese and one cup of frozen peas. She continued to stir the mixture until the water came to a boil and the powdered cheese dissolved. Olga then dropped the temperature to low, covered the fry pan, and went into the living room to see what her new roommate was up to.

"That's a nice room. Who usually sleeps in there?"

"No one, it's a guest room."

He picked up a photograph off the living room's wall unit. Steven turned to look at Olga. "These your kids?"

"My niece and nephew. I never married."

"Why?" he asked bluntly.

"That's not an appropriate question for a young man to ask a lady," Olga scolded her guest.

"Sorry, my mom always said that I was all mouth and no brains."

"Where are you parents?"

"Don't know," Steven shrugged, displaying the same defeated posture she'd seen in the parking lot when he realized he had nowhere else to go. "They said they'd call when they had arrived in Arizona, and I haven't heard from them since. That was two years ago come this fall."

"And you haven't ever heard a word?" Olga couldn't help but

question the young man, who suddenly appeared so small and defeated.

"A few weeks after they left, I was worried, so I called the state police in every dinky town between here and Arizona. But not one knew anything. I don't know, maybe they forgot our phone number."

Olga stood back and stared at the boy as he carefully set down the family picture he'd been analyzing. "No brothers or sisters?" she asked.

"My brother Michael is dead, hit by a car when we were little. And my older sister Monica is married. That's who they went to see in Arizona."

"Why don't you call your sister and see if they made it safe and sound?"

"I can't remember her husband's last name," he shrugged his shoulders again. "But the way I see it, if they wanted to talk to me, they'd have left word at the hospital. I've been working there for the last four years, and anybody who wants to find me, always knows to call there."

"Well, let's check on supper," Olga turned and walked toward the kitchen, anxious to finish the meal and get on with her personal investigation.

"What's in that?" Steven asked, watching Olga crumble cornflakes over the top of the steaming casserole.

"Taste it first and then tell me what you think."

"Do you have any ketchup?"

"I said taste it, not drown it," she firmly reminded the young man.

Digging in his fork, Steven carried a mouthful up to his lips, just taking a second to blow on the hot food before shoveling it into his mouth. "Mmmm, this is good. But I always liked macaroni. This one of them frozen casserole dinners?"

"No, I made it while you were unpacking."

"My mom used to make food and freeze it for bingo night. Then when me and Monica got home from school, we just popped it in the oven for an hour, and then we were ready to eat before Dad had to go to his night shift job."

"That's nice," Olga smiled, trying desperately to comprehend the dynamics of Steven's home life. "What did your dad do?"

"He worked security for a whole slew of companies. But he hated it," Steven added between bites. "Said he would have been a cop if the department hadn't been forced to hire all them blacks and nips in his place."

Nearly dropping her fork, Olga sat motionless in her kitchen chair as Steven continued with his family history.

"Dad always said that the US was getting overrun with foreigners, and if we weren't careful, every kid would soon have dark skin and slanted eyes."

"But you, you're a little..." she stammered, looking for just the right words to convey the fact that Steven himself had olive-colored skin with jet black hair, and high cheekbones.

"I know," he smirked. "My mom was Mexican, but Dad said that was fine, since they'd fought side by side with our boys in the war."

As she tried to figure out exactly which war Steven was referring to, Olga sat back and watched as he downed his second plate of her tuna and macaroni casserole. "Do you remember the date when your sister Monica was married? The year, maybe the month?"

"Why?"

"Well, if we could pin down the date, maybe we could find a record of their nuptials and you'd be able to locate your parents.

He picked up his plate and walked to the kitchen sink. Steven spoke without turning back to face Olga. "I'm twenty-three years old and all I ever finished was high school, but I know one thing for sure… my parents aren't dead; they've just run away. You know, when I was a kid, I didn't know that parents could do that," he continued to run the water over his plate even though there hadn't been a single scrap of uneaten food to wash down the drain.

Olga joined her guest at the kitchen sink, setting down her dirty plate and cutlery. She patted him warmly on the shoulder as she turned to deal with the leftovers. "You think you could handle some casserole for lunch tomorrow?"

"You bet," Steven turned and smiled as Olga buttered two pieces of bread, wrapped up some peanut butter cookies, and set aside an apple and a can of soda to go with the Tupperware dish full of leftovers.

"And Steven, if you don't bring home my Tupperware, you'll be eating cafeteria sandwiches the rest of the week. Deal?"

"Deal."

Sprawled out on the couch, flipping through the channels, Steven looked for any program that might remotely interest him. After living without a television for the last year and a half, he was unfamiliar with many of the weekly sitcoms or the new batch of reality TV shows. He finally settled on a rerun of *Friends,* and setting the remote back down on the coffee table, he eventually drifted off to sleep.

As she sat at the kitchen table sipping a cup of tea, Olga wondered just what in the hell she'd been thinking. She'd inadvertently jeopardized her nursing career, her retirement pension, and possibly her personal safety. She knew nothing of Steven, including his last name. And in the course of the last three hours, she'd committed a major infraction of hospital policy, had invited a total stranger to move into her house, and for all she knew, she was now harboring a possible arsonist.

She rationalized that even though his youth did sound rough; she also knew that anyone who could string together enough words to make a complete sentence was capable of fabricating a tumultuous past. She could possibly call Helen over, maybe run the situation by her, but then she wouldn't have any private time to do her little investigation.

As she looked over at the young man soundly sleeping on her couch, Olga decided that it was time to trust her intuition, and her intuition told her that she would be fine. Steven was exactly as he appeared to be, a down and out twenty-three year old orphan, and his temporary stay might be good for them both. She had plenty of handyman jobs that needed attention. He obviously needed to regroup and get back on his feet, and in the meantime, they'd live together as roommates.

Olga shut off the television, nudged the young man, and pointed in the direction of the spare room. She waited until he'd shut off the lights and climbed into bed before she turned and made her way to the box of canisters.

When she opened the lid, Olga was surprised to see that the contents in the first container had already settled. All the strands of tissue and small bone fragments had drifted to the bottom, the upper layers were a lighter mixture of blood and saline solution, depending on which procedure had been performed on the patient.

She dug through the box to find a container without saline, tucked the canister under her arm, and made her way toward the bathroom.

Sequestered behind a locked door, she took a deep breath and unscrewed the lid. Peering down inside, the seasoned nurse was not bothered by the contents. Just two months prior, she had assisted in emergency surgery while the attending physician had to debride a stranded hunter's leg wound that had already been infested with live maggots. Actually, Olga had smelled much worse that was drained from a neglected abscess. The contents of this canister were simply morally repugnant.

After setting the open canister down into the sink in case of spillage, Olga opened her medicine chest and pulled out a sterile cotton swab, dipping it repeatedly into the middle of the fluid. She lifted her skirt above her right knee, and balanced her foot on the edge of the toilet. She dabbed the bloody liquid in a circle right around the outer edges of her previous wound. Slowly, she painted the skin with the bloody liquid all the way around the patch of rejuvenated skin.

Olga decided to repeat the procedure with a fresh swab, so she stirred the canister, making sure she'd run the cotton over at least half a dozen pieces of tissue. Dabbing her leg again, she continued until she was satisfied that she'd covered the desired area with the bloody fluid. She tossed the swab in the garbage, reached up for gauze, and bandaged her imaginary wound. Quickly, she wiped the two droplets off the side of the bathroom sink, twisted the lid back on the canister, and returned it to the cardboard box.

Scheduled for her usual day shift, Olga rose to the sound of clinking dishes in her kitchen and the smell of burnt toast wafting under her door. She threw on bathrobe, and quickly made her way out of her bedroom.

"Morning," Steven called out, wet hair slicked back, obviously fresh from the shower. "I didn't know if you eat breakfast; most of the girls I know don't."

"I'm not a girl, I'm a woman," Olga rubbed her eyes, and

grabbed the kettle to boil water for her morning coffee. "What are you eating?"

"Oh, just a little creation of my own," he bragged. "First you scramble a bunch of eggs, add a bit of milk, chop up some sandwich meat, salt and pepper, and pop it in the microwave for a couple of minutes. Throw your bread in the toaster, and by the time she pops, you've got instant eggs without the messy fry pan or pot of boiling water."

"Not bad," Olga smiled, reaching up into the cupboards for her instant coffee while she couldn't help but notice how clean Steven had left her kitchen. He must have wiped the cupboards after buttering his toast, and then thrown the eggshells directly into the garbage. The smells of cooking may have lingered, but he'd erased any evidence of his mess. "I appreciate how clean you've left the kitchen."

"I appreciate the food."

Maybe this wasn't the world's biggest mistake after all. Time would tell, but right now, Olga had to shower and dress for work. "I'll be leaving at seven thirty if you'd like a ride. I don't even know what time your shift is," she admitted.

"Actually, I realized that I don't work today. So I'm just gonna hop a bus and see if I can recover anything from the fire. Firemen said there wouldn't be anything left, but now that it's cool, I wanna have a look and dig around for myself."

"Come here," Olga beckoned to the kitchen window. "See that red and green gnome in the backyard?"

"You mean that elf?"

"Yes. Well, there's a house key underneath the base. If you have a chance, I'd appreciate it if you would cut yourself a copy and replace the original back under the gnome."

Steven just nodded, a lump caught in the back of his throat.

"I've written down the address, zip code, and phone number

here, in case you want to call it in to the hospital, or change your mailing address at the post office. The paper is by the phone."

"You should have gotten married. You're a good mom."

As she watched him make his way back into the spare room, Olga shook her head and carried her coffee mug into her bedroom. She dropped her bathrobe and then kicked off her house slippers. She suddenly focused on the bandages still attached to her right leg. It was now or never, so without any further delay, she started to unwind the gauze.

The dried and crusted blood clung to the padding; the underlying skin on her leg was unchanged after her experiment. "Nothing new," she muttered, looking carefully over the patch of skin she'd painted with the blood and tissue. The original knife wound was still undetectable. The patch of new skin, measuring roughly the size of an oatmeal cookie, was now in its place. Yet the outer ring that Olga had coated appeared unchanged. Her skin was still aged, and wrinkled; it looked as old as the remainder of her leg.

"Thanks for everything. I'm leaving now," Steven politely called through the bedroom door.

"Will you be home by seven for supper?"

"What's for supper?" he teased.

"Guests don't ask what being served."

"Sure, I'll be here," he laughed back. "You want me to load the box of canisters back into your trunk before I go?"

"Might as well," Olga shook her head, walking over to her dresser to pull out a clean set of scrubs. "I'll see you at seven. And by the way, we're having pork chops."

Three buses later, Steven finally stepped off at the Santa Maria

Trailer Park and made his way across the park toward the lot that used to be his home.

"Steven?" a young voice called out as a kid pulled up beside his right leg on a bicycle.

"Pedro. What's shaking, buddy?"

"Heard you were dead. Momma said you burned to a crisp in your trailer the other night. What happened to you?"

Steven made his way past his neighbor's trailers, and finally spotted the blackened disaster that he used to call home. All ringed with yellow caution tape, he suddenly couldn't imagine how a single one of his belongings would have survived the blaze. "Holy fuck, man. Look at this mess," he muttered to himself.

"You said the *F word*, you said the *F word*," the young kid chanted over and over as he pedaled his bike in circles round and round on the gravel driveway.

Steven lifted the tape and stepped under to check out the charred remains that used to be his home. Careful to watch where he was stepping, mindful of all the nails and curled tin, he gingerly made his way across the lot to exactly where his kitchen would have been. Even the neighbor's tree was scorched; the tattered branches were hanging weakly in the morning sunshine.

"Cops are looking for you," the park manager announced from the road. "So is Jerry."

"What does Jerry want?" Steven called back, almost losing his footing as he stumbled across a tangled mess of wiring.

"What do you think he wants, boy? His trailer's leveled, his tenant is AWOL, and he wants to know who in the Sam Hell is going to pay for the damages. To be honest with ya, I'd be right pissed, too."

"What'd the cops want?"

"They want to talk to you about the fire. Investigating stuff, you know?"

"I was at work when it started. When I got here, the place was already swarming with cops and fire trucks."

"Hell boy, who do you think left you the message at work?"

Steven nodded his head, climbing back out from underneath the caution tape. "Thanks, man. Doesn't look like there's anything left to pick up," Steven regretfully surmised. "Thought the flames might have spared at least a few of my things."

"Nah, I think you're shit out of luck," the manager shook his head. "What you want me to tell Jerry? You know he's going to call me tonight, wondering if you came sniffing around."

Steven debated his answer for half a second, finally turned, and faced the manager dead on. "Tell him he can keep the damage deposit."

As they chuckled together, both men stood back and scratched their heads in the early morning sun. "So where you staying, boy?"

"A nurse from work is letting me crash with her while I get on my feet."

"A nurse, hey? You lucky dog."

"She's old like a grandma, so let up," he corrected his friend. "And she's been real nice, no reason for her to give a kid like me a break. But she is. Here's where I'm staying if… if they… you know, if they…" he stumbled with his explanation.

"If your ma and pa ever call looking for ya," he completed the young man's sentence.

"Yes," Steven nodded his head up and down.

After scratching the number down on a scrap of paper tucked in his breast pocket, the manager turned and patted the boy on his shoulder. "Wanna come in for some coffee? I'm sure the wife would like to say her good-byes before you pick up and leave us for parts unknown."

Glad of the diversion, Steven followed his lead.

"Welcome," Mae called out as they both stepped into the kitchen from her front porch. “Wondering if you was gonna stop by and take your leave of us?”

After grabbing a chair and accepting a cup of coffee, Steven sat back and watched Mae fill a plate with freshly baked cinnamon buns drizzled with white icing. “I’m going to miss you both,” he admitted, grateful for the friendship they’d shown him since his parents had left on their *holiday*.

“Old man Brinnley is looking to rent out his trailer, fourth row, second one from the road. He’s getting ready to move into some senior’s lodge. You want me to check on the rent?”

“I can’t afford a whole trailer to myself,” Steven admitted. “I was just damn lucky that Jerry only charged me half while Mom and Dad were away. And I can guarantee you that old man Brinnley ain’t going to cut me the same deal.”

“Cheese?” Mae asked, setting down a plate of sliced cheddar. “So then, where are you going?”

“I was telling John that I’m boarding with a lady from the hospital while I figure out my next step. I just wanted to see if there was anything left to salvage.”

Mae reached out and patted his hand. “Sorry hon, but by the time the fire department got here, your trailer was totally engulfed in flames. You know, you’re blessed to have not been inside.”

“Why?” he asked through a mouthful of baking.

“Well, by the time John spotted the smoke and called 911, the entire place was up in flames. I don’t really think anyone could have gotten out alive. You know how trailers burn.”

He took a moment to wipe his face on the paper napkin, and asked, “Did you hear anybody mention how they thought the fire might have started?”

“Well,” John rose from his chair to grab his cigarettes and lighter. “I heard an investigator from the fire department say that he was looking for some sort of accelerant or something. But after watching him work, I don't think he found anything."

"What's an accelerant?"

"Gas, lighter fluid. You know, stuff that burns really well," Mae jumped into the conversation. "They were looking to see if you started yer own trailer on fire."

"That doesn't make sense. Why would I burn all my own stuff?"

"That's what the cops said," John smiled and slapped Steven on the back. "As soon as they heard that you were the renter, not the owner, they seemed to lose interest in their own investigation."

Eventually, he bid his old neighbors and friends good bye. Steven walked across the park and made his way to the bus stop, not even bothering to turn around and take a final look at the place he used to call home.

CHAPTER SIX

"You may run from sorrow as we have.
Sorrow will find you. It can smell you."

—The Village, 2005

It wasn't difficult to tote the heavy box into the hospital. However, negotiating the elevators, the staff lounge doors, and every inquisitive snoop in between was another matter.

"Need some help, Olga?"

"No thanks, Jimmy."

"That looks like a heavy load of goodies," another staff member called out over his shoulder.

As she fielded her usual barrage of inquiries, Olga finally reached the safety of the lounge doors. She set her load of canisters down onto the bench in front of the metal lockers, and reached in under the watchful stare of the waiting group. She removed a gaily-wrapped package off the top, turned to the first nurse within reach, and handed her the box, encouraging her to unwrap it on the spot.

"What's with the present, Olga?"

"Nothing special, I was just cleaning out my deep freeze last night, getting ready for my fall bake, and I decided to pass out a few of my frozen goodies."

"Well, that's really nice," the nurse cooed, opening the box to find a cache of wax wrapped chocolate brownies."

"Enjoy," Olga smiled. "I'm just going to continue making my rounds and pass out some treats to a few of the other different departments."

"Aw, that's sweet," a second nurse commented as they all began dipping their fingers inside the box to retrieve a brownie to enjoy with their morning coffee.

After commandeering an empty cart, Olga lifted up her box and made her way down the hall to radiology. Within minutes, she'd also managed to drop off wrapped boxes at the hospital's admitting desk, and another at the pediatrics unit. After a few more stops, her diversion would be complete. She would quickly strip the remaining suction canisters in the bottom of the box of their wrapping paper, and dump them in the appropriate waste receptacles, and no one would even think twice about questioning her actions. She'd been able to pull it off, and she knew she was damned lucky.

Half an hour later, Olga was standing at the nursing station with a flattened cardboard box tucked under her arm, when Dr. Hood suddenly rounded the corner. Obviously lecturing a resident on the etiquette of dealing with the family of a deceased patient, he suddenly spotted his old friend Olga.

"Nurse Heinz, I hear you were asking for me yesterday."

"Yes doctor, I was."

"Well?" He stood at the edge of her station, calmly waiting for her to state her concern.

"I just had some questions regarding a patient's treatment regimen. They seemed to have escaped me at the moment, but if I think of them later, I'll track you down."

"Call me," the doctor smiled, tapping the phone permanently attached to his hip. "If you want, I'll be in my office between two and three."

"Thank you," Olga smiled, secretly hoping that she'd be able to sneak away during the middle of her shift and speak in private.

"Nurse, nurse," a man called out from somewhere down the hall.

"Excuse me," Olga nodded to the doctor and resident, before turning and moving toward the voice.

"Is there a problem?" she asked the man who was anxiously pacing up and down the hospital corridor.

"My uh… my friend, she's really getting quite anxious, and I, I mean we… well, we were wondering when… when…"

"When the doctor will be performing the procedure?" Olga guessed.

"Yes," he sighed, visibly shaken by the mere task of being present. "Is he almost ready?"

"I can check, but first let's see how the patient is doing."

Olga followed the young man into the room, and moved directly toward the patient. She looked down into her young face, and asked, "How are you feeling, dear?"

"I don't feel that well," she nervously muttered. "I'm kinda nauseated, and I'm really cold. Maybe I have the flu?" the young woman mused.

"How about a blanket from the warmer?" Olga suggested, turning to the man standing guard at the foot of the patient's bed. "Sir, could you please go back to the unit desk and ask the nurse for a red blanket? Tell her Nurse Heinz sent you from patient room five."

"I guess," he shrugged his shoulders before turning and reluctantly walking out of the room.

She waited until the door closed shut, and then Olga turned

and picked up the ear thermometer, and carefully measured the girl's temperature. "No fever, but maybe it's something else?" she suggested with a wrinkle of her brow.

"Do you think I should wait until I feel better?" the young woman asked, eyes turned up to the nurse's face, desperately searching for any kind of support.

Olga pulled up a stool, and nestled in at the patient's side. "Sweetie, do you want to terminate your pregnancy?"

"It's the best thing for everyone concerned," she quoted as if reading off a cue card.

"Who is everyone?"

"Well, Mr. Harper… I mean, Paul. He doesn't think that it would be a good idea right now."

Olga swallowed hard and fought to bite her own tongue. How in the hell did these girls get past the orientation counselor? This patient wasn't here under her own accord, the girl had obviously been coerced, and it hadn't taken longer than two minutes for Olga to figure it out.

"Mr. Harper… he's your boss?" Olga took an educated guess.

"Yes," she nervously whispered, eyes darting back and forth between the nurse's face and the closed door.

"Don't worry about him," Olga waved her hand. "I sent him for a *red blanket*, and the other nurses will keep him busy for at least fifteen minutes. It's kind of nursing code."

"That's really cool," the girl snickered, her face breaking out in the most beautiful of smiles.

"Dear, I'm not a counselor. I'm just an experienced nurse who's seen a lot over the years. But can I give you a piece of advice?"

"Yes," she vigorously nodded.

"This hospital is not going anywhere. We terminate pregnancies five days a week, twelve months of the year. What made you believe that you had to come in today?" Olga inquired, rising from her stool to pick up the young woman's chart. "I see from your file that you're only eight weeks pregnant. You realize that you have another entire month to decide, and you'd still qualify for a first trimester abortion."

"Paul wants this taken care of before he goes on vacation with his family at the end of August. He said he doesn't want to be worrying about what I'm going through, when he can't be here to comfort me."

Olga stood and gave the stool a little shove, somewhat surprised at just how vigorously she had booted the metal casters when it bounced off a neighboring wall. "If I were you, I'd take the month to really decide if this is exactly what *you* want to do. And in the next four weeks, I suggest that you make an appointment to see a professional counselor. I can suggest a few names, if you're interested?"

"Yes, please," the woman smiled, reaching out toward Olga's hand. "I'm sorry for wasting your time."

"This is not a waste of anybody's time. And if you decide that *you* would still like to terminate the pregnancy, I promise that no one will think less of you for today's cancellation."

"Thank you," the young woman smiled through the tears.

"Well, if you'll excuse me, I think I had better go and find your boss before he runs out and buys a red blanket."

———————

Olga watched as an orderly moved through the unit and completed the same routine that she and Steven had rushed through the previous night. She suddenly realized that the young man had only cleaned half the rooms. That meant that at least three or four canisters of freshly aborted tissue would still be sitting in the machines and waiting for disposal.

"But so what?" Olga muttered to herself. Why in the world was she suddenly so interested in the disposal of the canisters?

"Nurse Heinz," Dr. Hood smiled as he approached her position.

"I was just heading down to the cafeteria to grab a snack. Interested in joining me?"

"Yes doctor," Olga smiled, stopping off at the unit desk to announcc her break.

Seated with two teas and a shared fruit platter, neither spoke while a nearby table of cleaning staff finished their coffees and rose up to leave.

"So, what's the matter, Olga?" Martin suddenly broke the ice. "You're stumbling around the hospital as if you've got the weight of the world on your shoulders, and then today you tell me, in front of a resident I might add, that you can't recall some particular facts regarding a patient's treatment."

Olga accidentally brushed the doctor's hand while reaching for a strawberry in the center of the Styrofoam plate. She shook her head and popped the berry into her mouth. "You could always read me, Martin."

"Let's hope. After fifteen years, you'd think I'd be able to tell what my girl's thinking."

"Tell me something. What's new in the field of human cell regeneration?"

"Are we talking organ, brain, bone? What's your pleasure?"

"Organ. Specifically the epidermal and dermal layers of the skin," she specified. "Have you read anything of interest lately?"

"Not lately. There were quite a few articles published in the late nineties in conjunction with all the ground-breaking stem cell research."

"I remember all the hoopla," Olga nodded her head. "But have you seen anything within the last couple of years in any of your medical journals regarding research in the form of aborted fetal tissue applied as a topical for epidermal absorption?"

"Not that I can recall," the doctor thoughtfully sipped his tea.

"And we're both aware that molecular and nano-particle absorption in the skin stops at the stratum corneum."

"Correct me if I'm wrong, Martin, but hasn't research proved that some molecules will travel down the hair follicles and successfully reach the dermis layer?"

"Yes, that's been proven. But why in the world are we even talking about this, Olga?"

"I had a student nurse ask me an interesting question the other day, and to be honest, I wasn't sure how to respond."

"What was the question?" Martin asked, stirring in yet another spoonful of sugar into his lukewarm tea.

"Well, first she reminded me that the only time tissue or organs significantly form is during the gestational period inside the womb. After birth, the limbs and organs almost never form any further, the tissue only matures in dimension and cellular strength."

"Yes," the doctor precisely placed his dampened spoon in the center of his paper napkin.

"So… this student nurse then wondered if surgeons were able to harvest some tissue from the womb, let's say for example nose tissue for ethmoid bone and nasal septum development; could this harvested tissue be applied to the face of an adult who'd lost their birth nose in an accident, thereby regenerating new growth of the lost nose?"

"That's a very interesting proposal, isn't it?" Martin mused. "But you wanna tell me how a doctor is supposed to harvest the said tissue? This I'd really like to hear?"

"Don't look at me. It wasn't my idea. I was just wondering if there was any merit to her comments. I really like to encourage my nurses to think outside of the box."

"Olga, you've been attending too many motivational conferences. I remember when a nurse was told to be pleasant, treat the doctors like Gods, and make sure to check her stockings for runs."

"Oh lord, Martin. You're teasing me, aren't you? Please tell me that you're just trying to get a rise out of me and don't actually want the nursing staff to treat you like a God," she playfully slapped his right hand.

"No," he casually returned Olga's fleeting touch. "But seriously, your concept is somewhat intriguing," the doctor admitted. "At any rate, you and I both remember what happened to the institutions delving in stem cell research. It was almost like the Salem Witch Hunts. Files were confiscated, grants revoked, and worst of all, appointments were rescinded. I don't know about you, little lady, but with retirement just round the corner, I'm not interested in rocking any boats."

"Like I said, I just think it's important to encourage young staff to grow, to educate themselves on new advancements and techniques."

"That's fine," Martin winked, downing the remainder of his tea. "But don't do anything stupid that might jeopardize your retirement. I can't imagine what it would be like to be blackballed from the field at our age."

Olga stuffed her paper napkin into her teacup and rose from the chair. "Don't worry, I'm not going to ruffle any feathers, I just thought I'd run it by a doctor I could trust."

"You can trust me. Hell, I remember when you used to love me," Martin winked back.

"That was a long time ago," she consciously lowered her voice. "Back when we were young and foolish."

"I'm still foolish," he whispered across the table.

"But I'm not. Thanks for the snack," Olga said, and made her way toward the basement stairs.

"My door is always open," the doctor shouted after her.

Without turning back, she lifted her right hand up above her shoulder and repeatedly pressed her pointer finger against the pad of her thumb. A personal signal devised to promise a limited separation. An old lover's good-bye from a relationship long past.

As she roamed around the house in her flannel pajama pants and an old tee shirt, Camille turned her nose up at the two flavors of ice cream stuffed in the rear of the kitchen freezer. She didn't like cherry and couldn't even stomach the thought of pistachio. Who in their right mind would want to lick a frozen treat with green nuts poking out the waffle cone? "Mom, do we have any other kind of ice cream?" she yelled, both arms braced on the kitchen counter as she repeatedly blinked her eyes.

"What you see is what you get," her mother called back from the sunroom.

"Is anyone going to the store today?"

"Shopping list on the fridge, money in my purse," her mother called back.

Camille grabbed her mom's wallet, yanked out a hundred dollars, and ripped the scribbled list off the fridge door. "I'm taking the convertible," she yelled back, staggering up the stairs to her bedroom to change before leaving the house.

"Fuck," Camille cursed five minutes later when the convertible stalled on the driveway for the second time.

"What, you forgot how to drive a stick?" her older brother teased from the sidewalk.

"Piss off," his sister hissed, unsure why she was having such trouble driving a car that she must have driven a thousand times before.

"Hey, hey," Joshua yelled, running up to the driver's door in an attempt to grab the handle. "What'd the Mustang ever do to you?" he laughed. "Just relax and quit trying to force the shifter into reverse. Just lightly pull her back."

Camille turned and leveled a look of utter disgust at her brother. When she finally found the gear she wanted, she tromped her foot down on the gas, and roared backwards out of the driveway.

"Slow down," Joshua yelled at Camille. "There are kids playing down the street."

Camille didn't hear her brother, or the blaring horn. The last thing that registered was the sight of the beautiful monarch butterfly, caught in the mesh grill of the oncoming cherry-picker truck.

CHAPTER SEVEN

"Your God gathers in the good ones… and leaves the living to those of us whom fail."

—The Thorn Birds, 1983

Olga swung open the door, walked down the hall and stepped up to the nursing station. She checked the roster to see how many procedures were left to complete. Three were left on the charts, so she made her way to room number five to see if the doctor and student nurse required her assistance.

When she came into the room, Olga found the patient's bed was already vacant. The cotton sheet was stained with droplets of fresh blood, and the dirty instruments littered the stainless steel tray. Olga's eyes eventually rested on the vacuum aspirator, the canister only two feet from the floor; they purposely situated the receptacle low, to keep it out of the patient's line of sight.

Olga reached for the canister, her fingers were greeted by the escaping warmth from the blood, and tissue as it began to settle in the container. The procedure couldn't have been performed more than ten minutes before, and the scrambled fetal matter had yet to cool, and congeal.

With her face eye level with the canister, Olga found herself staring directly into the swirled mass, trying to discern any kind of pattern, for no obvious reason. Eventually, she straightened and shook her head and rubbed her eyes, unsure of just how long she had been mesmerized by the reddish swirls. "I know you're hiding something," she muttered to the tissue, leaning over to remove the canister from the aspirator. Then without giving further thought to her actions, she began collecting a few necessary items and stuffing them deep into her pockets.

She grabbed a handful of butterfly bandages, some cauterizing agent, and a scalpel. She finished by folding the canister up inside a large clean towel. With the white cotton tucked under her right arm, Olga opened the procedure room door and began making her way towards the nurse's lounge.

Joshua didn't realize that he wasn't breathing until he involuntarily choked from lack of oxygen. "Camille!" he was finally able to scream out, forcing his feet to run down the driveway to the rear bumper of the cherry-picker truck.

As he raced up the truck's left side, toward the buckled side door of his sister's mustang convertible, Joshua was stopped dead in his tracks as the trucker swung open his driver's door and almost fell out onto the pavement.

"I didn't see her," he mumbled, shaking his head, attempting to clear away the impending fog that was threatening to settle down on his brain, in conjunction with the obvious head trauma. "She came out of nowhere," he rambled, wiping the trickle of blood that was escaping the gash in his thinning hairline and dripping down over his right eyebrow.

Joshua pushed his way past the driver and rushed over toward the front of the car. "Call 911," he shouted back over his shoulder.

Joshua stopped and stared straight across the rumpled hood and through the shattered windshield of Camille's car… but all he saw was emptiness. She wasn't there. *She's not in the car. She's not in the car*, Joshua chanted, over and over in his head.

"I can't find my phone," the truck driver stumbled up toward where Joshua was standing, both his eyes blinking as he fought to focus on the scene.

"Well, then run inside and call!" Joshua spun on his own heels and angrily shouted at the man. "Go call 911," he yelled a second time, turning and flapping his arms at his side in desperation, at he swung his head toward the family's two-story brick house.

"I'll go," the man mumbled, turning to walk away, when without warning, he crumbled like a house of cards and landed in a heap at Joshua's feet.

"Hey buddy," Joshua called out to the driver, dropping to his knees to check on the only visible victim at the car crash. "Are you alright?"

No response. The man was out cold.

Joshua glanced up and down the residential street, wondering where all the people were. Hadn't anybody heard the crash? Where was everybody when he needed help? With a backward glance at his sister's empty car, he turned and sprinted across the street and up the driveway, bursting through the front door of the family house.

"There's been an accident," he yelled at full volume, the sheer tone of his voice beckoning his mother, his words distorted by the volume. Picking up the phone, Joshua punched in the three digits, panting as he waited for the operator to answer.

"911, what is your emergency?"

"There's been an accident: a big truck hit my sister's car."

"What is your address, sir?" the operator began to compile the information needed to dispatch the appropriate assistance.

Joshua handed the phone off to his wide-eyed housekeeper, turned, and ran back to the front yard. As he raced down the driveway, he instantly noticed that the driver was fighting to raise himself up on the asphalt, holding his head with his right hand while his left hand and forearm fought to support his upper body weight.

"I called an ambulance," he told the man. "Just sit where you are; they'll be right here," he muttered, pivoting in his shoes to scan the neighborhood sidewalks for any sign of his missing sister.

"She don't look so good," a child's voice called to him from the passenger's side of the car.

"What?" Joshua demanded.

"She's got blood and glass on her face." The kid sitting on the seat of his bike pointed down into the front seat of the black mustang.

Once again forgetting to breathe, Joshua quickly scrambled around the truck driver's body and rushed up to the kid's side. "Oh my God. Camille!"

She lay crumpled across the two front bucket seats, the left side of her face was bleeding profusely, and the yellow and black fragments of a monarch butterfly wing adorned her blood soaked hair as if placed in lieu of a fashion barrette.

Steven wandered around the backyard of Olga's house and wondered exactly what he was supposed to do. The lawn and flowerbeds were not manicured, but they were well maintained. The odd weed poked its head out of the gardening soil in the midst of the perennials beds, and tiny swatches of errant grass sprouted near the base of the fruit trees. But overall, the yard looked really well taken care of.

He was still licking his lips from his lunch of tuna casserole and peanut butter cookies, when he stepped into the gardening shed and pulled out the weed-eater. After starting up the gas-powered machine, he moved in circular motions around the trees, the annual shrubs, and any other place the lawnmower wouldn't reach. Eventually, he set the weed-eater back into the gardening shed, and opted for a pail and a pair of gardening gloves. Dropped to his knees on the edge of the flowerbeds, Steven leaned over to pluck out the unwanted intruders.

"Well, well," Olga announced an hour later from the house's back door. "Looks like someone's been making themselves at home."

"Not much to do out here. You keep everything in pretty good shape."

"How about you just finish up with the weeding? I'm going inside to start supper."

Steven nodded, diving back down into the dirt and reaching for the tuft of pigweed.

Back inside the kitchen, Olga stood at the counter and continued preparing her pork chops. Setting a Teflon pan on the stove, she poured in a couple tablespoons of olive oil to heat while she prepared the meat. She whipped a raw egg with a half a cup of milk and a dash of salt and pepper, and set it aside to rest. She grabbed a fresh plastic bag and dumped in a half a cup of fine breadcrumbs, and a half-cup of corn meal, and then she shook it vigorously. As she rinsed the raw pork chops under the kitchen tap, Olga gave a jerk of surprise when Steven walked up behind her back.

"What are you doing? Is this a medical thing?" Steven teased, watching Olga set the chops down on a dinner plate covered with paper towel for absorption.

"Have you ever eaten a pork chop and bitten into a small sliver of bone?"

"Sure, everybody has. It's just part of the pork chop," Steven reasoned.

"No, it's not part of the meat. The bone slivers come from the butcher, when the high-powered saws slice the pork loin into chops. Simply rinsing off the meat will remove any of the bone shards that we can't see."

"God, you're smart."

"Don't confuse smart with old," Olga teased. "When you're my age, you'll be surprised at how much information you've accumulated."

He watched her dip the pork into the egg mixture and then gently set it down into the breadcrumbs that she'd dumped onto a dinner plate. Steven stepped back when Olga laid the meat down into the sizzling oil.

"You don't use butter? My mom always did."

"Butter burns too fast. With oil, I can get a nice sear on the outside, trapping in the meat's juices and not have to worry about scorching the dairy in the butter."

Leaning against the counter and watching Olga cook, Steven couldn't help but make a comment. "Now that I see you in here," his arm waved encompassing the entire kitchen. "I can see why they call you the *Cookie Lady*. You really know your way around a stove."

"I guess it's been a little bit of a hobby since I was a nursing student back in the late sixties. When I was in training, I worked for one summer in a medical clinic in east Harlem. Free checkups for the local families, counseling on personal hygiene, and family nutrition, all paid for by the city. You wouldn't believe how many suffered from malnutrition; the family budget wouldn't stretch far enough to cover the costs of food after paying the rent and utilities."

"So what's the connection between baking deserts and working in a free clinic?"

She stopped her story long enough to lift the pot she'd been boiling on the back burner. She dumped the pot of parboiled potatoes into a strainer. "Many people who live on a fixed income need a little help stretching their food budget," she explained, as she drizzled the potato-halves with olive oil and sprinkled them with Parmesan cheese. "Unfortunately, there isn't a cookbook anywhere that helps families, whether they're working or retired, to prepare nutritious meals on a limited budget. I'm writing a book with be a collection of recipes using everyday ingredients, no special processing equipment, no fancy techniques," Olga summed up, dumping the potatoes onto a cookie sheet and sliding them into the preheated oven. "Just simple recipes for the average person to follow and serve. No extra chapters on holiday entertaining or seafood appetizers."

"No shitake mushrooms or filet mignon?" Steven teased.

"Why, is that your favorite meal?"

"No, that's just what that cooking lady Mrs. Weatherbee was making on television while I was eating my lunch."

"Mrs. Weatherbee?" Olga mused. "I don't know a single working mother who watches her shows or follows her recipes. I think that woman really caters to a little *Stepford Wives Club*. Who has time to create castles by gluing sugar cubes together with royal icing for the holidays?"

"Someone sounds jealous," Steven teased. "Want your own show? I hear her slot is up for grabs."

Shaking her head, Olga reached into the fry pan to flip the browning pork chops. "I don't know anything about the lady's business dealings, but I will tell you one thing," she lectured her boarder. "No matter what we hear on the news, we're still only getting half the story. The truth about that recipe scandal is just that...scandal."

Steven grabbed a couple of plates, silverware, and glasses and began to set the table. "Do you ever plan to publish your recipes into a real-life cookbook? One that people can actually buy and use?"

"I'm just about ready," she admitted. "I'm just working on the finishing touches, a few ethnic recipes."

"I can remember a few good ones of my mom's, especially her baked bean burritos. Maybe I can show you one day and you can add them to your book?" Steven commented, stepping around Olga to reach up into the cupboard for a glass. After he filled it with tap water, he spun back toward where he'd been standing at the same moment that Olga pulled the fry pan off the stove. As she turned to move the pork chops onto a baking dish on the counter, they both collided in the middle of the kitchen floor.

The meat flew out of the super-heated pan, and three of the four chops jumped off the Teflon and awkwardly landed on the floor. The third chop was jarred upward when Steven's right shoulder slammed into Olga's left side. It flew through the air, and then landed on the top of Olga's clenched right hand where she held the fry pan's handle.

She dropped the pan onto the linoleum floor in an attempt to brush the burning pork fat off her skin. Olga began to yelp, as the slick of fat sealed in the searing heat, which moved downward past the epidermal layer of her skin, giving her a second-degree burn.

"I'm so sorry," Steven cried. He rushed over to Olga as she clutched her hand to her chest, breathing rapidly, her eyes wide with pain. "Let me see it," he demanded.

After taking a deep breath in an attempt to settle her stomach and her emotions, Olga took control of the situation. "Turn on the cold water tap," she ordered, as tears began to silently stream down her face, and she carefully shuffled her feet over the greasy kitchen floor.

Steven scrambled to turn on the water, and stood to the side, staring as Olga submerged her right hand under the running faucet. Her skin already puffy with the newly formed blisters.

"Holy shit," Steven moaned. "That's gotta hurt like hell."

Taking a very deep breath, Olga squeezed her eyes shut. After two more deep breaths, she was almost ready to speak.

"Want me to take you to the hospital?"

Olga pulled her hand out from under the cold stream of water, and bent to inspect the damage. "Second degree," she announced as if diagnosing a patient's wounds. "Looks like it's burned down to the hypodermis, but the patch is smaller than two inches in diameter, so I think I can treat this at home," she surmised with a nod of her head. "Can you go bring me the first-aid kit under the bathroom sink, please?"

Steven flashed through the house like a bullet.

"Here it is," he announced, flipping open the clips on the lid to reveal the contents. "Bandages, gauze, rubber gloves, burn ointment," Steven announced aloud. "Do you want some of this," he passed the tube toward Olga just as she turned her back and shoved her hand back under the kitchen tap.

"No, I'm going to keep it submerged for at least another ten or fifteen minutes under the running water. Do you mind bringing me a chair from the other side of the counter? I'm feeling a little dizzy."

Steven grabbed a three-legged chrome stool, and set it down directly behind Olga so she was able to rest her legs and lower back. "Do you want me to clean up the mess?" he asked.

"Yes, that would be really nice. But first, could you hand me a couple Tylenol from the first aid kit?"

After swallowing the two extra-strength capsules and washing them down with a full glass of water, Olga stayed put on her stool while Steven picked up the lukewarm pork chops and set them on the counter.

"There's a bucket and some floor soap in the utility room. Do you mind?"

Steven shook his head, tears threatening to form in the corners of his eyes. "Just tell me what to do," he whispered, shuffling off to the utility room.

By the time Steven had finished the floors, Olga was ready to bandage her arm. "Please shut off the oven and pull out the potatoes. If you're still hungry, I believe the pork chops are fine since the floors were just washed and hot enough to kill any germs. If you won't tell, neither will I," she tried to lighten the mood with a joke.

"I'm so sorry. I didn't mean to bump into you. I didn't know you were turning," Steven attempted to apologize for the second time.

Gingerly patting the skin dry surrounding her burn, Olga set down the cloth on the counter. "That was an honest to goodness accident, so I want you to stop worrying right now. Deal?"

"Deal."

"Now I'm going to go to my room, bandage my arm, and take a little nap. Hopefully the painkillers will set in and I'll be able to return a little later for some tea and toast."

"What about your supper?"

"I... I brought a snack home from the hospital," Olga lied. "Just hand me the brown paper bag from the fridge."

Steven complied, watching Olga tuck the first-aid kit under her arm before accepting the paper bag and moving off toward her bedroom door.

"I'm going to be fine," she stopped to comfort the young man. "It was an accident, Steven, remember? I'm gonna be just fine."

Steven turned and stared at the cookie sheet of crispy browned potatoes halves and fried pork chops. The food looked aesthetically pleasing, but unfortunately, he'd lost his appetite. He dug in the cupboards until he found a roll of foil, and reluctantly loaded the food into the empty baking dish and wrapped it all up for later.

Now that she was behind her closed bedroom door, Olga could test her theory. Sitting on the edge of her bed, she fumbled with the first aid kit. She finally flipped open the lid to reveal the gauze and bandages. She unrolled the top of the paper sack and revealed the canister of bloody tissue, and gingerly removed it and set it down on top of her legs. Carefully positioned between her thighs, Olga twisted off the lid, mindful not to jostle the sloshing liquid.

"Here goes," she muttered. She dipped in a cotton swab, swirling it round and round the tissue before carefully dabbed her multitude of blisters, almost as if running up and down a fluid filled mountain range.

She repeated the process until the entire area was covered in congealed tissue. Olga set the canister on her nightstand and began wrapping her hand. Not the world's easiest task, especially since she was right-handed. With the bandaging finally completed, Olga took a deep breath and forced herself to clean up before lying down and stretching out her back muscles.

With the canister stowed under the bed, and the first-aid kit balancing on her nightstand, she lay back on her throw pillows and closed her eyes, intentionally willing the pain to ease. Hopefully, she'd be able to fall asleep; otherwise, the night was going to be very long and very uncomfortable.

Her wish was almost immediately granted, and an hour later when Steven crept into her room to check on how she was feeling, Olga was snoring, lying motionless in the same position on her back.

CHAPTER EIGHT

"...I learned that ... in families there are no crimes beyond forgiveness."

—The Prince of Tides, 1991

As she took a stroll down the back alley, Helen instantly noticed that Olga had been working around the trees in her back yard. How in the world did that woman find time to nurse at the hospital, work on her cookbook, and keep her yard so well maintained? They were roughly the same age, but Olga was a dynamo, and as usual, the lights were still on at ten o'clock.

"Knock, knock," Helen called out, rapping her knuckles against the metal frame of the back door. "Tea kettle on?"

Steven reluctantly dragged himself up off the couch and shaking the cobwebs out of his head, stumbled toward the back door. "Can I help you?" he answered, swinging open the screen door to face Helen.

"Where is Olga?"

"Sleeping. Who are you?" Steven protectively demanded,

unwilling to step aside and allow the lady entrance until he understood exactly who she was and what she wanted.

"I'm Helen Horowitz. I'm Olga's neighbor. I live across the back alley in the white stucco house," she turned and pointed.

"I'm Steven Whitters." He relaxed and offered his hand to the visitor. "I'm rooming with Olga for a couple weeks. We both work at the hospital."

Helen nodded, returning the handshake as she took a step forward over the threshold of the back door. "Do you mind if I come in?"

"No, I guess not," he shrugged his shoulders, stepping aside and allowing Helen to stroll in and take up a position at the back door's landing.

"You said Olga was sleeping? That's unusual. It's only a few minutes after ten."

"Well, we had a little accident tonight."

Helen didn't wait for a further invitation; she turned away from him and marched straight toward her friend's bedroom door. "Olga," she whispered, slowly turning the doorknob as she tiptoed into the darkened room. "Are you sleeping?"

Olga moaned and turned her head away from the irritation, but never woke from her slumber, her heavy breathing a testament to her deep state of REM sleep. As she scanned Olga's body from the left side of the bed, it took Helen a few minutes to notice the bandaging on her friend's right hand. She gazed around the room, eventually adjusting to the minimal light and noticed the first aid kit sitting on the nightstand. There were no blood spots on the bedspread or soiled tissues in the bedside garbage. Helen concluded that whatever the wound, it was fairly minor. She quietly backed out of the room, carefully shut the door, and turned to face the young man named Steven, who was supposedly Olga's new roommate.

"Was she still sleeping?" he asked, his concern appearing genuine.

"Yes. Now tell me what happened," Helen demanded, walking toward the kitchen to make herself a cup of tea.

As he recounted the details of the burn, Steven nervously watched as Helen lifted up her mug and continued to sip at the herbal tea.

"So you're telling me that Olga wouldn't go to the hospital; she bandaged her own arm, and then took a couple pain killers and went to sleep. Is that right?"

"That's correct," Steven nodded, feeling as if he was under a police interrogation. "She didn't want to go to the hospital. She said it was only a second degree burn, and since it was smaller than… than…"

"Than two inches," Helen finished his sentence, "she figured she could self-medicate and treat at home."

"That's it. But how did you know?"

"I nursed at the same hospital with Olga for over twenty-five years, but when my husband Gerald was diagnosed with prostate cancer, I took a leave to stay home and care for him. Then after he died, I decided it was time to retire and hang up my whites."

"Oh, I see," Steven nodded. "I'm not a nurse, I'm just an orderly. But I've already worked there over four years, and I know that your husband was probably happier at home than he would have ever been on any ward."

As she rose to put the kettle back on the stove, Helen began to relax. "Why don't you tell me a little bit about yourself, Steven? Tell me how you came to be living with Olga."

Steven joined Helen for a second cup of tea, and recounted his story, including the details of the fire, but omitting the fact that Olga had caught him drinking on the job. "I was damn lucky to have met someone like your friend, or else I'd probably be staying downtown at the Y."

"She's an extraordinary woman. I think that's one reason I'm so protective of her. She's always lending out a helping hand, and I'm afraid that one day, someone might just sit up and bite the very hand that feeds them."

With their hands clamped down around each other's fingers, the entire family of Camille Greenway sat linked together in the emergency's waiting room.

"Where was she going?" her father whispered, turning to his wife, but essentially throwing the question out in the air for anyone to answer.

"She was going for groceries," Camille's mother whispered, as if speaking aloud might somehow cause her daughter pain. "She wanted ice cream, and didn't like the flavors we had in the house."

"She was acting kinda funny when I talked to her," Joshua spoke up.

"What do you mean?" His older brother Archie demanded in a harsh tone. "Are you telling us that Camille was acting funny, and you still let her drive?"

"She was already in the car and had the gear in reverse. I don't think I could have stopped her, even if I tried."

Archie jumped to his feet, breaking contact with his mother, and moved past his parents and plopped down in the seat next to his brother, Joshua. "Did you even try? Or were you in too much of a hurry to fill your face and get back to swim practice?"

"Don't yell at me," Joshua argued back, suddenly intimidated by his brother's looming presence. "At least I noticed; you wouldn't have even bothered to stop and talk to her."

"Enough," barked their father. "We're not going to cast blame out here while Camille's fighting for her life in there." He pointed to the swinging doors. "We're a family, and we're going to stick together, no matter what," he emphatically stated, leaving little doubt to his sincerity. "Now everybody just sit back and take a deep breath. We're probably going to be here for the rest of the night." He silently prayed, desperately hoping that a doctor wouldn't emerge from behind the closed doors to break the news that they'd been unable to save Camille's life and the family was free to go home.

CHAPTER NINE

"There are moments in life... moments when you know you've crossed a bridge. Your old life is over."

—Limitless, 2011

As she watched the dehydrated parsley flakes swirl clockwise, and ultimately sink to the bottom of the paper cup, Tammy Greenway sat with her husband and her two sons, and idly wondered why this heated liquid was called *Cup O' Soup.* It actually was nothing more than powdered chicken stock, littered with ground vegetable residue. It was not really fit for human consumption, was possibly a health hazard all in itself.

"You should really try to drink that," Ed urged his wife. "I don't think you've had anything for hours."

"I can't swallow," she finally admitted. "My throat feels like its swollen shut."

Ed nodded as he leaned down and removed the cup from his wife's shaking hand. "Maybe later."

"Mr. and Mrs. Greenway?"

"Yes doctor," Ed answered as everyone jumped up to their feet.

"I was wondering if we'd be able to speak? Maybe you can all follow me. I'll try to grab an unoccupied conference room."

The family nervously trudged down the hallway, unconsciously forming a single line, but grateful for the chance to stretch their cramped legs, and anxious to hear what the doctor had to say.

"Please be seated," the doctor waved his arm toward the chairs, stepping to the side to allow everyone entrance before turning back to close the door. "Camille is out of the woods," he smiled as he delivered the good news. "However, there were a few abnormalities on her admitting chart that I'd like you to enlighten me on, before we talk any further about..."

"What abnormalities?" Tammy interrupted, reaching under the table to grab her husband's hand.

"Well, as with any accident, I ordered a toxicology screen to check for alcohol, prescription medication, or illegal drugs."

"And?" Ed prompted the doctor, not very happy with where the conversation was heading.

"And we found an alarming amount of Valium in your daughter's system. We believe that at the time of the accident, her reactions and perception were severely compromised by the tranquilizer. We don't usually see this level of over-medication unless we're investigating a possible suicide attempt."

"Are you telling me that my daughter was trying to commit suicide?" Ed barked at the physician. "Cuz if you are, I think you're wrong."

"No, Mr. Greenway. I'm not. Please don't misunderstand what I'm trying to explain here. We are just a little concerned that the Valium your daughter Camille was prescribed to combat the emotional side effects of terminating her pregnancy may have been too strong a dosage, or possibly a case of incorrect ingestion. Do you remember the name of the physician who wrote the prescription?"

"She's seventeen years old," Ed mumbled, his fingers falling limp in his own lap.

"I understand," the doctor offered another polite smile. "But even young adults can make mistakes consciously, or even unconsciously, taking more of their medication than originally prescribed. I'd like to find out what dosage was intended, how the prescription was filled, and whether or not your daughter was taking her medication as ordered." Looking around the room at the stunned faces, the doctor finally realized that he was conversing on a lateral plane. "Do I understand that no one in this room knew Camille had recently terminated a pregnancy?"

"My baby was pregnant?" Tammy spoke up, her voice easily betraying the mounting pain in her heart. "I didn't know," she mumbled. "When did she term… terminate it?"

"As far as we can tell, it would have been within the last seventy-two hours. To be honest, we probably would not even have checked. However, due to the trauma from the crash, your daughter experienced some abdominal bleeding."

Archie turned away and growled through gritted teeth into his younger brother's ear. "What's the name of that little fucker who's been sniffing around our house?"

"Todd Parker, or Parkinson," Joshua whispered back. "Why?"

"Cuz we're going to pay him a little visit," Archie vowed, slowly turning back to rejoin his parent's conversation.

"Is she going to be fine?" Tammy quietly whispered, reaching forward as the doctor pushed the tissue box from the center of the table toward her chair.

"If you're asking about her future ability to bear children, I don't see any problems. However, we're going to have to be extremely conscious of any opportunistic infections for the next thirty days. Almost a self-imposed quarantine, if you will."

"But there was so much blood on her face," Tammy remembered upon her arrival at the hospital

"The blood was fortunately caused by the multitude of minor lacerations concealed in the scalp on the left side of your sister's head. And although she has suffered from a concussion, again, we believe there will be no permanent damage."

"And how's the truck driver," Joshua asked.

"Virtually the same diagnosis. A concussion with scalp lacerations. However, I'm having the emergency room doctor check him for neck or back trauma."

"Well, that's all pretty good news," Ed Greenway took a deep breath, clenching and unclenching his fingers. "It could have been a lot worse. I think we should be very grateful that no one was seriously hurt."

Nodding her head in agreement, Tammy wiped her eyes and blew her nose one last time. "Can I take my daughter home tonight?"

"It's almost three in the morning," the doctor reminded the family. "I'm planning to keep her for observation for at least another twenty-four to forty-eight hours."

After rising from his chair, the doctor reached forward and shook the hands of all four family members. "Please feel free to have the nurse page me if you have any further questions and good luck with the police. They're waiting outside to speak to you."

"The police?" Ed repeated.

"Well legally, your daughter was under the influence when she got behind the wheel of a motor vehicle that was involved in an accident causing injury."

"I guess that's true," Camille's father painfully admitted, his usually ruddy skin tone suddenly taking on an ashen pallor.

The first break of daylight was beginning to peek through Olga's bedroom sheers, the beams dancing on her eyelids, since she hadn't bothered to draw the blinds the night before. As she shielded her face with her right arm, she rose up in the bed, and swung her legs over the side, while yawning and stretching her back.

When she realized that she was still wearing her housedress from the previous night, Olga stepped out of her room and made her way straight to the bathroom. Her was bladder full and her teeth were in desperate need of a good brushing.

As she sat down on the toilet, she folded her hands in her lap and stared down at the bandages haphazardly wrapped around her right hand. Not exactly her best work, but they'd still somehow managed to hold together through her sleep. Opening and closing her hand, Olga was pleasantly surprised that there were no jabs of pain, or even the usual tightness usually brought on by stretching the skin as the blisters puffed up, filling with fluid.

Olga stood by the sink, and washed her hands as well as possible, considering the gauze. Then she immediately prepared to undress a wound, for the second time inside of a week. "Well, let's see what we've got," she spoke aloud, verbally encouraging herself to proceed. After she unwrapped the length of gauze, Olga stopped and stared down at the pad that still covered her burn.

Ordinarily, the area would be extremely inflamed and rimmed with pinky-red tissue. The interior of the burn would be covered with a multitude of blisters, ranging in height from just above the skin level to a couple of millimeters. It depended on the depth of the damaged tissue, but the blisters may or may not contain bloody fluid. Either way, it wasn't going to be pretty, and Olga was curious to see just how badly she might scar.

As she gently peeled back the pad, nothing could have prepared her for what she saw. The skin wasn't just healed; it was absolutely perfect—so perfect that it didn't even look like it belonged on her hand.

Olga scrambled in the medicine chest to find a magnifying glass, desperate for a closer inspection of the previous night's burn site.

"How you doing?" Steven gently knocked on the bathroom door. "I heard you get up. Do you need to go see a doctor?"

"No, I'm fine," Olga answered, the understatement of the year.

"How's it look? Do you need my help changing the bandage?"

"No, I'm alright," she shouted back through the door, scrambling to find a roll of clean gauze to conceal her hand. "I've just about finished wrapping it."

"Really, I just wanted to see how you'd faired," Steven admitted, visibly disappointed that he was being kept out of the loop.

"Why don't you put a kettle on for tea? I'll be out in a second."

As he puttered around the kitchen, Steven popped some sliced bread into the toaster, pulled out the margarine and jams from inside the fridge door, and began to set the table.

"Good morning," Olga chirped; her overly positive spirits slightly disarming. "No eggs this morning?"

"No, last night after your friend Helen left, I ate two of the chops and half the roasted potatoes. Believe it or not, I'm still full," he emphasized by rubbing his stomach.

"Helen was here?"

"She stopped by for tea, but since you were already sleeping, she just talked with me for awhile and then eventually went home."

"Did you tell her about the burn?"

"I had to explain why you were in bed before ten o'clock," he offered with a shrug of his shoulders. "She looked in on you, but you had already conked out and Helen decided not to try to wake you."

She made herself a cup of tea while debating just what she was going to say to her neighbor. Olga was so lost in thought she didn't notice that she'd just lifted the steaming copper kettle off the stove with her bandaged hand.

"Just how bad is your burn?" Steven demanded, rising up from his position at the kitchen table.

"Why?"

"Cuz you're moving around the kitchen like it never happened," he motioned his head toward the kettle, afraid the Olga might be experiencing some form of delayed shock. "I think you better let me see your hand."

"I'm a nurse," she reminded him. "I am one hundred percent capable of assessing my own wounds."

"Never the less," Steven brushed off her attempt to assure him. "Let's see," he continued to nag, stepping around the kitchen counter, and reaching for her hand.

As she instinctively pulled her arm out of sight, Olga felt the horizontal handle of the oven door press up against her lower back. With no further retreat possible, she stood her ground and faced her roommate. "I'm fine. Just eat your breakfast, and get ready for work."

"Show me your hand, or I'm going to call your friend Helen over," he threatened, the tone of his voice leaving little doubt to his convictions.

Eyes locked together, Olga evaluated the young man, taking one last chance to weigh the sincerity of his threat.

"And I know she lives across the back alley in the white stucco house."

"I think we overreacted a little last night. It wasn't nearly as bad as we thought," Olga began to set the stage.

"Let me see it," Steven demanded one last time, his right hand beginning to move around Olga's side.

"Let me do it," she shook her head, disgusted that she was

allowing herself to be bullied by a twenty-three year old kid. Pulling her hand out into plain view, Olga slid off the loosely wrapped bandaging, turning her hand palm up and then palm down to satisfy his curiosity.

"I don't fucking believe it."

"You'll watch your mouth in my house," Olga barked.

"Sorry," Steven muttered an apology, not even lifting his eyes from Olga's skin. "I was sure it was a lot worse than…" He stopped mid sentence, finally raising his face to catch Olga's eyes as his own fingers gently wrapped around her hand. "Did you see this new skin?"

"Yes," she nodded, fighting to stop the smile from spreading to the corners of her mouth.

"It's incredible. This skin is just like baby skin," Steven whispered, dropping his face only inches from the back of Olga's hand. "This is a miracle."

"I think you're taking this a little too far," she chuckled, extracting her hand from his grasp. "Tea?"

"Tea?" Steven repeated in astonishment. "Screw the tea. I think we should head over to the hospital and have somebody look at your hand. It's rejuvenated, or revived, or something. We can't keep this to ourselves!" he exclaimed.

"Well, we kinda have to," she reluctantly nodded, dropping two tea bags into her pot as she turned to pat the side of the copper kettle, checking the temperature of the previously boiled water.

"Explain it to me," Steven simply demanded, stepping away from the stove and dropping down into one of the kitchen chairs.

When she realized her husband was still occupied with the two police officers jotting down information regarding his fleet insurance policy, Tammy moved away from Ed and continued to pace back and forth outside Camille's hospital room. The doctor had promised her that she'd be able to see her daughter shortly, and no matter what, she wasn't leaving until he followed through on his promise.

"Mrs. Greenway, you can comc inside now," the nurse beckoned.

With a backward glance at her husband and sons as they continued to converse with the officers, Tammy wiped her eyes for the hundredth time and entered her daughter's room.

"She's still sedated," the nurse explained, stepping aside to allow Tammy admittance.

As she rushed up to Camille's side, she stood and stared down at her baby, wondering how in the world she'd ever be able to make all her daughter's pain go away. "How is she feeling?"

"After she arrived by ambulance in the ER, we were able to stop her internal hemorrhaging. Then we sutured the lacerations in your daughter's scalp. Since then, she has been resting quite comfortably," the nurse reported.

"The doctor said she had terminated a pregnancy," Tammy finally choked out the simple statement. "Was it performed here?"

The nurse picked up her chart and scanned the compiled information. "No, it appears it was an outside clinic. We have no record of a Camille Greenway coming through our system."

"Was it, was it done…" Tammy wiped her nose and struggled to clear her own throat. "Was it done properly? Was my daughter damaged?"

"No ma'am. The emergency doctor's notes clearly state that wherever the procedure was performed, an experienced doctor under sterile conditions must have done it. The only reason your daughter hemorrhaged was due to the trauma inflicted on her abdomen at the time of her car accident."

"Thank you," she turned up her face and smiled at the nurse.

"To be honest, I didn't even know she was pregnant. No one in the family did."

"That's not uncommon with a girl your daughter's age."

"I can't imagine how she could go through something like that all by herself. Camille is a very strong girl, but an abortion… What was she thinking?"

"I don't know anything about your daughter, Mrs. Greenway, but from my experience on the floor, the average young girl does not go through the procedure alone. Rest assured someone—chances are the father—was probably there to hold her hand."

Somewhat comforted by this information, Tammy continued to stroke her daughter's arm, desperately hoping that Camille's eyes would spring open and she'd be able to tell her how much she was loved.

"Tammy, there you are," whispered her husband as he slowly made his way into the room. "How is she?"

"The nurse says she's going to be fine. I just can't believe that she was pregnant," Tammy admitted. "How did I miss it?"

"We all missed it."

"What did the police have to say? Are there going to be any charges against Camille?"

"Possibly," he sighed, "After all, she was under the influence of a Class-A narcotic when she backed across two lanes of traffic into the path of that truck."

"I couldn't bring myself to say anything during the meeting with the doctor, but I think *I'm* missing a half prescription of Valium," Tammy sheepishly admitted.

"Really?"

"Well, I won't be a hundred percent sure until the next time we head up to the cabin, but if it's not there, then it's definitely missing."

After rubbing his forehead with his right hand, Ed signaled his wife to follow him out of his daughter's room. "The police reminded me that if charges are pressed against Camille, the driver of the truck will be in a strong position to press a civil suit, seeking damages up to six figures."

"What?" she shrieked, instantly covering her own mouth as she scanned up and down the hallways to see if anyone had caught her outburst. "This nightmare is never going to end, is it?"

"Whenever the insurance companies get involved, nobody wins except the lawyers."

Tammy nodded her head in agreement; allowing herself to be wrapped inside the comfort of her husband's outstretched arms.

Steven and Olga both called in sick. It was the first time in ten months for Steven; Olga was unable to remember if she had ever. At her kitchen table, they both repeatedly examined her right hand, alternately comparing it to the original skin on the back of her left.

"I don't understand," Steven kept chanting, as if the mere admission of his ignorance was enough to grant him infinite wisdom.

"I don't understand it either," Olga admitted, "but I might have an idea."

Steven pulled back from his huddled position over Olga's hand. "What's your theory?"

"It's kind of farfetched, so bear with me, and just hear me out before you start with the questions. Deal?"

"Deal."

"Remember when you knocked over the aspirator at the hospital, and sent the canister crashing into the floor?"

"Yeah."

"Well, I'd cut myself quite deeply just above my knee less than twelve hours before. The wound was bandaged, but since it was unstitched, it was still relatively open."

"You're a bit of a klutz," Steven smiled, nervously attempting a joke.

"Anyway," Olga continued with her explanation, "When the canister broke, the fetal tissue splashed up on my uniform, and soaked through the bandages, down to my skin and inside the cut. The next morning, it was as if the cut had never existed at all. In its place was fresh tissue; brand new skin," she shrugged her shoulders, "just like the patch on my hand." Pushing back her kitchen chair, Olga discreetly pulled her housedress up above her knee, revealing the *baby skin* now adorning her leg.

"It's so soft," Steven muttered; pulling his hand back the second he realized that he'd been stroking her leg without invitation. "To be honest, I'm having a hard time with the idea. If I hadn't seen your burn last night, I don't think I would have believed half your story."

"I know. Me too," Olga admitted. "But I've been injured twice, and both times the fetal tissue repaired me beyond my original condition."

"You used tissue again last night?"

"Yes, there's a canister under my bed," she admitted, watching Steven jump up from his chair and hurry to her bedroom.

"I can't believe you stole this," he motioned toward the darkened liquid. "I'd never have imagined it in a hundred years," he swore.

Olga stood, brushing the dress material back down her leg, unconsciously stroking the new skin on her right hand. "It's like... it's like a research project. I just can't walk away from it until I understand what I've found."

After setting down the canister on the counter, Steven pulled a carving knife from the wooden block, opened his left palm, and before Olga could jump up from her chair fast enough to stop him, he sliced a swath downward across the length of his palm. "Oh God, that hurts," he wailed. "I've seen it done in movies before, but I never knew," he continued to moan as Olga rushed up to his side. She grabbed his palm and wrapped a dishtowel around the clenched wound.

"You fool," she yelled. The knife could have slipped and you could have severed every tendon in your wrist. Are you crazy?"

"No, but I'm really in pain," Steven almost cried, stomping his right foot in anguish.

Olga stood motionless in the kitchen, stared at Steven, and then back at the canister. Did she dare?

"Aren't you going to help me?" he begged, his eyes beginning to water with the pain.

Olga shook off her trepidation and finally began to move, suddenly turning her back on Steven and marching off toward the bathroom.

"Hey, where are you going?"

"Hang on," she shouted, returning a moment later with a handful of cotton swabs and a collection of bandaging. After settling Steven at the kitchen table, Olga assembled everything she needed for dressing the wound. "Are you sure you want to do this?"

"Yes!" he barked through gritted teeth.

She laid out a clean tea towel and set Steven's hand down on the table, gently opening his palm to survey the wound. The gash was at least three inches long and still bleeding profusely. "Squeeze it again," she instructed him, taking the opportunity to open the canister gently.

"Are you going to mix it?" Steven asked, watching the congealed levels of fluid slowly slosh back and forth in the circular container.

"I suppose," she admitted, returning with a wooden spoon and tentatively dipping it down into the mixture. For the first time, Olga noticed an unpleasant odor; the dead fetal tissue was beginning to decompose. “This doesn’t smell right,” she sadly announced. “I’m afraid of giving you a lethal dose of blood poisoning, instead of administering a cure.”

Steven took a whiff from the open container, and instantly pulled back his head as he wrinkled his nose in disgust. “I don’t know if it’s such a good idea either.”

“I think we need a new canister,” Olga admitted, and she began to wrap the young man’s hand with the sterile padding and gauze.

CHAPTER TEN

"Arnie, do you think there's a difference between a reason and an excuse, because I don't think there is?"

—Traffic, 2000

Barely rested, but freshly showered, Archie prowled the house and backyard, anxiously waiting for his younger brother Joshua to wake.

"Coffee?" his mother asked, sitting on the rear deck, downing yet another cup as she re-crossed her arms and legs in an unconscious effort to comfort herself.

"Mom, have you been to sleep yet?" Archie demanded. He was concerned that his mother was living off the caffeine and cigarettes that the housekeeper kept replenishing without even being asked.

"I've tried twice, but I can't relax. Every time I close my eyes, I see that awful car wreck in front of our house. How about you, dear; were you able to sleep?" Tammy asked, slipping a manicured fingernail between her teeth without even noticing.

"Just a little, but I have something I need to take care of this morning, and Joshua promised to help me," he vaguely explained, pulling up a chair and grabbing a smoke out of his mother's pack of cigarettes. "Where's dad?"

"He went in for a meeting with his insurance agent."

"But it's Sunday."

"True, but he offered to buy him brunch at the golf club, and the man accepted."

"Have you phoned the hospital yet? Do you know how Camille is?"

"Yes, I called. They say she's still resting comfortably, and they don't expect her to wake for at least another three or four hours. So as soon as your father returns, we're going to head back down to the hospital. Do you want to come?"

"No, remember? I told you I have something to take care of with Joshua."

"Yes, I remember now," Tammy confided.

Under closer inspection, Archie noticed that his mother appeared groggy, as if she was heavily medicated—more than likely, that was the cause of her disoriented thoughts. "Dad must've have shit when he saw you smoking."

"No, he just shook his head and left. I guess he figures he has bigger fish to fry."

"What's for breakfast?" Joshua interrupted his older brother and mother, sliding open the kitchen's screen door before stepping out onto the patio.

"Coffee and smokes," Archie toasted by raising his mother's cup with a lit cigarette clenched between the fingers of his right hand. "So go get dressed, we have a little business to take care of."

Joshua nodded his head, turned and shuffled off back into the house.

"Will you meet us at the hospital?" Tammy questioned her son for the third time.

"We'll stop by as soon as we're done," he promised, roughly butting out his cigarette and giving his mother a weak smile.

While he impatiently waited on the driveway for his brother, Archie strummed his fingers against his gearshift, his eyes casually checking the position of the baseball bat barely concealed under the leather jacket in the back seat.

"His name's Todd Parkinson, and he's captain of the lacrosse team," Joshua announced. "I found his address and cell number in Camille's address book. Shit, she really knows a lot of guys."

Archie raised his eyebrows and shot his younger brother a disapproving look.

"I mean, she sure has a lot of friends," Joshua stumbled over his own words, eventually settling on directness as he passed Archie the recorded information. "So what's the plan?"

"Hold on a sec," Archie growled, backing out the driveway even faster than his sister had the day before. "So here's the deal, bro. You've got five minutes to come up with a plan while I drive to this fucker's house," he explained, looking down at the note for the second time to confirm the address. "Cuz if you don't, we're going with mine," he motioned toward the aluminum bat.

Dressed in street clothes, with a large canvas shopping bag slung over her shoulder, Olga walked through the doors of the hospital and made her way up to the designated unit for day surgery.

"What's in the bag," one doctor quipped as she walked by, his mouth instinctively watering like Pavlov's dog.

"You'll see," Olga smiled back, shaking her head as she continued to scuttle down the hallway.

She casually leaned against the nursing desk, picked up the day's roster, and began scanning the patient rooms, checking which were empty, and which had already housed a procedure. She nearly jumped out of her skin when a hand landed on her waist. Olga spun around to face Dr. Martin Hood.

"A jeans skirt?" Martin couldn't help but notice her casual attire. "Must be your day off, my dear. So, what about supper this evening? Just as friends?" he added, so Olga wouldn't assume he was pressuring her for a date. "I'm craving an authentic bowl of spaghetti like we used to enjoy down at Antonio's."

"Sounds good, but I have plans with Helen tonight," she lied.

"Rain check?"

"That'd be great," Olga smiled as she impatiently tapped her toe, waiting for Martin to rush off to whatever emergency required his immediate attention.

"Well, I have to run," he smiled. "I'll call you?"

"Sure," Olga nodded as the doctor finally turned and began making his way down the hallway. As she took a moment to watch him leave, Olga was surprised at just how much he'd slowed in the years since the breakup of their relationship. His graying hair was really beginning to thin, his scalp peeking out from the back of his head. His gait slowed, Martin's back appeared to be the slightest bit stooped, as if the mere act of bending might cause him pain.

"Time stands still for no man, not even the brilliant," she muttered, turning her attention back to the roster. According to the duty nurse's notes, room four should be empty, three procedures already completed before noon, nothing scheduled until after the break.

After slipping down the hall and into the vacant room, Olga immediately stepped up to the waste receptacle, snapped off the plastic lid, and reached down inside to retrieve a fresh canister. She dropped the container into her bag and straightened her back, closing the metal snaps sewn onto the canvas. Just as she was about to step back into the hallway and leave, the fight broke out.

"Let me in there," the man shouted, stomping his work boots on the floor as two hospital security guards fought with all their might to hold him back. "Gladys!" he continued to shout. "I know you're in there, and I want you to come out right now!"

A fiery red-haired woman stepped out of patient room number eight, and began shouting back just as loud. "Harold, you get your hairy ass out of this hospital and back into your truck, because I'm not going anywhere with you until the doctor finishes his job."

"Gladys, don't do this," he warned. "You ain't got no right."

"No right?" she screamed, which drew every single member of the floor's staff toward the ruckus. "Then why don't you tell me just what my rights are, Harold Harding? Go ahead," she prodded the angry bear of a man. "You stand there and tell me that my rights are all about the cooking, and the cleaning, and raising all the kids. And cuz you won't use no rubbers; then I don't have no damn rights. Ain't that the way you see it, Harold?"

"Gladys, this is private. Now *please* get yer clothes and let's go," his tone began to change from that of a forceful demand to a heartfelt plea.

"Come on, buddy," the two burly guards attempted to muscle him back toward the elevator. "Let's take this outside."

"I'm not going anywhere without my wife!"

"Your wife? Did you just call me your wife?" Gladys continued yelling, moving closer, now only six feet from the man's position. "To be your legal wife, you'd have to ask me to marry you, and we'd have stood before a preacher, and you'd have promised to take care of me forever. Well Harold, you ain't done no such thing, so you just better rethink what you been calling me, cuz I ain't nobody's wife."

His head bowed, arms falling limp at his sides, he finally gave up the fight. "Gladys, I can't marry ya, cuz I ain't yet divorced."

"But you said yer first wife was dead. You better fess up right now, Harold Harding," she demanded, both hands flying up to her hips.

As he slowly shuffled his feet to close the small distance between them, Harold sheepishly stuffed his hands in his pockets, searching for just the right words to explain. "My wife Suzy never died, she done ran off with her friend," he admitted, gently taking Gladys's arm in an attempt to steer their conversation to a somewhat more private location.

"You told me she was dead, but she really left you for another man?"

"No, that's not it," Harold shook his head. "She's one of them *jar lickers*," he whispered, his voice low, his right hand covering his mouth.

"A what?"

"A jar licker," he carefully pronounced. "You know," he tried to make his point by nodding his head and winking his eyes. "She liked to have her rim licked, but didn't want no pickle in her jar."

"For Christ sakes, Harold," Gladys shook her head in disgust. "Are you trying to tell me that your ex-wife was one of them lesbians?"

"Shh," he warned, turning to look if any of the gathered staff had heard her question. "No need for anyone to know my private family business."

Gladys nodded her head in agreement, and motioned for Harold to drop his head so she could whisper in his ear. "If I knew the truth, I wouldn't have come here."

"So can we go?" he asked, his voice as soft as a child's.

"Sure, I'll just grab my clothes."

As the security guards waited to escort the couple from the hospital grounds, Olga turned and made her way to the elevator on the floor, wondering just how her roommate was fairing back at home.

As he surfed up and down the limited television channels, Steven was determined not to give in to the pain and head for the emergency room. A shot of painkillers, a little antiseptic bandaging, and he'd be fine within the hour. But he was damn determined to test Olga's theory, so he continued to sit on the couch, cradling his left hand in a bath towel as he waited for her return.

"Steven," Olga called out. "Are you in the living room?"

"Yes," he answered, rising from the couch and walking over to the table. "Seemed to take a lot longer than I thought it would," he commented, trying not to sound like a whiny preschooler.

"There was a little distraction on the floor, but I got it," Olga announced, carefully lifting the aborted fetal material out of her shoulder bag. "And by the way, what did you do with the old one?" she couldn't help but ask.

"I flushed the liquid," he admitted with a shrug of his shoulder. "The empty container is in a plastic grocery bag under the sink. I didn't want to just drop it in the trash full of blood, so I rinsed it out and wrapped it up."

Olga nodded a silent agreement, and carried her offering over to the table. Very slowly unwrapping Steven's hand, she peered down at the cut, still leaking blood, the wound was attempting to seal itself at both ends. "Are you ready?"

"Yes," he simply answered.

Olga unscrewed the lid, dipped a sterile cotton swab into the fresh tissue, and began dabbing it onto Steven's wound. A multitude of layers applied, she finally sat down to examine her work. "That's as much as I ever put on. Guess we might as well bandage it up."

As he sat back and watched Olga finish dressing his self-inflicted wound, Steven began to evaluate the ramifications of what they'd just done. He wasn't sure of the exact charge, but he was damn sure that stealing aborted *baby guck* from a hospital room was good for at least a couple years. "Nobody saw you do this, right?"

"Nobody saw," Olga reassured her patient, screwing down the plastic lid on the canister. "I guess we'd better figure out where to put this," she looked the young man directly in the eyes.

"It seems to spoil fast, so I guess it's gotta go in the fridge."

She gingerly set the canister down into a brown paper lunch bag, folded it closed, and set it deep within the rear of the kitchen fridge.

"Now what?" Steven asked, attempting to roll up the soiled bathroom towel with one hand.

"I don't know," Olga admitted, I guess we wait and see if it works again."

"And if it does, then what?"

"Well then, we should probably contact somebody, let some professional research institute take a shot at testing our theory," she summed up in a flourish.

"Why?"

After unconsciously moving to wash her hands with hot soapy water under the kitchen tap, Olga returned to the table to continue the conversation. "We can't keep this kind of discovery to ourselves. We have to do something with it."

"I agree," Steven answered, his brain racing a hundred miles a minute. "I just haven't figured out what yet."

As they sat in the car, Archie and Joshua had already switched discs at least five times, bored with the lack of selection, nervous about waiting in broad daylight to ambush some young guy they barely knew.

"He might not be home for hours," Joshua tried to reason with his brother. "We're going to sit here till midnight, hoping the kid shows up, and then when he does, we pray that he's willing to hop in your car and go for a ride?"

"That's the plan," Archie admitted, his eyes never leaving the front of the Parkinson's house.

"That's not a fucking plan, that's a prison sentence waiting to happen. Might as well head to the cop shop and turn ourselves in right now."

"I told you to come up with something better, but you didn't," he sneered, throwing his hands up in the air.

"I'm going home," Joshua announced; reaching for the car's inside door handle in frustration.

"Stay put," Archie ordered in no uncertain terms. "What the fuck's the matter with you? Don't you wanna see that little piece of shit pay for knocking up our sister and forcing her to have an abortion at some god damn free clinic?"

"Yeah, but I'm not going to blow my scholarship over it."

"Then get out!" Archie shouted, leaning over to push his brother out of the front seat of his car.

"What are you doing?"

"I said get out," Archie argued back, throwing his full weight into the argument.

"Hey, what's going on? Is there a problem?" a voice shouted from Joshua's open car window. "Do I need to call the cops?"

Both brothers froze, deeply embarrassed that they'd been caught in the middle of a brotherly squabble.

"Who are you?" Archie abruptly shouted, as if he had any right to be demanding answers.

"Todd Parkinson. Why?"

"I'm Archie Greenway, and this is my brother, Joshua. We've come to talk to you about our sister Camille."

"What about her?" Todd asked, stepping one foot closer to the car. "Is she sick, in hospital?"

"Now why would you guess that?" Archie mused, stepping out of his driver's door and strolling around the hood of his car. "Did a little birdie come and tell you that your girlfriend was ill?"

"Camille and I broke up," he announced, eyes downcast.

"Oh, you broke up. Isn't that just convenient?" Archie's interrogation continued. "Why'd you break up?"

"Personal shit," he shrugged, looking to Joshua for some measure of support.

Instead of support, Joshua surprisingly jumped in on the act. "Did it have anything to do with the fact that she was pregnant and you wanted nothing to do with her?"

Todd dropped his knapsack to the ground, and simultaneously took two steps backward, as Joshua swung open his door and exited the car. "Look," Todd said, "I really like your sister, but it didn't work out. She was pregnant, so I paid for the abortion. End of story."

"Fuck you and your *end of story*," Archie rushed up and shoved Todd so hard the kid stumbled backwards, eventually losing his balance, and falling flat on the ground.

"I'm sorry," he shouted, taking his time rising to his feet. "The abortion wasn't my idea; it was your sister's."

"She's only seventeen, did you know that?" Joshua again added his two cents.

"So am I," Todd muttered as he bent to pick up his knapsack. "Which hospital is Camille in?"

"Why do you care?" Archie threw over his shoulders as he stomped off back around the car and leaned into the back seat. "You see this?" he threatened the kid, lifting out the aluminum bat. "I could crack your skull wide open and leave you on the sidewalk to die. Maybe just break your ankle instead."

"That would sure derail your little lacrosse plans, wouldn't it?" Joshua chimed in, somehow spurred on by his brother's raw fury.

"What do you want from me?" the kid finally begged, unsure whether they had actually come for a pound of flesh, or whether they would be satisfied with simply berating him.

Joshua stepped up to within a foot of Todd's face, glaring down into his eyes as he began to speak. "Our sister was so drugged up on Valium after her abortion, that she had a car accident. I just wanted you to know that I got your number, buddy. You got my brother so mad, he wants to crack your head, and my sister is an emotional train wreck. But see, I'm the cool-headed one, and although it may not look like it, I'm your biggest problem."

"Really?" Todd questioned the threat, feeling his courage return once he felt sure that he wasn't going to get his ass kicked. "What're you going to do to me?"

"Absolutely nothing," Joshua chuckled, turning to walk back to the car. Settled once again in the passenger's seat, he leaned out the window to make one final statement. "Did I mention that my best friend is Grizzy Davidson? As in coach Davidson's son? I'd sure hate to see the coach send an unfavorable letter spelling out your discipline problems to whatever college your parents paid-off to accept your ass."

"Do you know how college coaches treat discipline problems?" Archie interrupted, thrilled with his younger brother's approach. "Trust me, you little piss ant, you've haven't even experienced pain and humiliation until you get on the bad side of your college coach."

"What do you want from me," Todd surrendered, the wind totally gone from his sails.

"Simple," Archie answered, tossing the impromptu weapon back into his car through the open back window. "If you ever breathe a word of Camille's pregnancy to anyone, you're dead. And second," he swung open his door. "Don't ever talk to our sister again. I don't care if she calls, writes, or shows up on your doorstep. You see her—you better turn and run the other way. Got it?"

"I hear you," he answered, his voice and posture revealing his defeat.

"Then don't fuck up," Archie warned, slamming his car into drive and peeling out of the kid's neighborhood.

CHAPTER ELEVEN

"Of course it's unfair. We're women.
Our choices are never easy."

—Titanic, 1997

Dr. Martin Hood sat in on the executive committee meeting, unable to fathom why the meeting had even been called for a Sunday afternoon in the first place. He was sure nothing could be a bigger waste of his time. He had the minutes from the previous meeting in front of him, and a copy of the agenda listing all the motions and discussion points for the day's meeting. Armed with this much information, he couldn't possibly imagine why the assembled bureaucrats would actually require his presence. They never requested his opinion without arguing his position even before he completed his statement, and in all likelihood, every vote scheduled for the afternoon's meeting almost surely had been previously decided.

"Dr. Hood, are you in favor or not?" an unidentifiable voice echoed from across the room.

"I'm voting in favor," he raised his hand, clueless as to what the issue at question actually was.

"Well, that's a majority," the chairman brought his hands together, slamming shut the leather-bound agenda and rising from his position at the head of the conference table. "I want to thank you all for your expertise and your understanding regarding this most difficult policy ruling. Ladies and gentlemen, this meeting is officially adjourned," he nodded, turning toward the secretary taking notes. "And Dr. Hood," he shouted across the mahogany table, "May I see you a moment, please?"

Martin took a deep breath, reminding himself that he had absolutely no more time for an extra committee or advisory board appointment, and walked over to the chairman as everyone rushed to exit the room. "What can I do for you, Dick?" he lifted up the corners of his mouth in his best imitation of a smile.

"Well, for starters, I just wanted to say thanks. Never in my wildest dreams did I ever imagine that we'd have your support. But don't think I'm not grateful," Dick Mansfield continued to jabber on. "And now that I feel we actually might be working on the same team, I'd going to recommend the committee rethink your proposal for the community health clinic."

"Well thanks, Dick," Martin genuinely smiled, thrusting out his hand to join the chairman's extended fingers. "I know you were a little worried about the availability of funds, but I'm positive that if you and your boys really try, you can squeak out a few extra bucks from the budget."

"That's the beauty of it," the chairman turned and whispered his departing comments in Martin's ear. "By helping me pension a few of the senior staff, you've just freed up a hell of a lot of spending capital. I think we're going to be able to work out a deal," he reached up and patted Martin warmly on the back before turning and leaving the conference room.

"Senior staff?" Martin called out to the empty room. "I'm senior staff," he mumbled to himself, finally opening the agenda for the meeting, his index finger following the eighteen points downward until his hand stopped on number nineteen. *Vote required: Mandatory retirement packages for all staff over the age of sixty years with full-time employment benefits.*

"It doesn't seem to hurt anymore, and the throbbing pain has kind of evaporated," Steven suddenly noticed. "It's only been a minute since you swabbed me with tissue, but it's like I've instantly been sealed, or repaired."

"Maybe you should just sit on the couch and rest awhile."

"That's a good idea," Steven agreed, moving toward his favorite recliner in the living room. "I'm just surprised that there's no tingling of the skin, no itchy rash…not even a burst of heat or flash of cold. It's weird," he admitted. "I can't even tell if there's anything happening underneath these bandages other than the lack of pain."

"Well you wouldn't rather be in agony, would you?" Olga never even bothered to raise her head.

"No. So how much longer?" Steven asked; Olga's face still buried in piles of handwritten of recipes scattered across the couch and adjacent coffee table.

"It's only been a couple of hours," she reasoned with the impatient young man. "I think we should at least wait until after supper."

Steven groaned his displeasure at Olga's firm decision. From his peripheral vision, he noticed the shadow crossing the living room window. "We've got company," he announced, instantly jumping to his feet as the form continued to make its way to the back door.

"Oh hell," Olga cursed. "I'm not in the mood for some door to door salesman. Hang on. I'll get rid of him."

"Helen," Olga remarked the minute she swung open the front door. "I didn't realize it was you. I'm not used to you walking past the front."

"I just thought I'd bring in your mail and see how you were doing," she dropped her eyes down to her neighbor's right hand as she set the envelopes down on the floor. "Where's your bandage?"

"Oh, I'm fine," Olga reassured her, unconsciously slipping her hand behind her back. "The redness and swelling have all gone down, never even blistered. I guess I'm a fast healer."

"I guess," Helen repeated back. "So," she attempted to change the mood of the conversation, "you got time for a quick cup?" she asked, bringing her right foot forward to step into the house without even waiting for an invitation.

"Actually, it's not a good time," Olga explained, standing her ground as Helen quickly pulled back her shoulders. "Steven's home sick, and I wouldn't want to pass you the bug."

"Oh, I see. Why didn't you tell me that you were looking at taking in a boarder? Kind of caught me by surprise."

"I wasn't actually planning it. Steven's house-trailer burnt down and he was left in the lurch."

"In the lurch," Helen repeated, as if having trouble believing her best friend's story. "Is everything alright, Olga?" she whispered. "Just give me a signal. Blink twice if you want me to call the cops," she continued, suddenly afraid that her neighbor might have fallen prey to some sort of home invasion.

"Helen, there's nothing criminal going on here. Why don't you come on in for a cup of tea?" she relented; afraid that brushing off her friend might just bring further unwanted attention. "Can you excuse me while I check in on Steven?"

"Sure," Helen answered, waiting until Olga had stepped back from the door before she entered.

As she rushed to the living room, Olga was grateful to see that

Steven had already retreated to the privacy of the spare room. "I had to invite her in," she whispered her apology through his open door. "We'll have a quick cup, and then I'll send her on her way. You going to be fine in here?"

"I guess," he sighed, already bored with watching television, not the least bit sure what he'd do to occupy his time in the seclusion of his bedroom.

"Good, and no peeking." She pointed at the bandage, her voice firm. "Just lie down and try to take a nap. I'll come and get you as soon as she leaves."

Door closed, blinds drawn, Steven lay down on the bed and closed his eyes, sure that sleep would evade him. He was wrong.

Olga stood motionless in the living room just out of Helen's sight, and desperately tried to figure out what to do to conceal the rejuvenated skin on the back of her hand. She decided to use the quick remedy of burn ointment. She turned and walked straight past her guest and into the bathroom. "Should we have some cookies?" Olga called out, hoping to stall for a little more time while she slathered on the heavily medicated cream.

"Tea's ready," Helen answered back, already nestled in behind the table by the time Olga joined her. "Oh, and can you grab the milk?" she asked, reaching across the table to pop a shortbread biscuit into her mouth.

When she swung open the fridge, Olga's heart nearly stopped beating as she recognized the brown paper bag lurking behind the mayonnaise jar on the top shelf. "I'm out," she announced, stumbling back to the table and clumsily sitting down in her chair."

"Want me to take you for groceries? You could probably use a little neighborly assistance."

"What?" Olga asked, finally tuning into the last couple of words of Helen's statement.

"Are you self-medicating?"

"Just a few over the counter painkillers. Nothing stronger," Olga promised, forcing herself to pay attention. "I'm fine, really."

"Let me see your hand," Helen coaxed her friend, reaching across the table as she gently picked up Olga's right arm and brought it in for a closer inspection. "Looks like you dodged another bullet. I can't exactly see the skin under the layer of cream, but..." she stalled, raising the hand only inches from her nose, "I don't see any blistering redness to indicate second degree burns. You'll be fine."

"Thank you, doctor," Olga teased, pulling back her hand and settling it down in her lap.

"Where's your roommate?"

"Sleeping. He's quite sick, so I don't expect he'll surface before late afternoon."

"You look worn out, Olga. Is something else the matter?"

"I had coffee the other afternoon with Martin. Now he wants to go out again for supper," she admitted; a move designed to throw Helen off her tracks.

"That's why you're looking so worn out. You've been worrying about *him* again and not sleeping." She shook her head in disgust. "You've got to put the doctor behind you and get on with your life. Your preoccupation with that man just about derailed your career, and by the looks of things, it almost caused a serious burn."

Olga dropped her head to reorganize her thoughts then raised her face with a further explanation, surprised at how easy it was to concoct a false story. "Having Steven stay with me curbs any temptation I might have to invite Martin over, especially since all three of us work in the same hospital."

"Good thinking," Helen agreed, reaching for the teapot to refill both their cups. "I can see you're trying really hard sweetie, but I'm afraid you just might slip into your old routine. And this time, I don't know if you'd be able to fight your way back."

With the game suddenly changed, Olga felt her emotions rise as the genuine memories came flooding back to greet her. "I thought we might live together here one day," she admitted to herself as much as her friend. "But who was I kidding? Martin was never going to be happy living in this little old neighborhood."

"It's been nearly ten years," Helen gently reminded her. "I think it's time that you moved on, maybe considered dating someone else."

"I'm not interested in making supper for a bunch of seventy-year-old widowers who're looking for someone to do their laundry. Martin and I had a real connection."

"I remember. Didn't you do most of your *connecting* in the supply room, doctor's lounge, and basement laundry?"

"We were a lot younger. Hell, I was only thirty-nine when I started seeing Martin. I thought he was the love of my life, I thought…"

"You thought he'd get divorced and marry you," Helen whispered the remaining words in Olga's train of thought. "But he never did, he stayed with his wife Mary right up until she died. Then when he finally came to you, it was too late. You felt like the consolation prize, and your relationship just didn't feel right. Have I hit the nail right on the head?"

After dabbing her eyes with the right sleeve of her dress, Olga took a small sip of her tea, forcing the liquid down her throat. "He only came to me once he'd run out of options," she admitted, her voice strained as she fought to speak through the welling tears. "If Martin had really wanted to be with me, he would have divorced his wife and asked me to marry him."

"But his wife was dying of cancer," Helen reminded her friend. "No one would have ever forgiven him if he'd have left. You know that."

"I course I do," Olga cried. "I'm the one who told him he had to stay. But he never even tired, he never even argued with me," she ranted, a weak attempt at playing devil's advocate having blown right up in her own face.

"He was damned if he did, and damned if he didn't. That was a no-win situation for both of you," Helen gently whispered, trying to comfort Olga. "I don't know if realistically there was any way for either of you to find the peace and happiness you deserved."

"Helen, you told me years ago that when you met your husband, you knew within a week that he was the one. Well," she stalled to reorganize her thoughts, "Martin was mine."

"See, that's the part that bothers me," Helen divulged. "It's been ten years since his wife has passed, and if you two were meant to be, why haven't you picked up where you left off before?"

"Maybe it just took us ten years before we were ready to try again?"

After popping yet another shortbread into her mouth, Helen took a minute to wash the remaining crumbs down with her tea. As she continued to play with the rim of her cup, she stalled, wondering just how to handle the remainder of the conversation. "You just about had a nervous breakdown when you ended it with Martin the first time, do you really think you're up for round two?"

She felt shocked at the depth of her suppressed emotions, but Olga just shook her head side-to-side, totally unsure of what the future was about to unfold.

CHAPTER TWELVE

"I don't know—you meet thousands of people, and none of them really touch you. And then you meet one person, and your life is changed forever."

—Love & Other Drugs, 2010

After carrying the thick plastic garbage bag into the rear of her yard, Olga set it down under a tree, and then went into her garden shed, and dug around the darkened building for something heavy. She settled on an old spade, and yanked the handle up out of the storage barrel and made her way toward the soft shady dirt between the fruit trees and her neighbor's fence. Olga raised her shovel above the canister, still wrapped in the plastic bag, and proceeded to smash the plastic walls with the back of the curved shovel.

Five or six blows later—sweat beading on her top lip—Olga was finally convinced that the pieces were small enough to be unrecognizable. She carried the shattered chunks in the bag toward her alley, opened the metal can, and dumped it all into her trash.

She wasn't willing to risk that an unsuspected neighbor might recognized the hospital's container, so she'd done her best to disguise its origins.

Back in the kitchen, she decided that it might be a good idea to make some kind of supper, especially since she hadn't really eaten anything substantial for the past twenty-four hours.

From the moment her neighbor Helen had stopped by for tea, Steven had fallen into a deep sleep, and amazingly enough, he was still snoring like a hibernating bear. After checked on him at least three times, she was confident that he was fine, just in the deep stages of REM sleep.

As she opened the fridge and leaned in to pull out a thawed package of ground beef, Olga couldn't help but catch a glimpse of the other hospital canister still hiding out at the back of her top shelf. Slowly closing the door, she stood up and wondered just what she was going to do. During Helen's earlier visit, Olga had averted discovery by checking for the coffee cream herself. But what if another guest decided to peek in the bag, by assuming it was one of her baked treats? She had to find another method of storage, and with only one refrigerator in her home, the options were somewhat limited.

Olga dropped the uncooked ground beef into the stainless steel bowl. She made a conscious effort to discard the bloody plastic wrappings in such a way that they had no chance to drip down and contaminate her kitchen counters. She always used disposable paper towels and a disinfectant spray for raw meat wipe-ups—Olga was fastidious about cross contamination.

She dropped a packet of powdered onion soup mix, a cup of breadcrumbs, and a cup of dried rolled oats, onto the meat. Then Olga turned to grab two raw eggs from the fridge, and cracked them open into a small cereal bowl. After whipping the eggs with a fork until sufficiently scrambled, she dumped the mixture into the bowl. It was an old cooking trick to break-up the protein strands. This created a tender meat mixture, instead of a hamburger patty or meatball you could bounce off the sidewalk.

Before mixing the raw ingredients by hand, Olga first prepared her work area. She preheated her oven to three hundred and fifty degrees. With an ungreased cookie sheet positioned beside her bowl on the counter, Olga lastly ran a sink of hot soapy water, before preparing to dig her hands into the raw meat.

Raw ground beef was such a virulent substance; every experienced cook knew to take extra precautions to protect their family's health from the bacteria hidden within the ground beef. As she thought about the suspected healing powers of the raw fetal tissue, Olga couldn't help but compare how one container was life giving, and one could be life suppressing. At the hospital, she had treated more than one case of the dreaded salmonella poisoning associated with undercooked hamburger patties.

She shook off the unpleasant memories, and dropped her hands into the bowl and began working the mixture together with her fingers, clenching her hands as she combined the eggs and meat together with the remaining dry ingredients. When it was thoroughly mixed, she began to pinch off clumps of the hamburger mixture, and roll them into bite-sized meatballs. She lined them up side-by-side on the cookie sheet, not bothering to worry whether her raw meatballs were the perfect symmetrical shape.

When her bowl was empty, she put it into the sudsy dishwater, and carefully washed it and her hands. Olga popped the three-quarters full tray into the oven and finished her clean up. With her mind still whirling, she knew she needed to figure out what to do with the container of tissue. It was dangerous to store it in her home refrigerator. Without proper handling, she knew it would begin to disintegrate immediately, and nothing was more hazardous to her health than biological waste.

Olga set the oven's timer for one hour, and returned to her garden with a glass of ice tea to catch some air and contemplate her options. Early pioneering families had no refrigeration, yet they stored wild game and domestic foul for months on end. As she recalled a few of her granny's stories, Olga began scribbling notes on the pad of paper and pencil she always kept tucked inside the pocket of her apron, jotting down the ideas as they popped into her head.

"Canning," she murmured aloud. Many homesteaders stuffed blanched fruits, vegetables, and partially cooked poultry inside the narrow confinements of a glass jars, and further boiled the jars with special sealers lids until all bacteria was eradicated. It created a vacuum seal when the jar was immersed in the extreme heat. But Olga was positive that cooking the aborted fetal material would not be the answer; the heat would probably alter the biological complexity of the tissue, thereby neutralizing its ability to heal. No, she needed another method of preserving the material.

She recalled stories of preserving beef and pork by salting, but that was just adding a chemical—in this case extremely high quantities of sodium—also possibly altering or destroying the healing ability.

Neither of those options were the solution she was looking for. She needed to safeguard the tissue without cooking or adding chemical preservatives. As she looked out across the garden, Olga's eyes fell on her apple trees. The solution came to her as if she'd been hit on the head by a piece of falling fruit.

She raced back inside the house, directly into her utility room, and pushed a small step stool up against her clothes dryer. Climbing up the two steps, she reached deep into the wall-mounted cupboards, pulled out a cardboard box, and returned to her kitchen. Olga opened the flaps and pulled out a large, six-tiered food dehydrator.

"Perfect," she smiled, digging in the bottom of the box for the appropriate trays.

"What are you doing?" Steven asked, his mere presence making her jump, especially after nearly forty years of living alone.

"Forget about me. How are you doing?" she asked, moving around the counter toward the table.

He took a seat, and rubbed the sleep from his eyes as he tried to wake himself fully. "I can't believe it's nearly seven, I slept like a log."

"How do you feel? How's your left hand?"

"Feels the same as the right." He turned both hands palm up and then palm down. "Guess we better take a look under the bandage."

Olga nodded, and returned to the kitchen for a pair of scissors. Carefully, she snipped open the gauze across the back of Steven's hand. The remaining bandaging fluttered to the table, and the bloodstained pad landed soiled side up.

Olga smiled as she searched Steven's face for his response. She leaned back and watched while he instinctively pulled the palm of his hand up to his eyes and inspected the rejuvenated tissue, lightly brushing the new skin with the fingertips of his right hand.

"Oh my god. It worked." He lowered his hand to the table, carefully comparing his left to Olga's right. "I think it's safe to say that what happened to you wasn't a one-time miracle."

"*Once a miracle, twice a blessing, three times a cure.*"

"What was that?"

"Oh, just an old nursing adage," she nervously chuckled. "But we're definitely on to something, and I think we have to come up with a storage plan. Remember how the canister from yesterday spoiled overnight?"

"For sure. It was disgusting."

"Well, to be honest, I was thinking about dehydrating the tissue. You know, pulling out all the moisture so it wouldn't further decompose without cooking the tissue."

"With that?" Steven stood up and walked over to the electric machine Olga had just begun to assemble. Starring down at the white plastic trays, he shrugged his shoulders. "Well, let's give it a try."

Without further delay, Steven locked the front and back doors while Olga pulled out the liquid trays, bought to dehydrate pureed strawberries and apples for fruit leather.

"I think this might work," she admitted, pulling the canister of tissue out of the bag and setting it down gently on the counter.

"So you just gonna pour the stuff in the trays?"

"Unless you have a better idea," Olga nervously snapped, tying the strings of a fresh apron around her back.

"We're not making cookies," Steven reminded her, shaking his head at the brightly colored gingham.

"Sorry, old habit," Olga explained, turning to shrug her shoulders. "Now, can we get on with this?"

Unscrewing the canister, Steven handed Olga the open container, watching her very slowly stir the tissue with a disposable straw before carefully pouring it out onto the solid plastic trays.

"I think I'll use more than one," she moved toward a second tray. "I want it to dehydrate the entire canister as quickly as possible."

Steven nodded his silent agreement, and ever so gently lifted the first tray. He set it down on top of the circular fan, waiting patiently while Olga filled the second.

When she finished filling the final tray, Olga stopped, righting her canister as soon as the last lump of tissue plopped out onto the donut shaped tray. "Do you think we should dry it all? Even the solid tissue pieces?"

Steven leaned over to look down inside the canister, unaware that his nose was wrinkling at the sight. "I think we have to."

"I agree, at least until we figure out exactly whether it's the red blood cells or the solid tissue parts that are carrying the healing properties."

Steven stood back and watched as Olga reluctantly spooned the remaining chunks onto the tray. He forced himself to pick up a plastic straw from the open package on the counter, and began spreading out the tissue lumps as evenly as possible.

Olga bent down to adjust the temperature dial on the machine. When she straightened her back, she found Steven immobilized, frozen in time as he stared down motionless at one of the trays.

"I think I see a tiny baby foot," he muttered, as bile began to rise in the back of his throat, threatening to make an entrance within the next couple of seconds. He dropped the bloody straw on the floor and ran off toward the bathroom.

Olga was unwilling to look down and either confirm or deny his findings. Instead, she just quickly loaded the remaining trays on top of the dehydrator, capping them off with the lid and then plugging in the electric motor.

"I'm sorry." Steven returned a moment later, his eyes watery, and his stomach completely empty. "I just couldn't believe it. I really saw a…"

"I know," Olga patted him on the shoulder. "I think that we got so excited about our discovery, that sometimes we forget exactly where our miracle cure is coming from.

The buzz of the oven timer set Steven off again. This time he jumped, as he spun around in the kitchen to locate the origin of the noise. "What the hell was that?"

"I guess supper's ready."

"I'll pass," he mumbled, turning and making his way toward the back door in search of a little fresh air.

Still perched on the edge of the flowerbed's brick border, Steven yanked out another errant blade of grass, bringing the tender shoot up to his lips. He let his eyes continue to wander around the backyard, finally settling on a plastic stake poking its head out of the black soil.

"Lobelia," he muttered aloud, somewhat amused that the plant's name reminded him of a woman's *private parts.* Flipping over the stake to read the back, Steven continued to mumble. "Spikes of small, purple flowers, lance-like leaves, three feet, zones five to eight."

After turning the plastic back over, he leaned down and shoved it back into its original hole. His head raised, eyes scanning the flowerbeds in the garden, Steven casually wondered what the marker meant by *zones.* Maybe it had something to do with the placement of the flowers in the beds, or the colors, especially since everything in his sight was bright purple. He wasn't sure, but one thing was certain, Olga would know.

Olga Heinz was really quite a remarkable lady. She obviously knew not only what the zones were, but also why they were necessary. He really respected her, and she was starting to remind him a lot of his mother.

His mother had always managed to make sure there was good food on the table, enough money for new running shoes in September, and at least one present under the tree for each child come Christmas morning. She undoubtedly left her children alone a little more than was socially acceptable during her weeknight bingo sessions. But hell, even as a young boy, Steven had recognized his mother's need for a little diversion. She'd worked full-time at the drycleaners, where her minimum wage paid for all the food, the kid's clothes, and she still managed to pay for her gambling habit. Any prized toy he'd owned had been purchased right after a win, and although there weren't many, there were enough.

Each child had been assigned jobs when their mother was away at bingo. The oldest, Monica, was responsible for serving and then cleaning up the hot supper always left in the oven, while Steven was responsible for tending to his younger brother Michael. Their father, a nightshift employee, was an all but absent figure in their lives. This void necessitated the children to form their own family unit, each relying on the other for emotional and intellectual support.

Monica helped Steven with his schoolwork, Steven repaid the favor by routinely cleaning up the kitchen and sweeping the floors in return, affording his big sister a few precious moments to run to the local playground and hang out with her other thirteen-year-old girlfriends. Baby Michael, Steven's assigned duty, toddled around the house, encouraged to amuse himself with the pot drawer, usually more enamored with any other treasure that might fall from either of his sibling's school bags. While he frequently called his older sister Mommy, the baby of the family was just glad to have anyone pay a little attention to him, since he spent most of his energy chasing either his brother or sister around the house.

They weren't exactly the *Cosby's*, but then who really was? Steven was just grateful that his family had stayed together throughout his entire childhood, a rarity in his lower, working class neighborhood. Still, as a grown adult of twenty-three, he missed his family. Or what was left of it.

After Michael had died in grade school, struck down while crossing the street, everything seemed to slowly fall apart. Steven's mother stepped up her bingo to seven nights a week, and his father even stopped coming home to sleep—leaving messages on the machine that he was working double shifts. In Steven's senior year of high school, his sister Monica's boyfriends and extracurricular activities kept her anywhere but home. Steven found he was suddenly the forgotten family member, and by the time he managed to reach his own high school graduation, he felt like a bachelor, living alone in the family's trailer.

He'd left repeated notes for his parents and sister regarding the graduation exercises, but no one bothered to let him know if they would attend. So on the final day, he walked into the school office and declined his family's allotted tickets, gladly watching a grateful classmate scoop them up, with her extended family obviously clamoring to attend.

Graduation came and went. It was not until the school mailed his passing grades that his mother stepped forward with a quick apology and a twenty-dollar bill tucked into a *dollar store* card. She had recorded the family's best wishes in pen, signing on behalf of his father and sister, and laid the card on the kitchen table while she continued to pack her ink daubers and lucky charms into the pockets of her bingo bag. After she planted a quick kiss on her son's head, his mother had turned and hurried out the door, anxious to catch the four fifteen bus.

After stuffing the cash into his back pocket, he left the card on the table and walked out the trailer, straight to the student employment office. Steven was determined to get a job and start saving up enough to get a place of his own.

A couple of years later, Monica had sent word back home that she'd met someone during her vacation in Arizona and was planning to get married in late summer. They were all invited to the wedding, and were asked to please reply as soon as possible. So bright and early the next morning, Steven had marched into his boss's office down at the hospital and had requested time off to attend his sister's wedding.

The answer had been a resounding *no*. A twenty-year-old kid working at his first full-time orderly job didn't take unscheduled holidays during the Labor Day weekend, no matter who was getting married. Steven would be working, probably double shifts to help cover for the senior staff already on vacation. If he tried to be cute and called in sick, his boss had promised that he'd be fired on the spot. Steven had just nodded his head and sucked it up. When he eventually returned home later that night, he was caught off guard by the strangest sight.

His mother and father were both home together, zooming around the house, throwing a selection of possessions into scattered cardboard boxes. He was been shocked—unable to remember the last time he'd seen them both home at the same time. His mother had immediately stopped what she was doing and explained that they were rushing off to Monica's wedding, and were packing a few extras belongings for his sister to set up her house with.

Steven couldn't imagine what they'd possibly deemed as extra. He was horrified when his father started wrapping the cord around the base of the television, but he held his tongue and watched them continue to pack.

"Don't worry kid, I'll get a bigger TV as soon as I'm back," he'd promised his son.

As he sat on the couch, chewing on an apple, Steven watched his parents strip the trailer, taking everything from dishes, to ornaments, even all the counter-top appliances.

"I've left you two of everything," his mother had explained, her back turned as she continued to wrap their dinner plates in newspaper. "I'm giving all my old stuff to your sister Monica. We'll buy new when we're home."

Their promises were starting to sound hollow, and they would no longer meet Steven's eyes as they raced back and forth between the rooms, randomly packing whatever caught their fancy.

Steven eventually tired of their antics, dropped to his left elbow, and leaned down the length of the couch. He peered into his parent's bedroom, and watched his father suddenly empty all the papers from his locked metal filing cabinet, down into cardboard boxes. They were both packing as if they were hell bent, and running for their lives. As the clock neared midnight, Steven eventually became bored with the action and dozed off right where he lay.

When he rose at first light, he'd found his parents drinking coffee at the kitchen table, surrounded by boxes, as if secured in a cardboard fortress.

"Join me," his mother had invited him, patting a kitchen chair as his father stepped away from the table, explaining that he was leaving for a quick shower and shave. She passed her son another envelope and explained that the enclosed cash was for groceries and the next month's rent, due and payable in a couple of days.

Accepting the cash, Steven had reluctantly helped his mother stack the boxes into the U-haul trailer that had mysteriously appeared in the night, securely attached to the back of his dad's old Pontiac.

Forced to hasten his goodbyes, Steven had quickly changed into his hospital uniform, grabbed a slice of bread and a raw hot dog, and waved good-bye to his parents, silently praying that his mother had left him enough money for rent and groceries until they actually planned to return.

That had been nearly two years ago.

CHAPTER THIRTEEN

"We are who we protect, I think. What we stand up for."

—The Da Vinci Code, 2006

Olga lifted the plastic lid off the dehydrator, and bent down to check the trays. She had already changed their order from top to bottom at least three times, making sure each tray received equal time in first place. Finally satisfied that the job was complete, she unplugged the machine and began unloading the tray's contents into a huge plastic bowl.

"It's done?" Steven asked, leaning against the doorjamb that separated the living room from the kitchen.

"It's splitting into pieces, and curling. I think it's as dry as it's gonna get before the tissue burns."

"So now what?"

Olga tapped the tray to make sure that all the dehydrated pieces had fallen into the bowl. She turned and ran a sink of soapy water, dumping the trays into the steaming liquid. "I was thinking that we could turn this into something more manageable," she explained, picking up a curled piece roughly the size of a potato chip and crumbling it easily in the palm of her hand. "Something more like a healing powder," she explained, as she slowly opened her fingers and allowed the oatmeal-sized pieces to flutter to the bottom of the bowl.

Walking through the kitchen past Olga, Steven reached up into the cabinet and grabbed a drinking glass. He pivoted on his heels as he turned toward the sink, and stopped dead in his tracks when he caught his first glimpse of the bloody red dishwater, colored by the small flakes of tissue instantly dissolving in the heated liquid. With a sigh, he set the empty glass back down on the counter and turned to leave the kitchen.

"Can you give me a hand?" Olga asked, as she turned to rummage through her pantry for the mortar and pestle she knew was hiding somewhere in the back. "This is gonna take a fair bit of grinding.

"Sure," Steven conceded. He took another deep breath as he dropped into one of the kitchen chairs.

She slid the marble bowl and snub-nosed pestle across the table. Then she spun and grabbed the bowl of dehydrated tissue, and set it down on Steven's right. "I guess we grind it up, and then package it," she mused, turning to walk back into her kitchen.

As he shook the sides of the bowl, Steven wrinkled his nose at the mere sight of the scarlet-colored chips. There were small lumps of what appeared to be bone protruding from the surfaces, and the flakes of material ranged in thickness from paper-thin to that of a lightweight cardboard. Their movement in the bowl made an eerie rustling noise, a sound that reminded Steven of walking over layers of dried poplar leaves.

"Do I just pick them up with my fingers?"

"No," Olga quickly answered back, standing with her hands poised on her hips. "We both have to remember that this is dried human tissue, and we must treat it as possibly contaminated biological waste. We have no idea whether any of these women were infected with hepatitis, AIDS, or any other blood-borne diseases. And now that I think of it, I'd better bring some masks home. We don't want to inhale the airborne powder either."

"Yuck," Steven moaned, shaking his head and moving back from the table. "I don't know about this? How do we know that we're not passing one patient's disease onto another? Hell, we could already be infected with something really bad."

"I'm making the research leap of faith that the healing properties of the tissue somehow counteract any lingering blood-borne diseases."

"I'm just an orderly, but that sounds like an awfully big leap."

"Just put these on," Olga instructed her young helper, whipping out a fresh pair of disposable latex gloves from a box under her kitchen sink. "I think that from now on, whenever we are handling the canisters or the dried tissue, we must treat it accordingly."

"Okay," he agreed, shoving his hands into the fingers of the powdered latex. "So what should I do with the stuff once it's ground up?"

"Here," Olga proudly announced, producing a box of empty glass spice bottles, complete with shaker tops and lids. "I've been saving these for years. Couldn't think of a use until now." She turned to dig into her cutlery drawer for a small plastic funnel. "And I think it's important that we keep the patients separate. Each canister of dehydrated tissue should have its own batch number. Don't you agree?"

"I guess so," he said with a shrug.

"Until we determine whether or not every canister of fetal tissue has the same healing properties, we have to keep them separate for research purposes."

"Well then, let's get this over with." Steven took a deep breath and dropped his hand into the bowl, picking up a few of the crumbly chips and placing them straight into the bottom of the marble mortar.

Olga lined up four of the freshly sterilized spice bottles and then proceeded to fill them with reddish-brown powder. When that task was completed, she carried the mortar and pestle to the kitchen sink and began to wash the polished stone in her sink with boiling water and liquid bleach.

"God that stuff smells," Steven remarked, wiping the table and countertops with a handful of disposable paper towels. Olga had forbidden clean up using her cotton dishcloths just minutes before.

"The smell is a good sign. It means that the disinfecting agents are still active, so just suck it up," she teased, trying to lighten the mood.

"Suck it up? Where'd you get that from?"

"I hear a lot of the phrases used around the hospital. Most of them I dismiss, but *suck it up*—somehow, that one just kind of stuck."

Steven laughed to himself, and quickly finished the remainder of his clean up and walked up to where Olga was positioned at her kitchen sink. "What's next, boss?"

"Testing," she simply replied. "We need to check and see if the dehydration has altered the fetal tissue's healing powers."

"I agree, but I don't think I'm up to another slice."

"I agree. Two wounds are more than enough for me, too," Olga admitted, draining the sink just before she peeled the bright yellow gloves off her hands. "I thought we might take our little show on the road."

"Where to?" Steven asked, watching Olga carefully position the dehydrator trays for air-drying.

"I know a shelter downtown where many street people congregate, looking for food, and clothing. Unfortunately, many of those men and women are usually sporting a multitude of injuries. Everything from simple cuts and scrapes, to hidden stab wounds and fractured bones are commonplace with these people. I guarantee that we could easily find a couple of test subjects, without drawing a lot of attention to ourselves."

"You're talking about people like the homeless drunks who hang out under the bridge, aren't you?"

"Yes."

"Well, if they're homeless, how in the hell are we going to check on their progress?"

Olga frowned at Steven's use of language, and wiped the dampness off her hands, before untying her apron. "Just because they're homeless, it doesn't mean they don't have a routine. Trust me when I tell you that whoever we treat, we'll be able to check up on their progress within twenty-four hours."

"Really?"

"I've spent many shifts volunteering at the shelter. I'm right about this."

"Why so many shifts?" Steven asked as he stepped out of Olga's way.

"I… I just wanted to help," she stumbled, caught off guard by Steven's questioning of her motives.

"I suppose they're probably dying for medical assistance?"

"Yes, that's an understatement. The city's shelters are always posting requests for volunteer pediatricians to evaluate the children, ophthalmologists to check the seniors' eyesight, and a host of other requested specialists."

"But let me guess. They never show?" Steven sneered, as his mind whirled back in time to the overcrowded children's ward at the community hospital. As the entire family stood at Michael's bedside, they held a vigil, hour after hour. There was nothing else to do but helplessly wait for his baby brother to die. "I bet all the doctors are too busy waiting for the society ladies to come in for a face lift or a tummy tuck. Nobody wants to get their hands dirty. Nobody bothers to take the time to treat some little kid, who's slowly dying in a back ward, because his parents didn't pay up their insurance premiums, and nobody's got the money for surgery."

While silently holding her position at the counter, Olga slowly folded her cotton apron, and gently placed the gingham on the laminate counter. "Volunteer work is a huge commitment. And not only do many doctors' private insurance companies not cover shelter or community service work, they've even been known to discourage it."

"Why?" he demanded in a harsh tone.

"Well, I've heard a handful of reasons, but the most obvious seems to be that the doctors would be diagnosing patients without proper resources, and completing procedures with limited equipment, thereby multiplying the risk of mistakes and malpractice lawsuits. It's a numbers game, and the insurance companies don't like the risks."

"That's frickin' bullshit! People just want to be helped. Are you trying to tell me that some little old homeless man who's been cracked on the skull with an empty wine bottle is going to call a lawyer if the doctor's stitches are pulled too tight on his forehead?"

Shaking her head, Olga turned and reached up above the refrigerator to pull down her purse and retrieve a set of car keys. "So, are you coming with me?"

CHAPTER FOURTEEN

"Keep your friends close, but your enemies closer."

—The Godfather, Part II, 1974

The sorted piles of manila files covered almost every available inch of the boardroom table. Some stacks were only a few files high, while others were at least fifty files plus. Every file was assigned to an individual, and every individual's file varied in thickness, the largest measuring in at least two inches. Assembled around the table was a quorum, brought together for one specific purpose. The advisory committee was going to continue with their deliberations, reviewing file after file, until they had narrowed their choices down to a final list of ten.

"Why don't we just pick the ten oldest staff members and call it a day?" one of the men suggested. "They must be the closest to retirement, and a mandatory package really won't surprise them," one participant rationalized, bored with the ongoing procedure.

"The oldest don't necessarily translate into the most problematic," the chairman reminded everyone. "Look at the head of our maintenance... Mr. Mendez," he flung open the file on the top of his pile, using it to make his point. "This guy has been with the hospital for over twenty years. He started part-time after his retirement at a previous job at the age of fifty. Within a couple years, he was working full-time, and now he's seventy-three years old and his record is spotless."

"Nobody's record is spotless," a lady at the far end argued back.

"Well his is," the chairman retaliated, opening the file to dig for a few quotable facts. "Mr. Mendez hasn't called in sick or taken any kind of paid medical leave for any reason in the past ten recorded years. He runs an entire department—a department, I might mention, that is one of the few operating within budget—and you think he should be pensioned off because he's the oldest hospital employee. You're wrong, Isabella." He dropped the file on the table, crossing his arms at his chest.

"Alright, point taken, Dick," the lady said, "So what's your suggestion? Should we just grab ten files at random, make sure everyone is over... let's say, sixty, and recommend them for mandatory retirement?"

"That's ridiculous," another member of the board spoke up. "We've got to establish some sort of criteria for our decisions. I don't think grabbing the top files and then punishing people simply by their age would be an adequate method of selection. And I don't have to remind you of the possible law-suits for age discrimination."

Dick Mansfield, the chairman of the advisory committee, interrupted what appeared to be the beginning of a heated argument by rising up from his chair and simultaneously clearing his throat. "How about this? We've already set up an advisory committee to help trim the fat off our staffing by putting into a place a program for mandatory retirement for senior staff. Correct?"

Everyone nodded.

"Well then," Dick continued, "I suggest that we should heavily consider which of the senior staff have *cost* the hospital more than they have *contributed*."

"And how do you propose to measure that?" Isabella demanded, a curious grin spreading across her face.

"Simple," he said as he slid back into his chair, before grabbing one of the heavier files adorning the boardroom table. "For example, we have a senior nurse named of Olga Heinz. She has a respectable service record, with only one reprimand for insubordination. It looks like it was regarding an altercation with a resident, back in ninety-eight. Oh, hold on..." Dick continued to read from Olga's personnel file. "Nurse Heinz appealed the reprimand, and the disciplinary board overturned the decision in her favor because of the new evidence."

"What evidence?"

Flipping the page, Dick scanned the notations for further information. "I don't know," he finally admitted, "it doesn't say anything else about the evidence. But anyway, that's not really important. It's her personal medical record that I'm interested in. Nurse Heinz had taken two extended medical leaves. The first," he reported, his fingers running down the columns in the file, "lasted for nearly a year."

"A year? That's a long time. What was the problem?" Isabella inquired without even lifting her head, busy scribbling Olga's name down on her pad of paper.

"Mental breakdown," Dick reported. "Looks like she then had a relapse a couple of years later, and took another six months of paid medical leave."

After rising from her chair to clear a space in the middle of the boardroom table, Isabella straightened her back and turned to Dick Mansfield. "I guess we've nailed our criteria. Why don't you pass me the file," she asked, beckoning with her outstretched hand, "and we can get on with finding number two."

The Lilac Tree—or as many referred to it, the Second Street Shelter—always reminded Olga of a futuristic daycare, where the young children had been replaced by adults. The people who milled back and forth aimlessly around the entrance appeared to be searching, looking for someone to drive by and pick them up; even though the reality of the situation was that no one would ever come.

"You worked here?" Steven couldn't help but ask; his eyes wide with shock. He was surprised that someone like Olga would risk her personal safety to clock a few volunteer hours. "This is really a rough part of town. You must have been dealing with all the hardcore alcoholics and junkies. How'd you handle them?"

"One at a time," she smiled, waving at a familiar face crossing the street, right in front of her car. "Let's go inside and see if they can use a little help tonight," Olga encouraged Steven. She stepped out of her car, and adjusted the fanny pack at her waist.

"Lead the way," he answered, shaking his head and wondering just what he'd signed up for.

"Nurse Heinz!" a woman's voice shrieked from across the main floor of the shelter.

"Doris," Olga shouted and waved back, nudging Steven to follow her, and she began making her way across the floor.

Seated in the counselor's office/storage room/first aid station, Olga listened as Doris quickly rattled off a few of the latest happenings at the shelter. "And just when we thought we'd seen it all, the board of health comes in and tells us we need a commercial dishwasher if we're going to serve hot meals. Can you believe it? We're trying to stop people from scavenging through the garbage in restaurant dumpsters, and the health board threatens to shut down our kitchen if we don't have a heat sterilizing dishwasher."

"That's appalling," Olga agreed, turning to wink and smile at a large group of faces that had begun converging at the office window.

"I see your fans are beginning to gather," Doris teased, standing up to shoo away the more adamant who had begun to press their faces against the glass. "So Steven is it?"

"Yes," he smiled, shifting in his chair, a little uncomfortable with the attention.

"Olga says that you're an experienced orderly at the hospital, and you might be interested in joining her for a few volunteer shifts. Is that true?"

Looking first at Olga, and then back at Doris, Steven nodded, unsure of what he was agreeing to. "I'm just an orderly," he announced, his voice betraying his nervousness.

"I know," Doris smiled, "and we're glad to have you. I hope you won't mind filling out this simple form. I need you to sign the bottom, authorizing me to conduct a criminal background check. Will that be alright with you?"

"That's fine with me," he shrugged, accepting the clipboard and pen.

As Steven quickly jotted down a few basic particulars about himself, Olga couldn't help but ask a few more probing questions. "Who's been completing your medical checkups?"

"We've cut that program," Doris sighed, shaking her head in disgust. "It scares the hell out of me to know that most of these people are going without any medical attention at all."

"Why?" Steven interrupted, handing the completed form back to the shelter director. "The county hospital now has an emergency room open to the public, whether or not they carry insurance."

"That's true," Doris admitted, sadly offering Olga a smile before turning to reply to Steven. "But if the patient is intoxicated, or under the influence, they will make them wait until they're sober for treatment, without even a cursory exam to determine the seriousness of the injury. Unfortunately, that leaves many of our people without medical care as they choose to leave, uncomfortable with the strong police presence and scrutiny in the waiting rooms."

Steven took the information in, and nodded, carefully constructing his next statement before speaking. "Well, then I guess a nurse and an orderly are better than nothing at all."

"I like him," Doris slapped both her palms down onto her knees. "I think he's going to fit in just fine."

As he wandered around the room and waited for Doris to finish Olga's tour of the renovations to the lady's washroom, Steven found himself drawn to a lively card game in the back corner.

"Fifteen two, fifteen four, fifteen six, and five for the spades, gives me eleven" one old man proudly announced, right hand shaking as he reached for the back red peg stuck in the wooden crib board.

"Hold on Metro, I don't see no fifteen six," his card partner argued back, taking his turn to count the four cards freshly lay down on the table. "Fifteen two," he pointed to the five and the queen. "Fifteen four," he continued, tapping the five and jack, "and five for the spades. That's nine, not eleven," he argued in his own defense.

"Sorry," the old man relented, painfully rising from the chair. "I gotta take a leak," he announced, as he began shuffling toward the men's washroom.

Stepping aside to allow Metro easy passage, Steven couldn't help but notice how the elderly man dragged his left leg, suddenly wincing when a woman rushed across his path and he was forced to make an unexpected side step. He slowed to wipe the beads of sweat that had instantly appeared on his brow, took a deep breath, and continued his journey toward the washroom door.

Steven glanced over his shoulder to make sure no one was

watching before slowly turning to follow the injured man into the men's washroom. After taking the first empty position at the wall urinal, Steven stood and fumbled with the metal zipper on his denim jeans, while he waited for the man to limp into a private stall.

As if on cue, Metro picked a stall and slowly locked the door behind his back. He dropped his pants into a rumpled heap on the tiled floor—his painful sigh immediately signaled relief, as he was finally able to take the weight off his throbbing left leg when his bare bottom made contact with the toilet seat. While he urinated from his sitting position, he reluctantly took the opportunity to examine the wound that festered on the calf of his left leg.

Steven nervously paced outside the stall. He stepped away from the wall urinals and quickly bent down, dipping his head to peer below the stall door to sneak a quick glance at Metro's bare legs.

His skin appeared to be very dark, a combination of what looked like unwashed flesh and dark body hair. Metro's calves were very thin, and it took a second before Steven's eyes even noticed the soiled bandage haphazardly wrapped just two or three inches above the ankle bone. The man's fingers were shaking; patting the wound as if an adjustment of the bandage would be much too painful to bear.

After straightening his back, Steven shoved his right hand into his coat pocket, and squeezed the dehydrated tissue within the glass spice bottle. He'd possibly found a test subject, and since they were already alone in the bathroom, the opportunity to approach the man in private probably wouldn't be any better. Unconsciously turning toward the mirror, Steven was shocked to see the fear peering back at him from his own eyes. He yanked his hand out of his pocket, walked over, and splashed a handful of water on his face, eyes casing his surroundings one last time before he made his move.

"Evening," Metro nodded his head, as he slowly emerged from the bathroom stall. "Just gonna wash my hands and I'll be on my way," he explained, careful not to annoy the unknown stranger.

"No rush," Steven smiled, slipping his hand into his right pocket. "I see you're favoring your left leg. Did you hurt it?"

"I'm favoring it some," Metro confirmed, shaking the excess water off his hands before taking the opportunity to rub them, palms down, over the front of his soiled jacket.

"I know what it's like," Steven nodded his head up and down in agreement, pivoting on his feet to face the man. "I hurt my hand really bad, and my friend gave me some special medicine and it healed me right up."

"Don't got no medicine or no money for any," Metro shook his head, turning away to now check his appearance in the cracked wall mirror.

"I think I might have a little extra left over, and I don't mind sharing it with you."

Metro turned back toward the young stranger, and shoved both hands deep into his jacket pockets. "I told you I can't pay," he reiterated, just in case the kid thought he might have a couple of bills folded up and hidden somewhere in his pockets.

"I know," Steven smiled, dropping down to his knees. "Now let's see exactly what you've got."

Metro slowly lifted his left pant leg as high as possible, and was somewhat surprised to see the young man forcing his fingers into a pair of rubber gloves. "You a doctor?" he asked, that old wary feeling starting to creep up his spine.

"No, my name is Steven, and I'm not a doctor. I'm just being careful not to spread any germs on your wound. You know how dirty bathrooms can be," he insinuated, casually nodding his head toward the urinals.

"My name is Metro Bobbins, and I'm really glad to make your acquaintance." He thrust his hand down toward Steven's face.

After quickly returning the greeting with his gloved fingers, Steven refocused his attention on Metro's wound. "So what happened to your leg? It kinda looks like a really bad gash," he guessed, from the tattered tissue protruding around the soiled bandage.

"I was climbing over a fence when that damn barbwire just reached up and grabbed me." Metro winced; his breath catching in his throat as Steven gently tugged at the remaining bandage still clinging to the dried blood and matted leg hair.

"So where was the fence?" he asked, attempting to steer the old man's attention away from the impromptu debriding of his wound.

"Behind those big fancy restaurants—the ones with the blue dumpsters. You know which ones." Metro's attention abruptly turned to his freshly unwrapped leg.

"I know," Steven agreed, scrambling to spur Metro onward with his verbal explanation. "But where'd you find the barb wire?"

"Well, that's the thing," Metro started ranting again. "The restaurants—they got all mean and put up barbwire fences all the way round and round their garbage bins. Can you imagine why someone..."

Steven wasn't listening; his total concentration was focused on the task at hand. He would have loved a basic first aid kit with sterile gauze and clean tape, but if his miracle treatment proved sound, by morning they'd just be redundant anyway. "So, what's the best meal you've ever found?" he spurred his patient on one last time.

As Metro launched into a detailed memory of *special fried rice*, Steven liberally doused the infected, two inch laceration, with the dark red powder, careful to cover the entire wound. As the test patient continued with his story, the simple act of shifting his own weight from his left foot back to his right sent a tiny rivulet of puss oozing from the unstitched wound.

Steven quickly pulled his face back, and wrinkled his nose, shaking off the disgust as he pushed his saliva back down his throat. Forcing himself to lean in one more time, he covered even the small river of decomposing tissue with a last dash of the healing powder. "Well, that should do it," he announced, rising to his feet as he searched the room for something clean to dress the wound with.

As if reading the young man's mind, Metro produced half a roll of gauze, the outside already soiled from its storage in the depths of the woolen coat pocket. "Here you go," he passed the wrapping downward.

"Thanks," Steven smiled, turning the roll over in his right hand as he attempted to look for the tattered edge.

"It's just tobacco and burger crumbs," Metro interjected, watching the young man as he picked at the roll, the debris flaking off and falling to the bathroom floor. "It's clean," he promised with a genuine smile in his eyes.

Steven nodded his understanding, reaching around the old man's dirty calf to begin bandaging the freshly powdered wound.

Sequestered in a leather recliner, with the fingers of his right hand unconsciously strangling the stem of his Waterford crystal goblet, Dr. Martin Hood reflected on the events at the committee meeting. Somehow, in his ignorance—or his infinite boredom—he'd unknowingly voted for Olga's termination. The woman he loved was about to be put out to pasture and it didn't look like there was a damn thing he could do to save her.

"Save her?" he mumbled to himself. Shit, he was part of the lynch mob that was ready to slip the very noose around her neck. How could things have gone so badly, so quickly? He needed to see Olga—to talk with her. Maybe if he explained in detail what the committee was planning, they'd be able to thwart the decision together. They had over fifty years of combined service at the University Hospital, and Martin was willing to pull every string he could muster to save Olga's career. She was more than a senior duty nurse; the woman had become an institution. Olga Frieda Heinz had extensively trained more young men and women than all the staff combined.

Whenever the elevator doors sprung open and a new class of graduate nurses and resident doctors flooded her unit, she struggled to take them all under her wing. She would gently remind the new hires that their years of schooling were essential, but that on the floor, a strong dose of compassion could prove to be their most powerful medicine. It was a message that they'd all heard from well-meaning professors. Still, it somehow took a seasoned veteran to reinforce its practical meaning.

He remembered a time when on the post-op ward, the husband of a patient had called repeatedly for a nurse. His wife was in recovery, and she was crying in pain. The man's children were upset because of their mother's tears. The man seemed very upset and nearing his breaking point. He demanded that the newly hired nurse give his wife additional pain medication.

The new nurse got the patient's chart but couldn't do anything for the patient. She had already received maximum sedation, and without a change to the doctor's orders, the nurse's hands were obviously tied. The young nurse located a resident doctor, gave him the chart, and tried to convince him to up the patient's dosage. They began to argue, with the nurse trying to consider the family's needs, and the doctor only concerned for the patient's welfare.

When Olga saw the pair of them disagreeing on what appeared to be a professional level, she had decided that she should not intercede as long as the conversation stayed civil.

The doctor had spoken to the patient earlier, and she asked to have slightly less medication. She was going to require further surgery and she wanted to be able to speak to her children about it. Additional meds would have had her asleep during their visit.

Martin remembered that particular doctor was one who especially didn't like to be challenged by nurses. He had told the young nurse that he wasn't a miracle worker and he wasn't God; he couldn't stop the woman from crying.

When the doctor left, the patient's husband went to the nurse's station and asked Olga if she could help. She took over the situation and found a solution that satisfied everyone, without even looking at the chart.

An hour later, while the family gathered in a semi-circle around their mother's bedside, she was able to speak to each of them and give all three of her teenage children comfort. They all agreed when she explained in whispered breaths how she required a second surgery to remove all the cancer. The children were able to pull strength from the reassurance in her voice. They were able to have a memory of their mother that was warm and uplifting, instead of one clouded with worry and sorrow.

What Olga had done to remedy the situation was to cover the patient's eyes with gauze padding. She had explained to the patient's family that this was to protect her eyes from the uncomfortable glare of the recovery room lights.

The children had only briefly questioned the bandaging. But it seemed like their mother was not suffering as badly. The gauze had allowed the patient to momentarily suffer her pain without additional meds, but in a way unbeknownst to her children, since the sterile padding soaked up any and all of her tears. Olga had been touted a miracle worker.

That had been just one of many examples of her nursing skill that Martin fondly remembered. As the supervising doctor on that patient's chart, he'd once again just stood back and marveled at Olga's magic.

With his eyes focused on the stemware still perched on the arm of his leather chair, Martin never moved a muscle as the blood red wine threatened to spill over the far edge. He was fully aware of the ivory Persian rug below him, which cushioned the hand-carved legs of his chair. He could envision the resulting damage, should the fermented grapes ever splash down onto the delicately woven threads. But tonight he didn't care—the carpet was just another possession in a long line of possessions that he suddenly didn't give a damn about.

As his glass precariously teetered on its perch—the fingers of his right hand only an inch from the stem—Martin suddenly shook himself free from the past and jumped to his feet. The goblet instantly responded by tumbling through the air and released its contents onto the carpet in the process. A millisecond later, as the crystal met solid resistance and splintered into tiny shards, many embedding themselves permanently into the weave of the rug, Martin came to a conclusion.

Without bothering with even the slightest attempt at a cleanup, he strode over to the corner desk and grabbed the telephone. He punched in Olga's phone number from memory, and waited patiently while the phone continued to ring. Ten rings later—still no answering machine hooked to the line—Martin continued to pace the room until he suddenly heard a man's voice pick up, on the other end.

"Hello?" the guy repeated for a second time.

Unsure what to do, Martin stopped, and checked the telephone's display to make sure he'd dialed the correct number. Convinced that this was indeed Olga's home phone, he found himself stuttering on the line, a habit he'd trained himself to break as a teenager. "I… I… I was looking for Olga Heinz."

"One second," Steven answered, setting the phone down on the kitchen counter while he called out for Olga.

Martin heard her shout back, "Take a message."

Steven asked into the phone, "Can I take a message? I guess she's kinda busy."

Martin gave his name and number, and said, "Please have her call right away. It is urgent." After he hung up, he thought about what his next move would be.

After he scratched down Martin's name and number on the message pad by the phone, Steven returned to the kitchen table and watched Olga draft a final set of columns.

"We're going to have to track Metro's recovery, especially if the treatment turns out to be a success."

"I just can't see how it's gonna work. His leg was so dirty, and the pus…"

"Have a little faith," Olga encouraged him. "We might have just stumbled on the equivalent of penicillin for the twenty-first century. This could turn out to be one of the most monumental discoveries in the history of medicine."

"Or not," Steven mumbled, resigning himself to the unpleasant task of grinding up the remaining batch of dehydrated fetal tissue. "We might just be paving our personal paths to the unemployment line," he moaned, snapping the rubber gloves firmly around the wrists of each hand.

CHAPTER FIFTEEN

"And you know, maybe we can figure out a way where we can give back some of what we've taken to other people who really need it."

—Fun With Dick and Jane, 2005

After rising early, Steven had just about finished his second bowl of cereal when he suddenly heard knocking on the front door. He glanced over his left shoulder to Olga's room, and then back to the front door. He reluctantly pushed away from the kitchen table and made his way toward the intrusion.

"Steven Raymundo Whitters?" the first man in the suit asked.

"Yes," Steven answered, already wary of the two authority figures standing on the front steps.

"I'm Agent Mathers, and this is Agent Ferby, with the FBI. We'd like to come in and talk to you, if possible."

"About what?" he demanded, the hairs on the back of his neck instantly standing up at the mere mention of their organization.

"Steven, is everything all right?" Olga called out from two steps behind her houseguest's back.

"I don't know," he admitted. "And how exactly did you guys find me?"

"The hospital gave us your address," the lead agent offered with no further explanation.

After gently guiding Steven to one side of the open door, Olga stepped forward to greet the uninvited visitors. "My name is Olga Heinz, and this is my home. I suppose you gentlemen wouldn't have a problem showing me your identification before I let you in my house."

"No ma'am," they both chimed in unison, reaching into their breast pockets to produce badges and photo ID

Satisfied, Olga stepped back and invited both men in, and offered them each a seat at her kitchen table.

"We've come to speak to Mr. Whitters regarding the disappearance of his parents, Arnold and Carmen Whitters."

"I don't know where they are. I haven't spoken to them in years."

As he nodded his head in agreement, Agent Mathers removed a notepad, and glanced down at his own notations before speaking. "There was a fire at your residence, effectively destroying all your belongings and family memorabilia?"

"Yes," Steven answered, nervously playing with the breakfast spoon left behind after Olga had quickly picked up his cereal bowl and milk jug. "I didn't have nothing to do with that fire. It started when I was at work. You can ask John."

"We've already spoken to the park manager, your friend John, and his wife…"

"Mae," the second detective completed his partner's train of thought. "They were quite helpful."

With the last statement still hanging in the air, Olga suddenly changed her mind and adjusted her position from that of a friendly observer to Steven's protector. "Are you here to question Steven about the fire, or is this related to something else?"

Both agents turned and looked at each other, almost as if partaking in a silent conference. Then finally, after what felt like an eternity, Agent Mathers said, "We are not here to question Mr. Whitters about his possible involvement in the trailer park arson. We are here regarding our investigation into his parents' disappearance."

"Are you telling me someone did set my trailer on fire?"

"Yes son, it appears that's going to be the findings on the final report. However, we believe that the fire was not set to endanger you or destroy your belongings. We believe the fire was deliberately set to erase any possible clues as to your parents' whereabouts."

Olga stood up and tightly cinched the housecoat's belt securely around her waist. "What exactly do you know about Steven's parents? Why would someone burn down a trailer to hide their whereabouts?"

The directness of Olga's questions caught the men off guard, and in response, they returned an offensive play. "Ma'am, is it true that you took Mr. Whitters into your home directly after the fire?"

"Yes."

"Can you tell us why?"

"Steven needed a place to stay, and I needed a little help around the house. Seemed like a good match at the time."

"Do you still feel the same way?"

"Yes," she bluntly retorted. "And furthermore, gentlemen, I no longer feel comfortable with your questions. If you wish to continue, I think Steven should first consult with a lawyer."

"Do you agree, son?" Agent Ferby quickly interjected.

"Yes sir," Steven nodded his head. "I think I'd better talk to a lawyer before I answer any more questions about the fire or about my parents."

After she relocked the front door while both agents reluctantly walked down the sidewalk toward their nondescript dark sedan, Olga spun back around just in time to catch a glimpse of Steven nervously chewing the nails of his right hand. "Still hungry?" she teased.

Pickup up the cue, he roughly shoved both his hands into his jeans pockets. "What do you think that was all about?"

Olga filled the glass coffee pot with tap water, and slowly shook her head side to side before formulating an answer. "The FBI doesn't come calling to your house unless they believe that someone inside is involved in something very serious, and obviously, very illegal."

"It's not me. I didn't start any fire."

"I don't believe that the fire is their number one priority right now. I think they're much more concerned with the whereabouts of your parents. Steven, you really don't know where to find them? What if it was an emergency?"

"Like when my trailer burned to the ground, and I had no home, or clothes, or furniture?"

Olga picked up his sarcasm—his angry tone undeniable. Steven's family had effectively abandoned him, and any parents in their right minds wouldn't have left their child hanging in what had to be one of the most traumatic events of his young life. When putting all the events in perspective, she couldn't help but wonder if Arnold and Carmen Whitters were even capable of contacting their son.

As if reading Olga's mind, Steven began to question the obvious. "Do you think my mom and dad are okay? Maybe… maybe they're already dead?"

She admitted that she had absolutely no idea about his parent's well being, so Olga poured herself a quick cup of the freshly dripped coffee, and took up her usual position at the kitchen table. "Tell me more about your dad's job."

"Well, he worked security for a bunch of different places. Nothing really special, as far as I can remember. Why?"

As she sipped from her cup, Olga struggled to organize her thoughts. "Chances are that it's not so much what your father *did*, as what your father might have *seen*. What kind of companies did he work for? Can you remember any of their names?"

"Not really," Steven admitted, frustrated at the lapses in his own memory. "He was always moving around from job to job, and for the last couple of years, he was usually working nights, so we barely had a chance to speak."

"Well, I'm pretty sure the security at several hospitals is contracted through a single company."

Wrenching his hands free of his denim pockets, Steven grabbed a cup of coffee and joined Olga at the table. "You know, I think you're right. As far as I can remember, no matter where Dad worked, he always seemed to be wearing the same navy blue uniform. If I could just remember the name of the company, then they'd probably be able to tell us where he was employed. Don't you think?"

"How are you planning to dig up that information?"

"John and Mae said they have a bunch of boxes at their place, and maybe if I plough through some of Dad's stuff, I'll be able to find an old pay stub or something else."

"Maybe," Olga agreed, rising from her chair to refill her empty cup. "You know, when I saw the FBI at the door this morning, I thought they'd come to see us about the powder. I was really scared that they'd come looking for the canisters we'd taken from the hospital."

"You think they'd ever do that?"

"Well, we have stolen hospital property, and we've interfered with the proper disposal of medical waste. I'm pretty sure we could at least be charged with some form of theft. I guarantee it'd be more than a slap on the wrist."

"Maybe we should just take everything to the dump and forget about it all.

"Maybe," Olga agreed. "But before we fold our tent, I'd really like to know how that man faired down at the Lilac Tree Shelter. Wouldn't you?"

"Then we'll take everything to the dump and have it destroyed?" Steven reiterated.

"I agree. If the powder did nothing for the homeless man's leg, then we'll have to sit down and re-evaluate its supposed healing powers. We might have just stumbled on a coincidence where a medication in the fetal tissue reacted with the anesthetic from the procedure, or something the doctor administered to the patient, or…" Olga trailed off, her mind listing a few other possibilities. "Our two cases may have just been freaky, onetime miracles that will never be explained by modern medicine."

"You're right," Steven agreed. "We may never be able to reproduce the healing affects again. So, then we can stop taking the tissue?"

"Deal," Olga agreed.

"Deal," Steven repeated to confirm their agreement.

"Mr. Mansfield, Dr. Hood is here to see you. He says it's rather urgent," the secretary announced to the group of assembled businessmen.

"Well, then send him in," Dick boisterously announced. "Highly unusual for a doctor to actually appear when you require a medical opinion—I say we take advantage of his expertise. Don't you gentlemen agree?"

The assembled medical professionals nodded their heads, moving their chairs over to make room for the doctor at the conference room table.

"Martin," Dick greeted him with a warm handshake the minute he appeared in the office. "Why don't you take a seat and join us. We could really use your opinion regarding one of our more pressing concerns."

"I actually needed to speak to you alone," Martin attempted to whisper out of the corner of his mouth. "It's kind of a personal matter."

"Well, I always have time for my friends," Dick smiled, patting the doctor squarely in the back. "Just take a seat, and I promise we'll wrap this up in just a few minutes."

Martin obliged by taking a seat and reluctantly accepted a cup of coffee from Dick's secretary just moments before she closed the office doors.

"So where were we?" Dick asked, shuffling a stack of papers on the table in front of his high-backed chair.

"Time frames," the assistant on his right read from a note pad.

"Here's where you fit in, Martin. Pass him a sheet, would you?" Dick directed one of the men on the other side of the table.

After carefully taking time to read the collection of diseases listed on the stapled pages, Martin shook his head and tried to understand the purpose of the meeting.

Dick took a cue from the doctor's look of uncertainty, and brought the meeting instantly back to order. "You're going to find a list of communicable diseases that are regularly encountered in most community health situations. As a senior staff doctor, can you please tell us how many would be classified as life threatening, possibly terminal? We're trying to assess our medical expenditures in correlation with the benefit to the community." After taking a deep breath, Dick flipped open his file and dropped his hands directly on top of the pages. "We need your help Martin, to assess whether or not we can afford to treat the average range of diseases that will darken our door step if we open a community clinic. Essentially, we need to know if we're talking penicillin and fiberglass casts, or Interferon and respirators?"

Martin dropped his eyes once again to the list, picking out many of the common sexually transmitted diseases, in addition to the entire range of breathing disorders. He noted that most were afflictions brought on by repeated exposure to the acrid smoke of crack cocaine and other illegal drugs. "Well, on their own, many of these are not life threatening. However, considering the multitude of conditions that one patient may suffer from, the combinations have proven to be fatal. I've even seen one young woman succumb to a severe case of pelvic inflammatory disease that was left untreated and festered, resulting in a case of toxic shock."

"PID," one of the men spoke up. "Isn't that a disease that just hookers get?"

Martin abruptly pushed back his chair, and rose to his feet, unconsciously rolling the list of afflictions into a white paper tube. "There isn't a single disease in existence that has not crossed socio-economic boundaries. We have young college girls from affluent families treated at in our own ER for the same conditions that many of the homeless suffer from on a day-to-day basis. The difference is the treatment. Daddy's little girl can afford the antibiotics and follow-up exams, many of her counterparts cannot."

"What about AIDS?" Dick interrupted, watching Martin continue to pace the perimeters of his office. "You can't tell me that isn't terminal?"

"I won't even try," Martin shook his head. "The World Health Organization warned us ten years ago that the numbers would hit forty million infected worldwide. Do you remember the conference a decade ago?" he demanded, as he scanned all the faces in the room.

Everyone nodded their heads in agreement, more than familiar with the catastrophic predications.

"Well, it is ten years later, and the numbers *have* exceeded the predicted forty million. AIDS is a fact of life. Choosing not to open a community health clinic, simply because you're afraid the infected might drain your budget… is just plain cruel. We had a chance, as a community, to educate society, especially since AIDS is a preventable disease. And what did we do?" Martin demanded, banging his rolled-up paper against the tabletop for emphasis. "Well, let me tell you. We did nothing! We were so worried about offending the PTA that now, over ten years later; we're now reaping the unfavorable rewards of that very lack of action."

"So, what can we do to combat the problem?" Dick interjected.

"We can't combat it without education," Martin argued. "We now just have to live with the consequences of our lack of action. We, in the medical community, helped to create the growing numbers through our own apathy. So now, we should be prepared to help treat the consequences generated by our lack of action. We owe this community as much."

"Correct me if I'm wrong, Dr. Hood, but treating an AIDS patient does not necessarily mean including rounds of the experimental treatments presently flooding the pharmaceutical market. Isn't that correct?" Dick Mansfield spoke up to clarify any mounting confusion.

"Experimental?" Martin asked, confident he knew what the man was alluding to, yet wanting to hear the verbal explanation.

"At present, we do not have an accepted cure for Acquired Immunodeficiency Syndrome. Until we do, we have to consider all treatments as experimental," Dick reiterated. "Therefore, other than treating the direct symptoms brought on by the disease itself, we cannot be expected to indulge in every new drug that's being tested by one or the other pharmaceutical giants."

As he slumped back down into his chair, Martin watched everyone nod their heads, agreeing with the preliminary mission statement of the proposed health clinic, which obviously would read *Treat and Street.* He felt immediately defeated by the group's reaction. Dr. Martin Hood released the papers from his hands and watched as they rolled off his lap and fluttered to the carpeted floor. He'd known for years that medicine was now big business, but until tonight, he hadn't fully realized that there was no room left for compassion in the mix.

"Thank you gentlemen," Dick Mansfield said as he shook hands with the last departing guests after the meeting finally adjourned. "Well Martin, you sure clammed up. What the hell happened? First, an impassioned plea for increased spending, and then suddenly, total silence. I don't know how you did in college, but I'll bet you never won a single debate for your team."

Still glued to his chair, the doctor finally looked up at the hospital administrator. "We don't agree on much, do we, Dick?"

"Depends," he cautiously answered.

"But we have a long history of battles won and lost together. Don't we?"

"Yes, we do," Dick agreed, walking up and taking the closest seat on Martin's right. "We've been through hell and back a few times—especially when the maintenance staff threw in with housekeeping, and then tried to convince the kitchen staff to form a union. Remember that?"

"Yes, I remember. Look, I'm asking you for a favor, Dick. I have a friend who's in trouble, and I need you to do whatever you can, pull whatever strings you have to, to get this lady out of hot water. Alright?" he demanded, his tone a little harsher than originally intended.

"No insurance? Let me guess. Your lady friend needs some kind of surgery or procedure, and she's inadvertently allowed her policy to lapse. Well Martin," Dick leaned over and patted him on the shoulder. "It'll be a little difficult, but I think I can get her pushed through the cracks. What's the point of having the corner office if every now and then you can't push your weight around a little?"

"Dick, my friend is Nurse Olga Heinz, and I need you to pull her off your mandatory retirement list," he blurted out as if the statement had escaped his lips by their own accord.

"Nurse Heinz is *your friend*?" Dick Mansfield repeated, heavily emphasizing the word friend.

"I love her, Dick," Martin admitted. "I would have married her years ago if not for… for…"

"For Mary's cancer?"

"For Mary's cancer," Martin whispered. "You have to help me. You can't hold me to that vote. Hell, I didn't even know what I was voting on."

"I know that," Dick agreed. "But unfortunately, I think it might be too late. The decision to terminate the names on the committee's list has already begun moving forward."

"Slip Olga through the cracks," Martin pleaded, spinning both their chairs so that he sat knee to knee with Dick Mansfield. "I never asked you for a personal favor before, and I'm begging you to help me now."

"You don't need to beg," Dick mumbled back. "We *old school boys* have to stick together."

Taking a deep breath, his first in twenty-four hours, Martin finally sunk back in the leather chair and allowed himself to relax.

CHAPTER SIXTEEN

"Because no man can be friends with a woman that he finds attractive."

—*When Harry Met Sally, 1989*

"Oh, come on," Camille pleaded with the nurse for at least the hundredth time. "I really, really need to talk to him, and my parents won't let me have a phone in my room."

As she smiled to herself, the nurse leaned in closer to check the patient's bandage, mindful of the tender area surrounding her lacerated left temple. "Exactly who is this Todd? Your brother, your boyfriend?' the lady gently teased.

"Just a friend," Camille turned away from the nurse, attempting to focus her attention on anything outside the hospital window. "Todd used to be my boyfriend, but he cheated on me, so we broke up."

"I'm sorry," the nurse patted the young girl's left wrist. "How has your breathing been? Any trouble since we taped your ribs?"

"Not really, but it's definitely easier to take a lot of short breath than any big, deep ones."

"That's normal, just be careful not to pant. You don't want to hyperventilate accidentally," the nurse warned. "Just take as regular a breath as possible, and don't forget to gently press down on your stomach should you need to cough or find yourself laughing."

"Don't worry, my world's not all that funny right now," she moaned into the right side of her tear-stained pillow. "The police were already here to see me."

"I'm sure your parents have already advised you on your legal matters," the nurse attempted to respond without taking sides or assigning any blame. "They seem like very compassionate and intelligent people."

"Dad said he's getting me a lawyer, someone with a lot of experience."

Smiling, the nurse bent to pick up her bandaging supplies just as a male visitor timidly poked his head in the room.

"Camille?"

"Hello," the nurse replied. "You must be Todd. I'll leave you two alone," she winked at her charge. "Just ring if you need anything," she smiled one last time, patting the boy on the shoulder before gently closing the door.

"How are you? How are you… feeling?" Grizzy gently asked.

"Fine," Camille hissed. "I was feeling fine until you walked in here."

"Well, I just wanted to see for myself. I stopped by your house, and one of your brothers told me that you'd had a bad car accident, so I just wanted to come by and see if you needed anything," he obviously lied.

She stalled by straightening the creases in the cotton blankets covering her chest. Camille debated whether she would grab the call button clipped to her pillow and summon the first available nurse.

She thought it might be a good idea to demand that security hold her attacker until the cops could arrive to arrest him.

"Are you going to be pissed at me forever?" Grizzy interrupted her internal debate.

She shook with fear as much as with frustration, but she finally found her voice and was able to speak. "I don't know what to say, Grizzy. You wanna tell me exactly what the fucking statute of limitations is on a rape!" Do I get to hate you for the summer, or is this something I'm able to carry around for… let's say… maybe five years?" She began to sob, her hands rushing up to the bandaging wrapped horizontally around her lower chest.

Grizzy quickly checked right and then left to insure that the room held no witnesses before pulling up a chair and dropping down into the plastic seat. "I'm really sorry. I was piss drunk, and I don't really know what happened."

"You want a recap? You want me to tell you?" Camille wailed, the pain of her jagged breathing nauseating her further with every forced breath. "You raped me," she continued to sob, as if the word itself was somehow violating her over and over again. "Why did you do that to me?"

Unconsciously tapping his right leg, Grizzy searched the drab colored walls as if the answers to Camille's anguish were somehow transcribed in the paint. "I… I thought you always liked me." He threw his hands in the air.

"So you ripped off my jeans," she stopped to take two quick breaths, "and then you forced yourself inside me. Did you know?" she began to choke. "Did you know that… that I bled for two days? You really hurt me!" her voice trailed off into a tormented whisper.

Unaware of his own tears, Grizzy sat paralyzed, watching Camille fall apart right before his eyes.

"And I got pregnant, too!"

He closed his eyes and shook his head, as if attempting to erase the lingering residue of a bad dream, Grizzy still wasn't able to block out the sounds of Camille's sobbing. Her pain was torturing him. Still, something kept him glued to her bedside chair. "I know. Todd came to see me for money, and I paid him, but he never cashed the check."

With her eyes open, and her attention focused on the far wall, Camille continued to fixate on the clock as she fought to block out the mere presence of her unwanted guest. The ticking of the second hand helped to regulate her breathing, and after two more trips around the face, she found that she had indeed recovered enough of her wind to speak. "We tried, but the bank wouldn't clear your check in time."

"Oh."

"Oh what?" Camille demanded, still flushed and beginning to sweat, the beading on her forehead instantly absorbed by the white cotton gauze.

"I was just wondering is all," Grizzy mumbled, the lump in his throat inhibiting him from relaying anything longer than short, choppy statements.

"Well, I'm damn lucky that Todd helped me out. He paid."

Rolling his eyes, it was now Grizzy's turn to find a focal point and attempt to regroup. "I'm sorry that I hurt you."

After unclenching her cramped fingers, Camille finally released the wrinkled blanket fibers, flattening her palms to alleviate some of the tension. "It's over," she released the statement with an audible sigh.

"Are you and Todd gonna, maybe… get back together?"

"No!" she blurted out. "And don't try to act like my friend. Cuz you gave up that job the night you attacked me out in that field."

Realizing that he'd probably pushed her as far as he dared, Grizzy decided that it was time to hit the bricks before Camille started crying again and he lost his cool and cried, too. "Todd won't talk to me, and I guess I deserve it, but I just wanted you to know…"

"What?" Camille angrily demanded—her patience was beginning to evaporate as the headache began to cut a swath through her temples.

"You weren't hitting on me the night of the party. I was the one hitting on you. You didn't deserve what happened, it was all my fault."

"I know," she agreed, picking unseen lint balls off the surface of her bedding in an attempt to ignore the pounding in her brain.

"Well, I better go," Grizzy announced, awkwardly pushing the chair back into its original position.

"Don't do it again… to anybody," Camille half warned and half pleaded as he slowly turned and shuffled out of her life.

Metro purposely wiped his hands on his pants before attempting to pinch off the black mold dusting the corners of his loaf. He'd been hiding it for a couple of days, and without refrigeration, the slices had begun to turn. Luckily, the damage seemed limited to one corner, so as soon as he'd freshened up his bread, he make a little lunch with the chicken he'd been given.

"Ner liked crust anyways," his impromptu dinner guest suddenly announced. "Don't 'pose you got any mustard in them pockets?" the young girl pointed to his coat, hoping to draw his attention away from the precious drumsticks.

Shaking his head with a smile on his lips, Metro's good eye never left the take-out Styrofoam container. "Not tonight Ruby, maybe tomorrow," he promised. "But right now, we got bread."

Carefully dividing the chicken, mindful that the soggy skin would be extra difficult for Metro to chew without his bottom dentures, Ruby completed the task as they both settled in with their designated portions. "Mustard be good with this," she teased again through a mouthful of sandwich, winking at Metro as she reached down into her own coat and pulled out a huge can of beer. "Share?"

With his mouth falling open, Metro could barely remember to swallow as his undivided attention was diverted to Ruby's offering. Mesmerized, he watched her as she set down her sandwich and cracked open the aluminum can.

"It was just rolling round on the floor—don't think he even knew." She winked, and lifted the can to take a long pull of the lukewarm suds. Immediately wiping her mouth, Ruby released a beer belch before turning to pass the can off to Metro's shaking hands.

Oblivious to the fact that his half-eaten sandwich sat unprotected on his lap, Metro threw back his head and began guzzling the contents of the oversized can.

"Taste good?" Ruby asked the minute she finished ripping another bite off her remaining lunch.

"Yes ma'am," he growled, licking his lips as his shaking fingers circled the half-empty can.

"Trade?" she nodded down at his sandwich, the only real sustenance his body had seen in days.

Passing off his food with his left, his right brought the can back to his mouth, instantly filling his throat with the liquid gold.

Ruby watched him down the piss warm beer as she chuckled to herself and continued to wolf down the second sandwich. She'd been working most of the night, and after the last trick, her stomach had really started to growl. God how she hated wasting money on food, so when she spotted Metro shuffling down the street with a take-out container stuffed under his arm, she knew she'd hit pay dirt.

"Any more?" he asked, the foam still dripping off the graying stubble of his chin.

"Nope," Ruby laughed, with her stomach full and her ass cold from squatting on the damp wooden crates in the alley. "How'd the leg heal?" she remembered to ask, twisting her miniskirt so the ripped seam was hidden in the back. "Want me to take a look fer ya?"

Nodding, Metro began pulling up his left pant leg—grateful to have someone else check his wound and save him the pain of bending his lower back.

"You drunken old fool," Ruby laughed aloud in the mocking tone she usually saved for *johns* who couldn't get it up. "You got the bandage on the wrong leg."

Metro shook his head in disagreement, and strained to bend at the waist, struggling to figure out just what kind of scam Ruby was attempting to pull over on him now. "That's the leg," he argued, struggling to position his calf for a better view.

He unpeeled the tape and watched the dirty gauze slide down his calf to circle the sock bunched at his ankle, Ruby jumped back up to her feet and wiped her hands on the sides of her skirt.

"I ain't giving it away for nobody," she warned him. "So if you want help, stop messing 'round. I gotta crash, so let's hurry up and see the other leg."

Confused, Metro sat motionless. Not the least bit bothered at having to take the lead herself, Ruby once again dropped to her haunches and pushed up the mud stained material of the old man's other pant leg. Neither spoke, both just as surprised as the other when they were unable to locate the festering wound.

"You all cured up," the prostitute mumbled in disbelief. "Holy fuck, we's got ourselves a goddamn miracle."

Metro continued to rub the calf of his left leg, oblivious to the shooting back spasms running up and down his lower spine.

"I just saw you last night, right?" Ruby struggled to get the facts straight in her own mind. "Out front of the Lilac, right?"

Suddenly anxious to get as far away from Ruby as possible, Metro nervously pulled down both legs of his pants and struggled to rise to his feet. "I gotta go," he blurted out without raising his eyes.

"But I'm sure it was just yesterday."

"Gotta go," Metro repeated, reaching out to steady himself on the brick wall as he pushed past the cramps shooting through his lower back.

"Hey Metro, what about your bread?"

He never turned around. He was too busy making a beeline straight for the Lilac Tree Shelter.

After carefully steadying herself, Camille took the deepest breath she could muster before blowing her nose for the second time.

"Looks painful." Tammy Greenway gave a nervous smile to her daughter, and rushed over to pluck the wet tissues off the folds of her bed. "Are you alright, dear?"

"Mom, I'm fine. Please, can you just quit stressing?" she begged. She turned away from her mother's prying eyes, and wiped her face, working hard to shake off the tears still threatening to spill down her cheeks. "It's just been a rough morning."

"Well, I have a little good news that might actually make you feel better," her mother promised. "The doctor said that you're released!"

"Today?"

"Right now. The nurse called me after rounds, and I rushed right over to pick you up. Aren't you excited about going home?"

Instinct told Camille to jump up and clap her hands, yet the reality of the situation somehow prohibited it—never mind the fact that her ribs were screaming at the mere thought of having to dress in her own clothes. She finally noticed the duffle bag her mother had placed near the foot of the bed. "What's in there? I hope it's not more flowers or gifts."

"Clothes," her mother chirped. "One of your father's button-up shirts, a pair of jogging pants from Jacob's closet, and a pair of my flip flops."

"No underwear from the pool boy?"

"You know your clothes are very form fitting," Tammy admonished her. "Luckily, the nurse who called and told me about your release reminded me that you'd need something fresh to wear that wouldn't bind. This is not the time to worry about how you look…" Her mother's voice trailed off as she spun around to hide her face. "You should have seen yourself two days ago. You were covered in glass, and blood, and…"

"I'm so sorry," Camille apologized, helplessly watching as her mother's shoulders began to shake. "I can't remember anything about the accident."

Tammy turned and propelled herself toward her daughter's side, clamping her fingers around the lowered bed rail attached to the frame of the bed. "The hospital psychologist told your father and me that the accident was possibly just a cry for help."

Camille unconsciously stopped breathing, waiting for her mother to drop the proverbial bomb.

"He told us that you'd recently terminated a pregnancy, and were extremely over-medicated when you decided to drive the Mustang. We couldn't believe what we were hearing. The doctor reported that you were taking prescription Valium, probably prescribed after your…"

"Abortion," Camille flatly stated.

"After your abortion," her mother repeated, the words sounding alien as they crossed her lips. "Are you alright, Cammy? Why didn't you come to us? Maybe we could have helped you."

"How?"

"Well, for one thing, I wouldn't have let you go through everything alone."

"Todd was with me."

"We figured as much."

"Stop it! For the love of God, fucking stop talking like that!" Camille shouted across the bed at her mother's bewildered face. "You sound like you don't have your own opinion. All you can do is repeat whatever Dad says. Don't you ever think for yourself anymore?"

"What's the matter? Why are you so upset with me?" Tammy began to tear up, seemingly on the verge of a full-scale breakdown. "I don't understand why you're so mad at me. I've been worried sick about you."

"Forget it. Never mind. I don't know what I'm saying."

As she reached up to wipe away the tears with the back of her hands, Camille's mother felt the moment slipping away from her grasp. She was so close to a breakthrough with her daughter—an honest to goodness *mother and daughter moment*—that she couldn't believe how desperately she wanted to run away and hide.

As she sensed her mother's sudden indecision, Camille held her tongue and watched the tug of war rage on her mother's face.

"Was Todd the father of your baby?"

"Why, does Dad think I was some kind of ho?"

Tammy reached across the blankets and rubbed her daughter's forearm. "Your dad and I have never spoken of this. I was just thinking that maybe part of the reason you were having trouble dealing with the pregnancy, and the termination, was because you weren't pregnant by choice."

With a shake of her head, Camille turned away from her mother's face, and painfully attempted to shift her bodyweight.

The action immediately broke the physical contact between mother and daughter. “Nobody my age gets pregnant by choice.”

“I know, sweetie.” Her mother reached out, this time attempting to stroke her daughter’s damp cheek. “I was just wondering if you’d had unprotected intercourse by choice, too?”

CHAPTER SEVENTEEN

"You want somethin', go get it. Period!"

—The Pursuit of Happyness, 2006

As soon as Metro tasted his first sip of coffee, he realized that he'd forgotten to add his usual two lumps of sugar. Unfortunately, in his haste to commandeer the most coveted seat in the house, he had added a generous splash of cream, but had somehow missed the box of white cubes. But all was not lost. He was sitting up on the stage, exactly where he wanted to be. Front and center.

"Coffee hot?" one of the staffers from the shelter leaned over and asked.

"Yes sir," Metro nodded back, unwilling to meet his eyes should the Lilac Tree counselor mistake his friendlessness for an invitation to sit down and join him.

"Oh, by the way. How you feeling? I saw you were limping just a couple of nights ago. Did you twist an ankle, or was it just a rough bout of arthritis?"

As his eyes darted back and forth, Metro checked to see if

anyone was eavesdropping on their conversation. Satisfied, he finally lifted his face to answer the questions. "My leg was sore, but it's better now. Thanks for asking," he nodded, returning to his coffee to end the questioning.

"Well, take care Metro," the staffer smiled, as he lifted the black garbage bag to continue with his volunteer collection of discarded paper cups and balled up sandwich wrappers. "Just yell if you feel like a little company."

Diving back down into his now lukewarm cup, Metro just shook his head and continued to scan the room for any sign of the guy who had fixed his leg. "Sam, Cecil," he continued to mumble, unable to remember Steven's first name.

"Doris," one of the volunteers called out to the senior counselor as she took her turn and patrolled the shelter's main floor. "I thought you should know that Metro appears very agitated, and he's sitting up on the stage all by himself. Look at him," the guy turned Doris's attention up toward the folding chairs and padded vinyl card table.

"You're right, he's looking for something or someone," Doris agreed, thanking the volunteer and making her way toward the raised platform.

"Maybe he's got a gun under his coat, and he's waiting for his victim?" the volunteer nervously suggested.

"Why don't you go see if anyone needs help unloading supplies in the kitchen," Doris encouraged the overzealous man.

After reluctantly agreeing, he turned and walked away, leaving Doris with the uncomfortable task at hand.

She casually approached in what she hoped was her most disarming manner, and slid into the vacant chair across from Metro. "Looks like you're really enjoying the view up here."

"Don't want to make you mad, but..."

"But what?" Doris gently prodded, noticing how Metro continually fidgeted with the folded rim of his paper cup.

"I don't want company."

"Are you looking for someone?" she took a stab, not the least bit concerned that Metro may be readying himself to spray a hail of bullets down at the assembled crowd. "You look a little nervous."

When he realized that the counselor probably wasn't going to leave him alone until he talked, he opened his mouth and the excuses started falling out. Metro ended with his need for a further cup of coffee, finally excusing himself from Doris's probing eyes and shuffling back to the refreshment table.

"Hey Metro," one of the kitchen staff called out to him. "There's a guy looking for you by the bins. He said his name is Steven."

"Steven, Steven" he began to chant, as if trying out the possibility of a new mantra. "He's here?" were the last words Metro muttered before turning around and rushing off in the direction of the used clothing bins.

After she dropped Steven off at the shelter's front door to check on Metro's progress, Olga decided that it was time she did a little research of her own. Whether or not her roommate was going to choose to be involved in her find, Olga wasn't prepared to park her little miracle cure in the closet until Steven made up his mind. She had a plan in mind, and until Steven was positive that he wanted to be involved, it was probably better for her to delve into this world, all on her own.

As she parked and prepared to lock up her car, Olga twisted down the rear view mirror and quickly checked her appearance. Stripped of all jewelry, dressed in a basic monochromatic sweat suit, she was pretty sure her appearance wouldn't be very memorable.

She didn't want to be confused with a client, yet at no time did she want to stand out and become an object of curiosity. Curiosity usually developed into suspicion, and suspicion often evolved into paranoia. Paranoid people, in turn, had a funny way of taking matters into their own hands, and Olga had lost track of how many stab wounds and bullet holes she'd patched up under the banner of paranoia.

After locking her purse in her trunk, and discreetly tucking her car key into the right cup of her brassiere, she finally gave herself the okay and walked across the street and down to the basement's entrance.

The smell greeting her nostrils wasn't really as unpleasant as she would have imagined, however the unsettling sounds more than made up for her level of discomfort. Years of hearing patients cry out while they suffered with their pain was difficult enough—yet hearing a whimper when you were unable to distinguish whether it was man, woman, or child, was unsettling, to say the least. Were they crying out in physical pain, or was it the torment of mental anguish? Not being able to verify the source was very difficult, and Olga found that the unknown just drew her deeper into the underground recesses of the building.

Another few steps and she was finally standing right in front of the second door concealing all the answers. Although she was scared to move forward, her need to unearth the source that sound overcame her trepidation.

Once again sequestered in the men's bathroom, Metro held his position, staring right into Steven's face. He had a whole list of questions for the young kid, and at this point, he really wasn't in the mood to have the interrogation turned on him.

"Did you feel any sort of burning or tingling in the last twelve to twenty-four hours?"

With his right hand still cradling the paper coffee cup, Metro took the opportunity to pivot and toss it in the open garbage can.

"I can see that you feel much better," Steven noted, jotting down the test subject's obvious mobility. "Do you mind if I take a look at your leg?" he asked, setting his notepad on the corner of a sink before dropping down to his haunches.

"No!" the unwilling patient barked, "Something happened to me. I don't know what you did, and nobody is looking at my leg until you tell me what happened!"

Steven hadn't foreseen this bump in the road, and he wasn't the least bit sure of how he was going to handle the situation. He stood up. "I… I didn't do anything really special, it was just a… a new medicine," he forced out, "We're trying to keep it a secret because we don't have approval, so we're kinda, we're kinda trying it out for free."

Pondering the answer, Metro shuffled his feet and debated his further co-operation. He really did want someone other than Ruby to take an interest in his healed leg, but he didn't know this kid from a hole in the ground. What if he'd given him some kind of dope, something that made him think he was all cured when he really wasn't? What if the kid came back because he planned to shake him down for some kind of payment? "I just don't feel right about this. Are you some kind of doctor, maybe one of those training kinds that's still learning and taking your classes?"

"No, I'm not a doctor or a nurse," Steven reminded the man.

"Course you're not a nurse," he chuckled. "You've got stuff," the grown man clumsily motioned toward his Steven's crotch.

"Yeah, I got the stuff," Steven smirked.

With the ice broken by the small joke, Metro suddenly bent

down and lifted up his pant leg, motioning for the kid to lean in and take a closer look at his left leg.

"It does look good," Steven confirmed. He bent down even closer to inspect the wound site on Metro's left calf.

Hell, looking good was a little of an understatement. Not only was the open gash and subsequent infection healed, but the site now had a swatch of brand new tissue.

Metro said, "I know a woman who's got really bad burns. Her husband threw a pot of boiling pudding in her face, and by the time she scraped it off, some of her face came with it. Can you help her too?" he asked, genuinely concerned for the lady's wellbeing.

Olga grabbed the length of steel pipe that had been welded on to replace the broken door handle—suppressing the most unwieldy of her fears—and forced herself through the clinic's entrance. Although she'd never been there before, its reputation had become legendary, and more than once, she had dealt with the after-effects in her hospital's emergency room.

Even now, she still had trouble rationalizing that she was standing in the middle of *The Changeroom*, the most notorious underground clinic in town. Over the years, the owners had changed, as had the name, but in the end, the supposedly unethical and illegal medical treatments were still taking place.

Day after day, at a very alarming rate, bodies were surgically altered. Some patients had parts enhanced, others had things reduced, and occasionally the odd body part was physically sliced off—as long as the cash was paid up front and the patient's referral checked out. In addition to the benefit of cash fees, clients did not have to contend with any hospital review board overseeing the efficacy of the surgical options. No one cared that the patients might be paying to have themselves maimed out of a sick psychological need. Patients never had to worry about the scheduling problems, follow-up appointments, or the reams of paperwork associated with insurance policies and medical benefits. Cash spoke volumes.

Essentially, everyone walking through the door was treated like a paying customer, not a patient. For behind these doors, it wasn't just a hospital, it was also a business, and if you wanted your hand held, you'd be much better off by heading down to the local emergency room. This was a *cash only* clinic, where dreams were supposedly realized and nightmares were finally corrected. Unfortunately, the line between dreams and nightmares was cloudy at best. When the client set down their greenbacks to order up their dreams, they weren't always buying what was best for them.

"Lady, hey lady," a man yelled from across the crowded floor. "You picking up or dropping off?" he demanded, immediately noticing that Olga wasn't carrying a change of clothes or any of the other personal items required before day surgery.

"I wanna see a doctor," she abruptly snapped back, more out of nervousness than actual annoyance.

"Here you go," the intake worker and in-house bouncer handed Olga a blank form. "Fill in as much as you can, I'll put you on the list, and hopefully you'll get to see a doc this afternoon. Did you take care of your payment?"

Nodding, she nervously accepted the pen and paper thrust in her hands, along with the blank referral form. "I'm not exactly sure what kind of procedure…"

"Not my department," the thirty-year-old intake worker barked. "Just fill in the blanks, take a seat, and I'll get to you as soon as possible. And can someone take this woman to the exit," he nodded his head in the general direction of the young lady still sobbing in the chairs.

Turning to look for an empty seat, Olga jumped when the man's voice boomed from across the room one last time.

"Petula, Petula Rodriguez," he briskly announced, leaving little doubt that it was the next client's turn to follow him into the back.

Olga watched as the twenty-something year old woman rose from a chair near the back wall, and sauntered toward the inner office. Olga quickly moved toward the vacated seat, grateful for a chance to sit and hopefully blend in. She dropped down into the plastic lawn chair and waited for the idle chitchat to resume.

"How do you spell… castration?" the young woman seated on her left whispered toward Olga's ear.

"Pardon me?"

"You know, cutting off your balls," the girl continued to whisper, her voice hoarse and her breath reeking of stale tobacco smoke.

"C-A-S… T-R-A… T-I-O-N."

"Thank you, sweetie," she smiled, returning to print the world under the *operation category* of the form.

Discreetly shifting her eyes to read the girl's form without having to turn her head, Olga squinted to decipher the notes scribbled down between the lines.

Name:	*Gerald Ralph Newberg*	Nickname:	*Gerri*
Age:	*Twenty-three*	DOB:	*Jun/05/81*
Birth Sex:	*Male*	Living As:	*Female*
Surgery:	*Castration*	When:	*Now!*
Occupation:			

"Sorry to bother you again, but can you tell me how to spell *unemployed*, like when you have no job?"

Olga took the opportunity to introduce herself, shaking hands with Gerri as she graciously offered her to fill in the remainder of the clinic's form.

"Well, I have a job… sort of. It pays cash. I just don't know what to call it," the young girl smiled impishly.

"Just say the word, and I'll spell it for you."

Nervously biting her bottom lip, Gerri fidgeted with gold lamé purse strings draped over her bare knees just below the hemline on her mini skirt. "I'm a *fluffer*."

Dropping her head to record the word, Olga stopped, her wrist poised directly above the paper. "What exactly is a fluffer? What do you do?"

Gerri leaned back against the plastic of the chair, and crossed her legs while nervously searching for just the right words to describe her job's requirements. "I work in the film industry. I help actors get ready for their screen time."

"Oh, like hair and make-up?" Olga smiled, immediately appreciating why the young male/female was comfortable wearing such heavy foundation and had obviously chosen such a highly coiffed wig. "Have you done anyone famous? Someone I might have heard of?"

Yanking the form back from Olga's hands, Gerri slammed the clipboard down on top of her own knees. "Not hair and make-up. It's cocks! I make sure the guys have hard-ons before the director starts rolling the film. Get it?" she demanded. Olga obviously embarrassed by the revelation, was not sure how to handle her outburst of emotion.

"Oh, I see."

"Oh, I see," Gerri repeated in a mocking tone, the raised volume of their conversation now drawing the attention of a few casual observers. "I'm not a prostitute, you know. I don't fuck for money!" she blurted out to the entire room.

Caught off guard by the young woman's anger, Olga carefully weighed her next statement. "I'm sorry. I wasn't judging you. I don't know anything about the adult film industry, and I'm sorry if I offended you. I'd just never heard the term *fluffer* before.

Knocked off guard by the sincerity of the apology, Gerri relented. "I… I just stroke it and kiss it, is all. They've gotta save it for the screen. Know what I mean?" she chided.

"For the screen," Olga repeated, nodding her head as the reality of the situation suddenly hit home.

"I can also waitress, but the money sucks. You know what it's like to pull an eight-hour shift and have the bus boys suck half your tips off the tables? It really bites."

Smiling, Olga looked up just as the empty machine in the corner was replaced with a fresh pot. "Coffee?"

"Sounds good," Gerri agreed. "Let me. Least I can do for all the spelling."

Sipping the hot, but not especially tasty brew, both continued their wait side-by-side in the busy holding room.

"So, what's your pleasure?" Gerri asked, turning to appraise Olga's handwritten form. "You want some kind of surgery or treatment that the husband won't let you have?"

"Yes," she agreed, suddenly content with that explanation. "I was thinking of some liposuction, and since I'm paying cash anyway, I didn't think I needed anyone's approval."

"You go, girl," Gerri patted her on the knee. "I saved up my cash for two years for this operation, and I ain't gonna have any little red-neck doctor down at the county hospital tell me it's not ethical. How in the hell would that man know what it's like, trying to live as a woman with a set of balls hanging around and ruining the lines of my skirts every… single… time… I step out the damn door. You know what I mean?"

Not quite sure what to say, Olga stalled by taking another sip of her coffee. It wasn't that she'd never been exposed to any gender reassignment surgeries in her lengthy career—she'd never been so up close and personal before. Never had she been granted a behind the scenes interview with the patient before the actual surgery. It was a little unsettling, to say the least.

"I think it's kind of like buying a pair of pantyhose. They all look the same in the packages, but only *you* actually know which pair is gonna feel good on your body, right?" Gerri fought to explain.

"But correct me if I'm wrong, but you'll still have your penis after being castrated. You know that, don't you?"

"I can't afford everything right now," Gerri confided, "so at least this way, I'll kind of take care of two birds with one stone."

Starting to understand where she was going with the explanation, Olga finally felt comfortable enough to speak. "You're talking about the hormonal change in your body, such as the lack of testosterone?"

"Exactly. My equipment's supposed to shrink," she nodded with a smile. "My voice will rise a notch or two, and I shouldn't have to shave so often," Gerri gently patted her own right cheek.

"And you're absolutely sure this is what you want to do? Because once it's done, it's really done, and there's no going back."

"I'm so sure; I almost paid for a *do it yourself* at my own house."

Olga's quizzical look confirmed that she wasn't totally following what Gerri was alluding to with the *do it yourself* reference.

"Well, my boyfriend knows a guy that'll come to you with his stuff, and take care of it right in the privacy of your own home. But since I live in a small apartment and have a roommate, I thought I'd better do it properly and come down to the clinic."

"Do it properly," Olga repeated, trying on the statement for size.

"Yeah, I heard there can be a lot of blood, so I thought it would be better here," she waved her hands to encompass the entire room. "Besides, I think it'd be a lot safer. Don't you?"

Olga's throat felt as tight as a drum. She couldn't swallow another sip of coffee or utter a single sentence, and for lack of reply, her ensuing silence was mistaken for agreement.

CHAPTER EIGHTEEN

"Sometimes in order to see the light, you have to risk the dark."

—Minority Report, 2002

Before Olga realized, it was nearing late afternoon and she'd have to run to pick up Steven at the Lilac Tree Shelter. Hopefully, he would locate the homeless man with promising results, and will be prepared to continue researching their miracle cure.

"Heinz," the name rang out through the congested holding room. "Olga Heinz," the man's voice repeated for the second time. "It's your turn."

"Coming," she called back, turning to face Gerri before rising and heading off to her long waited appointment. "I have to go," she announced with audible disappointment.

"Want to grab some lunch after?"

"You read my mind," Olga smiled. "Where?"

"How about Romanoff's Deli on the corner of sixth, just two

blocks up the street? I should be right behind you, if you don't mind waiting for fifteen or twenty minutes?"

"I have the time, and I think lunch would be great."

"Heinz," the man barked, reaching for another file off the top of his intake counter.

"I'm here," Olga called out, winking back at Gerri before turning to present herself for her initial consultation.

A consultation would be a very generous description of the following twenty minutes of Olga's life. The first half was more of a grilling process, conducted by the same man who had served as receptionist and clinic muscle. His concerns were all about the cash. He asked her if she familiar with the costs associated with her surgery. He presented her with a *fees schedule* and asked her to locate her procedure on it, and then commit to the price. The process felt more like Olga was buying an appliance than having a consultation for surgery. It was also made abundantly clear that the clinic offered absolutely no after care.

During the second half of her consultation, Olga was further informed that not only was she responsible for her own ride home, but she'd be responsible for any follow-up medical treatment, such as staple or stitch removal. The clinic's front man also told her that if she was really in a bind, she could stop by, and for fifty bucks, he'd help her out himself. What a prince.

As he scanned her freshly penciled form, the man highlighted the word liposuction, and Olga's age. He noted the cash fee she had agreed upon, and that she was ready for surgery at their first available convenience. "This all looks fine, but what about your referral form?" he continued to quiz her from his position behind the desk.

"Well," Olga began her little speech, testing the waters to see just how firm the clinic was on its referral policy. "I was in a relationship with a doctor for over ten years, until his wife died of cancer. Now, I think I just need to freshen myself up," she nervously smiled, patting her own thighs. "I'd heard about your clinic for years. My doctor friend always said that if someone needed work done quickly and privately, your clinic was probably the place they'd end up."

Obviously satisfied with Olga's answer, the man suddenly rose from his chair and exited the room.

"Nurse Heinz," the doctor unceremoniously announced as he strolled into his own office, coffee cup firmly clenched in his right hand. "It's been a long time since we've crossed paths. I must say that I'm surprised to see you. Never thought a woman like you would darken my door."

"Dr. Clifford?"

"The one and only," he smirked, setting down his cup and linking his fingers together on the top of his desk. "I hear you're looking for a little liposuction to slim the outline of your inner thighs. Want to accentuate that good old Adductor Magnus muscle, do we?"

"I'm sorry Dr. Clifford, but I thought you had retired after your uncle passed?"

"Maybe moved to the Cayman Islands to manage my family's substantial residential holdings? Or was busy allocating funds for the family's philanthropic ventures?" he recited as if quoting a newspaper headlines.

"Yes. That's exactly what I'd heard," Olga agreed with a nod.

"Well, you had it half right. My uncle did pass away, but the only thing he left me was the title to this office building, and the keys to this basement clinic. So tell me, Nurse Heinz, how do you like the family's *Little Shop of Horrors* so far?"

"Why didn't you come back to the hospital—return to your practice?"

"You never were a woman too concerned with the hospital's daily gossip, were you?"

"Dr. Clifford, I think..."

"I know exactly what you're thinking, Olga," his tone began to soften; silently reminiscing about the life he'd left behind. "Trust me when I say it's impossible. Once word leaked to the medical community that my uncle was the guy who owned and operated this very clinic, my fate was sealed. There wasn't a reputable trauma center in the state who wanted to link their name to mine."

"But your career—a lifetime of professional accomplishments? What about your classes down at the University? Couldn't you continue to teach?"

"As soon as the will passed probate, I was a social pariah, and you have to remember that even our university's budget is largely funded through alumni donations. Nobody—and I mean nobody—wanted their money associated with the butcher who owned the Changeroom."

"Well, why didn't you just close it down then?"

"Oh God, how I wanted to," he emphasized with a wave of his hands. "But by this time, I had no other source of income, and somebody had to play for my ex-wife's private… whatever," he tried to sum up with a wave of his hand.

"You and Susan are divorced, too?"

"A casualty of my profession," he half-heartedly admitted. "I guess Susan was tired of all the prestige associated with my new clinic."

Olga looked him over and was surprised to notice that her old colleague's white lab coat was actually frayed at the collar, and the cuffs were stained with ink or some other dark substance. His office was decorated in *Mid-century Flea-Market*, and her woman's intuition told her that at least half of his clients earned their fees working somewhere in the sex trade. In all, Olga came to realize that Dr. Marcus Clifford was just a shell of the man she remembered. As the minutes passed, she almost forgot why she'd stopped by in the first place.

He said, "So enough about me. I hear that you and Martin Hood are unfortunately no longer a couple. I looked for you at his wife's funeral, but I guess you decided that it wasn't appropriate to attend."

Olga just nodded, her silence putting a quick end to their joint trip down memory lane.

"I hope you don't think me too forward, Olga and it's not like I couldn't use your cash, but I really don't think you need any liposuction. You're an attractive woman, and in my opinion, you'd be throwing your hard-earned money toward an unnecessary procedure."

"Thank you, doctor," she nodded her head, grateful to see the man she once knew shining up through the dirt and grime.

"How about a tour?" he offered in exchange.

They started with his examination/procedure room, and Olga was relieved to see that even though the equipment was dated, the room appeared adequately sterile.

"I only operate on Mondays, Wednesdays, and Fridays. Tuesdays and Thursdays are set aside for consultations, paper work, and of course, clean up. I'm down to a staff of two, and with equipment repairs and supply costs continually rising; I'm not sure how long I'll be able to hang onto Tony."

"Tony, the charmer you have working your intake desk?"

"That's my man," he chuckled, "Doesn't hurt to have a little muscle in this neighborhood either. The junkies tend to think twice about walking in and trying to hold us up ever since Tony *piped* the last guy who stumbled in brandishing some rusty old steak knife."

"I didn't really come about liposuction."

"I figured so." The weary doctor stopped long enough to drop both his hands into the pockets on his lab coat. "So are you moonlighting for the FDA, checking on generic prescriptions?"

"No. Nothing that covert. I'm just doing a little private research for a new topical healing agent."

"Funding?"

Turning her face away from the doctor's eyes, Olga stepped around the gurney and rested her hand on the top of the threadbare cotton. "Private money mostly. Hush-hush. You know how drug development goes."

"I vaguely remember," he mused, the tone of his voice betraying his resentment.

Suddenly, flashbacks of Dr. Clifford's extensive work in developing the hormone adrenaline to be used in the saline injection during tumescent liposuction flooded back to Olga. His work had been brilliant, but in lieu of lucrative patents, he had turned over his findings to speed up the approval process.

"Dr. Clifford," Tony interrupted their reunion, "it's time for your next patient."

"I'm sorry to keep you so long, Doctor. I actually have somewhere to be myself."

"Please stop by again," he genuinely encouraged her. "I'd love to hear more about your research."

"I will," Olga promised. She stepped forward to shake her old friend's hand. "This has been a nice surprise."

"Tony, please walk my friend, Nurse Heinz, to her car. You can take her discreetly out the back staff door. No use ruining both our careers."

Tony never questioned a word; he just followed the doctor's orders; exactly what he'd been hired to do.

When Steven finally tired of roaming up and down the main floor of the shelter, waiting for his ride, he eventually found Doris and left word that he was running an errand. He had decided to look up Metro's friend with the facial burns, and daylight was wasting.

Just as he'd been told, the lady lived in an older house just off Tenth Street, and down the corner from the gas station. After knocking lightly on the front door, Steven was surprised when a uniformed woman in latex gloves and a surgical mask opened the door.

"Can I help you?"

"I was looking for Miranda," he replied, reading the scribbled name off his notepad. "Her friend Metro asked me to look in on her after the accident with the pudding," he rambled, trying to sound more like a friend than a door-to-door salesman. "Is she at home?"

"Yes she is. Why don't you step inside? I'm just changing her bandaging, and I'll be out of here in a jiff."

As he followed the home care attendant into the house, Steven's nostrils were instantly assaulted with the combined stench of garlic and antiseptic. He could have never imagined such a combination—only after entering the kitchen did he locate the source. Picking jars and baby cucumbers lined the counter tops, and a large enameled pot stood simmering on the stove. Steven cautiously moved past all the canning supplies and made his way toward a seated woman with her back toward the door.

"I'll be right with you," she politely addressed her unseen guest, clenching her fingers and wincing in pain as the final stages of the bandage change were completed.

With the dressing in place, and introductions made, Steven accepted Miranda's invitation for a cup of tea and took a seat behind the table.

"You're not a doctor, but you help down at the shelter?" she confirmed.

"Yes, that's where I met Metro. And how did you two become friends, if you don't mind me asking?"

"Metro and his wife were our neighbors back in the eighties, when our kids were young. They moved away, and we lost touch. Then about five or six years ago, my church was volunteering down at the Lilac Tree Shelter, and we met up again. From what he's told me, his wife had passed, and he'd lost touch with his children. Sad, just terribly sad," Miranda muttered, as she carefully poured the boiling water into the antique blue willow teapot.

"Metro's homeless?"

"He's chosen a bottle of whiskey over his family, and God help him," she stopped to cross herself, "that bottle is going to kill him."

After accepting the fine bone china with the tiny chip in the rim, Steven couldn't help but miss his own mom. Not that she'd been the *stay at home and can vegetables* kind of mother, but she was still his mom, and at moments like this, he truly missed having a family home.

"...so as I was saying," Miranda continued, "my Bert was spending too much time with Metro, so I just had to lay down the law. The bowl of pudding that night was an accident, and I know it won't happen again," she announced with mock confidence.

Steven shook off the flood of personal memories that struggled to invade his thoughts. He stood up from the table and slowly walked over to the kitchen window. "I have a special treatment that's being tested on bad wounds. It fixed Metro's leg, and he thought it might be able to help you."

"Doctor said there was nothing much that could be done," she warned, the good spirits quickly fading from the tone in her voice. "Said I was going to have some red splotches, maybe a little tightening of the skin on my right cheek forever."

"Well, I can't guarantee that my medicine will work, but I can guarantee that it won't hurt you," Steven promised, braver and a little more confident since his encounter with Metro.

"Alright," Miranda agreed. "You come back tomorrow at the same time when my bandage is being changed, and you can put a little on me before home care covers me with their greasy salve."

He could visualize the problem of attempting to explain his experimental treatment to a trained professional, so Steven found himself scrambling for an alternative plan. "My co-worker is a professional nurse. How about if we both stop by sometime tomorrow morning? Then, she can change your dressing, too. It'll save home care from making an extra trip, and you can have a real nurse check the healing of your burn."

"I like that idea," Miranda agreed, shaking Steven's hand to seal the deal before he downed his tea and look his leave.

Gerri was almost ready to fly the coop when she finally spotted her lunch date racing up the street toward the deli.

"I'm so sorry," were the first words out of Olga's mouth as she slid across the vinyl booth to face her lunch date. "My appointment took a lot longer than I thought."

"I gathered that, especially when that no-neck orderly came out and announced that the doctor wouldn't be seeing anyone else today."

"Sorry," Olga felt compelled to repeat again.

"No matter. The day wasn't a total waste. I made a new friend."

"I'll drink to that," Olga agreed, lifting her empty cup to signal the waitress that they were ready for her to take their order.

They decided on Cobb salads with peppermint tea. As Olga sat back and watched the dried leaves bleed color into her boiling cup of water, Gerri couldn't help but ask. "Can I be dead honest with you?"

"I'd be disappointed with less."

"Well, are you with some kind of Board of Health, looking to shut down the clinic? Cuz you weren't there for any surgery. Even I can tell that."

As she pushed her cup aside to make room for the incoming salads, Olga took advantage of the break in their conversation to formulate her answer. Genuinely fond of her new acquaintance, she opted for an explanation as close to the truth as possible.

"Dr. Clifford and I had worked together for many years. I'm a nurse, and he used to be one of the resident doctors in the research department at my hospital."

"You're a nurse! she exclaimed. It seemed to Olga that the news cheered Gerri up for some abstract reason. "That's why you knew how to spell all those fancy medical terms."

Nodding in agreement, Olga smiled while Gerri took a travel-sized bottle of sanitizing gel from her gold purse and liberally dropped a dollop into the palm of her left hand.

"Want some?"

"Thank you. That would be helpful."

Hands cleansed, and ice broken, both ladies dove straight into their salads.

"My turn," Olga announced between bites. "So tell me, why castration? Why not just not continue living as you have been until you've saved enough for a complete sex change?"

"I don't qualify," she mumbled through a mouthful of grated cheddar cheese and chopped boiled egg. "A couple years ago, I tried to kill myself after a really bad break-up, and now I can't get past any of the psychologists, with that stamped on my county file. They all want hours and hours of therapy first, but nobody has any idea about who is supposed to pay for it," she summed up in a huff. "So, I'm doing what I can."

"Castration is pretty invasive surgery. Painful, and a fair bit of fluid loss is usually quite common. What kind of arrangements have you made for your recovery?"

Suddenly turned off by the bright red Catalina dressing that covered the remainder of her salad, Gerri pushed away her plate and delicately dabbed the paper napkin across the curves of her lips. "I'm gonna take a cab."

"No, not the ride home," Olga gently corrected Gerri. I mean your recovery time. You know that you'll be basically incapacitated for at least a week, unable to walk, or even complete basic daily tasks. You'll need someone to bring you food, and water, and to change your bandages. The simple act of urination is going to bring you to your knees."

Shocked by the explicitness of Olga's revelations, Gerri felt the room spinning, her Cobb salad threatening to make an unwanted entrance all over the deli's polished floor. "I need some fresh air," she mumbled, swallowing hard to fight the nausea.

Olga took the cue and threw a twenty-dollar bill on the table. She rushed to help Gerri to her feet, and expertly guided the wobbly girl outside the deli's front doors. "Are you feeling better?" she asked the minute she'd spotted a newspaper box for Gerri to lean on.

After extracting herself from Olga's grasp, Gerri stood tall and tossed her hair back over her shoulders. "I'm absolutely fine, sweetie." She laughed in a rather deep, masculine chuckle.

"But I thought…"

"I know what you thought, but please trust me," Gerri cinched her arm around Olga's waist to propel them down the sidewalk. "You see, I *can* take care of myself."

"I get it," Olga laughed, "and it just cost me a twenty."

"Sorry," Gerri apologized, slipping her right hand down into her purse.

"No, no. Lunch is on me, I insist. It was a lesson well learned."

"Fine," Gerri conceded. She gently reached for Olga's wrist to check the time on her watch. "Oh sweetie, time's up. I gotta run."

After hugging as if long time friends, they quickly exchanged phone numbers in the middle of the sidewalk and reluctantly parted ways.

As she drove back toward the shelter, Olga attempted to make double time by taking two side streets and one very cluttered back alley. When she finally pulled up in front of the Lilac Tree, she was unable to spot Steven anywhere in the crowd, but then she was over two-and-a-half hours late.

Forced to settle for a lukewarm cup of coffee while she waited for Steven to reappear, Olga strolled over to Doris's office and gently wrapped her knuckles on the door. "Got time for a break?"

"Come in, come in," Doris beckoned, pencil tucked behind her right ear, phone receiver cradled in her neck.

Olga felt exhausted just from watching Doris juggle the phone lines, the continual stream of people demanding sound bites of her attention, and of course, and there were the backbreaking boxes of paper work. Olga was impressed with Doris's stamina. Maybe it was just her own age, but there was no way she could even imagine fulfilling those kinds of professional demands.

"Sorry. I'm all yours," Doris said.

Just as Olga opened her mouth to ask where she could sign up as a volunteer, the phone began to ring for the umpteenth time. Doris glanced down at the number, and raised her face with an apologetic look. "I have to take this, sorry," she announced with a roll of her eyes.

Olga waved a polite little goodbye, turned and was about to leave when Doris frantically started waving her hands in the air.

"Help me," she whispered, simultaneously reaching up with her left hand to cover the mouthpiece. "I have a batch coming in. Can you stay? Please?"

A batch of cookies? A batch of clean laundry? Olga had no idea what Doris was talking about, but the woman apparently needed her help, so she nodded her head in agreement and decided to stay.

After another cab ride, Steven was finally back at the shelter, which was quickly beginning to feel like his second home. He was relieved to spot Olga's car on the side street. He paid the driver and trotted up the front steps. It had been a long day, and he wanted nothing more than to head home, grab a bite to eat, and compare notes on their day. He had so much to report; it might not be a bad idea to organize his thoughts on paper first, in some kind of bullet points.

"There you are," Doris beckoned Steven over the second she spotted him in the shelter's foyer. "I'm sorry, but I haven't had a chance to give Olga your note. But don't worry; she just arrived here a few minutes ago, and she's back in the kitchen."

Steven picked up on the polite dismissal, and sauntered over to the hub of the chaos.

"Everything is stowed except for the milk. I don't have the slightest clue what we're supposed to do with the ten gallons sitting back there in them crates," the cook continued to moan. "My vegetables are gonna freeze if they're packed in that fridge like sardines, and now you tell me that I have to fit in all those jugs. I just can't do it." He gave up with an exaggerated flourish.

Steven decided to be bold; he pushed his way through the assembled crowd and resurfaced into the middle of what was starting to feel like an impromptu pajama party.

"I'm sure we can fit another couple mattresses over here on the floor," Olga instructed the crew. "Just remember to leave a walkway in between—don't want anybody stepping on anybody's toes."

"Olga, Olga! I'm back," Steven shouted over the din. "What are you doing?"

After squeezing past the volunteers hauling in the temporary bedding, she rushed over to where her roommate stood his ground. "The shelter on eighteenth was shut down for twenty-four hours with some kind of infestation. We're setting up emergency housing, and I'm in charge while Doris runs down to city hall for a temporary license. Wanna help?"

"What kind of infestation?" he teased, hands positioned on his hips.

"Four legged," Olga threw over her shoulder. "Now come with me. I need a little assistance organizing all our guests before we have a little revolt on our hands."

For the next hour and a half, they juggled mats, shuffled intake forms, and generally worked to appease a group of men and women who were more than a little disturbed by the forced evacuation.

"Where are we?" one of the newly transplanted women demanded, a six-year-old girl tucked deep behind her back. "My old man's gonna be looking for me in the morning. How in the hell is he gonna find me here?" she demanded.

"A message was posted on each of the shelter doors," Steven repeated for the hundredth time that evening. "It has the address and the phone number for the Lilac Tree written in big black letters. He'll find you."

"He better," she growled, not the least bit encouraged by Steven's reassurance.

"Excuse me ladies and gentlemen," Doris shouted from her position at the edge of the stage. "Can everybody hear me?" she called out again, stalling to make sure she had the crowd's full attention before she rattled off her list of instructions.

"The lady said quiet!" Steven barked, his outburst immediately achieving the desired results.

"Thank you. Now if everyone can just pay attention, I promise it won't take long."

Twenty minutes later, with a very short list of do's and don'ts relayed to the assembled crowd, Doris stepped off the stage with a final set of instructions for her volunteer staff. She dispatched three to the kitchen to help the cook, a couple to organize games and activities, and then she asked Steven to be on security patrol. She and Olga would attend to any lagging medical concerns.

Resigned to pacing back and forth across the shelter's floor, Steven gently swung the flashlight from his wrist. Not exactly sure about what he was supposed to do next, he finally chose to put the flashlight to use and check the basement storage rooms for any extra blankets.

Three steps down the back stairs, he began to pick up the faintest of whimpering sounds. He decided that it was his duty at least to check out the origin, if not the motivation for the crying, so Steven flicked his beam on high and began moving forward.

"Oh, oh my god, that's good," the young girl continued to moan, her voice now taking on a tone of ecstasy when Steven suddenly realized that what he had misinterpreted as sobbing was actually pleasurable moaning.

"Excuse me, you've got company," he announced, trying his best to keep the mood light, positive that the couple would be terribly embarrassed after being interrupted.

"Who's there?" a male voice demanded from the bottom of the stairs.

"I'm Steven, and you both shouldn't be down here. Come toward the light of my flashlight, and I'll guide you both back to the main floor.

The only noticeable reply was the flash of the butane lighter as the group continued to cook up their rocks of crack cocaine, which they had carefully positioned on the swatch of tin foil.

Shaking his head in disgust, Steven combed the wall for a light switch, only to find disconnected wires where the plate should have been. "Alright, let's just cut it out and head back upstairs," he announced with as much authority as he could muster in the dank basement.

"Fuck off!" another voice retorted. "We ain't hurting nobody, so just piss off and leave us alone."

Not sure if he should move in for a closer look, or run for reinforcements, Steven swallowed his fear and carefully inched forward. "Look, I don't give a fuck what you're doing down here, but I think you should take your show on the road."

The young girl threw her head back with her mouth open and eyes closed, and again moaned in a release of drug-induced euphoria. "Ohhh goddd…" The moan escaped from her throat and rushed past her blistered lips.

"Want some?" the third kid at the party offered as he turned—his animated face illuminated by the glare of Steven's flashlight. "Good shit," he promised, as if the supposed quality of the dope was the only issue.

"Let's go," Steven announced for the second time. "Pack up your stuff and head up the stairs, or I'm gonna call the cops, and you can deal with them."

After reluctantly standing up from their crouched positions, the two men and the one young girl began slowly dismantling their little party, disappointed that they were about to lose the privacy afforded by the darkness of the shelter's basement.

"Gimme the rest," the man closest to the stairs demanded of the other.

"What rest? You got it all. I gave you the whole thing!" the other shouted back. "Ask Cassy, she saw me give you the eight ball. She knows!"

All eyes turned to the young girl cowering in the far corner of the basement. With her back pressed flat against the concrete wall, she reminded Steven of a petrified deer caught in the blinding headlights of an oncoming vehicle.

"Leave me alone!" she screeched, whipping a kitchen paring knife out of her coat pocket and brandishing it, as if forced to protect her very life.

Glued to his spot on the landing of the basement stairs, Steven stood by helplessly as one of the guys unexpectedly rushed the young girl named Cassy. The man was instantly rewarded with a swipe of her blade, as she caught her attacker directly on the chin. His spurting blood did little to impede his intended attack as he landed with a thud on top of her body.

Stepping forward in a heroic attempt to rush to the young girl's aid, Steven was caught off guard by a powerful body check when one of the guys fled the scene and ran straight past him up the stairs. The flashlight was instantly knocked from his grasp the minute he lost his footing. So Steven was resigned to watch helplessly as it clattered to the rough concrete of the basement floor. As it spun in a three-hundred-sixty-degree circle, the light cast surprising shadows, and flashing images of violent anger only countered with intermittent blankets of darkness.

"Get off me," Cassy continued to screech. "I ain't got your dope, but I got this," and without another seconds warning, she began flailing the knife as if slashing a path through a jungle forest.

"You got me again, you bitch!" the last guy screamed, scrambling first to all fours, and then suddenly rising to his feet in an attempt to clear out before the girl's next strike.

"I'll kill you, too," she hissed at Steven, motivated by her success with the first two attackers.

"I'm here to help you," he tried to argue, unable to rise quickly enough to move out of Cassy's path of destruction. "I'm not here…"

His reasoning apparently fell on deaf ears when the young girl leapt from her crouched position and landed squarely on top of his chest—the resulting thud extremely painful.

The moment Cassy's knees met with the solid resistance of Steven's rib cage, the air was forced from his lungs, and when it rushed back in a second later in an attempt to re-inflate the void, it was met with the intruding presence of a bloody kitchen blade.

CHAPTER NINETEEN

"Some of the worst things imaginable have been done with the best intentions."

—Jurassic Park II, 1997

As she stared deeply into her bathroom vanity, Camille twisted her neck to the right and then the left, simultaneously reaching out to adjust the folding side mirrors for a better view of every facet of her face.

"Are you up?" her mother called through the locked bathroom door.

"Yes."

"I've got a fresh pot of coffee brewing. Would you like to join me for a cup before I head out?"

She leaned in just a little closer, so her nose was just a few inches from the bathroom vanity. Camille unconsciously held her breath as she inspected the scabs adorning her left cheek. They were preliminary, the nurse had explained, mostly comprised of dried blood. Dark and chunky, they were frightening. But once they were shed, the nurse explained that the secondary scabs would be much lighter in color and consistency. They'd in turn be comprised mostly of clear plasma, and when they fell off, the condition of the underlying tissue would be a lot more telling. At that point, the renowned plastic surgeon that her parents had hired would be able to look Camille square in the face and tell her if she was going to be pock marked like a burn victim. Damn, wouldn't that be a fun appointment?

"Camille, are you coming out?" her mother shouted one more time. "I picked up some fresh star fruit," she tempted.

"Alright. I'm coming."

While sipping the coffee heavily flavored with fresh cream and raw sugar crystals, Camille shifted uncomfortably in her kitchen chair.

"How about another seat cushion?" her mother suggested, reaching over to an empty seat and tugging at the flowered upholstery.

"Mom, slow down, I'm fine. Besides, it's not my butt. It's my shoulders and my back. They're so stiff," she complained, shifting for the third time in the last five minutes as she worked to find some measure of comfort.

Tammy picked up her fork and stabbed at the sliced fruit still spread across the serving platter. "I don't know what you find so appealing about this," she rolled her eyes, forcing herself to chew on the freshly peeled flesh. "It's almost tasteless

"Then why are you eating it?"

"Your father says I need to try new foods. Expand my horizons."

Chuckling under her breath, Camille shook her head and picked up her own fork, filling her plate with strawberries, kiwi, and of course, a generous helping of star fruit. "What happened to you, Mom? When did you grow so old and lose your own sense of self?"

"My sense of self? Camille Greenway, I don't have the slightest idea what you're talking about. Why can't we just sit back and enjoy our coffee?"

"I've been doing a lot of thinking lately, Mom, and it seems to me that somewhere between the time when I was a little kid, and now, you kind of died inside."

Her turn to shift on the seat cushion, Tammy paused before answering. "I don't really understand why every time we speak these days, you find it acceptable to berate me. What are you blaming me for? You always seem to be so angry, as if everything that happened is somehow my fault."

Camille dropped her fork on top of her fruit, and let her hands fall down into her lap. "I don't know what to do about school."

Confident that she'd finally uncovered the source of her daughter's angst, Tammy picked up her linen napkin and folded it precisely before laying it crosswise over her plate. "Thank you for confiding in me, Cammy. To be honest, with everything you've just been through, I've had a few reservations about school myself. Maybe a year off wouldn't be such a bad idea. You could always take a few courses here at the community college if you found yourself needing a little academic stimulation."

"No Mom, that's not what I was talking about. I was talking about my major; about possibly shifting my classes from liberal arts to premed."

"Premed?"

"Why? Don't you think I could do it?"

"Oh Cammy, you know that if you set your mind…"

"Please," she immediately interrupted the parental achievement speech. "You haven't had a clue what I've been interested in for ten years. Ever since you stopped shopping for my *Care Bears*, you lost track of me."

"That's a little harsh," her mother fought back.

"Really, I don't think so. I know you kept a running record in your purse of every toy that I owned so you wouldn't duplicate or miss. And then one day, well, you just kind of… kind of gave up caring. Why is that?"

"I never gave up caring about you. That's ridiculous," her mother argued, her face flushed, her palms beginning to sweat. "I was just so busy."

"Busy?" Camille shrieked, her voice taking on an edge of desperation. "One day I had a mother, and the next day," she paused, looking for just the right words. "You were gone."

"It's not that simple, Cammy. You don't remember what it was like back when you were a young child. When you were five, all you worried about was a new canopy bed, and the fact that your dad wouldn't let you have a bunny cage in your bedroom. You were just too young to know what the family was going through. But at five, that's the way it was supposed to be."

"I know, I know," she admitted. "I was a kid, but I'm not now. So tell me, Mom, what happened when I was in preschool? That's when everything changed, right? When I was in preschool?"

"I'm not sure…"

"You keep telling me to act like an adult, to take responsibility for my actions and stand up for what I believe in. Isn't that the rhetoric you've been jamming down my throat since I hit puberty?"

"Yes, but…"

"Well, *quid pro quo*, Mother. I think it's time you leveled with me and let me know what happened around here when I was a little kid. What in the hell happened to bring this family to its knees and steal my mother?"

"Cammy dear, you've been through so much. Are you sure that

you want to get into this right now? Why don't we just wait until your father gets home?"

"No!" she shouted, gritting her teeth as she slammed both hands palm down on the table in a fight to rise to her feet. "I wanna talk about this now!"

"But your father and I, we just..."

"Fuck Dad! I wanna talk to *you*!" Camille cried. "You're my mother, and I wanna know why you abandoned me?"

Tammy Greenway suddenly felt the dining room floor reach up to greet her, the Persian rug welcoming the delicate bones in her right cheek.

Olga circled Steven's hospital bed for the tenth time, re-checking his monitors and his drainage tube. Dressed in her uniform, she appeared to be an average duty nurse, but gauging the look of pain on her face, you'd think she was nursing her very own flesh and blood.

"Excuse me, Nurse Heinz, there's a call for you at the station desk," an orderly announced.

As she followed the young man out the door, Olga almost ran straight into his back when he stopped dead in his tracks and suddenly spun around. "How's Steven doing? Is he gonna be alright?"

She reached forward to give the boy a motherly pat on the shoulder, and pasted on her best face before addressing his question. "Steven is a very strong young man, and you know he's receiving the best care here at the University Hospital."

He looked at her skeptically and then repeated his last statement. "So, is he going to be fine?"

Sighing, Olga let down her guard. "He's been moved off the critical list, and now that's he's stable, I think it's fair to say that we are going to see a steady recovery. Steven's lucky to not have any organ damage, and since last night's surgery repaired the knife's path, there's no further internal bleeding."

"We were all kind of worried when we heard that one of us had come through emergency."

"You can tell everyone who asks that Steven will be fine, and I'm the one who said so."

"That'll work," he agreed, turning to escort Nurse Heinz back to the station desk.

Ed Greenway sat on the foot of his wife's bed and witnessed her drug induced sleep, uncomfortable with the realization that the same symptoms from his wife's past were beginning to resurface.

"Supper's ready," Camille whispered from the open door. "And since it's just you and me, I thought I better wait."

"Where are your brothers?"

"Practice, and a date."

"Alright then, let's eat," Ed relented, rising from his position and following his daughter as she slowly moved toward the kitchen nook.

"Ta da," Camille announced, spreading her arms over the assembled containers of take out. "I know you don't like pizza, or western Chinese food, so I ordered Greek."

"Greek? I didn't know you could order it in. How'd you manage?"

"I called about twenty restaurants, and finally, I found one that used fresh black olives instead of the canned ones you hate. Then for a small delivery fee, they agreed to bring it out."

"How small a fee?"

After picking up the empty emergency cash jar and shaking it upside down, Camille clearly made her point about the cost.

"Let's hope it's worth it," Ed teased as he dropped into one of the kitchen chairs.

With their plates nearly empty, and their appetites definitely appeased, they both continued to pick on the remaining lumps of crumbled feta cheese peeking through the leftover salad.

"Dad, what's the matter with Mom?"

"You heard the doctor. She fainted from lack of glucose. Basically, your mother had forgotten to eat."

"No, I'm not talking about today," Camille, corrected him. "I'm talking about the last ten years. I'm old enough to remember what Mom used to be like, and I'm smart enough to know that she's not anywhere near the same. Unfortunately, I can't remember what it was that changed her."

"Camille, you've been through so much yourself, are you sure…?"

"Daddy, I'm positive. You're gonna have to tell me what happened. I really need to know."

Ed got up to throw the empty containers in the trash, and busied himself with the clean up while stalling for extra time. "I really think we should put the leftovers in something else. You know how your mother hates to eat out of cardboard containers."

He bent down, and dug deep in the cupboards. After pulling out a couple plastic containers with what he hoped were matching lids, he said, "Did you ever notice that the clothes dryer somehow eats socks and the kitchen cupboards eat plastic lids?"

"I've noticed," Camille nodded, playing along with her father while he carefully sidestepped around the pink elephant standing right in the middle of the room.

With the counter cleaned and leftovers stowed, Camille joined her dad in front of the television. "What's on?"

"Nothing special. You choose," he offered up the remote, one of the most prized possessions in the Greenway household.

Flipping up and down the satellite menu, they sat in silence as Camille scanned the highlighted movie channels for anything that might catch her attention. "I give up," she announced, tossing the remote back across the couch into her father's lap.

"You still wanna talk?" he picked up on her cue.

"Yes," she admitted. "I really wanna talk."

"Well," her father admitted, "it looks like it's just you and me kid, so ask away."

"Alright. Mom's different, and I know that for a fact. I just really wanna know what happened to make her change."

As he flipped the remote over in his hands, Ed Greenway stopped to look at his daughter. She was a beauty, even with all the scrapes and bruises—a lovely young woman just coming into her prime. "You look just like your mother, especially when we dated in college."

"But Mom's a redhead."

"True, but half of the resemblance is your attitude and your zest for life. And as for your hair, that was a gift from Grandma Greenway. You remember her, don't you?" he teased with a wink.

"I do, now please tell me the truth, and no more stalling. What happened to Mom, and why did she shut down?"

"Well, when you started preschool, your mother desperately missed her little baby. She felt so alone, so isolated, a very serious case of *empty nest syndrome*, with you and your brothers off at school. I didn't know how to help, so when your mother suggested that another baby might be the answer, I quickly agreed."

"So when she couldn't get pregnant, she got depressed?" Camille guessed.

"No, that's not the way it played out. You see, your mom actually got pregnant immediately, and carried the baby to full term. It was only after the birth that we realized the baby's limitations."

"What kind of limitations?" Camille struggled to understand—suddenly feeling like she might have opened a Pandora's Box of emotions that her father might not be able to control.

"Your little sister was born with severe Down Syndrome. It's the most common chromosomal disorder with pregnancies in older women. Especially since fourteen years ago, when the baby was born, your mom was already forty-one years old."

Camille nodded her head in agreement, but still struggled to digest all the information. She felt like she needed to somehow reach out and comfort her father. "I'm so sorry, Dad. Burying a child could kill anyone. But maybe if you had have told us kids, we could have helped her deal with the baby's death."

"Camille," he interrupted her train of thought. "I never said the baby died."

CHAPTER TWENTY

"You know, you don't throw a whole life away just 'cause he's banged up a little."

—Seabiscuit, 2003

After picking up the blinking phone line, Olga was forced to identify herself and then patiently stand by while the secretary on the other end of the line transferred her call to the chairman of the hospital.

"Dick Mansfield," the voice boomed.

"Hello, this is Nurse Olga Heinz. You had called personnel looking for me, sir."

"Nurse Heinz," the chairman repeated as if reading her name off the top of a file. "I would like to see you in my office as soon as you're available."

"Is this urgent? Should I call for a shift replacement?"

"No, it's not critical. Why don't you finish your shift and just stop by after three this afternoon."

Olga nodded as if her connection was visual before finally

clearing her throat to reply, "I'll be up to see you as soon as shift change is complete."

"Thank you, nurse. I'll be looking forward to…"

"Excuse me, Mr. Mansfield," Olga interrupted his string of pleasantries. "Can you please tell me what this is regarding?"

"Let's just say it's a personal matter, and I'd much rather not discuss it over the telephone."

"I understand," she conceded, nervously hanging up the handset.

Once she returned to her duties at hand, Olga found her concentration more than strained. When a nurse was suddenly required to assist in the manual sterilization of a quarantined patient room, she jumped at the opportunity. Dressed in full mask and gown, and then double gloved as if working with maximum sharps, the sterilization team moved toward the patient's room.

"All ready?" Olga asked; preparing to snip the plastic quarantine tape stretched diagonally across the door.

"Who was in here?" one of the cleaning ladies softly whispered. "I've never had to do anything like this before."

"A set of twin girls, victims of a motor vehicle accident," Olga recited from the limited notes off her patient chart. "ER determined that they might have possibly been exposed to Asian Bird Flu during an exchange trip to Toronto, Ontario. Both teenage girls succumbed to their injuries after the accident, so we're here to implement protocol and reclaim the room. Any other questions?"

"Are we safe?" one of the ladies muttered, turning her head to make sure no other hospital employees were watching. "I don't wanna take anything home to my family. My husband would kill me if I made the kids sick. You know what I mean?"

Olga knew exactly what the woman meant. A cleaning job that entailed working with a sick patient's bodily wastes, and unknown quantities of used medical supplies must surely be a nightmare for the families of the hospital's janitorial staff.

No one ever worried about the day-to-day struggles of the cleaners, or the sleepless nights every time a plastic bag tore and released miniscule droplets of liquid onto the weave of their cloth uniforms. Janitors were the unseen army who worked behind the scenes. These men and women filed down the halls and into the vacant rooms only after the families had exhausted their vigils, and the bodies had been moved to another ward or the basement morgue. They really were the final soldiers to scour the battlefields.

"We'll be fine," another of the cleaning staff comforted her co-worker. "Don't worry, the nurse is coming in with us, and one thing I've learned about cleaning here at the hospital," she carefully explained, "They'll never put *one of their own* at risk."

Olga turned and was greeted by both women, who nodded their heads to confirm they were ready to dive in and complete the task.

Once they were sequestered in the patient's room behind closed doors, Olga quickly assigned specific duties to both helpers before they all slipped into their routines.

"Garbage?" the younger asked, concerned that someone might unintentionally break the plastic seal during transportation.

"We'll take it with us, and ladies, I think we're done." Olga pulled down her facemask to make her point.

"Nurse Heinz, we were just wondering if we could ask you a question," the elder of the two stepped forward as she too removed her facial mask.

"Yes. Go ahead. I'll try and answer as best I can."

"Well, Stacey down in administration heard that the hospital is pushing for mandatory retirement packages for senior medical staff. And I, well actually… all of us, well we…"

"Yes?' Olga encouraged her to finish her train of thought.

"Well, we were wondering if that includes housekeeping, too."

"I honestly don't know. To tell you the truth ladies, this has all kind of taken me by surprise. I hadn't really heard anything about retirement packages. But I promise you, I will be checking on it. Actually, I myself have a meeting with the chairman, Mr. Mansfield, the minute my shift is over."

Neither lady spoke, they just shared knowing glances.

"Let me thank you both for an excellent job," Olga smiled, suddenly uncomfortable with the fact that neither woman was interested in meeting her eyes.

"Are we done, nurse?"

"Yes, you may head back to your stations," she officially wrapped up their joint-work project. "And thank you again."

"Good luck," the older woman called out over her back as they both briskly walked down the hall.

"Good luck?" Olga repeated, as if saying the words aloud would give her clues to decipher their hidden meaning.

With all the extra paper work associated with a physical attack causing bodily harm at the shelter, Doris barely had enough time to sneeze, never mind sit down with another set of inquisitive cops.

"Let me get right to the point and maybe I can help you cover a lot of your basic groundwork," she announced. "For starters, gentleman, no patron who visits here at the shelter has been able to identify the young girl in question. And if they won't confide in any of the staff, I guarantee they won't be confiding with either of you. Secondly, we do not make it a habit of allowing indigents to use our basement stairwell to shoot up. Therefore, no one has any sort of sign-in records for the girl. And thirdly, I want you to know…"

"Excuse me, ma'am," one of the agents interrupted her little speech. "We are not from your local police detachment. We are with the Federal Bureau of Investigation."

"FBI?" Doris repeated to clarify the agent's last statement. "You've come down here to investigate a stabbing in the shelter's basement? Seems a little overzealous, don't you think? And if you're so worried about the welfare of my staff and the shelter patrons, why didn't you stop by last winter when three of our regulars died of exposure? That's a real crime, if you ask me."

"Ma'am, we have some very important questions to ask you about one of your volunteers, a Mr. Steven Whitters. Do you think you'll be able to help us?"

"Well, of course I'll co-operate to the best of my ability. But what kind of information do you think I might be privy to?"

"Can you tell us, did Mr. Whitters complete any type of volunteer application form?"

"Yes, but it's fairly generic," Doris attempted to explain. "Most of our volunteers are placed by word of mouth, so it's basically just some contact numbers in case of an emergency, and a signed release to check for criminal records."

"May we?"

Doris handed the agent a photocopy of Steven's paperwork, but she still couldn't help but feel like a traitor, as if she was somehow betraying an unwritten code of volunteer confidentiality. "He hadn't worked here for very long, so beyond what's included on his application form, I really can't be of much help."

"Do you mind if we walk around, maybe talk to a few of the volunteers, or your patrons?"

"Help yourselves, but don't be disappointed if everyone clams up. I gotta warn you, people in here don't respond well to authority, and your suits aren't going to win either of you guys any bonus points."

"We'll take our chances," one agent said, as they both dropped their business cards on Doris's desk.

As she watched the men circulate up and down the Lilac Tree's main floor, Doris felt like she was watching a dress rehearsal for a school production of the *Red Sea.* For no matter which direction the two agents strolled, the crowds parted down the center to allow them unheeded passage. They were about as inconspicuous as the devil at a church picnic. Still, the agents refused to give up, and before departing, they had managed to insult or at least annoy half of the center's visiting patrons.

"Thank you for the access," one agent concluded before their departure.

Doris had just smiled, knowing that they had effectively wasted her time as well as their own.

"Doris," one of the volunteers called out. "You have a call from Nurse Heinz down at the hospital. Sounds kinda important. Wanna take it?"

"Hell yeah," she barked, tossing the departing agents a wave before running back across the floor to the semi-privacy of her office.

As Olga waited for Doris to pick up the phone, she sat at a corner desk in the nurse's station with her head in her hand and closed her eyes. When Doris finally answered, Olga tried to sound as upbeat as her exhaustion would allow. "I'm sorry my dear, but I won't be able to meet you in the hospital cafeteria after my shift. I've been called upstairs for an impromptu meeting with the hospital's management, and I have no idea how long I'm going to be tied up."

"Everything alright, Olga?"

"Yes, Steven is stable and recovering fine from his surgery. I think it's more than fair to say he's out of the woods."

"Actually," Doris interrupted her, "I was asking about you. I know Steven's fine, I already spoke to someone down in admitting, and they confirmed that he was stable. But why are you going upstairs. Is it promotion day?"

"I doubt it, especially since there is really nowhere up for a head duty nurse to go."

"So then, why do you sound so nervous?"

"For God's sake, I'm not nervous," Olga argued, suddenly aware of the shrill ring of her own voice. "I'm just tired, is all."

Doris took a deep breath, and said in a softer voice. "You haven't slept for what, something like thirty-six hours? You've been up all night tending to Steven, and I don't know if you're going into this management meeting with a clear head. Can you postpone?"

"No, Dick Mansfield's office doesn't reschedule. This wasn't a request, Doris, it was an order."

"I didn't realize that one of the suits was capable of ordering nursing staff around."

"The chairman of the hospital board is not one of the suits—Dick Mansfield is *the suit*. He's in charge of all funding for all departments."

Olga went on to explain what she knew of the hospital hierarchy, really more to try to understand it herself than to teach her friend any specific lesson. She knew that Doris was far more experienced with the flow of money, political maneuvering, and the red tape associated with large organizations. Olga's job had always been in the trenches; she had no clue about the motives of generals. She had always tried to respect Doris's expertise and advice. All the same, she didn't really see any cause for concern over one little meeting.

Doris interrupted her lengthy description and asked, "Have you thought about taking someone in with you?"

"No, why would I do that? It's not a disciplinary action, it's just a meeting."

"Really? Well, if this Dick Mansfield is truly as important as you claim he is, why is he bothering to meet with a lowly duty nurse like yourself? Wouldn't he just staff out any of his concerns to some overpaid flunky?"

Olga sat straight up in the chair and rubbed her forehead as she fought to follow her friend's line of thinking.

"You know what else bothers me about this whole thing?" Doris continued.

"No, what?" Olga moaned.

"Let's say that the chairman has a genuine concern that he believes for some reason can only be addressed in person with one of the hospital's duty nurses. Why the emergency? Why wasn't the meeting scheduled through proper channels?"

"I don't know. Maybe he just had an opening and decided to fit me in?"

"Bullshit, Olga! Something is coming down, and I'm warning you. Please be careful. I've dealt with these kinds of people for more years than I can remember, and I smell a rat!"

Olga felt exhausted, she just wanted to lay her head back and close her eyes. She felt tears beginning to well. "Doris, I don't have the energy to argue with you and keep my head on straight for the chairman. I'm going to the meeting, and I'll be fine."

"Will you call me as soon as you're out?"

"As soon as I'm out of the meeting, I'm going to check in on Steven, pick up a few groceries, and then head home to put my feet up. Can I phone you later from my house?"

"Do you still have my home number?"

"If you haven't changed it, it's still in my address book."

"Please be careful Olga. I have a bad feeling that you might be walking into some kind of ambush."

"I'll call you later. I promise," she signed off the conversation. By an act of sheer will, Olga stood, secretly yearning to just put her feet up and close her eyes for at least another fifteen minutes. Olga forced herself to move down through the hospital corridors, zigging and zagging through the underground tunnels. She finally reached the basement of the adjoining office tower.

After stepping off the elevator, she said to the receptionist, "Nurse Olga Heinz to see Mr. Mansfield." Ushered past one receptionist and two personal assistants, she finally gained entrance into the chairman's inner sanctum. Seated in a small generic conference room, she waited for the appearance of another staffer, someone who would surely ask her how she took her coffee while she was expected to wait for the chairman to make his timely entrance.

"Nurse Heinz, nice to meet you," the voice announced from behind her back. "I'm Dick Mansfield, your Chairman of the Board here at the University Hospital."

"Hello, sir," she rose to shake his hand. "I'm sorry, I didn't see you..."

"Side door," he pointed to the entrance disguised as mahogany paneling. After he motioned for his guest to join him at the small round table, Dick graciously waited for Olga to take her seat. "Thank you for accommodating me this afternoon. Unfortunately, with my schedule, I sometimes have to fit in meetings with very little notice."

Olga allowed herself a small smile, took a deep breath, and tried to relax. This wasn't going to be as awful as Doris had predicted. Probably had something to do with her student nursing staff and their pending budget. Maybe another cut, possibly a motion to revoke overtime. Maybe it was the flex pay? Maybe...

"Well, might as well get down to business," Dick Mansfield interrupted her train of thought. "Nurse Heinz, you've been selected for mandatory retirement, and I'm here to offer you a very attractive package."

Camille continued to pick at the remnants of yesterday's Greek salad. It was never as good the second day; the dressing now tasted watery, and the cucumbers were soggy at best. Suddenly disgusted with her choice of snack, she tossed the contents of the entire bowl down in the garbage.

"Not appealing?"

"Not really," she smiled up at her mother. "Can I make you something hot to drink, Mom, maybe some peppermint tea with honey?"

"No, I'm not in the mood. Your father said he was going to pick me up for a late lunch this afternoon. Said he had a meeting near the house and he thought some spaghetti and garlic toast might hit the spot. Would you like to join us?"

As she mulled over the offer, Camille looked at her mother for any hint of trouble—some warning as to whether joining them would be a good or a bad idea. It was hopeless. Looking at her mother was like looking straight into the face of a fog.

"Camille, if you're going to come with us, your father will be here in ten minutes and I think something other than a sweatshirt and sweatpants would be appropriate attire."

"Sure Mom, you're right. But I don't think I'm going to go. I'm not really up to it, and I'm just going to try a few more leftovers and take it easy. Besides, Dad might want to talk to you about something. Maybe he just wants a little couple time."

Tammy smiled and shook her head, walking off to freshen her make-up before heading out of the house.

Half-hour later, with the house finally to herself, Camille found herself moving from room to room, almost as if she was searching for something that she just couldn't put her finger on. Finally settled in her father's den, she began punching on his computer, looking for the cache of card games she knew would be hidden somewhere behind a bogus icon. After taking a second to adjust the lumbar support in the office chair, Camille finally nestled in and began to play a fourhanded game of spades.

Three games later, she was restless again. As she painfully rose from the leather seat, her stomach began to growl—reminding her that nothing substantial had passed her lips since her stab at the day-old salad.

"Chocolate," Camille murmured to herself, suddenly thrilled at the prospect of finding her Dad's secret stash. "Now, where are you hiding, *my little pretties*?" she whispered in a singsong like verse, slowly spinning in a circle behind his desk.

Instinct told her that it wouldn't be a simple find, because to remain a secret stash, her Dad would've had to hide them from the housekeeper, her nephews, and most of all, her mother. But that wasn't going to derail Camille Greenway, *super snooper!*

First, she had to stop and then think like her father. Ed Greenway was over six feet tall, so his height was obviously going to play a factor in choosing a hiding place. In addition, moving the candy bars out of the bottom cupboards would definitely alleviate the problems associated with her snoopy little cousins. The second obstacle would be the housekeeper. The candy wouldn't have survived long tucked behind any of the objects that would need dusting. So after ruling out all the ornaments and upper shelving, the options were seriously starting to dwindle.

Last obstacle was her mother, and her sporadic interest in her husband's den. If wasn't very often—however once in awhile, she did pop in and use the computer or the printer. So ruling out both stations, Camille was left with a small section of neutral ground, and the neutral ground was situated just behind her father's head.

As she suspected, the upper cabinets of his rear credenza were stuffed full of his belongings. Stuff he didn't want to throw out, yet objects that had outlived their usefulness on his desk.

Carefully pawing through her dad's treasures so as not to disturb their original order, Camille was finally rewarded with an opened box of chocolate bars. Each bar individually wrapped, she was quite sure she'd be able to swipe one without sending out an alert.

After tearing off the paper, and then unfolding the foil sleeve, she snapped off one of the caramel filled pockets and popped the morsel into her mouth. There was no doubt—the chocolate tasted just like heaven, and within another minute, she'd managed to gobble down the remainder of the bar. Then just as she stood debating a second indulgence, her eyes spotted the small black-velvet photo album.

"Pictures," she laughed. They were probably goofy shots of her brothers' lacrosse games or her tap-dancing recitals. For a brief instant, just before flipping open the front cover, it suddenly occurred to Camille that the snapshots might be of a private nature. My God, what if they were naked shots of her parents having sex? The thought was just too weird even to contemplate. But then, she wasn't a ten-year-old virgin, so she knew could handle it. Either way, they'd be good for a laugh.

After settling back into the chair, Camille finally flipped open the cover, and took her first glimpse of the collected stills. They appeared to begin at the first trimester of one of her mom's pregnancies. As the months passed, her belly grew, as did her father's smiles. Five or six pages into the collection, Camille spotted the group shot that left her cold. This wasn't the pregnancy for herself, or her older brothers; this was the pregnancy of *that child*. Frantically flipping the pages to advance the term, Camille found what she assumed would be more group shots. Instead, it was a picture of a young girl and her own mother with their backs to the camera, throwing what looked like chunks of bread at an assembled group of ducks.

"Why don't I remember this?" Camille muttered aloud. "I couldn't have been…" she stopped to evaluate the photograph, "younger than four or five. I should remember something…" her voice trailed off one last time.

Hands moving as if motivated by an outside power, the pages continued to flutter by. Year after year, a photograph was filed in chronological order depicting a fresh-faced young girl—a girl who had obviously progressed from her preschool years, right through to the onset of puberty. The girl looked happy, almost too happy, as if oblivious to the problems of the world around her. And she had *that look.* There was no hiding it, and Camille was surprisingly saddened to see that her sister's Down syndrome was so telling.

"What's your name, little girl?" she whispered, pulling one of the photographs out of the album's protective sleeve to flip it over in her hand. As she'd hoped, there on the back were notations recorded in legible ink. *Stacey Maureen Greenway, Age Fourteen, Pleasant View Long Term Care.*

"Stacey," Camille tried out the name. "Stacey Greenway." She inserted the picture back into its original slot, and once again flipped through the fourteen-year progression.

Stacey's shiny blonde hair curled in waves around her unusually small head. Her features were somewhat distorted because her face appeared quite flat, but her overall appearance was still that of a sweet young girl. Her sparkling blue eyes were captivating, if not slightly unusual with their upward slant. Stacey's good-natured spirit seemed to rise straight up from the two-dimensional photographs, and as Camille sat back to analyze the face of a sister she'd never met, she suddenly felt a terrible sense of loss.

CHAPTER TWENTY-ONE

"Great ambition and conquest without contribution is without significance."

—*The Emperor's Club, 2002*

After turning the ignition off in her car, Olga reluctantly reached across the passenger's seat for her duffle bag, not the least bit conscious of her drive home. Granted, it was a trip she had made thousands of times, yet today was an absolute blur. Thankfully, she hadn't ended up on a neighbor's front law. She forced herself out of the car and trudged up the front walk. As she reached for the locked door, her hand froze before inserting her key, motionless while her mind evaluated the situation.

The pitch-black windows did little to ward off the wave of coldness invading Olga's heart. Her home was obviously empty, and with Steven still in the hospital's care, she was having a hard time convincing herself to step inside. Reluctantly, she dropped her bag on the house's doorstep, and decided to walk over to her neighbor's to see if she could garner an invite for a cup of coffee. She needed to vent, and sitting alone in her empty house wasn't going to do her any good.

"Well, hello stranger," Helen greeted Olga the minute she recognized her familiar silhouette. "Coffee or tea?"

"Either," she sighed.

With her hand poised over the coffee tin, Helen slowed her motions and turned to face her friend. "Maybe you'd prefer it if I opened a little wine? I still have a couple bottles that my sister gave me last Christmas. You game?"

This time Olga smiled her approval.

"So what are we toasting?" Helen casually inquired as she lifted her glass to inspect the color of the wine.

"My career."

"Then it's to your career," Helen toasted. "May you find fulfillment in your nursing as long as you choose to work."

"To *as long as I choose*," Olga mimicked her friend's toast. "And to those of you who knew when it was time to bow out gracefully."

As she raised her glass to her lips, Helen stopped short, staring across the kitchen table at Olga's face as she started to feel that something else was going on behind the scenes. "What are you trying to tell me?"

"Well," Olga sucked in a deep breath, fighting the tears that were beginning to well. "I've been selected for something…something very special, by our chairman himself, Mr. Dick Mansfield."

"And?"

"And he called me up to his office today to deliver the news in person."

"And?"

"And as of three o'clock this afternoon, I was officially retired from my position at the University Hospital."

"What?" Helen demanded, quickly becoming a master of the single word replies.

"Mandatory retirement," were the last two words Olga was able to choke out before she lost control and began to sob into her hands. "I've been put out to pasture," she mumbled into her own palms.

Frozen in shock, it took Helen a couple of minutes before she regained control of her senses. "Oh honey, I'm so sorry. Come here," she offered her shoulder. "They don't know what they're losing."

"No they don't," Olga tried to laugh through the tears. "But I'll tell you what," she took a second to grab a tissue off the sideboard and wipe her nose. "Two young nurses at half the price won't be able to handle my workload. And God help the patients when they need a little compassion. They'll be screwed!"

"Screwed?"

"Sure, screwed. Why not?" Olga began to chuckle at her own choice of words.

"Screwed," Helen repeated, rubbing the back of her neighbor and closest friend.

After taking a second to blow her nose, Olga threw back the remainder of her wine and reached for the bottle. "Guess I don't have to worry about thinking clearly on my feet tomorrow."

As Helen watched Olga dive into her second glass, she began to weigh her response, debating the merits of encouraging her to fight the decision, or helping her to accept the inevitable. "So what's your plan?"

"I'm not planning; I'm just digesting all the information. And just for the record, do you think there's a way past this? Or is the decision already written in stone?"

"From a legal standpoint, I don't know."

"Well, I guarantee that any lawyer I consult will tell me there is hope, and that I should take it to court."

"You know it's all about the fees," Helen quickly agreed, taking the opportunity to refill her own glass. "So what are you gonna do? Just roll over and play dead?'

"I just don't know!" Olga sighed, literally throwing her hands up in the air.

Helen got up to dump a bag of potato chips into a bowl to help sop up the booze, and returned to the table with a little different perspective on the situation. "If you still want to work, you could hire yourself out into the private sector. You know how all the agencies in town are dying for registered nurses for their in-home programs and their…"

"Helen please, just stop and take a breath for a moment," Olga begged her. "I don't need to work. Financially, I could probably retire today, and with careful spending not have to worry. But nursing was my reason for getting out of bed each morning. I didn't stay at the University for the paycheck. I stayed because it was my life. It's my whole world."

"So contract yourself out. It's not exactly the same, but I think you'll still find it quite fulfilling."

"Really, is that why you left?"

"I left the hospital by choice to open my hair salon. But if I'd still wanted to nurse and there was no other…"

"Bullshit! You can't tell me that bathing seniors and changing dressings from day surgery would have fulfilled your medical needs."

"I'm not you," Helen reminded her friend. "I'm not interested in changing the world."

Olga snatched a handful of chips out of the bowl, and ground the salty potato slices between her rear molars. "I know you're just trying to help, but I'm not ready to retire, and a homecare contract is not going to replace my nursing career."

"Fine. Then what are your other options?"

"I'm not sure. Like I told you, this just came down a couple of hours ago."

"I don't know if this is such a good idea, but I was wondering if… well… if it might be a good idea…"

"You're flapping Helen. Please just get to the point."

"Well, maybe Martin could throw his weight around a little and get you rehired. There, I said it," she gushed, relieved the suggestion was finally out on the table.

"I don't know. It's… it's such a tricky… I don't know. How in the hell would I even ask him?"

Helen pretended to pick up a telephone, and began to simulate a mock conversation. "Hello Martin, it's me Olga calling. I just got canned today and I think it's about goddamn time that you stood up for me and got my job back."

"Oh, that'll work," Olga snickered through watery eyes.

"Okay, you might want to put it in your own words. But in all reality, I don't think talking to the famous Dr. Martin Hood would be such a bad idea. Correct me if I'm wrong, but he's got his head shoved so far up management's ass that he'd be bound to have a little pull in a sticky situation. Right?"

As she mulled over the thought, Olga continued to sip her wine. "You know, you are right about one thing. Martin not only has a bit of pull, I think he actually sits on one or two of the same boards as Dick Mansfield."

"There you go," Helen encouraged, "Nothing like a little behind-the-scenes maneuvering."

Olga threw back the remainder of her second glass, suddenly jumped up to her feet, and said, "I have to run."

"Stay. What's your rush? I could heat up a frozen pizza, and we could open the other bottle and do it up properly."

"Rain check. I'm going to change my clothes and call Martin. I want to check into this as soon as possible. No use procrastinating."

"No point," Helen agreed; waving goodbye as her friend rushed off down the back alley.

With her duffle bag moved from her doorstep to the laundry room, Olga was making her way to the bedroom when she noticed the blinking light on her answering machine. She pressed the button and impatiently drummed her fingers as the tape rewound.

"Olga, it's Doris calling. I was just wondering how everything went. I'm still at the shelter. Looks like I'll be here 'til closing, so please call me when you get in. Doesn't matter if it's late. Use the staff nightline. Someone will pick it up. See you."

"Shit," Olga cursed, suddenly reminded of her afternoon's promise. After quickly punching in the Lilac Tree's staff number, she began tapping the toes on her right foot while waiting for someone to pick up the line.

Eventually connected, it seemed to take another year for one of the floor staff to locate Doris and bring her to the phone. Then when she did pick up the line, Doris sounded like she'd just finished training for the Boston marathon.

Out of breath and obviously winded, Doris grabbed the receiver from one of the volunteers and barked into the line. "It's about time you called. You… you had me worried," she forced out through ragged breaths.

"Well, I stopped by my neighbor's before coming home. But I'm here now, so you don't have to worry anymore."

"So, what was the emergency? You up for the Nobel Prize for Medicine?"

Olga debated whether she should tell a quick lie to wrap up the conversation. Instead, she rolled her eyes and stuck with an abbreviated version of the truth for right now. "The chairman of the hospital is implementing a plan to retire a few senior staff. He just wanted to talk to me about it."

Silence.

“I don’t really have a lot of time to explain any further. I have to run out Doris. I have another commitment tonight, so can we talk some more tomorrow?”

“Sure,” she reluctantly agreed. “But I have a feeling you’re only giving me half the story.”

“There is more to tell, but it can keep. I promise.”

Resigned to the fact that dragging out the telephone call would probably end up being as difficult as procuring government funding, Doris gave up and said good night with a promise to call back the following afternoon.

Back on track, Olga changed into a simple pair of beige dress pants and a short-sleeved cotton sweater. She stood in the middle of her kitchen, and suddenly began debating the merits of calling ahead versus showing up unannounced. Either way, the visit was going to be uncomfortable, so upon reflection, a surprise attack was probably in her best interest.

She had only visited Martin Hood’s house two or three times during their entire ten-year relationship, so Olga actually had to pay attention to the road signs and make sure she turned at the appropriate landmarks. Door to door, the trip was only forty minutes, yet by the time she neared his neighborhood, a wine headache had already settled across her temples. Olga opted to stop off at a gas station to purchase a pain reliever, some bottled water, and possibly use the facilities, so she pulled of the main drag and into a service station.

Once she got back behind the wheel of her car, she took a gulp of the water, swallowed two tablets, and then gently leaned back against the headrest. As she willed her headache to pass, Olga took a few precious moments and re-evaluated her position. She couldn’t be sure that dragging Martin into the middle of her dilemma was in anyone’s best interest. Seniority was one advantage, yet he was still only a doctor—not *one of the boys* up in management.

Maybe dragging Martin into her mess would just spell out his own demise.

"*You are the first of ten staff members I will be meeting with,*" continued to replay in Olga's ears. The chairman's words effectively haunted her as she slammed her car in reverse and backed out of the gas station, suddenly deciding to continue on with her original path. Martin may not be able to help her, but at least she could warn him. Maybe with enough of a head start, he might be able to divert any unwanted attention away from his own file. She owed him at least that much after all their years together.

Steven blinked his eyes another five or six times and fought to adjust his vision, before he was finally able to focus on the face of the nurse hovering over his bed. "Olga," he mumbled, throat sore and mouth extremely dry from the anesthetic of surgery.

"No Steven, Olga's gone home to get a little rest," the duty nurse explained. "She was here all last night, right through your surgery, and during your stay in recovery. Only after you stabilized did she head home to rest."

Nodding instead of verbally replying, Steven took another couple seconds to close his eyes and try to stabilize his surroundings. The room was still cloudy at best, and until he was able to speak without stumbling over his own words, he doubted that any of his surroundings would visually improve.

"How about a little water?" the nurse gently encouraged, bringing the straw up to his lips.

Gently sucking up the fluid, Steven was suddenly struck with a horrible thought. He'd been carrying a glass shaker of the healing powder when that young junkie had stabbed him, and as of this exact second, he had no idea where the container had ended up.

"Nurse," he called out again, struggling to reopen his eyes.

"Just rest. You're going to be absolutely fine, and I'm sure you'd like to hear all the details of your recovery from the doctor as soon as possible. So why don't you close your eyes for a little nap, and I'm pretty sure that by the time you wake, the doctor will be making his rounds."

"It's not the doctor," Steven struggled. "It's my stuff. My clothes," he swallowed hard again, fighting to formulate the words. "What happened to everything I was… was wearing? Where's my coat?"

As she stepped away from the bed, the nurse opened the narrow wall closet and revealed his belongings hanging neatly behind the door. "Oh, hang on Steven. I see a little note pinned on your jacket. *Shirt cut off by paramedics at scene. Signed, Admitting, University Hospital*," she read aloud. "Well, not to worry, I'm sure nurse Heinz will bring you whatever clothing you need."

"Can you do me a favor? Will you dig around in my coat pockets and tell me what you find?"

The nurse nodded and reached into the closet to extracted Steven's jacket. She searched both outside pockets, and the one tucked discreetly inside, but she was unable to unearth anything other than a solitary ballpoint pen.

"Nothing?" he called out from his limited vantage point on the bed.

"Just this pen," she answered, turning to hang up the jacket. "Might be a bag in here from admitting with your belongings. Are you worried about your wallet?"

"Yes," he lied, "and some other stuff."

"Well, I can't find a thing," she shook her head. "Why don't you just hang on a minute while I go to the station desk and make a call? I'll find out if we're holding anything for you in patient services."

Steven nodded and watched the nurse leave his room. God, he hoped that she'd be able to find his personal belongings. Maybe it was lost in the attack? The thought of the bottle containing dried human embryo tissue rolling around in the shelter's basement wasn't really a comfort either. Maybe the paramedics found it and just tossed it in the garbage? In retrospect, that might actually be the best-case scenario. No, he had a funny feeling the explanation wasn't going to be that simple.

"Steven, I checked with patient services, and they don't have a record of your belongings anywhere."

"What the hell?" he cursed, forgetting the extent of his injuries as he attempted to sit upright in bed.

"Just stay still," the nurse reminded him. "You have fresh stitches, and I don't think you'd like to rip open your incision."

After dropping back into a prone position, with sweat beading across his forehead, Steven let out a succession of shallow panting breaths. "I don't understand," he admitted. "Who would have… stolen my stuff?" he forced out through clenched teeth.

"Steven, no one stole any of your belongings. I suspect that Nurse Heinz just took them home."

Closing his eyes in response to the good news, the patient finally allowed himself to release a deep cleansing breath.

CHAPTER TWENTY-TWO

"Relationships are complicated. It's never just one thing that ends them."

—The Man from Elysian Fields, 2001

It was pitch black by the time Olga turned into Dr. Martin Hood's cul-de-sac. Luckily, every single residence had some form of ornamental lighting that illuminated the home addresses. When she pulled up to the curb in front of the Victorian style brick house, Olga immediately cut the engine and just sat back motionless in her seat.

In her cache of turbulent memories, Olga struggled to pin point the exact date of her last visit. It had been just after Martin's wife had died, and the sight of the man she so dearly loved, crippled with grief, had been almost more than she could bear. Olga hadn't been able to help Martin that night, just as Martin hadn't been able to help his wife for years before. His university education, his medical contacts, and twenty years of blue chip investing hadn't been enough to pry his wife free from the clutches of cancer.

That awful night, when Martin had collapsed on the marble floor in his front foyer, Olga had misread his tears of desperation as a sign of overwhelming grief. To her, it had been solid and undeniable proof that he was physically and emotionally devastated over the loss of his wife.

"Martin, Martin! Are you alright?" she had asked when she rushed to his side, helping him steady his weight on the polished floor. "You had better lie down," Olga had warned, suddenly afraid that since he'd already dropped down to his knees once, the next lapse in strength might actually land him flat on his face.

"I feel so woozy," he had muttered. "I was just looking in the closet when I heard the bell," he fought to explain.

"Don't try to speak," Olga had urged him, reduced to forcefully tugging Martin down onto his back.

"I need to find the right shoes, and they all look the same."

Olga carefully shifted her legs, his head effectively cradled on her upper thighs. "Don't worry," she tried to soothe him. "I'm sure you'll find them."

"They're special cream colored dress shoes… shoes that Mary wanted to be buried in."

"Really?" Olga couldn't help but question, a little surprised that his wife had taken the time to make such specific notes from her deathbed.

"My lawyer called. Mary had left a letter of instructions. The clothes were easy, but I can't find the damn shoes," he cursed, fighting to rise up to a sitting position.

"Take it easy. You don't have to jump up."

"I'm fine. Just a little embarrassed."

"Let's get you to the front room. I want you to lie down for at least another twenty minutes before you do any more searching."

"I can't relax. I have to find those shoes."

As Olga watched Martin struggle to his feet, she realized that unless she quickly intervened, he'd probably fall again, this time possibly resulting in a broken bone or two.

"Stay put. I'll check," she ordered. "Just tell me exactly what they're supposed to look like."

"Umh, let's see," he dug into the back pocket of his corduroy pants. "Cream colored patent leather... Manola Blahniks. They have a two and a half inch heel with scalloped edges. But I just don't know..." he began to mutter to himself.

"May I see that list?"

Martin obediently handed the paper to Olga; secretly relieved to pass it off. He had no idea how he was supposed to pack up the detailed pieces of wardrobe requested to dress his wife's dead body. It seemed like such a cruel task to pass onto the spouse of the deceased. For all the money he'd paid his lawyer over the years, it seemed like they could have somehow figured out a better way to break the news to Martin, other than handling him a typed document and telling him to drop off the listed articles at the funeral home by four that afternoon.

"She's being cremated," Martin reasoned. What does it matter what shoes she's wearing? No one is going to see her feet at the funeral. It just doesn't make any..." his voice trailed off, the emotion choking out the final words.

"It's all right Martin. I'll find the rest of the stuff."

"She didn't want an open casket," he continued to ramble. "Mary didn't want people to see her in a cheap wig with an inch of bad makeup plastered all over her face. She always liked to look nice."

"I know," Olga had nodded her head in agreement. "Your wife was a very beautiful woman, Martin, and I think it's only fair that she be cremated in some of own her finest clothing. Look," Olga took a deep breath, "You go to the kitchen and make us a pot of coffee. I'll dig through the closet and look for the appropriate shoes. Are you okay?"

Brushing the nonexistent dust from his knees, Martin turned toward Olga, reaching up and clasping her cheeks between the palms of his hands. "Thank you for coming over as soon as I called. I really don't think I'd have been able to do this on my own."

She closed her eyes, waiting for the obligatory kiss on the forehead that instinct told her was bound to follow.

Without disappointment, Martin bent down and brushed his lips across her skin. "I love you, Olga."

She opened her eyes but never lifted them off the marble floor as a shiver ran down her spine right to the tip of her toes. Never in her life had she felt so cold.

"Will you come with me to drop off the clothes?" he gently inquired, lifting her face by hooking his fingers under her chin.

"Oh, I don't know."

"Please. Just come along for support. I'll run them in myself. I promise."

"Alright," she finally conceded. "Go make the coffee. I'll finish with the list."

Martin was so grateful. He couldn't believe how fortunate he was to have a woman like Olga in his life. Her love was so strong, and right now, he was almost positive that her love was the only thing holding him together. Olga's courage would guide him through these most difficult days, and when it was over, and the appropriate amount of time had passed, he'd ask her on bended knee to be his wife. One day they'd both find the happiness they deserved.

Down the hall, Olga silently evaluated her life choices. She'd fallen in love with a married man whose wife had succumbed to a terrible death riddled by cancer. She respected Martin for his loyalty, never relegating his wife's palliative care to strangers. Yet at the same time, she despised him for not having the courage to fess up to his convictions. As soon as enough time had passed, she would sit Martin down and explain to him that their future did not look very promising. She believed that they needed some time apart, and that one day, they'd both somehow find the happiness they deserved.

Jarred back to reality by the approaching headlights in her rearview mirror, Olga once more looked up toward Martin's house. At that exact movement, a light was switched off in the lower level and a minute later flicked on in the story above. If she didn't move quickly, Martin would probably retire for the night, and then it would certainly be too late.

After rushing up the main sidewalk, her steps guided by the solar powered lights embedded deep in the manicured lawn, Olga quickly reached out and rang the front bell. She was anxious to make her move before she chickened out and lost her resolve.

"Who is it?" Martin's voice demanded from the small speaker mounted to the right of his front door.

"Martin, it's Olga Heinz," she clarified, as if his life was inundated by an entire list of women named Olga.

No verbal reply, just the sharp click of the front door as Olga was instantly granted entrance into the main foyer.

As she once again stood on the marble floors, she brought her hands together and rubbed them as if they were cold, encouraging the blood to move quickly through her veins.

"Olga, is everything okay?" Martin demanded, rushing down the stairs as he wrapped a housecoat around his bare chest, allowing the bottom to flutter open over the bottom half of his pajama pants. "Did something happen at the hospital?"

Suddenly embarrassed by her own spontaneity, Olga found it nearly impossible to voice a reply.

"Come in, come in," he motioned, reaching out to encompass both her shoulders with his right arm as he effectively directed her from the entrance to a brocade couch in the front room. "Would you like a glass of wine?" he asked, unconsciously warming both her hands between his own.

"This isn't social," Olga corrected him, pulling her hands out of his lap. "I'm really sorry to bother you when you're obviously working an early shift, but I…"

"Nonsense," Martin interrupted, fighting to hang on to any shred of normalcy still hanging in the air. "I thought you were in the neighborhood and just missed my company."

As she fought to smile through the veil of tears beginning to cloud her eyes, Olga concentrated on the task at hand, taking a hard look at the man sitting across from her.

Ten years since his wife's death, and he still lived alone in their massive, five-bedroom house. As far as Olga knew, Martin still didn't date, even though many mature women turned their heads when he strolled through the hospital. As if living in suspended animation, Dr. Martin Hood continued to exist, barely affected by the ravages of time, or the weight of loneliness that continued to bear down on his shoulders.

"I met with Dick Mansfield today. He called me in for a private meeting," Olga blurted out, too caught up in her own revelations to notice every single drop of color slowly draining from Martin's face.

"You saw Dick today?"

"Yes, at three o'clock. And five minutes later," she paused to take a deep breath, "I was officially no longer an employee of the University Hospital."

Cassy had been hiding out on the city's streets for so long, that she honestly couldn't remember how much time has passed. Thirteen when she left home, fourteen when she was knocked up and had her first abortion—everything else just kind of ran together after that. If her mind hadn't been so foggy, or if she'd been able to break out of her drug-induced haze, Cassy might have been able to remember the year she was born, and counted forward from there. She knew if she subtracted her birthday from the present calendar year, then she'd have a number, and she further reasoned—that number would probably be somewhere around nineteen. But she wasn't able to formulate those basic thoughts.

The mere effort she expended with the thought process had been an accomplishment in itself, and now Cassy's brain was so exhausted by the proposed mathematical computation, that she decided she just needed to turn a quick trick. A trick would give her a little money to buy some smoke. An entire eight ball was out of the question, but if she could find some guy who'd pay ten or fifteen bucks for a blowjob, she'd probably be able to pick up enough rock to get her head on straight. Then once she was thinking clearly, she'd be able to try finding Jimmy. He'd know what happened at the shelter, and why she had a bloody knife jammed deep in her coat pocket.

It was a simple plan, and right now, it was about all the young girl's consciousness could handle. As she stumbled along, Cassy forced herself to move off the sidewalk and into the bathroom of the convenience store. She pulled a handful of paper towels out of the dispenser, and ran them under the water, struggling to wipe the street grime off her cheeks. After scrubbing with shaking hands, she'd removed most of the smudges before stopping to look at her hair. Since it was greasy and tangled, she couldn't do much without a brush. Luckily, a stray rubber band picked off the floor allowed her to pull it back into a rough ponytail. Nothing else to do except tuck her stained grey tee shirt into her jeans, and hit the streets.

The absolute last thing Cassy every wanted to do to feed her drug habit was turn tricks for cash, but when forced to be on her own, she had resorted to selling her body on more than one occasion. That's why she needed to find Jimmy, or at least hook up with someone else as soon as possible. A boyfriend on the street wouldn't buy you flowers, but he usually kept you in dope. You'd share his crib, his food, and every now and then, he might even surprise you with a new bag of clean clothes pinched from a mall.

A good boyfriend wouldn't trade you for dope or pass you off to his friends, but even if he did once or twice, it was still better than walking the streets and selling your ass to strangers. You never knew if your next trick was going to be *that freak*, the guy who pulled a weapon on you and got his kicks from listening to you scream. *Any* boyfriend was better than being alone, and if Cassy couldn't find Jimmy by morning, she'd have to start looking for a replacement guy.

Two blocks past the store, she saw a small group of men hanging out near the stoop of a dilapidated house. From twenty feet away, she could already smell their smoke, and once the crack cocaine registered in her brain, she'd have crawled a mile through the sewers for just one toke on their pipe.

"Hey," Cassy nodded, walking up slowly to give the guys a chance to check her out and register the fact that she was unarmed and relatively harmless.

"Get lost, ho!" one barked in her general direction.

"I was just looking for a little party. Either of you boys interested?"

"Fuck off. Take your diseased ass off our block, bitch!" A second threat rang out from the group.

Intuition alerted Cassy that this wasn't a safe place to hang, but her desperate craving for the dope drowned out all the warning bells ringing in her head. If she were lucky, she'd pull a trick, pocket a little cash, and score some dope as a bonus. So fighting the urge to turn tail and run, the young girl willed her feet over the remaining steps. "A twenty will get either of you the best head of your life," she offered her services.

"You deaf, ho? Get your sorry ass off our corner before I beat you senseless."

Cassy stood motionless—the three guys evaluating her form—as she quickly fought to inhale the lingering smoke still hanging in the air from their last drags on the crack pipe. "I don't want no trouble," she begged. "I'm just hurting really bad. Y'all know what that's like, don't ya?"

"So the baby needs a bottle?" one asked, stepping away from the others to put himself directly in Cassy's line of sight. "Well, I'm really hurting for you too, bitch," he teased. "But you wanna tell me why I'm supposed to pay for something I can get for free?" he hissed, whipping his right hand around the back of her head to grab her neck in a viselike grip. "Kneel bitch!" he barked. "You so busy offering, now do your job."

Thrust to her knees, Cassy tried to shift position, not in an attempt to flee, just to try to move her bony kneecaps off the small pieces of gravel embedding themselves into her already bruised skin. "Twenty?" she desperately attempted a last minute negotiation as the guy reached up with his free hand to unzip his fly.

The sudden kick to her lower back would have sent Cassy sprawling face down into the gutter, had the first guy relinquished his stranglehold on her neck. Still held up like a farm chicken dangling from the butcher's hand, she almost lost consciousness from the pain.

"I ain't paying you five bucks. Now do it right, or I'll slit your throat!" the instigator laughed, thrusting his cock inside her gapping mouth.

Cassy gagged as she tried to catch her breath, and frantically twisted her head sideways in an attempt to clear her airway. She was effectively choking to death, and neither one of the three guys were lucid enough to notice.

"Paco, grab her head," the obvious leader of the group yelled, angry that the street ho had the strength or even the audacity to fight him.

Paco followed instructions, and rushed over from behind his brother's back, struggling to stabilize the girl's thrashing head before he finally gave up and just wrapped his own hands around Cassy's neck.

"I said hold her," Manny screamed, gritting his teeth as he thrust his cock deeper and deeper down her constricting throat. "Take it bitch!" he yelled at the top of his lungs seconds before he exploded and ejaculated his entire load.

"My turn," the third guy announced, pushing his way in toward Cassy's face. "You give it to me good bitch, or this time, I'll kick you in the head."

Laughing, Manny stepped away as Paco simultaneously released his grip on her neck.

Without warning, Cassy's lifeless form crumpled to the pavement, her eyes wide open, the warm semen spilling from the corners of her mouth and trickling down onto the greasy sidewalk.

"Get up!" Paco yelled, the only guy unable to see her turned face.

Manny quickly stuffed his limp cock back into his denim jeans before taking two small steps toward the crumpled heap. "Get up," he repeated, roughly attempting to rouse her with the toe of his leather boot.

Bending down across her chest, Paco leaned in and looked directly into her lifeless eyes. "Fuck bro, I don't think she's breathing," he announced.

"Well then, let's fucking roll," Manny ordered his small gang.

Jumping to his feet, Paco scanned the dark neighborhood streets to see if anyone was going to step forward and play the hero.

The shadows remained motionless, and the three guys turned and sauntered off down the sidewalk.

Still seated, this time both cradling snifters of brandy, Martin searched Olga's eyes for any sign of a breakdown. She was completely motionless, her face as blank as an untouched canvas.

"I don't want this," she suddenly announced, leaning forward to place her snifter in the center of the coffee table.

"Is something the matter? Do you want me to reheat it?"

"No, it's not that. I actually don't like brandy."

Martin stood, swooped in, and picked up the crystal glass, checking the liquid for impurities. "I'm sorry, I thought you did," he shook his head in amazement.

Olga shrugged her shoulders, and continued to stare at the empty fireplace.

"Hold on, you do like brandy," he announced after a moment's thought. "We used to take a bottle with us on picnics and sip it in the park, down by the water's edge. I can remember it clear as day."

"I never liked it then either," she flatly admitted.

"Oh, I see."

Her turn to rise, Olga stepped around Martin and made her way to the liquor cart. She lifted up a decanter of red wine, pouring herself a generous glass before returning to her chair.

"So, you still like red wine though?"

"Yes," she tried to smile, suddenly realizing that she'd unintentionally hurt Martin's feelings.

"So, what else?"

"What?" Olga asked, not sure if she'd blocked out an important piece of their conversation.

"Well, I was just wondering, what else did you pretend to like just to appease me?"

"It's not really important right now," Olga dismissed the question, not the least bit concerned that his male ego might be taking a kicking. "Martin, I have to be honest," she finally admitted, "I need to fess up about why I came here to see you tonight."

"Because we're friends?"

"Because I wanted to ask if you could try to help me get my job back. I can't imagine life without nursing."

Instantly pivoting to hide his face, Martin moved away from Olga in a bid to refill his glass and buy himself a precious couple of seconds.

"I know your seniority extends you a few privileges, and I wouldn't ask if I had any other options, but I don't."

"Olga, I…"

"I was wondering if you could please talk to Dick Mansfield for me. Maybe you could ask him to reconsider my mandatory retirement package? I really believe that I still have something left to offer, Something…"

"Olga, I don't…"

"It's not a money issue. If you think a salary cut might strengthen my position, I'd be more than glad to talk about…"

"Olga!" Martin shouted.

Shocked into silence, she finally closed her mouth and listened to what the doctor had to say.

"I already tried," he finally admitted in anger. "That bastard Dick Mansfield promised me that he was going to pull whatever strings he could to keep you on staff. He jerked us both around."

Speechless, Olga looked away from Martin and back to the

fireplace. Then without any warning, she raised her right arm and hurdled the hundred and thirty-five dollar piece of Waterford Crystal against the blackened brickwork.

CHAPTER TWENTY-THREE

"I'm sorry, if you were right, I would agree with you."

—Awakenings, 1990

Camille Greenway was quite comfortable researching any of her problems on the Internet. Pulling up Google, she quickly typed in a broad search for Long Term Care Facilities and waited. The list was massive, and after scrolling downward through the pages, her eyes finally settled on the name she'd been looking for—*Pleasant View Long Term Care.* After clicking on its home page, she was instantaneously rewarded with answers. Camille excitedly congratulated herself—she immediately clicked the print icon and waited for the laser copy to be delivered into her hands.

Stapling the pages together, she leaned back in her chair and began reading the information. *Personalized long-term care for the mentally and physically handicapped members of your family.*

"At least they're to the point," she mumbled, as she continued to read the professionally designed cover page. Sandwiched between all the printed data were nine digital photos of the facility and its grounds. Taking the time to look them over carefully, she found herself scanning the faces for any familiar features, the slightest hint of a family resemblance. She wasn't even positive that these were actual patients, and not an assembled collection of models hired for a shoot, so Camille finally relented and threw her research down on her bed. As she turned back to clear her computer screen, she just happened to notice an information number posted on the bottom of the page, neatly typed under the heading of Family Emergencies.

After immediately grabbing her cordless phone, Camille dialed the New York area code and then punched in the remaining seven digits. Two rings later, a woman who identified herself as the Pleasant View receptionist answered the line and politely inquired which department the caller wanted to be connected with. Stumbling over her answer, Camille finally forced out the word admitting, and waited to be transferred.

"Admitting, can I help you?" the lady chirped on the other end.

"Hi, my name is Camille Greenway. I'm looking to speak to my sister, Stacey Greenway. I think she lives in your facility."

"Oh dear, you have the wrong department. Let me transfer you to visits," and without another moments delay, the line was rerouted to a second department.

"Hello, you've reached the appointment desk here at Pleasant View. Unfortunately, we've just stepped away from the phone for a few minutes. Please leave your name and number, and we'll call you back as soon as we return. Thank-you from all of us here at Pleasant View."

Thrown off by the scripted message, Camille chose to disconnect her line instead of recording her personal information. She just didn't feel right leaving a message regarding a patient she'd never even met. But then how would she ever know for sure if there was a girl named

Stacey Greenway living at Pleasant View, and most importantly, if she was really her sister?

Camille grabbed the phone and dialed again, determined this time to leave her name. She reasoned that she needed to deal with this once and for all—contacting the home was about the only positive step she could think of.

"Good morning, Pleasant View. May I help you?"

Once again speechless by the live voice on the other end of the line, Camille was just about to hang up for the second time before she gathered her wits and started to speak. "Umh, my name is Camille Greenway. My sister," she paused, the unfamiliar word tumbling awkwardly off her tongue. "I'd like to speak to my sister, Stacey Greenway."

"Please hold," the lady announced.

Forced to endure two tracks of canned instrumentals, Camille jumped when the live voice suddenly returned to the line. "I'm sorry miss, but I don't show you on our visiting list, and at present, Miss Greenway does not have phone privileges."

Thinking fast on her feet, Camille realized she'd need a plausible excuse if she had any hope of getting past this lady. "I've just graduated from high school, and until my eighteenth birthday, my parents weren't sure I would be able to handle any personal contact. But now that I'm an adult, I've decided that I am capable of handling the stress, and I'd really like to speak with my sister," she announced, actually pleased with her own performance.

"Can you please answer a few personal family questions for identification purposes?"

Camille agreed and began to recite her parents' and brothers' full names, and their home address. Eventually, after what seemed like an endless round of questions and answers, the lady on the other end of the line was satisfied that the caller was exactly who she purported to be.

"Well, as I mentioned earlier, your sister Stacey doesn't take phone calls, but if you'd like to book a visit, I can check our appointment schedule."

"In person?"

"Yes miss, we find that our residents usually respond more positively to one on one contact."

"Alright, when should I come?"

After taking a couple of minutes to check availability, the secretary returned with a date and a time, repeating it twice while Camille recorded it on a note pad.

"Please don't forget to call should you have to cancel the visit. Our residents can become quite upset by no-show visitors. I'm sure you understand."

"I just have one more questions," Camille nervously admitted. "Can I bring my sister a gift? I mean… like what kind of stuff does she like?"

"I'm sorry miss, I don't know your sister personally, but I can give you a little general advice. Due to allergies, we try to discourage live flowers or candy treats. Experience has taught us that stuffed animals are usually appreciated, no matter the level of physical or mental disability. However, please make sure that all buttons or decorative clothing is sewn, and not glued. This helps us avoid any difficulties brought on by potential choking from toy parts."

"I see," she muttered, simultaneously scribbling notes.

Softening her voice, the older lady took a second to collect her breath. "What kind of toys did you like when you were a young girl?"

"I loved *Care Bears*. My mom used to collect them for me."

"Then I'm sure your sister Stacey will love them, too."

Steven woke to the sounds of increased pedestrian traffic, as the hospital corridors began to come alive. Experience told him that the kitchen would be sending up the rolling hot carts carrying the patients' breakfast trays, immediately followed by a round of morning meds. As soon as everyone had been fed and all the prescriptions administered, the ritual of preparing the patients for the doctors' rounds would quickly begin. Sponge baths followed by dressing changes were the next order of business, and before the staff had much of a chance for a breather, it was almost time to serve lunch.

"Good morning, Steven," an orderly rang out as he entered the room brandishing a tray of cooked oatmeal and weak tea. "How ya feeling?"

"Better," he admitted, his pain subsiding and his strength slowly returning. "You got my shift?"

"Overtime, too," the kid smiled back. "How long you gonna be laid up for?"

"I'm not sure," Steven admitted, wrinkling his nose as he lifted the plastic lid off his bowl and inspected the congealed top layer of his porridge.

"Just a little foreskin," his co-worker teased. "Why don't ya just peel her back and dig in," he snickered before turning to leave the room.

Shaking his head, Steven ripped open both sugar packets and began stirring the granules into his tea. He desperately needed to talk to Olga and find out what had happened. Hopefully she would have some answers, cuz lord knows he had a shit load of questions, all beginning with the most obvious—where was the shaker of tissue he'd been carrying in his pocket?

As she made her way down the hospital corridors toward Steven's room, Olga's heart began to pound inside the confines of her chest, while she felt the beads of sweat begin to converge on her upper lip. She hadn't experienced a panic attack in years, however the signs were strong, and definitely too familiar to ignore.

After ducking into the first empty patient room she found, Olga pushed her way into the small cubicle bathroom and slammed the door shut. She wildly searched the room, and finally located the towel dispenser hanging in plain sight. She yanked out a handful of paper towels, dropping two or three on the floor, before shoving the remainder under the cold-water faucet. Without even bothering to wring out the soggy paper, she shoved her face down toward the porcelain sink and repeatedly swabbed her burning cheeks and forehead. "Slow down, it's alright," Olga repeated to herself. "Just breathe deep," her voice commanded her body, as if conveying instructions from an outside source.

With her panting subsiding into a stabilized breathing pattern, Olga dropped the wad of paper towels from her right hand and slowly raised her face upwards toward the mirror.

She looked absolutely frightful. With water still running down her chin and dripping onto her chest, the eyes staring back at Olga from the bathroom mirror appeared puffy and rimmed in red. The skin covering her neck and face was blotchy; the slight twitch invading the muscles surrounding her right eye was undeniable. Career nurse Olga Heinz was slipping back into her old pattern; and the sense of terror that invaded her consciousness was irrefutable.

She needed to get back home, and she needed to dig up some of her old medication. Still more than rest and drugs, Olga desperately needed to get out of the hospital undetected—during the seven o'clock scramble, it wouldn't be easy.

As she forced herself to sit and rest on the closed lid of the toilet, Olga suddenly became aware of the voices walking in and out of the hospital room. It was obvious that they were prepping the bed for a patient—staff members were discussing the placement of the accompanying monitors that would be following the gurney down from the ICU

"It's done," Claire announced as Olga instantly recognized the student nurse's voice. "Why don't you go call upstairs and let them know we're ready for the transfer. I'm just going to make sure there's enough linen on the bed."

Just as Olga heard one set of footsteps leave the room, another heavier set rushed through the door.

"Is she here?"

"Who?" Claire asked the doctor.

"Nurse Heinz. I was told she's on the floor and I can't seem to find her anywhere."

"I'm sorry, Dr. Hood. I haven't seen her. Have you checked down in the coffee shop?"

"Yes," he barked in a single frustrated syllable. "And should you run into Nurse Heinz, please tell her that it's urgent. I need to speak to her as soon as possible."

"I can page her for you," Claire offered.

Debating the option, Martin declined. He left the room and made his way toward the elevator.

"Martin," Dick Mansfield called out down the hospital corridors. "My receptionist said you stopped by to see me this morning. Said it was some kind of emergency, and then buggered off without even leaving a message when I wasn't in. What's up?"

"I thought you promised to save Olga's job?" Martin angrily stabbed at the elevator call button.

"I tried, but the wheels were already in motion, and my hands were tied," the chairman fell back on his cache of worn out clichés.

"You understand what I'm up against, don't you Martin? This whole mandatory retirement issue is a lot bigger than just our nursing staff. Hell, we're in the process of introducing major policy changes here at the University Hospital, and..."

"But you said you'd take care of it!" Martin barked his response just as the elevator doors opened up.

"Why don't you come up to my office," Dick politely encouraged the doctor. "We can finish this conversation over a cup of coffee."

"Doesn't your word mean anything? I took your promise at face value. I don't know who's a bigger asshole, Dick—you for lying to me, or me for believing in you in the first place?"

"Dr. Hood, I suggest we take this upstairs," the chairman hissed under his breath, conscious of their assembling audience.

As he turned to face his adversary, Martin glared down into the eyes of the hospital's most influential man. "Why bother, Dick. You're just going to fill the air with bullshit, and frankly, I've had enough."

"Dr. Hood, I suggest you take a walk and collect your thoughts."

"I'm walking all right," Martin agreed. "And I won't be coming back. I quit!"

Dick Mansfield shook his head in disgust, genuinely disappointed that an issue as trivial as one nurse's mandatory retirement could influence a doctor of Martin's stature.

By the time Olga resurfaced from her self-imposed seclusion in the vacant washroom, every floor in the building was beginning to buzz with word of Dr. Hood's fight. As the hospital rumor-mill circulated, the staff instantly began taking their sides. At least seventy-five percent leaned toward Martin, thrilled that a lowly doctor had finally put the chairman of the board in his place. It was hot gossip, and faster than a crash cart could be rolled down the halls, the news travelled up and down the units.

"I never met him," Steven admitted to Claire, his eyes shifting to the door as Olga finally made her appearance in the room.

"Hello Steven," she cheerfully called out. "I'm very glad to see that you're awake."

"And lucid," Claire added with a wink. "But our boy here is having a little memory lapse."

"Is that true, Steven?" Olga quickly stepped over to the foot of his bed, and examined his chart for any notations of head trauma.

"She's just teasing me," he quickly interrupted, "Something about a screaming match, down by the elevators. I don't really know the men she's talking about. Do you?"

"You know how I feel about gossip," Olga reiterated, her tone leaving little doubt as to the seriousness of her opinion. "Gossip is the wasted pastime of the idle mind. I'm sure you both have something a little more productive to occupy your time with. Isn't that correct?" she turned to face the student nurse.

"Yes ma'am, I do," Claire agreed before turning to leave the room. "But, umh… I almost forgot. Dr. Hood said it's extremely important that he speak to you. The matter is urgent. Well, I think it still is," she mumbled, not sure what was actually important at this stage of the game.

"Please tell the unit desk to page Dr. Hood and let him know that I'll be in the staff lounge momentarily. Can you do that for me?" she asked, slightly annoyed that Claire was not moving as quickly as she would have liked.

"Yes ma'am. But I don't think Dr. Hood is still in the hospital. I heard he stormed out toward the staff parking lot right after he quit."

"Quit what?"

"His job," both Steven and Claire repeated in unison.

Olga shook her head, as she busied herself with checking Steven's vitals. "What in the world are you two talking about?"

"Claire was just telling me that Dr. Hood and the chairman of the board got into a screaming match just outside the elevator doors, and Dr. Hood quit his job," Steven calmly reported. "I don't really know the doctor well, but he always…"

"Martin quit?" Olga repeated, the words sounding foreign as they escaped from her very own lips.

"It was so weird," the young nurse picked up where Steven had left off. "He just totally lost his cool, and when old man Mansfield wanted to take the fight upstairs, Dr. Hood just blew him off and let him know exactly what he could do with his job."

"I have to find Martin. You said he left the building?"

"That's what I heard," Claire admitted. "I didn't actually see him leave myself. Do you want me to check with his office and see if he's still in the building?"

"Yes," was all that Olga needed to say to send Claire flying off on a mission.

"Are you alright?" Steven questioned his friend the second he was confident they were alone. "You've gone totally white."

"I'm just worried about Martin, I mean Dr. Hood. We've know each other for a long time and I'm…"

"It's okay," Steven interrupted. "I'd already heard about you and the doctor, but I figured it was none of my business, so I never admitted anything to Claire."

She smiled down at her friend, and finally remembered why she stopped by in the first place. "And how are you feeling, dear? You really had me worried when we found you down in the shelter's basement."

"It was awful," Steven admitted in a rush of emotion. "That girl attacked me just like a rabid dog. I couldn't get her off me, no matter what I did. I thought she was going to kill me," he admitted, the emotional statement swelling up his throat. "She was stoned out of her mind, she could barely…"

"A girl? Did you know her?"

He shook his head side to side, and motioned toward the bedside pitcher of water.

As she silently watched the young man sip the room-temperature liquid, Olga couldn't help but recite a silent prayer of thanks for his safety.

"Who was she?" he asked, finally passing off the empty glass.

"We don't know either. The police showed up with the ambulance, long after your attacker had fled the scene. You're lucky you didn't bleed to death down there in the basement. Everyone is still surprised that you managed to crawl to the top of the stairs."

"I barely remember that," Steven admitted, dropping his head back on the pillow to collect his thoughts. "But I do remember the powder," he closed his eyes, the exhaustion threatening to take control. "Do you have the shaker that I was carrying in my jacket?"

"No," Olga answered, unaware that the powder had been lost.

CHAPTER TWENTY-FOUR

"Boy, the next word that comes out of your mouth better be some brilliant fucking Mark Twain shit, cuz it's definitely getting chiseled on your tombstone."

—The Devil's Rejects, 2005

As she absentmindedly watched the cameraman and make-up lady struggle to change the fitted sheets covering the king-size bed, Gerri patiently sipped her coffee and waited to be summoned. She'd been on the set for the last two hours, but due to the late arrival of *the star*, she still hadn't been called up.

"I said red," a man's voice boomed from somewhere behind Gerri's back. "All I'm gonna see is teeth and cum if you throw Tyreek and Leticia down on them black sheets."

"The red are dirty," the lady shouted back. "I told you they had to be washed, but nobody ever listens to me. So now all you've got is either black, or those shiny green ones you hate."

"I gotta do the fucking laundry, too?" Terence moaned as he

walked past the main camera onto the impromptu set. "Let's see the reds, they can't be that bad."

After kicking at the wrinkled pile of soiled bedding, the cameraman shook his head in disgust. "This is gross man. I ain't picking it up. You wanna touch it, you come over here, and you peel it off the floor yourself."

"Fuck me dry," Terence cursed. "The green gives us glare, the red stinks like shit, and the black is gonna swallow up our tits an' ass. Am I right?"

Half strutting and half prowling, *the star* finally made his entrance onto the set. "Are we almost ready to roll? I'm not gonna wait around all day. You think I have nothing better to do than hang around here with you queens," he complained, the twenty steps from his change room to the set almost dislodging the loosely knotted towel at his hip.

"Tyreek man, we got a problem," the director admitted. "My reds are dirty, the greens are ugly as shit, and that leaves only the black ones."

"Black? What are you, fucking blind? You won't be able to see my fabulous dick."

"I know," Terence moaned, reaching over to switch off the set lights in an attempt to save a few bucks in bulbs. "Hey, I got an idea. How about we move this party to another room? Maybe the…" he stalled, racking his brain for a set location that hadn't been filmed in the past five or six videos.

"Your kitchen table is white, how about there?" the porn star suggested, mentally gauging the height of the laminate edge. "I don't think I'd need a lift box for my feet. Actually, it's probably the perfect height for fucking,"

Terence leaned over and grabbed the portable camera, suddenly eager to take the show on the road. "Where's my fluffer?" he yelled out—his interest suddenly rejuvenated in the day's production. "We can shoot the *meet and greet* scene in the kitchen, and then maybe move the action to the laundry room. The washer and dryer will make a pair of good, solid backdrops. I'm almost fucking positive that we haven't rolled any video down there before. And hey," he turned to shout one last time. "Where the fuck is the goddamn fluffer?"

"I'm here," Gerri called out, lipstick refreshed, disposable coffee cup quickly discarded.

"Well," Terence moaned, "what's the fucking hold up?"

"I forgot my bag," Gerri apologized over her shoulder as she rushed back to the entrance to grab her purse, heels clicking loudly on the ceramic tiled floor.

"Forget your goddamn shit, and hit your knees!" Terence loudly barked in her general direction. "And what the fuck is going on? Doesn't anyone remember why we're here?"

"I'm back," Gerri announced as she dug down into the depths of her knock-off Fendi, manicured nails scrambling to locate her selection of condoms.

"You aren't fucking, you're just here to blow him," Terence snapped, his temper threatening to boil over.

"But I use these," Gerri argued back. "That," she pointed to Tyreek's flaccid penis, "is not going in here," she brought her fingers up to her lips, "without one of these," she summed up by opening the palm of her left hand.

"I can't get rock hard with a rubber covering my dick. So bitch," Tyreek added for emphasis, "you better get ready to suck me bareback."

"Suck yourself!"

"What?" the director finally snapped. "I'm paying you a hundred bucks a day to keep his cock hard, and you need these?" he slapped the condoms right out of Gerri's outstretched hand. "You're fired. Get the fuck off my set!"

"Who's gonna suck me off?" Tyreek started to wail the moment Gerri turned on her heels and marched out the front door.

Standing alone in his office, Dr. Martin Hood struggled with the volume of his caseload. Resigning his position was not as simple as quitting a job at an architectural firm or a construction company. Lives literally depended on him, and he wasn't willing to walk out the doors of the University Hospital and leave his patients hanging in the balance. Before he left, he needed to know that each individual case had been assigned to a competent colleague. Many of his patients would need a face-to-face explanation for his sudden departure before they would be willing to continue with their present course of treatment, and for all intents and purposes, they deserved it.

"Dr. Hood," the secretary's voice broke his train of thought. "There are two security guards here. They're demanding that I let them into your office."

"What for?"

"Mr. Mansfield reports that you are no longer employed by the University Hospital," the guard carefully read from a typed index card. "And we are ordered to collect your credentials, your passkeys, and to box up all the files belonging to, or pertaining to, hospital business."

"Right now?" Martin asked, totally shocked that Dick would be taking such a militant stand.

"Yes doctor. Right now."

After emptying his pockets, Martin reluctantly detached his ring of office keys from those designated for his car.

"Do you have the keys for these?" the second guard pointed to the bank of filing cabinets adorning the rear wall.

"Yes," was all Martin could mutter, his hand slipping into the top drawer of his desk to retrieve yet another ring.

"What about your calls?" his secretary blurted out, her voice wavering as she fought to control her tears.

"I guess, just transfer them to my…"

"Mr. Mansfield has a letter of instructions for you as well," the guards informed the doctor's personal secretary. "So if you are ready Dr. Hood, we'll escort you to your car."

"But…"

"Don't worry about your personal belongings sir. Your secretary has just been informed to pack them up, and have them delivered to your home address."

"I wasn't worried about my pens and pencils," Martin sarcastically threw at the men's faces. "I was worried about my patients. I think they deserve an explanation regarding my sudden disappearance. Don't you?"

"We have orders to escort you from the premises immediately. Please, Dr. Hood," the senior guard attempted to reason with him. "We're just doing our job, sir. If you think you're being treated unfairly, just take it up with your lawyer."

Martin nodded in defeat, only slowing his departure long enough to affectionately pat his secretary on the shoulder as he made his way out his office door.

As she was reaching in her purse for her car keys, Olga was shocked to see Martin marching briskly toward her, obviously being escorted by the two uniformed guards flanking both his sides.

"So it's true?" she asked the minute Martin was within earshot.

"I'm fine," he turned to dismiss the security guards. "I can take it from here."

"Sorry sir. You have no security pass to activate the parking garage doors. And like I said upstairs, we have to escort you off the property."

"Oh, for Christ's sake," he finally let loose. "I'm totally capable of driving my car out onto the street! Olga, let me borrow your pass," he turned to sneer at the guards, thrilled that he was finally able to *one up them.*

"Heinz?" the guards suddenly turned their attention toward Olga. "Are you Nurse Olga Heinz?"

"Yes I am."

"Well, we also have instructions to collect your credentials and your keys to the med lockers."

"Get in the car, Olga," Martin firmly ordered her. "We're professionals, not a pair of common criminals who need to be thrown off the property."

Briskly stepping over to the passenger's door, Olga yanked open the handle the second after Martin beeped her in with his remote.

"You can tell Dick that we've left the property, and he can expect to hear from my lawyer."

"Yes sir," the guards replied in unison as Martin started his engine and roared up the ramp toward the main street exit.

Two blocks from the hospital, he finally pulled over and slammed his car into park.

Without speaking, Olga reached across the consol and squeezed the doctor's ice-cold hand. "I don't have a clue what to say. The last couple of days have turned out to be hell for us both. I guess our careers are over," she audibly sighed, the reality of the situation draining all the life from her body. "It's funny, but somehow with you still up near the helm, I thought the board's mandatory retirement decision might be overturned. I thought..."

"I know," Martin turned in his seat, covering Olga's left hand with his right. "I was hopeful too. Hopeful that somehow in your last two weeks, I'd be able to bring about some kind of policy change. I don't know what I thought I was going to do, but I, somehow I…"

"Thank you, Martin," she politely interrupted his train of thought. "But tell me, why in the hell did you quit?" she inquired with a nervous chuckle. "What can you do from outside the University's walls?"

"Will you marry me, Olga?"

Pulling her hand back into the folds of her lap, she looked down at her uniform, searching the dyed cotton for any sign of a message.

"Marrying you used to be my dream—the fantasy I'd comfort myself with when I was alone or hurting," she quietly admitted.

"Well?" Martin gently prodded her with a smile. "I am here to make your dreams come true."

"This is all wrong. A marriage doesn't replace a career."

"I know that," he argued back. "But I'm not trying to replace my career. Nothing could ever compete with my work at the hospital. That was my life, my…"

"Martin," Olga interrupted him one last time. "Let's just shelve any more talk of marriage until we both figure out where we're heading with our lives. You know, you might spend the next twelve months in the middle of a legal battle."

"I was bluffing. I'm not going to start a war with the entire legal department of the University Hospital. If they don't want me around, I'm not going to fight to stay."

"My sentiments exactly. And you know what else? I bet there are a lot of other institutions that would appreciate us."

Martin turned back toward his windshield, and began fidgeting with the lacing on his steering wheel. "I think I'm done."

"You're willing to just walk away from your practice? What

would you do with your days? A person can only log so many volunteer hours."

"Travel, maybe a contract or two with *Doctors Without Borders.* I'm not really sure at this point, but let's just suffice it to say that I need a change."

While unconsciously wringing her hands in her lap, it was Olga's turn to make a proposal. "How about a little research?"

"I think I'm a little too old to spend my days staring down the barrel of an electron microscope. Besides, once you've spent the bulk of your career as a clinical practitioner, you can't possibly imagine filling your days with grant requests and supply requisitions. It's not for me, Olga. I'm not the research type."

"I know. It was just a thought. I figured that maybe it was a path we could explore together."

"Research? You?"

"I have a pet project in the works."

He shifted his car's transmission back into drive, and eased his Mercedes onto the street. "So I take it you've suddenly decided not to fight your retirement either?"

"Well," Olga mused. "If I decide to fight it, you know that I can do both."

"I'm totally aware of your capabilities, little Miss Heinz."

"Would you like to come to the house?" Olga offered. "We can have a drink, toast our careers."

"Our careers?" Martin repeated, still struggling with the realization that he was officially unemployed.

After cautiously poking her head out of the back door of her house, Miranda checked the yard for any signs of an underlying breeze. Satisfied that the sky was calm and rain had subsided, she slipped on her rubber boots and snuck out into the garden. The city smelt wonderful, the air freshened by the multitude of falling droplets, washing the neighborhood clean of any dust particles and lingering debris.

She collected her favorite pail and picking stool, and settled herself in the midst of her pea patch. Mindful of the bandages that still adorned a large percentage of her face, Miranda carefully leaned in to pluck the bulging pods from the mess of tangled vines. Gratefully lost in the tranquility of her gardening, she was unaware of the footsteps crossing the grass on a direct path toward her position.

"I thought you were supposed to stay inside? Wasn't that your story?" the man demanded, infuriated that his wife was sitting out in plain view, acting as if she didn't have a care in the world.

Miranda nearly jumped out of her skin, took a cleansing breath, and then bent down to pick up the pea pods she'd accidentally dropped. "The doctor just said I had to stay inside when it was raining or the wind picked up. He doesn't want me to chance wetting the bandages or to let any kind of dirt or crud to work its way underneath."

"Whatever," Bert muttered, turning to make his way into the house.

"I've got a pot of chili cooling on the counter and a Caesar salad in the fridge. You want me to come in and make you some garlic toast?"

"Don't bother, I ain't that hungry."

The words hung over Miranda's head, the paper sack slung from her husband's side a testament to his plans for the evening.

"I don't mind. The vines are kind of muddy anyway. Let me fix you a plate."

Shrugging his shoulders, Bert turned and trudged off toward the backdoor of their home.

Miranda jumped up to follow her husband and abandoned her half-filled pail, hurriedly stomping her feet, attempting to knock off as much of the clumped garden soil as possible.

"Cup or a bowl?" she called out less than a minute later, quickly rinsing her hands under the kitchen tap.

"Cup, I guess."

While the small serving of chili heated in the microwave, Miranda quickly slid two slices of Texas toast under the oven's broiler. As she reached for the handle of the fridge to retrieve her bowl of pre-made salad, her worst fears were suddenly confirmed. Standing guard as if they were a platoon of soldiers, eleven long necked beers anxiously awaited their call into service.

"Are you working tomorrow? I was thinking of getting up early and making us some pancakes."

"No work this weekend," Bert yelled from the living room. "Don't need me for awhile. Boss said to call in Monday after first coffee. Maybe he'd have some work for me on Tuesday."

"I see," she half mumbled to herself, wondering how they'd handle thirty-six hours together in the house. "Well, supper's ready. Come on and eat."

"Maybe later," he offered, waltzing through the kitchen to grab a second beer. "I'm just gonna relax for awhile."

Grateful that she hadn't spotted Bert carrying a bottle of hard liquor, Miranda stopped the microwave and returned the untouched chili to the cooled pot. Twelve beers would get him drunk, but it probably wasn't enough to push him over the edge. As long as she stayed out of his way, maybe went to bed early, they might make the night without incident.

"Are you gonna sit with me, maybe have some popcorn and watch a little TV?"

It all sounded so innocent. The invitation, the snacks, the concept of spending a quiet evening together on a Friday night was a wife's dream. But experience had taught Miranda that drunks liked company, and when his alcohol level rose high enough, Bert would eventually start looking for a fight.

"Actually, I'm a little tired from working in the garden, and I was thinking of lying down. You don't mind, do you?"

"Whatever," Bert offered his standard reply, instead of communicating a genuine response.

'It's just that I'm feeling beat and don't wanna…"

"Night."

"Goodnight," Miranda nodded, aware that she'd been summarily dismissed and was now expected to retreat to their room.

Eventually tucked into bed with a brand new paperback and a bowl of gummy bear candy balanced on her chest, Miranda prayed that the night wouldn't shape up to be the disaster she had first imagined. If everything continued on its present course, sometime after the late news, she'd just sneak downstairs, turn off the television, and cover Bert with an afghan. By morning, he'd be relatively sober, a little embarrassed and interested in nothing more than strong black coffee and a half stack of pancakes with sausage, twelve dead soldiers strewn carelessly at the foot of his upholstered chair.

"I'm coming, I'm coming. Hold your shorts," Bert yelled out in response to whatever had jarred him out of his chair.

Miranda jumped out from under the covers, and rushed over to the bedroom window seconds before the cab driver sped off into the night. "Oh shit. Oh no. Oh shit," she unconsciously muttered directly into the folds of the bedroom shears.

"Miranda, Miranda," Bert shouted from the bottom of the stairs. "Pete stopped by and he ain't had supper. Come fix him a bite. You hear me, Miranda?"

"Coming," she answered, scrambling to shove her arms into the sleeves of her terrycloth robe. "I'll be right down," her voice called out a second time.

"She's always got some juice hidden somewhere," Bert continued to push the glass jars around the top shelf of the refrigerator.

"Hello Pete. How's Lisa feeling? Heard tell she was having a rough go with her allergies this summer."

"We got any Clamato juice? I can't find any in this mess," Bert groaned.

"Stand aside," Miranda nervously joked. "You couldn't find it if it was ready to bite you on the nose."

Relinquishing his position, Bert turned and joined his old friend at the kitchen table where they each opened a fresh beer and began rehashing the week's events.

"Shall I put on a fresh pot of coffee?" Miranda nervously offered, setting down the pitcher of tomato juice in the middle of the table.

"No way, little lady," Pete piped up, lifting his beer to clink bottles with Bert. "I got the foreman job and we're celebrating tonight."

Strike number one. He has established a reason to drink.

Heart sinking to the bottom of her chest, Miranda almost forgot how to walk, her feet suddenly glued to the kitchen floor. An unsettling notion, since no matter how hard she tried to compose her thoughts, the only idea racing back and forth through her brain was the need to run!

Finally jarred back to reality by the harsh rapping on the house's screen door, Miranda forced herself to move out of harm's way only a second before her husband shoved his chair back from the table and jumped up to greet his guests.

Watching the men file into her kitchen, filling all her chairs and devouring most of her food, Miranda stood by as helpless as a child. Seen but not heard, she darted back and forth between the table and her kitchen counters. Reduced to little more than a waitress, she continued to serve drinks and wash empty plates as the crew gobbled up her chili and proceeded to wolf down the last of her canned peaches.

"To Pete. The best damn foreman on the site," the toasts continued.

One after another, each man poured himself a fresh shot, took the floor, and then proceeded to raise his glass to the newest company foreman.

"To Pete," Bert took his turn at the impromptu podium. "May your wife finally stop bitching about the size of your pay check and remember her place."

Strike number two. He has begun teasing and taunting his victim.

Still stuck in the middle of the action, Miranda immersed her hands deeper into the sink of soapy water. As her eye muscles began to twitch from the fatigue, she couldn't help but mentally torment herself by tallying the damage. Three cases of beer, a half sack of some kind of wine coolers, and now a forty-ounce bottle of vodka sat half-empty in the middle of the kitchen table.

After glancing across the room at the wall clock, she was surprised to see that it was already a quarter after twelve. The evening news was long over, and Miranda knew in her heart that she wouldn't be flipping pancakes for her husband first thing next morning.

"Miranda," Bert barked for the umpteenth time. "The guys wanna know what happened to your face. Why don't you tell them," he leaned back in his chair, just daring his wife to say the wrong thing.

"Just a little accident. Dropped a bowl of hot pudding and it splashed up in my face, is all. Don't worry yourself none, I'll be healed up good as new," she leaned in to exchange the dirty ashtray.

"No scarring?" Pete continued to pry, looking over to Bert for additional answers.

"How the fuck am I gonna tell? Not like I was looking at some beauty queen to begin with." He flicked a lit cigarette in the direction of Olga's hand.

Strike number three. He has begun unleashing his pent-up anger.

Miranda bent down to pick up the smoldering butt, returned to the counter, wiped her hands on the dishtowel, and then decided it was time to make her move. She had to get out. She had to remove herself immediately from the center of the action before Bert lost his cool. She could feel it coming, and unless she took herself out of his swing radius, all hell was gonna break loose.

Three steps up the living room stairs, someone yanked out a handful of her hair.

"Where the fuck are you running to?" Bert hissed into her ear. "Did I say I was done with you? We need more juice, and I think the boys might like some popcorn."

"I… I think we're out of juice," she whispered back, slowly lifting her right hand up to try prying her husband's fingers out of her hair. "I can make some powdered."

"You lazy cunt," he cursed aloud. "You can't even get the shopping done while I'm working my ass off. I thought you'd learned your lesson last time."

One of the guys walked over to the kitchen radio and cranked up the volume, effectively drowning out Bert's threats and eliminating any last minutes prayers Miranda had for a rescue.

You're out! No one is coming to your defense.

"Get your fat ass upstairs, I think it's time I taught you a lesson!" he tightened his grip on his wife's scalp. "How dare you embarrass me on the one night I pick to celebrate," the ranting intensified. "I work like a slave and you spit in my face."

Propelled up the stairs by sheer force, Miranda wondered if tonight was going to be the night. Would he finally beat her so badly that she couldn't explain away her injuries in the emergency room?

Or would he maybe take it one step too far, and actually kill her? Either way, by morning, she realized that she might be free.

"Are you listening to me, or you daydreaming again?" Bert demanded, his breath reeking of alcohol and Pete's cigarettes.

After twisting her head ever so slightly, Miranda took one last chance to reason her way out of the ever-worsening situation. "I was just thinking that if I grabbed a couple hours of sleep, I'd be able to get up and make your friends a wonderful buffet breakfast. You know. Pancakes, omelets, maybe some French toast? You know, Bert, all your favorites. Bet the guys would never forget your hospitality," she attempted to buy her freedom.

He released his grip on her hair, and debated the offer for a couple of seconds before abruptly shoving her forward with all his might. "This ain't no fucking restaurant. Those sons of bitches can eat at their own damn table!"

She scrambled to her feet, and tried to rush up the remaining flight of stairs. Bert smashed his glass against the wall, and took up the chase.

Miranda knew better than to run. Hell, Miranda knew a lot of things. But past decisions had little to do with life at this exact moment, and all the lessons in the world wouldn't bring her any comfort right now.

CHAPTER TWENTY-FIVE

"I've loved you all my life, even before I knew you."

—The Firm, 1993

Steven reread the handwritten message at least ten times before finally setting it down on the edge of his bed. "And that's all she said?"

Claire shrugged her shoulders and then shook her head. "That was it. Nurse Heinz just said she wasn't allowed on University Hospital property, and she'd be waiting for your call to pick you up after you're released Monday morning."

"So, she called you at the unit desk?"

"Well, she didn't specifically call me. I just happened to intercept the call."

Still in shock and totally frustrated by the limited details, Steven picked up the pink message paper one more time. "There's gotta be more to this. What do you think is going on?"

"Well," Claire suddenly perked up, secretly thrilled to be able to share the hospital gossip, "You already know that Dr. Hood quit.

Well, it turns out that Nurse Heinz had just been served with papers for a mandatory retirement herself a day or two before."

"They fired her?"

"Retired her," Claire corrected her patient. "And from what I heard in the nurse's lounge this morning, she wasn't going to take it lying down."

"But Olga said she's not allowed on the property," Steven said, winching as he attempted to adjust his position and relieve some of the pressure on his lower spine. "Why was she tossed from the hospital?"

"That's the interesting part," Claire cooed, reaching behind the patient's head to adjust the pillows bunching up at his neck. "There really was no specific reason. She still had two more weeks of work, and was even on the shift schedule. No one knows exactly what happened down in the parking garage. All I hear is that there was some kind of altercation."

Both Steven and Claire immediately stopped speaking as soon as the new duty nurse marched into the middle of the room.

"Good morning. How are you feeling Mr. Whitters?"

"Fine ma'am," he quickly answered, nervously shooting Claire a look.

"I'm Nurse Brown. I'm now the head duty nurse on the floor. I hear that you're actually one of us. Is that true?"

"Yes ma'am. I'm an orderly."

"Well, your chart says that barring any further complications, you're due for release first thing Monday morning. Do you mind if I take a look at your dressing?"

Shaking his head no, Steven leaned his head back and closed his eyes, conscious of the nurse's hands gently roaming over the fresh bandaging.

"Nice dressing change," the duty nurse said, nodding toward

Claire. "I'd just like to see a little more drainage padding on top of the stitches next time."

"Yes ma'am." Claire nodded in agreement.

After signing off on the student dressing, the senior nurse smiled once more at Steven before turning to leave the room. "Oh, I almost forgot," she dipped her right hand down into the pocket of her smock. "One of the EMTs found this half-full bottle of red powder rolling around in the back of his ambulance. Thinks it might be yours. Is it?"

Steven's eyes sprang open, his heart pounding as he scrambled to come up with the right answer.

"I don't know. Can I see it?" he asked, reaching forward with his left arm.

Nurse Brown handed the patient the spice bottle, watching him carefully as he quickly attempted to gauge whether or not any of the powder had been removed from the container.

"What is it?"

"Uh, my mom's Mexican," Steven scrambled for an explanation. "She's always dropping off samples of new spices for me to try. Something about lower cholesterol or something else," he rambled.

Once she was satisfied with his response, the duty nurse again bid Steven goodbye, and continued with her rounds.

"Is it ground chili peppers? It kind of looks like it," Claire leaned over and grabbed the half-empty bottle.

Steven watched in horror as Claire unscrewed the lid and in one swift motion raised the glass bottle up to her nose for a whiff.

"Oh gross. This isn't chili peppers," she moaned. "Here take a sniff," she stepped forward to pass the bottle under Steven's nose. "Whatever it is, I think it's gone bad. Don't you?"

"I don't know," he nervously plucked the bottle from her fingers. "I'll have to ask my mom. I can let you know," he lied, tightly twisting the lid back down onto the bottle.

"Steven," Claire mused. "If you're still seeing your mom, how come you're staying with Nurse Heinz?"

Back against the wall, he realized his lies were starting to pile up. It wasn't as if he had never bent the truth before; it was just that down the road he might have trouble keeping all the half-truths straight. "My mom and dad live out of town, so she mails the spices to me. I think it's kind of her way of keeping me in touch with my heritage. You know, spicy Mexican food and all?"

"Well, stay in touch," Claire smiled back. "I like to cook. Maybe I could put it to good use one of these weekends when we're both off?"

"Maybe," Steven agreed, not sure if she'd just proposed a date.

"Well, I gotta run. I'll stop by later if I hear anymore, all right?

Steven nodded his head in agreement, and slowly dragged the bottle of healing powder back under his blankets, carefully hiding it from anymore prying eyes.

Dressed in light sandalwood colored Capri pants, a lime green tee shirt, and hot pink flip-flops, Camille Greenwood rushed down the stairs to grab her purse. "I'm leaving," she shouted to anyone who might be listening.

"Cammy," her mother called back. "I need my car by four this afternoon. Were you planning to be back by then?"

She stopped to calculate her travel time, in addition to the two scheduled stops, and Camille was confident that the time restriction wouldn't be much off a problem. "I'll be back," she threw over her shoulder before running down the front steps.

Only three blocks from the family home, a giant toy store loomed in another of the city's mega malls, attempting to beckon buyers with its flashing lights, and revolving signage. After turning into the lot,

Camille cruised past all the reserved *handicap* and *mothers with baby carriage* parking spaces before finally locating a spot in the rear. As she hurried inside, she stopped to accept a flyer and directions from the gaily-dressed clown before rushing off on her mission to locate the perfect stuffed toy.

Four designated rows, fifteen feet high and thirty feet long, were laid out before her. Each row was literally filled to the rafters—hundred of choices bombarding the shoppers' senses. Every color, shape, and size of stuffie was lined up five or six deep. Without a specific idea of what you were looking for, even the best-laid plans could be rendered useless.

"Need some help?" a sixteen-year-old at his first summer job called out from the end of the aisle.

"I was just looking for some Care Bears. You have any in stock?"

"Follow me," the kid answered, taking a quick right and walking up the neighboring aisle. "Collecting or gift?"

"Why?"

"Well, in the showcase at the front of the store, we have a few collector bears from the seventies. Their prices range anywhere from two hundred, to a little over a thousand bucks. We've got a vintage Bedtime Bear, collector condition," he bragged, as if the original packaging was somehow going to justify the price.

"I'm definitely looking for a gift," Camille chuckled, shaking her head at the mere thought of a thousand dollar stuffed toy.

"Then here you go." The kid waved his arms at one of the lower shelves before turning on his heel to answer a page in the puzzle department.

Deciding on a darling little butter-colored Sunshine Bear, Camille paid cash and rushed out of the store. Her appointment at the care facility was at eleven a.m., and she had at least another half-hour drive.

As she juggled a double latte and the two-page map she'd pulled off Google Maps, Camille negotiated the streets and back roads until she found herself parked in front of an impressive stretch of manicured lawn. No barbed wire or telltale security fencing, the only structure marring the scenic beauty was a tasteful two by three foot sign spelling out the words Pleasant View.

Convinced she was on the correct road; Camille pulled into the driveway and began the last leg of her journey. After happily parking her car much closer to the main door than she'd been able to at the toy store, she plucked her sister's present off the seat and began the short walk up the flower-lined sidewalk.

Still seated across from the center's visitor liaison, Camille nervously answered the woman's barrage of questions; correctly repeating the information that she'd originally reported on the telephone.

"We're sure glad to have you join us for a visit here at Pleasant View. Experience has taught us that our patients are much happier and respond well to our counseling programs when they have regular family visits."

"Thank you," Camille smiled back, unable to think of another reply.

"One last question, Miss Greenway. Would you be interested in speaking to a counselor after your first visit? Some of our guests have found it beneficial."

"I have a therapist," she bluntly stated, not the least bit interested in another trained professional attempting to delve into her psyche.

"Well, then there's no point in delaying," the lady clapped her hands. "If you'll follow me, we'll take a quick snapshot for your guest identification badge, and then I'll have someone walk you over to the visitors' building."

Finally seated in what appeared to be a very comfortable waiting room, Camille scanned the faces of the other visitors. A handful of young parents were trying to amuse their children, a couple of teenagers were zoning out to their iPods, and a handful of seniors were attempting to ignore the noise—it was a complete cross section of society.

"Camille Greenway?" a voice called out.

She jumped to her feet, and crossed the floor in three easy strides, instantly caught off-guard when a young girl stepped from around the reception desk and rushed up into her arms.

"Sister," Stacey Greenway squealed, "You my sister."

"Hello," Camille laughed back, returning the hug.

"Why don't you ladies help yourself to some soda and cookies? I'm sure you're going to have a really nice visit. And just a reminder, please say your goodbyes as soon as you hear the five minute bell."

"Yes Johnny," Stacey vigorously nodded her head, obviously thrilled at the mere prospect of being called to the visitors lounge.

"Do you want something to drink?" Camille turned toward snack table.

"Pepsi. I like Pepsi. No Coca Cola, just Pepsi. I like..."

"Pepsi," Camille finished her sister's line of thought. "Alright, we'll get some Pepsi."

After carrying two paper cups of cola, brand name unknown, and two oatmeal cookies, the girls plopped down into opposing chairs.

"So, how are you doing?" Camille asked her younger sister, unsure of what else to say.

"I'm fine. How are... you doing?" Stacey repeated, taking her time to pronounce all the words carefully.

"I'm great. And I almost forgot; I brought you a present."

"I be loving presents."

"Here you go," Camille bent over to untie the gift-bag, a little surprised when her sister responded by hastily shoving the remaining cookie into her mouth.

"Done," Stacey sputtered dry crumbs down the front of her dress. "Present please?"

Camille watched her fourteen-year-old sister delve into the tissue paper with the same enthusiasm as a six-year-old child on Christmas morning.

"Yellow, I know yellow," Stacey shouted.

"It's a Care Bear. It's called Sunshine Bear."

"Sun… Sun… Sun… shine Bear," Stacey repeated, her brain struggling to grasp the three-syllable name.

"Did you know that I had Care Bears too, when I was a young girl?"

"Yes."

Taken aback by her sister's quick response, Camille found herself momentarily speechless.

"Sunshine Bear. I like… Sunshine Bear."

"You sure have pretty hair," Camille reached out to stroke her sister's curls gently, amazed at the bright sheen of her red locks.

"Jimmy is red too."

"Is Jimmy your friend?"

"No, Jimmy my boyfriend," Stacey turned to point to a young boy sitting quietly across the room.

"Is that Jimmy's mother," Camille nodded toward the lady nervously patting his hand.

"No."

"Oh," she turned back to Stacey, still amazed that she was looking straight into the eyes of her baby sister.

"Daddy," Stacey shouted, jumping up from her seat and clumsily rushing toward his outstretched arms.

"Hello, my baby girl," the man called out the second their eyes met.

Camille just sat motionless, not sure how to greet the complete stranger.

CHAPTER TWENTY-SIX

"I'm going to need you more than you need me."

—Love & Other Drugs, 2010

As she lay on her back and listened to Martin's gently snoring, Olga felt strangely comforted by his rhythmic pattern. It had been at least ten years since they'd spent a night together in bed, yet as soon as they'd finished the wine and the last of their grilled cheese sandwiches, the pull had been undeniable.

Not drunk, yet definitely tipsy—not overly excited, but obviously turned on; Martin and Olga walked hand in hand toward her bedroom door.

As they stood silently in the dark, arms wrapped snugly around each other's waist, they both yearned for the comfort that would ultimately come from the familiarity of their lovemaking.

Each was aware that a union of their bodies would no longer bring on the kind of explosion that had fuelled their relationship of the past, yet they were still satisfied with what it could achieve. The basic fulfillment that comes from sharing an evening of intimate caresses and loving touches was suddenly within their reach.

"Snuggle in," Martin extended the invitation, lifting his left arm so Olga would have room to cuddle against his chest. "How long have you been lying there with your eyes open?"

"Not long," she lied, resting her cheek on the graying hair of his chest. "I've just been enjoying your warmth."

"Oh really? You used to call me the human furnace, didn't you?" he teased, squeezing her tightly toward the length of his body.

"Let me go," Olga gently struggled, aware that her motions were once again giving rise to Martin's excitement.

"Now look what you've done."

"It wasn't me," she half-heartedly argued back. "You're the one saluting the flag."

"Come here," Martin abruptly ended the question-and-answer portion of their morning by pulling Olga firmly up onto his stomach.

Two hours later, both showered and padding around the house in fuzzy bathrobes, Olga leaned into her refrigerator and began evaluating the choices. "We've basically slept through breakfast, so how about we skip right to lunch?"

"Whatever you cook is fine with me. You know, come to think of it, I've never tasted anything at your table that I didn't like."

"Thank you," Olga smiled, secretly thrilled to be complimented on a passion so dear to her heart. "Tell me, you still have a taste for spicy food?"

"I'll love it to my grave, but every now and then my bowels remind me that a good old fashioned bowl of mashed potatoes, steamed veggies, and broiled fish, wouldn't be such a bad choice," he winced with a wrinkled nose.

"Well, why don't you grab the Saturday paper off the front steps and I'll make us a little lunch. Maybe surprise you with a new recipe I've been playing with for my cookbook."

"You ever going to finish that? Seems to me you've been working on it for years."

"I will," she nodded her head. "Now get out of my kitchen and go amuse yourself with the funnies."

Martin took the not so subtle hint and vacated Olga's domain. He felt so completely at ease, kicking his feet back and relaxed on the living room sofa.

Back in the kitchen, with ingredients pulled from the pantry and refrigerator alike, Olga set about to first stimulate and then ultimately satisfy Martin's palate. It had been years since she had experienced the simple joy of cooking for a mate, and without realizing it, she found herself humming as she puttered around her kitchen.

Born to a generation accustomed to the division of labor, Olga had been raised to be in charge of her own household. She would have never expected a husband to help with the dishes, to fold the laundry, or to cook the meals. These were the tasks assigned to the *woman of the house*, and it would have been an embarrassment to your family to behave otherwise.

All her life, Olga had embraced this unwritten code—a set of expectations handed down from the Heinz women of generations past. Unfortunately, during this entire education, no one had bothered to inform Olga that the very husband who would make all her sacrifices worthwhile might not turn up.

"Are you still allergic to green chili?" she called out from the kitchen, barely able to see Martin's face behind the paper as she reached deep into the drawer for her can opener.

"Of course I am," he tossed down Olga's copy of the morning news. "Good lord, it's only been ten years. You think I've stopped carrying my Benadryl?"

"Just checking. Sorry to disrupt you."

Smirking as he attempted to delve back into the day's events, Martin found himself casually listening as Olga read off her recipe card.

"Mix fourteen-ounce can of refried beans with one cup of grated cheese, and half a cup of chopped Anaheim peppers. Drop three large tablespoons inside a small corn tortilla and roll tightly into a log-shaped roll. Ends may be tucked in or left open." Breaking once again, Olga turned, this time catching Martin's eye the minute she raised her face.

"Need some help?" he teased.

"No. I was just wondering if I should double the recipe. Exactly how hungry are you?"

"Considering the events of late, surprisingly, my appetite has returned."

"I guess we should talk about it," Olga sighed, generously spraying a baking dish with non-stick spray.

"I not sure what's left to say," he admitted, rising from the couch to join the conversation in the kitchen.

After placing the rolled tortillas in a single layer, completely filling the bottom of her dish, Olga tightly sealed the pan with a layer of foil before popping it in a three hundred and fifty degree oven for at least half an hour. "I don't want to spend my entire retirement, and most of my finances, on a legal battle that I probably won't even win," she admitted in defeat.

"But what if, by some twist of fate, you do win, and the hospital is forced to hire you back? Wouldn't it be worth it to have your career back, to be able to nurse again?"

She carefully measured two cups of instant rice into a glass bowl, and took the opportunity to measure her reply. "I could never be happy working for an institution that was forced to hire me back. You and I both know that it would just be a matter of time before they found some other little technicality to file a dismissal on."

"You could just be really careful. Make sure you dotted your *I's* and crossed your *T's*."

Olga shook her head in frustration, and vigorously chopped up a half a cup of white onion and a half-cup of green pepper before dropping them in a fry pan to sauté lightly in vegetable oil. "Aren't you the very doctor who explained to me that medicine is not an exact science, and many treatments are based on interpretations of the doctor's orders?"

"Yes, in theory. But…"

"But what?" the tone of Olga's voice hardened ever so slightly as she poured one cup of tomato juice and one cup of water into a microwave able bowl. "I'm just a duty nurse, and any minute of any day, a doctor could report that I was not following his orders to the letter. After three reports, I'm sitting back in front of the board. The very board that…"

"That Dick Mansfield chairs," Martin finished Olga's sentence as she turned her back to stir the chopped vegetables in silence.

"Life has taught me that we have to choose our fights. Draining my savings, to win a lawsuit that may prove to be redundant when I'm dismissed on an alternate charge a month later, seems a little stupid. Don't you think?"

As he snuck a pinch of grated cheese, it was Martin's turn to measure his reply. "Would you reconsider the fight if money wasn't an issue?"

"No," she curtly answered, mixing the boiled liquid and sautéed vegetables into the bowl of instant rice before covering it with plastic wrap.

"Then tell me Olga, what exactly are you going to do with your days? I know for a fact that the lofty pursuit of research isn't going to keep you satisfied. You're a *hands-on* type of nurse—you crave patient contact as much as an alcoholic craves the bottle."

"Well then, doctor, maybe it's time we shoved the proverbial microscope up your butt," she snapped back. "Your career in medicine was just as important to you as mine was to me. What in the hell are you going to do with your life now that you can't hide behind your designation? You realize that you no longer have admitting privileges. What are you if not a doctor? So now *you* tell me, Martin, what exactly is going to motivate you to get out of bed tomorrow morning?"

He dropped into a kitchen chair, and sat motionless, unable to formulate the simplest answer, never mind a rebuttal laced with witty repartee.

Mustard had always been one of Gerri's favorite condiments, but as the main ingredient in a white bread sandwich, it left a little to be desired. Still, it filled the aching void, and for that small miracle, she was grateful.

Forcing the last bite down her throat before chasing it back with a glass of tap water, Gerri couldn't help but open her refrigerator door one last time. Still empty, nothing hiding behind the mustard jar or half loaf of bread, she resigned herself to the fact that it was time to go shopping. Unfortunately, she was a little strapped for cash since walking out on her last paying job. She knew it wasn't the time to hang onto her pride when her stomach was growling and she was forced to steal toilet paper from a local restaurant, but she swore she'd never do it again.

After walking over to the basement corner that was designated as her bedroom, Gerri reluctantly slipped out of her high heels. Bending at the waist, she carefully peeled off her fishnet stockings before reaching up to untie the lacings securing the dress at her hip and shoulders.

Gerri stood in the shower, hot water pulsing down the gentle slope of her back. She ignored the pleasurable sensation and reached for the bar soap. Aggressively lathering her washcloth, she began scrubbing every inch of her face. Rinsing and repeating, the sudsy water coursed in rivers down her legs before pooling in the bottom of the shower drain.

Wrapped in a towel, wet hair hanging in knotted strands down the center of her back, she shuffled over to a small collection of cardboard boxes. She cursed under her breath, and flipped open the first lid, immediately disturbed by what she saw. As she reminded herself for the hundredth time—she was totally out of food, toiletries, and options. Gerri closed her eyes, before delving into her past.

Finally dressed, hair pulled back in the simplest of ponytails, she left the basement and trudged down to the corner on ninth where she knew others might already be waiting. Half a block away, Gerri could already count at least five others. Unfortunately, her odds of picking up a little extra cash were dwindling by the minute. She needed to quickly hustle over and take her position before anymore showed up to join the ranks.

As she nodded to a few of the other hopefuls, Gerri took her position leaning against a cinderblock wall, scanning her competition and evaluating her odds.

"I'm looking for one," the guy in a concrete batch truck yelled across the street from his cab window.

In unison, every single man stepped up to the curb, lining up as if preparing for a grade school spelling bee.

The driver scanned the lot, not at all impressed, suddenly opting for a verbal test to help him with his decision. "Anybody know what a trowel is?" he yelled out, scanning their faces for some sign of recognition.

One man sauntered down off the curb to take a closer look at the truck's mixing drum. "I've used a trowel for small jobs, but sometimes a simple two by four over the top of the forms does a better job."

"Get in," the guy nodded toward his empty passenger seat.

After returning to the wall, Gerri fidgeted with the leather work-gloves covering her hands. No chance to remove her nail polish, she had opted for a quick cover up instead.

As the greenhouse flatbed rounded the corner, the groans rising from the sidewalk were audible. This late in the morning, the men were just damn lucky to find work, but the fifty dollars they'd each pocket would be paid for dearly in sweat.

After the foreman divided up the motley crew, Gerri found herself assigned to the strawberry patch. Gratefully accepting a straw hat and water bottle, she chose the first available row and dropped to her knees. Ten feet into the patch, she realized that her gloves were only impeding her work, the bulky leather forcing her to pluck at the same weed two or three time before extracting it from the tangle of young plants.

"I'm Campbell," the man in the next row announced without any provocation.

"Gerald," she answered back, her given name sounding foreign on her own tongue.

"Lose the gloves, man. You're not getting anywhere.

She lifted her head to evaluate her co-worker's statement, and Gerri instantly knew he was right. If she continued at her present pace, she'd be lucky not to get canned. So without a viable option, she ripped them off and unceremoniously stuffed them down into her denim jeans, glancing over to see if Campbell had noticed the deep red polish adorning her nails.

"If we work together up and down the same row," Campbell explained, "then we won't break our backs stretching across the entire patch. You get it?" he demanded, rising to his feet to step over his row in an attempt to join Gerri at hers.

"Sure, I get it," she smiled, lifting her face to slug back a mouthful of water before diving back into the patch.

Afternoon heat continuing to blaze down on their backs, Campbell was the first to rise and unbutton his shirt, yanking the material out of his jeans to flow freely at his sides. "Feel like a fucking ice cube on a griddle."

"Me to," Gerri lamented, swiping her brow with the back of her hand.

"Two?" some kid yelled up the row, stepping off his quad to drop a couple of bagged lunches and fresh bottled water at the edge of the patch.

"Just us two," Campbell yelled back, waving his hand as he rose to retrieve their food.

While squatting under a shade tree, both dove into their paper sacks, barely taking time for a breather between bites.

As she finished up with her apple, Gerri leaned back against the tree trunk and closed her eyes. Her stomach cramped, shocked by the sudden deluge of solid food. Experience had taught her that the cramps would eventually subside—she just needed to sit back and wait them out.

"So what exactly are you?" Campbell blurted out between bites. "I saw you take a piss behind the harrows, yet you got tits like a woman," he pointed to Gerri's sweat soaked shirt.

Too tired to lie, she opted for the obligatory shrug. "I'm saving up for some surgery right now. I'm kinda in the middle of it, if you know what I mean?"

"No," the man chuckled aloud. "But I guess it don't really matter for greenhouse work."

"Not really," Gerri looked down at her tattered nails; disappointed to see that she'd have to cut them all back to the quick.

CHAPTER TWENTY-SEVEN

"You know, how did I know that this man was a gift I couldn't keep—my one chance of happiness?"

—Moonstruck, 1987

After filling a small bowl with sour cream, and another with salsa, Olga continued to set the table. With the bean burritos almost baked, she grated another quarter cup of cheese for garnish on top of the Spanish rice. "Martin, lunch is ready," her voice rang out through the house, unsure exactly where he was hiding.

"I'm here," he flatly replied, carefully adjusting his tiepin before taking a chair on the far side of the table.

Olga stopped dead in her tracks, and forgot what she was doing, immediately thrown off guard by the attire of her lunch companion.

Fully dressed in his shirt and tie, Martin sat patiently as if waiting to be served the first course in a four star restaurant.

"You're dressed," Olga muttered, suddenly feeling out of place in her bathrobe and slippers.

"Well, I have to take care of some business this afternoon, so I'll take my leave of you as soon as we've finished."

"You'll take your leave of me?" She repeated, the phrase instantly conveying the change in Martin's attitude. "What's the matter?" Olga pulled up a chair at his side.

"Last night was wonderful," he admitted, the fight to contain his emotions becoming more and more evident. "It was very special, but we must recognize it for what it was, not imagine it to be more than it could be."

As she refolded the napkin she'd previously set, Olga fought to control her own tears. "Then why don't you tell me what it was? Tell me exactly what last night meant so I don't imagine differently."

Martin picked up Olga's hands, and lovingly caressed her fingers. "It was a walk down memory lane. You know it, and so do I. Our lives are in the midst of a giant upheaval. We can't fool ourselves into thinking that it's the appropriate time to start a relationship."

"Martin, when will it be the appropriate time? Your wife Mary has been dead for ten years, and we no longer have to worry about improprieties at work. I just can't figure you out," she shook her head, pulling her fingers from Martin's grasp. "Yesterday you proposed marriage, today you dismissed our lovemaking as some kind of drunken reunion. What's going through your head?"

"I'm not sure," he admitted, exhausted by the mere weight of the conversation. "I'm heading home," he suddenly rose from the chair. "I need to think, to make a few decision about my next step. The last twenty-four hours has been hell, and I think I need a chance to regroup. Hell, I think I deserve a chance!"

As she watched Martin storm out her house, Olga knew in her heart that he'd never grace her doorstep again—not that he wouldn't be allowed, not that he wouldn't want to… just that he simply wouldn't.

Once again alone in her home, Olga set about cleaning up the lunch that had never been, somehow content in her loss. The threat of happiness had almost been worse than the reality of a life shrouded in solitude. Experience had taught Olga that dashed hopes were far more painful than no hope at all. She would now concentrate all her time and energy on developing the healing powder—leaving love and all its chaos to the young.

Besides, Steven would be returning home Monday morning, and she needed to prepare for his recovery. They were about to become a team.

Driving home without a map hadn't been as difficult as Camille would have imagined, since her papers had slipped out of her reach between the passenger's seat and door on her second turn. With the radio silent, she replayed the administrator's words over and over in her brain. *Possible adoption under evaluation, suitable parental figures finally located.* How in the world could her mom and dad just sign over custody of her little sister Stacey to some strangers?

One infant in every eight-hundred to one-thousand births is born with Down syndrome. Was it something her mother did, maybe something she ingested? Why were three of four children born normal? What had gone wrong during Stacey's pregnancy? What made her different? Was some kind of mutant gene going to pop up when Camille was ready to start a family of her own?

"My baby," she muttered aloud, her mind whirling as she began calculating the mathematical odds. As it stood, it looked like she had a twenty-five percent chance of giving birth to a Down syndrome baby. Now, after having already terminated one pregnancy, did she kill a viable fetus, or a defective one? Maybe the rape had been a blessing in disguise, helping her clean the slate of some bad blood?

"But, maybe not," Camille's mind continued to reason. What if the baby had been all right and she had killed it anyway? Then she'd still have the bad genes floating around in her system, the defective egg just waiting to make an entrance.

Without noticing, Camille's foot responded to her frustration by bearing down on the gas pedal, slowly inching her speedometer up and over the legal speed limit.

Would she be able to raise a handicapped child or would she just stick it in a home like her parents did? Maybe it was in the best interest of everyone involved, but she couldn't be sure. It was almost impossible to compare *what was* with *what might have been*, she reasoned, racing down the divided highway.

As she dug for the cell phone ringing in her purse, Camille pulled her foot off the gas and eased the car onto the shoulder. She had learned a hard lesson where motor vehicles were concerned, and she wasn't planning to take any calls while zooming down the road.

"Hello," she answered, surprised to hear her mother's voice on the other end of the line.

"Camille, are you alright, dear?"

"Yeah, what's the matter, Mom?"

"Nothing dear, I just thought I'd call."

After sitting silently on the line, Camille waited for a further explanation, knowing that her mother did not call just to see how she was.

"Well, to be honest, Cammy, I just had a call from… from the…"

"From the administrator of Pleasant View," she finished her mother's sentence.

"Why did you go there? And how did you know where to call for an appointment?"

Camille carefully debated her reply while she listened to her mother take repeated drags off her cigarette.

"I don't think the question is why *I* went to Pleasant View. I think the question is... why don't *you*? Did you know that Stacey is up for adoption, and there's some other family thinking of taking her home?"

"Cammy, this isn't something I want to get into on the telephone. When are you coming home?"

"I don't know," she honestly admitted.

"Well, I guess I don't really need my car, but why don't you come straight home anyway. We'll mix up some homemade burgers, and when your dad gets home, he can grill them. How does that sound?"

"What in the hell are you talking about? I need some answers, and all you're worried about is a family barbeque? You're fucked!"

"Camille Greenway. That language is absolutely unnecessary!"

"No, I think talking to you is what's unnecessary," she barked, clicking off her phone and dropping it back down into her purse.

Her mother wasn't going to be of any help, so she'd be forced to go straight to her father. He had the answers; she could feel it.

Without bothering to call ahead, Camille drove straight to her dad's country club, exactly where she knew he'd be golfing on a Saturday afternoon.

As she wandered around the clubhouse, she scanned the faces of each diner, not only looking for her father, but any of his usual partners.

"May I help you miss?" the club hostess finally caught her on the way up to the club lounge. "You seem to be looking for someone."

"My father, Ed Greenway. He's a member. I think I have my card," Camille reached for her purse.

"That's not necessary," the hostess smiled, and guided her directly over to her father's table, nestled in the rear of the smoker's lounge.

"Is there a problem?" Ed Greenway jumped to his feet the minute he spotted his daughter crossing the floor.

"Dad, I need to talk. Is that okay?"

"Sure," he turned back to address his golfing buddies. "Gentlemen, can you please excuse me for awhile. I'll try and catch up with you later on the links."

After walking out of the clubhouse, Ed found himself steering his daughter towards the golf carts. "Interested in taking a ride?"

Camille just nodded, climbing in beside her father as he inserted his club card to release the steering mechanism.

Settled beside the tree line north of the first sandpit, Ed shut off the cart and stretched his neck to look down the fairway of the fourth hole. "Did you hear that the club is thinking of building yet another nine holes? I don't know how they can afford all the prime real estate. Guess they're having a better quarter than I am," he chided his daughter.

"I went to see Stacey at Pleasant View."

"Why?"

"Why does everybody keep asking me that?" Camille turned the interrogation back on her father. "She's my sister. Why wouldn't I want to see her?"

Ed slid off the seat, and wandered around to the front of the cart to collect his thoughts. "I suppose you want some answers, don't you?"

"Dad, I have so many questions, I don't even know where to start."

"How about I tell you what life was like for your mother and me, fifteen years ago."

"I'm listening," she encouraged him, stepping away from the cart, and moving toward the afternoon shade.

"Well, after you and your brothers were born, your mother and I considered ourselves especially blessed. So when your Aunty Jane approached your mother to be a birth surrogate, we thought it might be the least we could do."

"Stacey's not my real sister?

"Well, she is family. See, your Aunty Jane had a cervical incompetence and couldn't carry to term, so your mother's uterus was implanted with one of your aunt's eggs after it had been fertilized by your Uncle Roland's sperm."

"Oh, now I see. But they were still married at the time, right?"

"Yes, of course they were married. And looking back, that's when their marriage really started to crumble. After your mom's second trimester, her pediatrician suggested an amniocentesis to check on the baby's development. He said we had nothing to be worried about—it was just a routine test he recommended for all women in your mother's age bracket," Ed suddenly stalled. "Do you mind if I smoke?" he dug deep into his pants pocket.

"Whatever," Camille shook her head as her father quickly lit up a cigarette. "Why don't you and mom just sit down and let each other know you both smoke. These little games are getting kinda dumb."

Taking his second drag, Ed laughed aloud. "We're sort of a family built on secrets, aren't we?"

"So keep going, Dad. What happened after the amniocentesis?"

"The doctor called both couples in and explained that the baby carried an extra chromosome-21, and would be born with Down syndrome."

"What did you do?"

"Nothing at first, we just all went home and tried to digest the news. But as the weeks passed, the trouble started to brew. First, there was what I call *The Blame Game.* Jane told Roland that he drank too much, so his sperm was defective. Roland countered back that it had to be Jane's egg, obviously coming from a reproductive system that was all screwed up to begin with. Then when they got tired of fighting with each other, they turned their attention on your mother. It just about killed her when they began blaming her for the baby's abnormality."

"That's when she shut down, wasn't it? When she stopped being our mom?"

"Yes it was," Ed ground his cigarette butt into the grass. "Your mom seemed unable to rise above the accusations. She couldn't get past the fact that her age might have contributed to the baby's condition. Nobody could reason with her, not the specialist, or the psychiatrist. She was inconsolable."

"So then whose fault was it?"

"Down syndrome doesn't work that way. It doesn't point a specific finger at a single cause. Sometimes it just happens, kind of a numbers game if you know what I mean."

"So when did Aunty Jane and Uncle Roland get divorced?"

"They separated when your mom was six months pregnant, and by the time Stacey was born, their relationship had deteriorated to the stage where they only spoke through lawyers."

Watching her father light yet another cigarette, Camille tried to process all the information. "So by the time Stacey was born, there was no family to take her in, was there?"

"No, not really. And your mother's psychiatrist repeatedly warned me that bringing a handicapped newborn into our house may only jeopardize her recovery from the mental breakdown."

"So that's when she had her breakdown?" Camille fought to organize the timeline in her head.

"By the time Stacey was born, your mother had already endured more heartache than she could handle."

"Well, I still don't get it, Dad. Who exactly are Stacey's parents?"

"That's another one of the problems. Since Jane and you mother were sisters, we never bothered to draw up the necessary legal documents surrounding her birth. After Stacey was born, when no one stepped forward to claim the baby, the hospital declared your mother as the birth parent, and the documents still stand to this day."

"Well, Pleasant View looks like a really nice place from what I saw," Camille gently rubbed her dad's shoulder.

"We picked the best care facility we could find, and we've been financially supporting her ever since."

"But the adoption, what's that all about?"

"Stacey's always been on a waiting list since she was admitted fourteen years ago. I guess they've finally found a suitable home. We should be happy for her."

Camille smiled and nodded her head, not the least bit comforted by the thought.

CHAPTER TWENTY-EIGHT

"Some people, you squeeze them, they focus. Others fold."

—The Devil's Advocate, 1997

Bert tapped his foot while waiting for the kettle to boil, finally noticing the first wisps of steam curling up from the spout. After carefully filling the china teapot with water, he set it back down on the tray beside the cup and honey pot. He grasped both handles, and began negotiating the bedroom stairs, mindful not to trip and send the entire tray crashing through the air.

"Still sleeping?" he whispered toward Miranda, her form motionless under the layers of the blankets.

No response. The exact same silence he'd been greeted with for the past twenty-four hours still hung heavily in the air. After setting the tray down on her nightstand, he leaned in closer toward his wife.

"Miranda, are you awake?" he gently shook her shoulder, reaching across the rumpled bedding to turn her face. "Good, I see you're up." He forced a small smile, noticing that her eyes were wide open, darting back and forth across the entire bedroom. "How do you feel?"

No reply.

"I made you some fresh tea," he explained, turning to pour a cup. "You haven't eaten anything since you took that spill down the stairs, so I thought if you drank some with a little honey…"

Miranda just continued to stare up at her husband's face, an errant tear escaping from the far corner of her right eye.

"Jesus Christ, Miranda, you're starting to scare me," Bert cursed aloud, turning to drag over a wooden chair from the bedroom dressing table. "You won't talk, you won't eat. I just don't know why you're ignoring me so?"

Eyes fluttering, Miranda lay absolutely motionless, the sporadic movements of her eyelids were the only testament to any sign of life.

"You know I'm sorry," he mumbled, staring down at his hands lying uselessly in his lap. "I was thinking of calling someone, maybe 911. But then I thought it'd be best to give you a good night's rest before I made any decisions. So now that you're awake, I guess I don't need no ambulance," he reasoned, as if debating paper versus plastic at the grocery store.

"Sure wish you'd eat something, though. How about if I help ya?" he offered, shrugging his shoulders as he rose from the chair and leaned over the bed. Timidly slipping his left hand under his wife's neck, Bert attempted to help her sit.

"Miranda, for Christ's sake, you gotta help me woman," he shouted down into her face as her head flopped sideways across the palm of his hand.

Her breathing was suddenly labored, possibly due to the bend in her windpipe, Miranda began to wheeze. Struggling to suck in enough oxygen, unable to satisfy her lungs, her consciousness began fading. With her eyes rolling back into the recesses of her head, Bert figured it was best to set her down.

"I'm sorry, I'm so sorry," her husband continued to chant; quickly laying his wife's head back down on the pillow.

As her breathing resumed to a somewhat normal level, Bert quickly stood up and straightened his back. "Guess you're not that hungry after all," he reasoned. "Do you wanna sleep a little longer, may have another nap first?"

Miranda's eyelids fluttered then stayed closed, tears now running in tiny rivers down both sides of her face.

Bert picked up the untouched tray, turned, and left the bedroom. His guts were churning and his head was pounding. Maybe he should lie down too, and when he woke up, they'd both be feeling a little better.

With his head nestled between his wife's fancy sofa cushions, Bert closed his own eyes and tried to relax. Ten minutes and three positions later, he still couldn't get comfortable on the sofa. Every time he closed his eyes, he saw his wife tumbling down the stairs like a sack of potatoes. Head over heels, she just rolled. Eventually landing with a thump at the bottom of the stairs, he rushed over, positive that she was probably dead. But when he reached her body, splayed out on the living room rug, there wasn't even a single drop of blood. Nothing. No broken bones, no bloody nose. It didn't even look like she'd been hurt.

His drinking buddies had taken one look at Miranda's crumpled form at the bottom of the stairs and bolted, running as if they'd seen a ghost on Halloween night.

Too drunk to know that he was too drunk to help, Bert had decided to take matters into his own hands. Only coherent enough to check if she was breathing, he figured that was enough of a positive sign to confirm that she'd be all right. So after deciding to clean up *the mess,* which at this point included his wife's unconscious body, Bert roughly hoisted Miranda up onto his shoulders and turned back toward the stairs.

He stumbled under her weight and his unsteady footing, but he finally made it to the bedroom door. Three more labored steps across the carpet, and he collapsed onto the bed in a heap, his body landing squarely on top of his wife's as his brain instantly joined hers in a foggy state of unconsciousness.

Hours later when he awoke, Bert found himself lying next to his wife, his bladder screaming for release, the heartburn rising up through his throat. "Miranda, get me some milk," he'd barked, rising to his feet to drop his pants and shed his work shirt before stumbling off toward the bathroom.

When he re-emerged from the hall, Bert plopped back down onto the edge of the bed, initially surprised to see that his wife hadn't moved an inch. With her arms and legs still sprawled out in the same position that she'd slept all night, his wife had obviously been too lazy to even sit up and fetch him a glass of milk.

"Miranda! Miranda!" he called out, his anger continuing to rise. "What the hell's the matter with you? I'm speaking to ya, woman!"

But there was no response; physical or verbal.

He rose to open the bedroom drapes, and flung his head sideways the minute the sunshine hit his face. With a sigh, he rubbed the sleep from the corners of his eyes, simultaneously turning back to check on his wife, already formulating a plan for his apology.

Suddenly frozen in mid-step, the daylight image of her lying with eyes wide open and mouth slightly agape, was unsettling, to say the least.

Bert fought the urge to turn and run, and instead forced himself to move in for a closer look. "Honey, are you awake?" he whispered, waving his hand in front of her face.

Once again, no response.

Dropping his head to her chest, he was somewhat relieved by the sound of her shallow breathing. Still, without any movement or verbal reply, he wasn't sure what to do. After deciding to make his wife as comfortable as possible, Bert had straightened out her twisted body, and then reached down to the foot of the bed and pulled up the covers. "You better sleep some more," he'd ordered his wife, unwilling to spend another second looking down into her eyes. "I'm going to clean up downstairs," and without another word, he'd disappeared to the main floor—convinced that he'd already done everything he could to make his wife comfortable.

"You have to use these," Doris gently pushed the box of sanitary napkins into the young girl's hands. "You're menstruating all over your clothes, and I'm afraid you're going to get an opportunistic infection."

The girl shook her head, and nervously scanned the shelter's floor for a recognizable face, anyone who might assist her in an interpretation.

"Cree?" Doris asked, at least trying to establish the girl's heritage.

After rewarding her patience with a vigorous nod, the girl finally smiled.

With half an hour of futile attempts, Doris had finally uttered only that single word that had been understood. "Now who in the hell speaks Cree?" she muttered aloud, awarded a second time with another smile.

Finally locating an elder, Doris managed to make the man understand that she needed a female interpreter to help with a young girl's female problems, or the girl's *moon*, as the elder politely corrected her.

Sequestered back in her office, the three women all sat together in a circle, and the two Cree women both looked at Doris to lead the discussion. "Well," she nervously smiled at the reluctant volunteer. "I need you to tell this girl that when she has her period, or moon, or whatever it's called, that she must either wear sanitary pads, or insert a tampon," Doris made her point by lifting both boxes.

As she listened to the woman translate the message into the young girl's native tongue, Doris watched the girl's expression change from bewilderment to that of total embarrassment.

"She said to tell you that she knows how to keep clean, but she had no money to go to the Laundromat, and nowhere else to wash her rags."

"Tell her these are better than rags," Doris ripped open the napkin box and pulled out a pad. "See," she peeled the paper off the adhesive strip. "They stick to your underwear, and then you toss them in the garbage," she reached for a roll of toilet paper from her windowsill and wrapped the pad before dropping it in her trashcan. "Can you make her understand all that?"

"Yes," the interpreter smiled. "And… and can I have the tampons?" she pointed to the brand new box.

"Go ahead, help yourself. And tell…" she waited, still unsure of the girl's first name.

"Her name's Corinne."

"Tell Corinne to come see me when she needs another box."

Huddled together deep in conversation, Doris left both women alone in her office, gently closing her door before taking off to make a round on the shelter's main floor.

With her first stop at the kitchen, she refilled her travel mug, taking a second to sit on a stool and enjoy a few stolen minutes of volunteer gossip.

"From what I hear, it's some kind of epidemic. Seems like

everyone's just following suit. You never know who's going to be next."

"Well, I heard different," one of the men interrupted the little coffee clutch. "I heard that they aren't quitting, they're actually being forced to retire. Some kind of mandatory program, or something just like it, for all the older staff."

"How'd you hear that?" a woman immediately challenged his information.

"My sister Ruth works in housekeeping down at the University, and she gets all her news firsthand. This ain't gossip," he raised his fingers and wagged them at the other women. "This is the God's awful truth!"

Interest piqued, Doris jumped right in. "Tell me what I've missed. What's this about the cleaning staff being forced out of work?"

"Not the cleaning staff—the doctors and nurses," she was immediately corrected.

Doris jumped off her seat, bolted out of the kitchen, and raced back to her freshly vacated office. She needed to call Olga right now, to find out exactly what was going on. Was she one of the nurses with her head on the block? Is that why she'd been called in for a private meeting with the *big boss?* Doris had a sinking feeling in the pit of her stomach that the answers weren't going to be good.

After flipping the old plastic Rolodex open, Doris spun the dial to find Olga's card and immediately punched in the number. Three rings later, the phone was answered.

"Hello."

"Hello Olga, its Doris calling. How are you doing, honey?"

She hesitated for a long time, and finally answered the question. "I've had a lot of turmoil in my life lately, and right now, I'm just sitting back and trying to evaluate my options." she softly shared her anguish.

"Nice speech. Take you long to write it?

"You need something specific?" Olga retorted back. "Or you just called to hassle me?"

"How about grabbing a bite tonight?"

"Sure, that would be nice. And for the record, it wasn't a prepared speech. It was all off the cuff."

"I'll see you down at the shelter by seven," Doris confirmed, hanging up the phone just as someone rapped on her office door.

"Sorry to interrupt," one of the volunteers called out, but I've got a lady down here in pretty dire need of medical attention, and she said the hospital already told her to take a hike."

Doris grabbed the wall mounted first aid kit, and ran out in hot pursuit. "Where is she?" the head counselor demanded, eyes scanning the floor for any signs of a disturbance.

Crouched near the far kitchen wall, Doris spotted the woman who was fighting off anyone who tried to help her.

After rushing up to her side, Doris immediately demanded that everyone gathered step back, reminding them that she was there, and it was all under control. This usually helped to establish two things. First off, it gave her an instant sense of authority, and secondly, the person in distress began to trust that she actually might be able to help them.

"I'm really sick and it hurts so fucking bad," the girl hissed through clenched teeth. "I don't know what to do. Can you make it stop?"

"What's your name sweetie?" Doris asked, instantly popping a thermometer into the young woman's mouth while she felt her forehead for any sign of a fever.

"Ruby."

"Tell me, Ruby, you using anything?"

"Not regular," she winced as Doris plucked the thermometer out of her mouth.

"Well, it reads a hundred and two. You're running a temperature, and I'm guessing it's because you have some kind of infection. Do you have any wounds, like a cut or a really bad scratch? Any track marks that are bleeding or draining pus?"

Ruby shook her head, but motioned for Doris to lean in closer. "I've got a little something stuck, and I think it's making me sick."

Looking around the room for another volunteer, Doris quickly motioned for help in moving Ruby toward the cot in the back storage room. She needed to make the girl as comfortable as possible before she continued with her assessment. "How do you feel now?" she asked as soon as Ruby had collapsed onto the makeshift bed.

"It still hurts," the woman whined, rolling on her side to pull her knees up toward her chest.

"Everyone, clear out," Doris ordered the onlookers. She checked her watch and realized it would be at least another thirty minutes before Olga stopped by the shelter. Without any hope of immediate reinforcements, she still decided to push ahead on her own. "You've been at the hospital, Ruby? Did a doctor check you out?"

"No doctor, just a nurse," she moaned, the sweat beginning to bead across her forehead.

Reaching across the cot, Doris pushed the damp bangs out of the girl's eyes. "What'd the nurse say?"

"She didn't say much… she…" Ruby stopped speaking, the breath catching in the back of her throat. "She asked me if I was positive, and I when I told her the… the truth," she took two shallow breaths. "She told me to go sit down; they'd get to me when they could… after they'd helped everyone else first."

Doris had heard this story before. Thankfully, it wasn't that common, but she also knew in her heart it was absolutely true. Some hospital personnel considered street people like Ruby a total waste of their time and supplies. It wasn't that they turned them away, it was just that they were attended to absolutely last.

"I waited for eight hours, and nobody called me. Then they told me it wasn't a hotel," she began to whimper into the water stained pillow. "They told me to get up off the chairs and sit up regular. But it hurts to sit up," she sobbed, totally giving in to the pain.

Doris tucked the blankets in around Ruby's shoulders, and then stood up and excused herself. She needed to make a few calls before the shift change, and one of them was going to be to the County Hospital.

"I'm here," Olga popped her head in Doris's office. "You just about ready to leave?"

"Well, yes and no. See, I'm ready, but I've got a *drop-in* who isn't." Doris nodded her head toward the wall closet with the larger trauma kit still locked inside.

"So, what do we know?" Olga asked, now toting the heavy leather bag as she followed the counselor across the main floor.

"She's a prostitute, a user, but not habitual, from what I gather. She's HIV positive, and she's running a pretty good fever."

"Regular?"

"Never seen her before. I'd peg her between eighteen and twenty-one, but you and I both know how hard it is to tell."

Nodding her head, Olga watched Doris ask the volunteer holding Ruby's hand if she could please give them a little privacy.

"Hi, my name is Olga. I'm a nurse, and I was wondering if you'd like me to check you over."

Ruby just nodded; her eyes watery from the freshly spilled tears.

After lifting up the girl's tank top, Olga began gently pressing her lower abdomen, checking for signs of appendicitis, or possible swelling from internal bleeding. "Were you in any kind of car accident, or maybe a fight?"

Ruby shook her head, as she wiped her eyes with the back of her hands. "This guy, he paid me fifty bucks, and I didn't even have to fuck him. It was kinda weird, but he said he'd done it before and it'd be alright."

As Olga snapped on her rubber gloves, Doris stood up to lock the storage room door.

"I tried for two days, but I don't think it's all out, cuz I'm getting sicker and it's really starting to burn, especially when I take a… a…" Ruby began to wretch; the dry heaves wracking her body.

Pulling the stethoscope out of the trauma kit, Olga began checking her vitals. "What's your name dear?"

"Ruby… well actually, it's Lurlynne," she admitted. "Are you going to fix me?"

"I'm not a doctor," Olga stressed, "and I really think you should be at a hospital."

The young woman turned her face away and began sobbing uncontrollably—feelings of worthlessness and rejection flooding over her for the second time that day.

"But," Olga continued, "I am going to try. So you'll have to be honest and tell me everything."

"He was here for a convention, some kind of big party for guys in politics," Ruby stopped to blow her nose. "Said he always wanted to *play Clinton*, you know like the old president?"

"I know," Olga's stomach turned, starting to get a gist of what might have happened.

"But it was really late and he couldn't find anywhere to buy a cigar. Well, I told him that time was money, and if he kept driving round, I was gonna have to charge him anyway," Ruby winced, shifting her hips to try to find a less painful position. "So finally, he bought a pack Panatela cigars, and we gave them a try. But they were really skinny, and kept breaking off. I thought I counted all the pieces, but I guess I was wrong," she shrugged, as if inserting rolled cigars in one's vagina was common practice.

Catching Doris's eye, Olga shook her head; always surprised at the level of depravity these women would endure to survive on the streets. "Sounds like septic shock to me, but without proper blood tests, a diagnosis is a bit of a gamble."

"So what would the hospital do for her?" Doris demanded, fully aware that their treatment of Ruby would probably be the only medical attention she'd have the strength to seek.

"They'd probably perform some type of fluid evacuation to flush out her vagina, removing any lingering debris, and then shoot her up with high a dosage of antibiotics to fight the infection. Twenty-four hours of observation, and should her temperature drop, they might release her with a stiff warning not to insert foreign objects."

"We can do that," Doris smiled, turning to pick up Ruby's hand. "You're going to be fine dear. We're going to take care of you."

"Doris, can I see you for a second, please?"

As they stepped out of earshot, Doris braced herself for the fallout.

"What do you think you're doing? Look around here," Olga hissed under her breath. "This isn't a medical clinic, and I'm not a doctor."

"No, but you're a nurse," she argued back. "And we've got the supplies."

"Supplies?" she argued back, her voice now drawing even Ruby's attention. "Is this your idea of supplies?" her voice peaked while she ripped open the worn leather duffle bag. "This is only a collection of bits and pieces that were left behind over the years. This isn't a medical kit. It's a lost and found box!"

"Well then," Doris clapped her hands together. "Let's wrap her up and drop her off at an emergency room. I'm sure that after admitting takes her history, they'll immediately push our little girl to the front of the line. I know she won't suffer another agonizing ten or twelve hours waiting for treatment. Don't you agree?"

While she adjusted the latex gloves where they bunched up

around her wrists, Olga quickly evaluated Ruby's medical condition. Her skin was red and flushed, and she was already beginning to alternate between fevers and chills. She'd also developed a rapid heartbeat in conjunction with her shallow breathing. If she was left untreated, Ruby's skin would change, becoming cool and clammy, all followed by a drop in her blood pressure and severe thirst. Eventually, this same shortness of breath would lead to respiratory failure. The prognosis was extremely poor, and the eventuality of it all would probably play out within the next two to three hours.

"Alright, I'll do what I can, but we're still going to need some antibiotics."

"I can handle that," Doris nodded with confidence.

"I'll take whatever you can find, but if you've got connections, I'd prefer either Streptomycin or Erythromycin."

"Anything else, doctor?"

"Yes," she barked, "Don't call me doctor."

CHAPTER TWENTY-NINE

*"I know you cannot live on hope alone,
but without it, life is not worth living."*

—Milk, 2008

Olga had tried to explain the procedure to Ruby, but she wasn't the least bit interested in hearing any of the details. She was putting all her trust in Olga's hands, and *hearing* that it was going to be messy or painful wasn't going to make it the slightest bit easier.

Another hour had lapsed since Olga's initial diagnosis, and as predicted, Ruby's condition had worsened. Without wanting to wait a second longer than necessary, Olga had ripped open the paper sack Doris had returned with, and quickly pulled out the vial of Streptomycin. After administering Ruby's first shot, she made a mental note of the time and continued with the planned procedure.

Ruby had already been stripped naked, and was lying on the foldaway cot, the thin foam mattress wrapped with black garbage bags and a double layer of clean sheets.

"Now, honey," Olga explained, I'm going to insert this speculum into your vagina. It's going to feel extremely cold even though it's made of plastic, but it shouldn't hurt."

Ruby turned her face away, feeling a sharp stab in her lower abdomen, almost as if someone had shoved a frozen Popsicle up inside her.

"The infection has already spread outward to her vulva," Olga reported, shaking her head as she continued to inspect the damage. "I'm now going to flush your vaginal cavity with this lukewarm douche and try to remove all of the loose tobacco, and any leftover pieces of plastic wrap."

Doris nodded while Ruby continued to shiver.

After repeating the procedure, until she was satisfied that the girl's vagina was now free of any foreign debris, Olga began cleaning up her patient. "You did great," she praised the young woman, carefully coating her vaginal lips with antibiotic cream. "Why don't you close your eyes and try to sleep. We're all done, and when you wake up, you're going to feel a little bit better."

Doris tucked the blankets securely around Ruby's shoulders and then down at her toes. She walked over to where Olga was dismantling her impromptu treatment center, and said, "So what'd you find?"

Without speaking, Olga handed her the white plastic bucket. "I wonder if little Miss Lewinsky had this same kind of problem?"

"You probably saved Ruby's life. You realize that?"

"Yes I do," Olga smiled at her friend, "that's why I'm really going to miss my nursing."

"So it's true, you don't work there anymore?"

While she stripped the rubber gloves off her hands, Olga dropped down onto a pile of boxes. "I could probably find another job; it's just that the University was kind of my life."

"You could work here? I'd pay you… ten times what I make," Doris teased.

"Ten times zero… is still zero."

"I know, but it sounds really good."

"I'm thinking of taking on a research project, something I can really sink my teeth into."

Doris peeled off her own gloves, and joined Olga on the boxed files. "A woman like you is meant to help people, not juggle test tubes. Look what you did today?"

"How much did I really help Ruby, or Lurlynne, or whatever her name is? Did you see all the bite marks on her inner thighs, the bruising in her pubic area? I wonder if I just patched that young woman up so she can go back out on the streets and get herself killed," Olga debated aloud. "Do you think I really helped her, Doris? Because right now, I don't feel like I've done this woman any great favors?"

"Every volunteer who has ever crossed the shelter's threshold has asked me that exact same question at least once. And you wanna know what my stock reply is?"

"What?"

"I don't know if you've helped or not. But how could you sleep if you didn't try?"

"That's definitely a stock reply," Olga teased. "And by the way, where exactly did those antibiotics come from? I didn't see a name on the vial, the tube, or the bag."

"You're not the only miracle worker in this room. But you're paying for the pizza, cuz I'm totally out of cash."

After she wearily climbed off the flatbed truck, Gerri was surprised to see she wasn't standing alone.

"Feel like grabbing a beer?" Campbell offered. "Decent pub 'round the block."

"I don't think so."

"Taste good after sweating all day."

How could she explain that she was just dying to get home and change out of her clothes, to strip off the memories of a forgotten life, and move back into the clothes of her future? "I'm worn out. I don't know if I have the strength to lift a bottle."

"Come on," Campbell threw his arm around Gerri's shoulder, spinning the two of them around as he attempted to propel them both towards the pub.

"I said no!"

"Sorry! No need to get so touchy. Just had a few bucks in my pocket and thought I might like to buy my new friend a beer."

After taking a deep breath, Gerri evaluated her position. "I don't really have cash to blow on booze right now."

"I know, that's why I said I'm buying," Campbell roughly slapped her on the back. "Come on. We'll share a quick pitcher, and then we'll both get going."

"One beer," she conceded.

Three pitchers later, the conversation had made its way around to sex.

"So… when you get up in the morning, you shave your legs or your face?"

"Both," she howled, "but I gotta give you credit. Nobody's ever asked me quite like that before?"

"You're a funny guy, Gerald. I like shooting the shit with ya."

"Well, since I'm drinking your beer and all, I think I should tell you that I'd be happier if you call me Gerri."

"Gerry, Gerald, what's the difference?"

"Well, it's Gerri with an I. But since we're probably not going to have any spelling tests tonight, I guess it doesn't really matter."

Digging in his pocket to pull out cash for another pitcher, Campbell stopped midway through the action. "You know, we'd have twice the money for beer if we just bought it at a liquor store and drank 'em somewhere else."

"Good point," Gerri laughed. "But first I gotta hit the can. Sit tight and I'll be right back," she promised, sliding off the wooden barstool and wobbling off toward the men's washroom.

Without turning his body, Campbell slowly reached down, gently caressing the warmth still emanating from Gerri's stool.

Even after all the years of working as an orderly, Steven had never realized just how loud a hospital ward could be. Rest may have been the company motto, but the reality of the situation was much different. If it wasn't the staff's voices, it was the equipment. Nothing seemed to move without beeping, rattling, or humming. He would have a better chance of grabbing a catnap downstairs in one of the waiting rooms.

"How are you feeling Steven?" Nurse Brown inquired as she stepped up to his bed. "It's nearly time for me to clock out, but I thought I'd just stop by and say goodnight."

"Goodnight," he answered back.

"First off, why don't we have a little peek at your incision? See if I need to change any of the dressings after I remove your tubes."

Steven watched the nurse pull back his bed covers. He lifted his neck, and strained to get a glimpse of the damage to his chest.

"I'm just going to lift off this bandage," she slowly explained, "and take a little peek underneath."

"How does it look, is it healing well?"

The nurse stepped away from the bed and into his private washroom, reappearing a minute later brandishing a hand mirror.

"I can tell you're dying to see, so how about taking a look for yourself."

Accepting the mirror, Steven reached down toward his stomach and tilted the glass upwards, instantly reflecting his two small wounds.

"You had three exterior stitches to close each puncture, complete with an attached drainage tube."

"Thought they'd be bigger," he admitted, suddenly feeling a little foolish for all the care and attention.

"One was extremely deep. According to your chart, it just missed many important organs."

Steven set the mirror down on his bedside table, and watched as the nurse expertly pulled out both tubes and discarded the attached bags. Once completed, she stepped out of the way just as a young resident stopped by to assess the need for closing sutures.

"I believe butterfly bandages will hold it," he smiled, patting Steven on the shoulder. "And I don't see any reason why you can't be released."

"Tonight?"

"How about tomorrow morning," the resident doctor made a few notations on Steven's chart. "Spend one more night with us, and we'll make sure all your drainage holes are sealed up. Then, we'll release you a day early on Sunday morning."

"Thank you, doctor," Steven relaxed, watching the nurse redress his wounds.

Finally alone with the news, he closed his eyes and silently rejoiced. He'd always been a fast healer. Even as a kid, he remembered his mom saying that band-aids had been a waste. He'd be healed up before she even got the box open.

But what if this time had been a lot worse? What if the girl had hit his spleen, or maybe something even more important? What if she'd stabbed him in the heart and he'd died down in the shelter basement?

He yanked open the bedside drawer, and reached in—his right hand scrambling to find the glass bottle. With some small measure of comfort he drew from his healing powder, he tucked it down under the blankets and tried to sleep.

Not surprisingly, sleep eluded him.

He just couldn't get past the fact that he was all alone in the world. For the past four years, Steven had always believed that in an emergency, when push came to shove, his parents would reappear. They'd have some kind of plausible explanation about to why they hadn't been in touch, and all would be forgiven. But for the first time, he realized that it just wasn't true. They weren't coming back, and no matter how much he needed them, he had absolutely no idea where to look.

"Hi Steven," Claire popped back into his room. "Heard the news. You're going home tomorrow."

He nodded; his voice caught somewhere down in his throat.

"Well, I just thought I'd stop by and warn you. There's a couple of cops or something, asking about you down in admitting."

"Oh shit," Steven moaned, not the least bit interested in another interrogation.

"Mr. Whitters?" a man stepped through the doorway, instantly flashing his city badge. "We're here to talk to you again about your attacker."

Taking her cue to leave, Claire turned and quickly vacated the room.

"I kinda remember you guys," he sighed, flashing back to the day he was admitted.

"We have a photograph, and we were wondering if you'd possibly recognize the girl."

Shrugging his shoulders, Steven turned toward the picture. "I… I don't…"

"Please look carefully, Mr. Whitters. Was this the girl who attacked you at the Lilac Tree Shelter?"

As he turned away from the morgue photograph, he struggled to dredge up any of the faces. "Like I told you guys already, the basement was really dark. I didn't see what they looked like."

"But you were positive that there were *three* assailants?"

"That's what I heard, and kinda saw, but maybe somebody else was hiding in the shadows. I don't know."

"We hear that you're being released tomorrow."

"Yup."

"And we'll be able to contact you at the residence of Nurse Olga Heinz?"

"Yeah, that's right. But can you tell me what makes you think that the girl in the picture is the one that stabbed me? Cuz she's dead, right? Doesn't look like she confessed or nothing."

"She was found in a back alley, not far from the shelter. It appears our Jane Doe was strangled during a sexual assault. We found that she was carrying a knife in her pocket covered with blood. Upon testing, we found the blood matched your blood type. So we made the connection."

"Good connection," Steven shrugged. "So that's the end of the road?"

"No, we're here for your permission. We need your okay for a DNA match."

"Well, you've got it. So if it's a match, then what?"

The detectives divided up as if moving in to conquer, and circled Steven's bed. The taller one said, "Mr. Whitters, I have to level with you. An unknown assailant, and her two accomplices, stabbed you in the basement of a community shelter. This is a shelter plagued with indigents, junkies, and prostitutes. Many, as you're probably aware, don't even use their real names. It's going to be very difficult to tie up all the loose ends."

"So that's it. You came to tell me it's probably over."

"On a good note, we believe your attack was totally unplanned. You were in the wrong place at the wrong time, and when you surprised those junkies, they only saw you as an obstacle standing in the way of their freedom."

"So?"

"So, from my experience, I believe it's over."

"I think *over* might be a little too strong a word," an unknown voice spoke up from the doorway.

"Who are you?" Steven demanded, eyes darting back toward the city police as if looking for their protection.

"FBI."

CHAPTER THIRTY

"You got a dream… you gotta protect it."

—The Pursuit of Happyness, 2006

Each toting a plastic four-liter jug filled with draft beer, Gerri and Campbell took off toward the park under the bridge on the west side of town.

"Wait here for a sec," Gerri set down her jug. "You've bought all the beer, so I think it's only fair that I pick up some snacks."

Nodding his head in agreement, Campbell stood guard over the booze while Gerri ran inside the corner store and grabbed a handful of paper cups, and a couple bags of potato chips.

Back on track, both staggered down the street toward the well-worn footpath.

"Holy shit," Gerri tripped down memory lane. "I haven't been around here since I was a kid. We used to steal wine from the monastery basement and then lug the jugs all the way down here behind the trees. You wouldn't believe the crap we'd see when we were squatting in the bushes."

As he shifted his jug from his right to his left shoulder, Campbell decided to share his own story. “When I was young, we used to hook-up in the bars and head down here for a little action. The cops couldn’t follow in their cars or their pedal bikes, and they were too damn scared to walk in on foot. You could almost get away with anything down here.”

“Maybe I watched you,” Gerri teased.

“Maybe,” Campbell agreed, his erection beginning to press against the denim of his jeans.

“How far are we going? This is heavy.”

“Don’t be such a girl,” Campbell teased, slapping Gerri on the back with his free hand. “It’s Saturday night and I’m feeling alright,” he attempted to sing some obscure little ditty that was replaying in his head.

“What’s that?” Gerri stopped dead in her tracks. “Looks like some kinda lights or something.”

“Excellent. They have her going already. Now we won’t be chewed by any fucking mosquitoes, or any of those damn black beetles that crawl under the leaves and nip at your ass.”

“That’s good,” Gerri agreed, suddenly anxious to reach the light.

“Now stay close to me—don’t want you wandering off and getting lost in the woods, cuz if I gotta come looking for you, it won’t be fun.”

As they continued down the path, Campbell’s last comment somehow didn’t sit right with Gerri, and she found herself unconsciously slowing her pace. “Is this the only path leading in and out of here?”

“Hell no. There’s gotta be a hundred trails crisscrossing up and down these hills. You get lost, and you could starve to death,” he laughed. “Well, that’s if the coyotes and wild foxes don’t chew you to death when you’re sleeping,” he added to increase Gerri’s fear.”

"How big is a coyote? Are they like cats or they about the size of a dog?"

"Damn, you really are all city, aren't you?"

Gerri kept trudging along, mentally noting all the converging paths, silently cursing herself for not paying closer attention a lot sooner.

"We'll be there in five minutes," Campbell announced, his senses picking up on Gerri's insecurity. "As soon as we come around the next bend, you'll be able to see the fire again."

As promised, the party scene was soon revealed. Unfortunately, the atmosphere was anything but friendly.

"Why is everybody staring at me?" she whispered under her breath, afraid to take her eyes off the group while they deposited the beer on a flat rock next to the fire.

"Pay no mind. They're just trying to figure out if they know you or not. Don't worry, stick with me and you'll be alright"

Gerri took Campbell's words to heart, and closely shadowed her new best friend. As he circled around the fire, collecting five-dollar bills from the assembled crowd, she never left his side.

When Campbell stopped to stuff the money down into his pockets, Gerri took the opportunity to question him a little further. "Why's everybody paying you so much? Don't they know how much draft beer really costs?"

"Just collecting a little party fee," he grinned. "Don't you worry your pretty little head about it," and this time he slapped Gerri firmly across the ass.

Shocked by the sudden change in Campbell's attitude, she started backing away the minute some guy walked over with a fresh glass of beer.

As she turned in circles, Gerri scrambled to pinpoint the exact path they'd walked in on, but with all the foot trails appearing to converge at the same fire pit, it was impossible to tell. "Uh...

Campbell, I don't feel that hot. Maybe I got a little sunstroke from work today. Can we leave?"

"You gotta be fucking kidding?" he roared. "I spend fifty bucks on beer, and then bring you down here to a real special party, and now you wanna turn tail and run. Well, fuck you!"

Nervously pulling her fingers right up to her teeth, Gerri was completely unaware that she was chewing on her nails until one of the guys made a joke of it. "Look at it bite its hands. Why do ya think it's so nervous for?" he pointed out across the fire.

"*Look at it bite its hands. Why do ya think it's so nervous for?*" Gerri repeated over in her head. Why were they calling her *it*? Why not *he,* or even *she,* for that matter. She was dressed like a man, looked like a man, and if nobody recognized her, she should have been perceived as a man. What was going on?

As she stepped back, she accidentally crunched a bag of potato chips in the process. At the sound, Gerri couldn't help but jump, letting out a small squeal of surprise in the process. As if cued by a giant teleprompter, the guys all began hooting and hollering, their voices quick to reach full decibel.

"Two bucks," one dark haired man called out over the roar.

"Four," another answered in return.

"Ten," was heard from the inner ring, instantly followed by another round of cheering.

"Twelve," rose from across the pit as Gerri's mouth fell open in utter shock. What were they doing? Why were they… bidding? She forced herself to ignore the fear creeping up her spine and pay attention.

"Fifteen smackaroos," another yelled.

"Put it up," his buddy shouted, obviously not convinced that the man had the cash to back his bid.

"Suck me dry, you motherfuckers," he cursed, waving a twenty-dollar bill high above his head.

"Calm down," Campbell stepped in closer to the fire, the grin on his face illuminated by the flames off the burning logs. "Jed just bid fifteen. Anybody man enough to top his bid?"

With her heart almost pounding through the walls of her chest, Gerri knew it was time to run. She didn't know exactly where she was and she didn't really care, all she knew was that she'd rather take her chances with the wildlife than the animals congregated by the fire. Turning, feet ready to take flight, she suddenly felt the hands clamp down on her forearms.

"Let me go, let… me go," she screamed, kicking her feet and thrashing back and forth as hard as she could.

"Twenty, you cheap fucks. I'll bid twenty for it."

Her worst fears confirmed, Gerri's legs gave out and she felt herself dropping to the ground. Unfortunately, the goons at her side wouldn't allow her to sit, and they jerked her upright with one fierce yank.

"Twenty-one," Jed nervously upped his last bid; pretty sure he had a dollar in coins floating around in his pockets.

As the cheering began to die down, Campbell realized that with a little prodding, he'd probably be able to get a couple more bucks out of the crowd. "Funny the bid's stuck at twenty-one, it's only twenty-one years old. Can't believe you boys are passing on *first call* for that price."

Gerri felt the bile began to rise in the back of her throat. Swallowing hard, she fought to keep the liquid down. Gulping extra large breaths of air, her brain fought to rationalize what she'd just heard. Campbell wasn't auctioning her off to the highest bidder—he was just auctioning her off to the man who wanted to be first in line.

The scream welling inside her chest rose as if it had a life of its own. And by the time it cleared her throat, it blasted out with the power of an air horn.

"Look at it fight," one of the guys yelled. "How about a little taste of what we're paying for?"

Both captors reached simultaneously across her chest, and viciously ripped open Gerri's cotton work shirt—the tattered nails of one man instantly scratching four deep gouges across the tender skin of her breasts.

The cheers rose to an almost deafening level, and Gerri reacted with the only means at her disposal. She dropped her chin down to her chest and began to cry.

With the shelter closed for the night, and front doors locked, Doris and Olga leaned up against the wall and slowly munched on their pizza. With the storage room door cracked open just an inch, they managed to keep an eye on Ruby while curbing their hunger.

"You know, I cooked a whole meal today, but ended up throwing it all in the freezer."

"Had to run?" Doris took the bait.

"No, just lost my appetite."

"Well, life has a funny way of changing our dinner plans."

Olga fought to control her laughter, covering her mouth to keep from accidentally spitting any food particles back into the pizza box. "I think that just might have been the understatement of the year."

"I have a way with words," Doris snickered—the long hours beginning to take their toll. "But seriously, what in the hell is going on with you?"

"Well, I'm officially unemployed—thrown out of the University Hospital like a disposable diaper, and about as recyclable."

"Olga, if it's just a job you're looking for, you could be working by Monday. But my heart tells me that you want more than evening shifts at some auxiliary hospital. You're not the oatmeal and suppository kind of nurse."

"Well not really. Especially when you put it like that."

"So what are you going to do? Retire, travel a bit? Maybe settle down and get married?"

"Why, what'd you hear?'

"Hold on, sister," Doris cautioned, dropping the slice back down into the box. "I was just joking with you, but from your reaction, I don't think it's that much of a joke."

"Well, Friday I did get a proposal."

"Really? What'd you say?"

"I said it was too soon, but before I could reason with Martin and make him understand why, he withdrew his offer."

"Martin, Martin," Doris continued to repeat, picking up her slice and chewing on the crust. "Is that the doctor from your past? The one who'd broken your heart?"

"That's the man."

"Obviously he has a few commitment issues. Sounds to me like he may not be as serious about the relationship as you are."

Deeply sighing, Olga chose to jump right in and explain the entire situation. "Well, he quit his job at the University in response to my mandatory retirement."

"Alright, I take it back. He's got it bad."

As she stood up to check on Ruby's breathing, Olga finally straightened her back and looked Doris directly in the eyes. "He buried his first wife from cancer, and right now, I just think he's awfully confused about what he really wants."

"Kids?"

"No, they never had a family."

"Well, there are people who believe that those who don't want to have babies are selfish in nature, and make extremely poor spouses."

"I never gave birth."

"Choosing not to have children and being unable to have children are two different things."

After mentally debating Doris's logic, Olga blurted out a thought that had been haunting her for many years. "I think I've always known that I was going to die alone, and truth be told, so did my mother."

Doris closed the pizza box before dropping it down to the hallway floor, and wiped her face with a paper napkin. "Getting a little morose, are we?"

"When my maternal grandmother died, she left all her china and plated silver to my mother, her only daughter in a family of five. Now my mother, in turn, gave birth to the exact opposite, four daughters, and one son."

"I'm following so far," Doris smiled. "Five and five," she raised each hand to wiggle all ten fingers.

"So, before my mother died, she decided to gift us all with our inheritance, to make sure it was done right. She was quite a meticulous woman, and had little tolerance for mistakes."

"Doesn't remind me of a soul," Doris teased.

"All my sisters received equal shares of the china, the flatware, and all her crystal figurines. Do you know what she gave to my brother and I?"

"No, enlighten me."

"Well, she divided up my father's coin collection."

"I bet those coins were worth a pretty penny."

Shaking her head in disappointment, Olga folded her arms across her chest. "She knew. My mom knew I'd have no daughters to pass the heirlooms on to."

"Alright fine, I get what you mean. But so what? Your mother's bequests didn't map out your destiny."

"No, I mapped out my own destiny. Since I was a young woman, my nursing career has always been at the forefront of my world. It wasn't just my job—it was my family, my life. I can't imagine what will motivate me now."

After rising to brush the crumbs off her pants, Doris bent back down and offered Olga her hand. "Come on. Ruby will be fine for a couple of minutes. I need to show you something and I don't have the strength to bring it all to you."

As they walked across the shelter's main floor, Olga couldn't help but notice the width of the room. During the day, it seemed so small and crowded, yet at night, it felt like an empty dance hall. "Where are we going?"

"Come on, just follow me," Doris opened the basement door and grabbed a flashlight hanging on the wall.

Standing side by side in the musty basement, Olga's eyes followed the flashlight as it bounced off the metal walls.

"Meet Big Bertha, our trusty forced air furnace. Bertha is a little like you and me. She's nearing retirement, and everybody wants to throw her out."

"It sucks," Olga agreed, lovingly patting the gigantic cast iron walls.

"Well, Bertha needs a facelift, and if we don't comply by the New Year, the city is threatening to cite us and force the repairs."

"Fundraising, the curse of any foundation."

"Our operating budget could be stretched to cover the replacement of a new furnace and alleviate all the headaches at once, but I know that with a good cleaning and a little tune up, we'd get another five or six years out of Big Bertha. Besides, I've already earmarked that budget for community outreach programs, not galvanized venting."

"Alright, I get your point. Now can we go back upstairs? I don't like it down here."

"For crying out loud Olga, what I'm trying to say is that whoever takes over my job has to do more than break up fights with the kitchen staff and hand out tampons. It's a complicated position with complicated choices, and I think you'd be perfect for the job."

"Are you leaving?"

"I'm retiring, by choice," she added with a wave of her finger. "My husband Jack has taken about all he can of the long hours and midnight phone calls, and I was hoping you'd consider the position."

When they reached the top of the stairs, Olga turned to face Doris in the light. "What in the world makes you think that I'd even be good at a job waded down by bureaucracy and piles of red tape? I get frustrated keeping track of basic hospital memos."

"I admit it, there'd be portions of the job that you'd probably hate, but you're smart and resourceful. You'd figure out a way around the bullshit, and with your medical background, you'd bring a whole new facet to the shelter."

Hands on her hips, Olga shook her head. "Slow down. You can't possibly expect any kind of answer tonight, can you?"

"I know, guess it was just wishful thinking. I was praying that you'd jump at the job and my search would be..."

Both women stopped speaking, their ears tuning to a commotion on the shelter's main floor.

"Where the fuck... are my clothes?" Ruby slurred, the fever rendering her almost incoherent, her body miraculously strong enough to allow her to stagger to her feet.

"You've got to lie down," Olga rushed up to her side. "You're not feeling well enough to get out of bed. You have septic shock, and the antibiotics haven't finished working yet."

"Give me my clothes," she continued to rant, her eyes so glazed that they almost reflected her surroundings like a mirror.

As Doris nodded her head back toward the cot, she started

counting down from three. The moment she'd hit the number one, both women pushed their reluctant patient down onto her back.

With her eyes closing out of sheer exhaustion, Ruby continued to mumble, the only response her body was able to offer.

When they stood back up, Doris and Olga looked down at their patient.

"We could tie her down," Doris offered.

"Without proper restraints, we run the risk of cutting off her circulation."

"How about knocking her out with drugs?"

"Look," it was Olga's turn to lecture. "Shooting her full of antibiotics was dangerous enough, but administering narcotics without the supervision of a doctor is absolutely ludicrous."

"Relax, it was just a thought. So what do you suggest?"

"It really old-fashioned and you're probably going to laugh, but I can almost guarantee it's going to work."

"I hope so," Doris once again nodded toward the cot as Ruby struggled to sit up. "Look, Frankenstein rises again!"

Olga pulled over a box of files to squat on, and positioned herself on Ruby's right side. She reached out toward her arm, and softly began stroking her skin, quietly offering words of encouragement with each stroke.

In amazement, Doris leaned in for a closer look.

"It's all right baby, just close your eyes, and try to relax," Olga cooed in Ruby's ear. "Your body is tired and it needs a little rest. You're safe here at the shelter," she continued, the tips of her fingers and palms of her hands in continual contact with Ruby's skin. "Nobody can hurt you, so close your eyes, and just sink down into the blankets. I promise not to leave you as long as you sleep."

As if on cue, Ruby's breathing slowed, her muscles relaxed, as she unconsciously turned her face toward Olga's voice.

Doris watched the scene play out in front of her own eyes.

She'd heard of *Touch Treatments* before, but had never experienced anyone putting it to practical use. In reality, it wasn't that farfetched a theory, since most street people craved only one thing more than food or their drug of choice. They craved the simple comfort that could only be found in another human's touch.

CHAPTER THIRTY-ONE

"Girlie, tough ain't enough."

—Million Dollar Baby, 2005

She was losing the darkness, and any measure of protection it might have afforded her. Gerri couldn't be exactly sure when, but she guessed that within an hour, the sun would be coming up, effectively swallowing up all the shadows and exposing her movements to anyone near her position. As she consciously willed her body to be swallowed up into the depths of the forest, Gerri continued to cower in the rotten compost collected behind the fallen trees.

It was still following her, she could feel it, and if she held her breath and never made a sound, she could almost hear it. Not one of the men who'd been chasing her for the first hour—they ran through the woods like a herd of cattle, breaking branches and stomping over deadfall. This moved quietly, barely breaking a twig or bending a branch.

After a second round of uncontrollable shivers, Gerri slowly unwrapped her arms from around her legs, and forced herself to stand. With her head still throbbing with lingering spasms, she slowly turned in a full circle, fighting to assimilate her surroundings.

It was closer now—she could feel it—even though her eyes were unable to distinguish anything beyond the immediate underbrush surrounding her position.

Suddenly, she reached out to grab at a tree in a desperate attempt to steady herself, but almost blacked out for a second time. This was getting very serious—she could feel it. She'd been bleeding for hours, maybe five, or six, and now the resulting dizziness and nausea were affecting her ability to keep walking. She'd be dead for sure, unless she kept moving, and with this thought pulsing through her brain, she pushed herself onward.

Still unable to sleep, Steven lay back in his hospital bed anxiously awaiting his release. Promised a visit on early rounds, he strained to hear any movement down the halls that might signal a doctor was on the floor.

"I'm sorry Steven, there's still no answer," the night nurse popped her head in his room. "I've been trying to reach Nurse Heinz for hours, but no one is picking up. Is there maybe another number I could reach her at?"

"Olga doesn't carry a cell phone, and you know her old work number," he shrugged, totally at a loss.

"Well, I'll be back to check on you a little later. And don't worry, I've left two messages, so I'm sure that the second she walks in she'll give us a call."

Steven thanked the nurse and turned his attention back to the business cards still sitting on his bedside table. The men from the FBI had been all business, that's for sure. Different agents than the original two who'd stopped by Olga's house; these guys had a specific list of questions, and they weren't leaving until they were satisfied with the answers.

"Mr. Whitters, are we to believe that you have had literally no contact with your parents or your sister for the past four years?"

"Yes, like a told you, I couldn't reach them even if I wanted to."

"And you've been supporting yourself since the age of nineteen, without any help from family?"

"Yes. Well until recently."

"And what happened recently?"

"My trailer burned down and I moved in with Olga Heinz."

"Nurse Olga Heinz, an employee who recently retired from the nursing staff here at the University?"

"Yes," Steven answered, not willing to split hairs with the agents on the finer points of Olga's termination.

"Were you aware that the fire in your trailer was purposely set?"

"I was at work, you can check with records."

"We did," the lead agent stepped up closer toward Steven's face, "But there seems to be a lapse in your attendance. You clocked out for two hours and nine minutes mid-shift. Do you mind telling us exactly where you were for the missing time?"

"If you checked with records, then you know that I reported a family emergency and ran home."

"How did you know you had an emergency?"

"The trailer park's manager called me.

Picking up the solitary *Get Well* card adorning the windowsill, the second agent read the handwritten name at the bottom. "Claire?"

"She'd a student nurse here. A friend."

"Then tell me, Mr. Whitters," the lead agent interrupted. "What did you do upon reaching your trailer?"

"Nothing really, it was already burned to the ground. All I could do was poke around a little in the rubble and pick up whatever wasn't torched. A couple coffee cups, nothing of any value. I lost everything, you know?" his voice taking on a tone of insolence. "The fire ate up all my furniture and all my clothes."

"Mr. Whitters, it's been brought to my attention that half of your rent was being covered by an outside source. Can you shed any light on that for us?"

"I always thought it was just Mom and Dad's way of helping me. I never really questioned it," he admitted, suddenly feeling foolish for accepting monetary gifts from what appeared to be an absolute stranger.

"Upon checking with your landlords, one half of your rent was paid on the first of each month by money-order mailed from somewhere in the continental US. And here's an interesting fact. Whoever was in charge of mailing the envelopes has ceased sending further payments since your trailer was destroyed. Someone is aware of your present situation and is not wasting money paying rent on a trailer that no longer exists."

"Do you know who was sending the money?" Steven asked, now beginning to compile his own list of questions. "I never knew for sure if it was my parents, and it always kinda bugged me."

"Mr. Whitters, we'll ask the questions if you don't mind. So now, is there anyone else besides your parents who might feel compelled to assist you with your accommodations? Maybe an aunt or an uncle, some long lost cousin, or childhood friend?"

Steven shook his head, took a chance, and threw one more question back at the two agents. "Do you guys know if anyone from my family is still alive?"

The morning sunshine had little warming effect on Gerri's exposed skin, since every inch was smeared with dirt and blood, and pasted with moldy leaves. From a distance, she was sure she'd probably resembled some sort of ancient bushman slinking back and forth through the forest. Up close, she knew the sight was probably much more disturbing.

God, how she needed water. Her mouth was parched and her head was pounding—her body effectively dehydrated from the night's intake of draft beer. But right now, Gerri had bigger problems to worry about. Since her first rape at the fire, she'd been bleeding from her rectum, the fresh blood dripped down her legs and depositing itself on the spongy floor of the underbrush, leaving a perfect trail for any animal with half a mind to track her.

As another stabbing pain suddenly shot up through her abdomen, Gerri doubled over as she gasped for breath, desperately willing herself to stay conscious. Passing out on the ground wouldn't accomplish anything. Whatever had been following her all night would most definitely come in for a closer look, and possibly take the opportunity to attack while she was incapacitated. Fresh blood attracted more than mosquitoes and nasty beetles. Anything with fur and sharp teeth might be tempted to take a bite.

As she rose once more to her feet, Gerri looked down and noticed the ragged appearance of her scrotum and penis. Scratched, possibly torn, the blood had clotted in what appeared to be dime sized lumps. Not the least bit concerned with permanent damage, planning to lop it off as soon as financially feasible, Gerri was much more concerned with her ravaged nipples.

Still dripping fine streams of blood, she winced at the mere thought of losing one of her prized breasts to infection. She'd paid good money for the surgery, and suddenly all her attention was focused down on her chest. She gingerly patted the mud-covered mounds, her fingers tenderly searched for any deep cuts or lacerations, anything that might expose one of her saline implants.

Satisfied that her upper wounds were mostly bites and scratches, she decided that it was time to come up with a rescue plan. She'd have to walk out of here on her own accord, because another night in the underbrush would surely spell her death. If she didn't bleed to death, she'd probably die from exposure or dehydration. It didn't look like anybody from the party had been following her for hours, so it was time to try to make her way back to civilization. Only one problem—she had absolutely no idea which direction would take her home.

As he took a leak in the bathroom just off the kitchen, Bert was suddenly struck by a strange thought. His wife hadn't been up to the bathroom for an entire day. She'd been either sleeping or ignoring him since she fell down the stairs, and knowing Myrna's frequent washroom breaks, it was really quite amazing.

He decided that the idea warranted further investigation, so Bert turned on the hallway lights and began to make his way up the stairs. Reaching their room, he slowly pushed open the door, secretly hoping that he'd find his wife sitting up in bed reading one of her paperback novels.

She wasn't.

"Miranda. Miranda," Bert called out, his voice suddenly tainted with what appeared to be the stirrings of impatience. "Don't tell me you're still sleeping, it's been," he stopped to glance at the bedroom clock. "It's almost seven in the morning. You're always up by seven on Sundays for early mass," he shouted down at her face.

Eyes momentarily fluttering, somehow unable, or unwilling to open fully, the movements eventually slowed down and ceased all together.

"Don't you have to go to the bathroom?"

This time, when Miranda never responded, Bert decided to take the matter into his own hands. Reaching over, he flung the covers toward the bottom of the bed, immediately exposing her body as it lay motionless in the same position as the day before.

"Oh fuck," Bert cursed, shaking his head as he leaned in closer for a better look. The sheets were noticeably dirty, her urine and what appeared to be blood, now stained all the cotton bedding.

"Oh come on woman!" he barked. "You're on your damn rags and you pissed the bed. Get up right now! This game you're playing is got right out of hand."

Nothing but the tear tricking down Miranda's right cheek displayed any signs of life.

Bert opted for a threat. He painfully straightened his back, still sore from toting his wife up the entire flight of stairs, and said, "I'm going for smokes, and when I get back, I wanna see you up. I've had enough of this bullshit—I've said I'm sorry—now it's time to get on with it. Besides, that lady will be coming again this afternoon to change the bandages on your face. You want her to see you like this?"

As if finally stirred by something she heard, Miranda struggled to open her eyes.

"Oh, so you are awake?" he sneered, his hands now resting on his hips. "I was almost ready to call the cops to come take your body away."

As her lips struggled to form a single word, Miranda's eyes squeezed shut with the effort.

"Now's not the time for excuses, so save it. Just get up and clean yourself. You're embarrassing me," he shook his head, slamming the bedroom door shut before tromping down the stairs to head off to the corner store.

Gerri gasped for a breath, and leaned against a tree. She felt a touch warmer in the midday sunshine, but ultimately, it was beginning to encourage her thirst. She'd encountered at least ten or twenty branching paths, all looking exactly the same, none promising any sort of exit.

She rationalized that climbing up hill was probably her best shot at finding civilization, so Gerri continued to plod along. Her feet were now bleeding from fresh cuts and rock punctures, and she debated which would last longer—her willpower or her strength. Both were fading fast, the entire concept might prove a moot point.

Over the last hour, she'd actually managed to catch a quick glimpse of the animal that had been tracking her all night. Having unknowingly doubled back on her own footprints, she'd surprised it. It was sitting hunched under some deadfall, licking at what Gerri assumed to be droplets of her own blood—it didn't exactly look menacing. But upon nearing its position, she was rewarded with a growl and a show of extremely sharp teeth as the stray dog snarled right up at her face.

Turning to shuffle off—running was an impossible feat in her condition—Gerri had chosen another path and continued with her ascent. In a rush to leave the furry, four-legged animal down the hill, she unknowingly stumbled back onto the party sight.

"Holy fuck!" somebody shouted the minute she stumbled into the clearing.

As she turned to run, to try to escape one last time, Gerri's world began spinning in circles just before she fainted dead away.

"Extra light, king size," Bert repeated for the second time to the convenience store clerk, brainwashed by corporate advertising to somehow believe that less tar somehow translated into less cancer.

"Thank you very much, please. And a lottery ticket?" the clerk asked, his East Indian accent only adding to Bert's rising level of irritation.

"Just give me my change."

"Have a nice day," the man smiled, dropping the coins into Bert's outstretched hands.

"Fucking rag head," Bert cursed under his breath, quickly unwrapping the cellophane before discarding the thin layer of foil.

"Got a smoke?" he heard from behind his back.

He turned to give the bum a sharp tongue-lashing, but Bert was surprised to see his old friend Metro toddling up the sidewalk.

"You look like shit, old man," he called out in lieu of a simple hello.

"Morning, Bert."

Stopping to light a cigarette for himself before treating his friend, Bert watched Metro pop one in his mouth and tuck another behind his ear before trading the package for a spark from his lighter.

"You had breakfast yet?" Metro smiled, sucking heavily on the cigarette before strategically moving it to the corner of his mouth.

You had breakfast yet, translated into two possibilities. Either Metro was going to invite Bert to join him down at the Lilac Tree shelter for coffee and donuts, or he was looking for an invite back to the house.

"Miranda's still sleeping, so I was gonna grab a cup. Wanna join me?" he asked, already turning on his heels to make his way to the local diner.

"Alright," Metro finally chirped, as if debating a host of multiple offers.

Settled in a window booth, Bert ordered both men the weekend special of two eggs, toast, sausage and pancakes, a good filler for Metro's empty belly.

"Saw Miranda last week, she's looking better. Sent me out with a jar of peaches, but I haven't had a chance to wash the jar yet."

"Not yet, eh?" Bert chuckled, almost positive that his friend had traded the canned fruit for a bottle of cheap wine.

"This is good," Metro finished lapping up his runny egg with the buttered toast. "Nothing like hotcakes on a Sunday morning," he added, reaching across the table to grab the syrup dispenser.

"Take it easy," Bert warned his friend, instantly yanking his own plate out of harm's way before Metro's soiled sleeve landed anywhere on top of his food.

Metro smiled, not the least bit offended by the comment, and continued with his the task, effectively drowning his pancakes in a sea of sweetness. "Miranda off to church?"

"Nah, not today," Bert leaned back to enjoy his second cup of coffee. "She's been sick all weekend, and I don't think she's gonna get her ass out of bed."

Chewing without speaking, Metro filed the information, presently concerned with finishing his breakfast and any leftovers that might be abandoned on Bert's plate.

"How you been doing, old man? Last time I saw you, you had a hell of a limp going on. Feeling better?"

"A hundred percent," he grinned, the diner's napkin leaving tiny swatches of paper on his three-day growth.

"Good for you. I was a little worried that you might end up hobbling on one leg."

"No worries," Metro concluded his breakfast, eyes shifting down toward Bert's plate.

"Help yourself," his friend conceded, pushing his leftovers across the table. "Metro, you ever heard of anyone being awake without ever waking up?"

Carefully grinding a pork sausage between his rotten molars, he took a second to evaluate his answer. "You talking 'bout voodoo, like some kind of scary curse?" he teased.

After accepting a third cup from the waitress, Bert struggled for a better explanation. "I ain't talking about some stupid movie, I mean in real life. Like you're lying down breathing and everything, but nothing else. You know, awake without speaking or sitting up?"

"Sounds like a coma."

"Yeah, a little," Bert agreed. "But don't people in comas keep their eyes shut and look like they're sleeping?"

"I think so," Metro mused, his curiosity now piqued. "Is something wrong with Miranda?"

CHAPTER THIRTY-TWO

"We don't choose the things we believe in; they choose us."

—Minority Report, 2002

With her head bouncing frantically from side to side as if only attached by a tiny metal spring, Gerri luckily remained in a state of unconsciousness, her body depleted of every last drop of energy.

"Are you sure this is a good idea," Niles badgered his brother Fred for the hundredth time. "I think we'd have been better off just running up the hill and calling someone for help. This ain't going to work," he continued to whine.

"Alright, alright," Fred set down one of the makeshift drag poles. "I'm tired of all your bitching and crying. You run up the hill, find a cop, and bring him down here. Then when this… this thing," he pointed back at Gerri "wakes up, you can help *it* explain to the police that *it* was the guest of honor at our *Basher* last night. Sound good to you, Niles? You think that'll work well?"

"Well fuck it all, it's just that if we bounce it all the way up this hill, we're probably gonna kill it anyway."

"Niles, we're giving it a shot. If it hadn't stumbled back into the party site, it probably would have died for sure by nightfall. At least we're giving it a chance to live," he reasoned, his logic flawed by the basic fact that they were part of the group who inflicted the original trauma.

"Well, how about we compromise?" Niles suggested. "Instead of dragging the body up on the hill lying on this," he pointed down at the makeshift sling constructed of two by fours and a ratty old tarp, "we fashion something a little more akin to a gurney."

"You think we have the strength to carry him all the way up the hill? You fucking daft? He, or she, or whatever, has gotta weigh in at least a hundred and seventy pounds. How far do you think your back will last?"

Suddenly startled by the moans beginning to escape through Gerri's cracked and bleeding lips, both men quickly picked up where they'd left off and continued dragging her lifeless body up the path. Unwilling to be anywhere in the neighborhood when the victim regained consciousness, they actually began to hustle.

"When we get to the top… what're we… going to do with it then?" Niles continued to question his older brother through ragged breaths. "We can't just drop… drop it and run," he wheezed.

"I don't know," Fred barked. "I hadn't really planned on any of this, so don't blame me if I haven't quite figured it out yet."

"Maybe we should go find Campbell? He'd know what to do."

Fred dropped one of the handles, and turned to glare straight into his brother's eyes. "You must really want an ass whipping if you're thinking of looking for Campbell. Do you have any idea what he'd do to us if he knew we'd spent the afternoon dragging it up the hill? We're supposed to be cleaning up the site, not playing nursemaid to some partied out old fag."

Rubbing his chin, Niles took a second to look over Gerri's form. "I don't think it's that old. Didn't Campbell say it was only twenty-one last night?"

"I don't give a fuck whether it's twenty-one or a hundred and twenty-one, let's just get it up the hill, and dump it off. We gotta get back down and finish cleaning up before dark. Campbell said he was thinking of having another *Basher* tonight, and didn't want a bunch of empty bottles and plastic cups littering up his campsite."

"Hey Fred," Niles called out another twenty feet up the path. "Did you get your chance before it ran off?"

"Wouldn't you know it that I was up next when it bit one of Campbell's goons on the face and made off for the woods."

"Hey, I saw that," Niles excitedly announced. "I was coming back from taking a shit in the bush, when that guy let go of its neck for a couple seconds, and it jumped up like a lion and took a chunk right out of his face. That was fucking amazing."

"That's three times I've paid in the last month and then missed my turn," he complained. "Member that black one—the one with that really long nigger hair that we nailed to the log?"

"Yeah, I got in on that one," Niles chuckled to himself, fondly recalling the sight of the fag's matted dreadlocks pinned to the base of the fallen tree.

"Well, I didn't get that one before it passed out either. Fuck me."

"See, that's your problem," Niles dropped his grip on the two by four before taking the time to explain. "You're so goddamn picky. What's the matter if they're already out of it?"

"I just like them awake is all," Fred shrugged his shoulders. "Like to hear them scream, lets me know they're feeling what I got."

Nodding, Niles was suddenly struck with any idea. "Got any more water in your bottle?"

"Why, you still thirsty?"

"No, but I bet if you splashed a bunch of water all over its face you'd be able to wake it up and make it scream."

Stopping to debate the possible scenario, Fred took a second to evaluate Gerri as she lay unconscious on the tarp. "Too dirty," he poked his boot into the flesh at her hip. "We'll get a fresh one tonight, and this time I'm going third, right after Campbell and the high bidder. Or next time he can clean up his own party site."

"Sounds good to me, brother," Niles agreed, wrinkling his nose at the mere thought of having sex with the body they were carting up the hill.

As she watched Ruby struggle against the lingering pain in an attempt to dress herself, Olga felt encouraged by her pinkish skin tone and the dramatic drop in her temperature. "Can I help you, dear?"

"These are some damn fancy clothes," Ruby laughed, her throaty voice a testament to years and years of sucking on the toxic smoke emitted from a crack pipe.

"They're not Dolce & Gabbana," Doris interrupted from the doorway, "but in a pinch, I can promise you that they're clean. So other than the label, how're they fitting?"

"She looks good," Olga smiled. "I think all we need is a little soup in her tummy, and our little girl will be ready to rejoin the world."

"Did Olga have a talk with you about your injuries?" Doris demanded, her voice suddenly taking on a motherly tone.

"Yes. She explained about the pills and to make sure not to take them with any other drugs or alcohol."

"Good," Doris nodded, slipping into her chair to quickly dig for a specific pile of papers. "How about sex?"

"We covered that too," Olga confidentially smiled. "Abstinence for at least thirty days, or she runs the risk of a severe, repeat infection."

"Thirty days, hey Ruby? Did you get that?"

"Thirty days," the girl repeated, not bothering to raise her head as she continued to lace up her sneakers.

Finally locating the appropriate file, Doris shoved the papers deep inside and dropped it back down on top of her desk. "Ruby, you planning on working tonight?"

"Well, I got a couple regulars, don't wanna lose their business."

"That's exactly what I thought," the counselor nodded her head. "Well, can you at least try and cut back. Stick to blow jobs, hand jobs, and maybe a little anal sex if they're willing to go *back door*?"

"Well, I can give it a try," she threw her hands up in the air. "But what am I going to tell my guys? Some of them only get out on the town once a week and they'll be looking for their usual *straight fuck*. I don't deliver, they might start looking somewhere else."

Pushing her chair back and lifting her own feet up onto her desk, Doris thought for another minute before answering. "Well, you're right. Some of your regulars might be pissed. So offer them a hand job for half price this week, and promise them the best sex of their life next week for half price again. I guarantee you they'll be back. There ain't a guy alive that doesn't love a deal. They'll be lined up waiting for their turn, ready to cash in their *half-off coupons*."

"Half-off," Ruby hollered, "How the fuck am I supposed to survive a week of half-off?"

"Half-off this week, or all off next week when you're lying dead on your back and some rats are screwing your corpse for free."

Absolutely shocked with Doris's vulgar imagery, Olga found herself staring wide mouthed at both parties, wondering who was going to throw the first blow.

"Alright," Ruby agreed. "That'll work, but only for one week. I put these guys off longer than seven days, and I'm gonna be the one looking for rats to fuck."

Handing Ruby her plastic bottle of antibiotics, Olga gave her a hug and watched her walk out of the counselor's office to join the waiting soup line.

"Next," Doris announced, dropping her feet to the floor as she began thumbing through a stack of pink phone messages.

"I don't think I could ever do that," Olga admitted, still in awe.

"Sure you could. Sometimes, the only way to get through to street people is to lay it right on the line without the bullshit or the candy coating. There's no use extracting false promises from these women that you and I both know they're incapable of keeping. Experience has taught me that you're better off dealing with the realities of their lives. If you truly want to help these men and women, try to understand them before you judge them. Then some of their decisions might not seem so foreign or offensive to you."

"You're going to be absolutely impossible to replace," Olga smiled, tears threatening to spill down her face. "I don't know if any of these people appreciate what they have in you. What are they…"

"Let's stop that right here," Doris shook her head side to side. "Another lesson I learned ten years ago was that sometimes, no matter how hard you try, you just have to accept defeat."

"That doesn't sound like any motivational class I've been too."

"No, I don't think it's being offered at this present time. But just listen to my reasoning for a second. If I sat here even just half an hour a day, worrying about the people I couldn't help, the ones who slipped through my fingers, I'd waste… one hundred, eighty two and a half hours a year," she read off her desktop calculator. "And that's a lot of time I could be working toward new programs, more fundraising, and the search for the perfect replacement," she finished up with a laugh. "Anymore thoughts on my offer?"

"Jesus, Doris, it hasn't even been twenty-four hours yet. You gotta give me a chance."

"Just fighting one of the battles I think I might win," she smiled; patting Olga on the shoulder as she suddenly rose from her chair and marched toward the knocking on her door.

"Word is they found another one. They're bringing him here and should be arriving within the next ten minutes. You want me to call 911?"

"No," Doris sucked in a large breath of air. "I think we'd better evaluate our problem first. We can't afford another false call down here at the shelter."

After closing the office door as she turned back toward her desk, Doris began muttering to herself. Suddenly struck with an idea, she turned toward Olga. "Can you stay for another hour? Help me evaluate this poor guy?"

Olga looked down at her watch, and realized it was already one in the afternoon. She'd yet to go home from the night before, and was still dressed in Saturday's clothes. Technically, she was a free agent—her appearance was not required until Monday morning to retrieve Steven from the hospital, but for crying out loud, she hadn't even brushed her teeth.

"An evaluation shouldn't take more than fifteen or twenty minutes, then we'll either treat him or ship him off to county. It'll be a simple aye or nay. Can you stay?"

Even before she'd had a chance to open her mouth, the insistent rapping at the office door interrupted them both.

Olga ripped Ruby's soiled sheets off the cot, and quickly threw down a fresh layer of blankets. "What are we prepping for?" she demanded, positive that with a little advance notice she might be better prepared.

"Looks like someone found another guy who'd been the guest of honor at a *Basher* last night."

"He's been bashed?" Olga repeated, familiar with the violence sometimes inflicted on homosexual males without any provocation.

"No," Doris shook her head as she dug through her boxes of donated medical supplies. "We're talking about a *Basher Party,* and it's way worse."

"I've never heard of this. Is it new?"

"Yes and no," she explained, happy to find fresh rolls of gauze and medical tape stuffed inside one box. "Gang bangs, or gang rapes, have been around for hundreds of years. Hell, they're even mentioned in the Old Testament. But this is organized, kind of social thing, actually making it all that much sicker."

"Organized, how?" Olga stopped what she was doing.

"Well, word on the street is that these parties have someone in charge. He's a guy who picks the place, and is responsible for supplying the booze and the entertainment. For this service, he charges a flat fee, anywhere from a couple bucks to fifty bucks a head."

"And the entertainment?"

"That's the sickest part," Doris continued to explain. "The guy in charge usually charms some homosexual, or transgender male, into accompanying him to some kind of private little party. You know, just a get together with the guys. Well, once he's there, the victim finds that he's being auctioned off for cash to the highest bidder. The winner gets to rape him first, and then after that, it just seems to be a giant free for all."

Appalled at the thought, it took Olga a few seconds to speak. "Can't the police find these criminals and throw them in jail?"

"We haven't found anyone yet who was willing to testify. You see, these poor guys are either living on the street, or one paycheck away. They're desperately afraid of what will happen to them after the police are done. Sure, the cops might find the ringleader, but what about everyone else at the basher party? They know they can't identify every single rapist, and sooner or later, somebody will more than likely come looking for revenge."

"That's absolutely terrifying," Olga announced. "It sounds like mob mentality for the new millennium, some kind of warped safety in numbers theory."

"That's exactly what it is."

"So, can you warn me then? What kind of violence are we talking about?"

"Anything imaginable really," Doris shook her head in disgust. "But lately, we've seen a lot more of sexual violence. Torn anuses, detached scrotums, fractured penises, and of course the standard ligature marks from forced fellatio."

"Holy shit, then why are you even bringing the guy here? Why aren't you calling 911 or taking him straight to the emergency room?"

"Because… they… won't… go," Doris reiterated as she bent down to slap the lids closed on her supply boxes. "Like I said, this is usually one of the most traumatic and physically painful experiences of their life. These victims aren't the least bit ready to relive their experiences for the judgmental physicians they're going to encounter in emergency. Try and understand me Olga, when I say that these poor victims would rather attempt to lick their wounds in private and avoid any measure of psychological counseling, than expose their lifestyle to ridicule."

"Well, correct me if I'm wrong, Doris, but unless they have a county file, they aren't even entitled, or for that matter, registered for any of the government's victim counseling program."

At a loss for words, totally overwhelmed by the reality of her community's desperation, Doris let Olga have the floor.

After a pause while she studied Doris's face, Olga said, "How can we be expected to help these victims deal with the tragedy they've been through when we're subconsciously helping to sweep their assaults under the rug? So tell me," Olga demanded. "What's your follow-up ratio? How many of these rape victims searched out counseling on their own initiative? How do you think they would have benefited from an organized program of…?"

"Enough!" Doris shouted, throwing a handful of sterile bandages across the room. "I have no follow-up data," she finally confessed in an anguished voice. "Two of the three cases that I'm familiar with eventually committed suicide and died."

CHAPTER THIRTY-THREE

"Everything that I've seen tells me that this girl is a loser—scarred and broken and maybe even dangerous—but I've never really seen anyone like her before. Instead of running away, all I wanna do is protect her."

—The Rainmaker, 1997

Still guarding the two-dozen yellow roses, a Harry Winston diamond, and a backseat full of market fresh groceries, Martin reluctantly continued his wait. "Where are you?" he mumbled, eyes glued on Olga's front door.

He reached for his phone, and dialed the house number for the hundredth time, rewarded with the same message. "That's it," he announced, "I've had enough." He threw down his cell, swung open the door of his car, and marched around the house toward the backyard. After unlatching the side gate, he made his way directly past the side flowerbeds, making a beeline for the garishly painted ceramic gnome.

"Come to papa," he whispered, tipping over the lawn ornament and exposing the long-standing house key.

Three trips later, Martin had successfully moved all his supplies into Olga's empty kitchen and begun to set up shop. He realized he'd been such a fool, and he needed to apologize in a very big way. Olga Frieda Heinz was the woman he'd wanted to be with for nearly two decades, his soul mate, the only one who shared his joint passion for medicine and home cooking. How could he have been so stupid to nearly to lose her love again?

"Vase, I need a vase," he spoke aloud, checking the upper cupboards before finally spotting a large crystal piece in the china cabinet. He filled it with lukewarm tap water, before dumping in the florist's food crystals, and carefully arranged the flowers in a circular pattern, mindful not to leave any gaping holes between the blooms.

"Knock, knock," a voice called out through the back door. "Coffee pot on?"

Martin Reluctantly turned to check on his visitor, and found himself standing face to face with Olga's best friend Helen Horowitz. "Come on in," he motioned, graciously stepping aside to allow Helen access.

"Martin, it's been a long time," she politely nodded her head. "I didn't know Olga had company. I thought I saw her working in the backyard."

"I think that was me," he casually explained, drawing Helen's attention to the house key still lying on the countertop as he quickly tucked the ring box behind the mix master.

"Olga's not home?"

"No, I'm just here to make dinner before she returns."

"Where is she?" Helen continued, suddenly very concerned with her neighbor's whereabouts.

"It's Sunday, so I guess she'd either be at church or down at that community center where she volunteers. I know she's not at work," he tried to lighten the mood.

Helen slid down into a kitchen chair before continuing with her questioning. "I heard that you quit in protest, after they pushed Olga out. That was a classy thing to do."

"Well, it was about time I stuck up for that woman. Unfortunately, I've taken Olga for granted for more years than I'd like to remember."

As she sat back watching Martin sort his recent purchases, Helen had to admit that she was a little impressed with what she'd just heard. Maybe he had finally stopped living in a dream world, and was ready to stake a claim to his relationship with Olga. "So, what are you up to right now?" she smiled, trying to extend the hand of friendship.

"I thought I'd surprise Olga with dinner. I brought fresh asparagus, pork tenderloin, and baby red potatoes. For desert, I was planning on strawberry mousse, her favorite."

"Quite the chef, aren't we?"

"I can hold my own. Well… usually." He suddenly turned on his heel. "But I'll be damned if I can find where she tucked her colander."

"Bottom cupboard, right of the sink," Helen gladly offered, as familiar with Olga's kitchen as she was with her own. "You need some help?"

"No, but I don't mind the company. Cooking can be so lonely," he teased, "especially when it's time to do the dishes."

"You wanna share a pot of coffee?" Helen suggested, rising from her chair to fill the machine with water.

"Sure, I think it might be a little premature to start in on the champagne."

Reaching across the counter to pull out the glass coffee pot, the fingers of Helen's left hand inadvertently hooked the velvet ring box poking out from behind the mix master's stand. Quickly shoving it back out of sight, Helen spun around to see if she'd been spotted.

"Do you know what time Olga usually gets home on Sunday afternoons? I really don't want to start roasting this pork loin until I have some sort of time frame."

Helen turned back around to hide her face; standing motionless, she debated her next move. "So is this dinner some kind of special celebration, a birthday, or anniversary of some sort? I figure it'd have to be something special to warrant a B and E."

"I didn't break in," Martin argued back, insulted that Helen would even assume he'd violate Olga's privacy.

"Hold on cowboy, I was just teasing you."

After setting the colander of freshly washed asparagus back down into the sink, Martin meticulously wiped his hands before folding up the cotton dishtowel. "I guess I'm just a little on edge. Tonight could prove to be a big night for me."

"I see that," Helen motioned toward the bottle of champagne still sitting on the counter.

"Oh hell, that should be in the refrigerator," he rushed across the floor and grabbed the partially chilled bottle. "I can't seem to get my head on straight these days," he offered, returning to the sink to rinse the baby reds.

As she continued with her mission to make a pot of coffee, Helen watched Martin work out of the corner of her eye. Satisfied that he was more than competent, she switched on the coffee and returned to her chair. "This may be none of my business, and I'm not saying it to be a busybody, but Olga can't handle another break up like the one she's already been through."

"Well, neither can I."

"I'm serious, Martin." Helen shifted gears from that of the friendly neighbor, to the concerned best friend. "She nearly lost her job, and her grasp on reality. Olga is one of the strongest women I know, but somehow, you almost made her crumble into a thousand pieces. I'm not sure what you have on her, but whatever it is, it's almost criminal."

"I love her," he began arguing his own case. "I've been a bloody fool for the last ten years and I've come here tonight to make it right. I'm going to ask Olga to be my wife. It's about time, don't you think?"

"It's been time for many years now, Martin, I'm just wondering if it's all a little too late."

The large, bruiser of a man, who had carried the lifeless body inside the shelter's main doors continued to stand guard over the storage room. As if waiting for some further command, he continued to stand his ground, not moving a single inch.

Doris recognized the posture, accustomed to the protection mode many homeless shifted into over a fallen comrade. She walked up and gently reached out to squeeze the man's shoulder. "You did good. Thank you so much for carrying him all the way to the shelter. Why don't you go have a coffee and some cookies? I think you could use a little rest."

As he turned to leave without any verbal acknowledgement, the man just nodded his head, and slowly shuffled down the hall.

"Is he already here?" Olga leaned over and whispered in Doris's ear.

"The patient's on the cot," she muttered, shaking her head as she forced her constricted throat to swallow.

"What's the matter, Doris?" Olga turned her attention to the shelter's director.

"You know, I could work here another hundred years and I'd still never understand man's inhumanity to one another. What possible kind of creature draws pleasure from the suffering of another?"

"Age old question," Olga shook her head. "And you're referring to the *Basher* victim, aren't you?"

"Might as well see for yourself." Doris led the way into the storage room.

The victim that Olga saw lying on the cot was not simply a man or a woman—this was rather the *rawest* form of human existence she'd seen in years. This person had a pulse, and a heartbeat, but the body wasn't much more than a mangled mess of tissue and bones. "I'm not even sure where to start," Olga whispered her heartfelt admission.

"ABCs," Doris repeated the acronym from her last first-aid course. "Airway, breathing, and circulation."

Nodding her agreement, Olga snapped on a double set of latex gloves while setting up to evaluate the victim's wounds. "Vitals first," she called out, quickly establishing that their victim was not experiencing any sort of respiratory, or pulmonary trauma. She quickly moved to the limbs, and began checking for broken bones or severe lacerations, which might signal external or internal injuries. "There's blood everywhere, so I can't be sure, but it looks to me like we've got multiple sites and varying injuries—especially surrounding the sexual organs. Without even looking, I'm betting there's severe anal trauma and lacerations in the distil portion of the rectum."

As Doris gently swabbed the victim's face with a wet washcloth, and a tub of lukewarm water, she couldn't help but shake her head. "He's so beat up, I don't know if anyone could even ID this poor man from a photograph."

"Let's hope it doesn't come to that," Olga offered, ripping off her soiled gloves to toss them out, in lieu of two fresh pairs. "So are we calling 911?"

"You tell me what the hospital is going to do for this guy that we can't do better."

"Doris, we're not a community clinic. I'm not convinced that he doesn't have internal injuries. Only an internist could verify that. And as for his other injuries, what are we going to do if he needs stitches. We don't have any of those kinds of supplies."

"I can get them. I could have them here within an hour."

Olga knelt down to pick up a clean washcloth, gently brushing the mud and forest debris off the body and onto the floor. "I need more than needles and silk. I need an intravenous drip to push a high concentration of antibiotics into his blood. I need…" Olga stopped to think for a second. "Doris, this is absolutely ridiculous. We can't do this here. Even with our best intentions, we might actually harm this guy by withholding proper treatment. How could we live with ourselves? And another thing," she dropped the cloth to pick up a cotton swab and clean the patient's encrusted eyelids. "How do we know that this victim isn't someone who does want to be rushed to emergency?"

"Take one more right," Steven instructed his old landlord as he pulled onto Olga's street. "The second house, pink roses in the flowerbed."

"I see," John turned and smiled at his wife Mae. "Looks like our boy really moved up in the world. Nice little spread you got here."

"Olga is a really great lady. I hope she's home to meet you guys."

"Lady has sure got some fancy wheels," John motioned toward the car parked in the drive. "Ever let you borrow them?"

"That's not Olga's car," Steven answered, reaching for his door handle the minute the car rolled to a stop.

"Slow down, let me help you," his old neighbor shouted. "You gotta take it easy, man. You've just been through hell and back."

As he jammed his house key into the front door, Steven rushed directly into the middle of Martin and Helen's conversation, with John and Mae not more than two steps behind him.

"Steven," Helen announced, "I didn't know you were coming home today. Olga said it wouldn't be until Monday morning. Change of plans?"

"Early release," he answered, leaning around her shoulders as he continued to stare at the man moving back and forth between the sink and the refrigerator.

"That's Dr. Martin Hood. He's an old friend of Olga's."

"I know Dr. Hood from down at the hospital. But what's he doing in the kitchen, and where is Olga? I've been trying to get a hold of her since yesterday."

"Maybe we should all just sit down and have a coffee," Helen quickly interceded, offering Steven's guests two of the first chairs.

Seated around the table, everyone sipped at their cups while nervously waiting to see who'd be the first to break the silence.

"So who was the last to hear from Olga?" Steven suddenly demanded, tired of waiting for someone else to speak.

"I think it was me," Martin nodded his head.

"When was that, Dr. Hood?"

"Steven, please call me Martin. And it was Saturday around noon. Olga made us a quick lunch," he offered, without bothering to explain that he'd spent the night and then run out on her before touching a bite.

"And you never spoke to her after that?" he turned to confirm the information with Helen.

"No. But that's not unusual. Why are you so concerned? What's the matter, Steven? You're starting to spook us."

"I'm not sure, but I just think it's a little weird that she didn't come home last night."

"How can you know that?" Martin demanded.

After stepping up to the answering machine, Steven pressed the play button, revealing a string of messages from the University Hospital encouraging Olga to call. "She wouldn't ignore those calls if she was home, so I know she couldn't have been here."

As she turned toward Martin, Helen felt a funny feeling beginning to churn in her stomach. "I think I'm going to head down to the shelter and see if Olga's volunteering her time."

"I'm coming with you," Steven announced.

"Me to," Martin joined in.

"And I think it's our turn to say goodbye." John stood up from the table. "Mae and I have some people stopping by this afternoon, and we have to run."

Steven turned to shake both their hands, and took the opportunity to thank them both one last time.

"Our pleasure." Mae stepped forward to hug the young boy. "We promised your mom and dad that we'd take care of you the best we could. I figure that rates a ride home from the hospital now and then. Take care of yourself, Steven, and we hope your friend Olga is alright."

"Me too."

With Mae's vacuum cleaner humming in the living room and John's baseball game blaring in their den, neither was aware of the two men repeatedly buzzing their doorbell.

After they received no response, the visitors abandoned the electronic doorbell and resorted to banging their fists on the wooden door.

"We got company," Mae shouted while bending down to unplug her vacuum, the on/off switch long since burnt out.

"Come on in," John ushered both men toward the kitchen table, warily accepting their business cards. "You guys wanna tell me why you're here?"

"Well," the first agent searched for just the right words. "We've actually come to ask for your help. We're conducting a little investigation regarding Arnold and Carmen Whitters, and we were wondering if you could maybe shed some light on the situation."

"What kind of information are you looking for?" Mae politely inquired. "We haven't seen either of them for years."

"Did you ever accompany Carmen on any of her evening trips to the surrounding bingo halls?"

"Mae?" John teased the men. "You can't get my Mae to sit long enough to finish one game, never mind a whole series. Carmen loved those satellite bingos; they'd take forever and run all kinds of hours."

"You sound like you've played a few games," an agent abruptly pointed out to John.

"Used to call bingo down at the community league on seniors' night. But gave it up after my surgery," he pointed to the horizontal scar across his throat. "Can't project my voice worth shit anymore, since they operated on my throat for cancer."

"So, over the past four years, have either of you had any contact with the Whitters?"

"No," John answered, "just like we told the first two agents who stopped by. Once they left on holidays, there's been no word ever since."

"We have email now too," Mae added with pride.

"But Arnold wouldn't know that," John quickly reminded his wife. "Can't send us an email if he doesn't know we have a computer."

Silently agreeing, Mae refilled her husband's coffee and tried to pass it across the table to him, annoyed when he wouldn't set down the agent's business cards and accept his cup.

"You were the man who called the fire department, is that correct?"

"Yes," John nodded, unconsciously tapping the edge of the cards down on the worn surface of the table.

Both men leaning in closer, the senior agent continued his questioning. "Were you able to recover any of the Whitters' possessions before the fire consumed their house trailer? Maybe, let's say, a box of keepsakes, or a family photo album? You know—irreplaceable heirlooms that you knew insurance wouldn't cover?"

"Nope," John answered, folding his arms at his chest. "You boys ever been round a trailer that goes up in flames? She burns like dried spruce boughs, and running inside would be nothing less than suicide."

"And the son, Steven Whitters, he wasn't able to retrieve any possessions either?"

"To be honest with you," Mae shook her head, "there weren't a lot of possessions inside to begin with. The boy didn't even have a television. He'd come over here now and then to watch a ballgame with John."

Since they were obviously finished with their questioning, both men quietly nodded at each other, and rose in unison from the table.

"You'll call if you think of anything relevant."

"We've told you everything we know," Mae threw her hands in the air. "It's not that we're gonna remember anything new, cuz there's nothing else to remember."

John nodded his head in agreement, unusually quiet.

"You have our numbers, so please call us if either of the Whitters attempts to contact you." And without any further pleasantries, the two agents turned and walked out to their car.

"Write down the license plate," John hissed under his breath, not wanting to appear too agitated.

"What for?"

"Do it," he ordered, leaving little doubt as to his sincerity.

Called to her office, Doris excused herself to handle the newest emergency while Olga remained behind to evaluate and ultimately clean up their last patient.

"Oh my poor child," Olga muttered, changing into her third set of gloves before attempting to clean and debride the mud and grass impacted in nearly all the victim's many orifices.

"Help me," a weakened voice pleaded—the lips barely moving, the throat swollen and obviously dry.

"You're alright," Olga attempted to soothe the young man. "You're at the Lilac Tree Shelter, and we're going to help you."

"I really... my back, my..."

"Were you anally raped?" she gently asked; the question obviously redundant.

"It hurts... sooo bad," the muffled cries continued to escape from the victim's lips.

"My name is Olga, I'm a nurse, and I'm here to help you."

"Olga?"

"That's right," she smiled, gently reaching out to stroke a blood-streaked shoulder.

"Nurse... Olga Heinz?" the victim repeated, too weak to sit up, but still struggling to do so anyway.

"Yes. Do you know me?"

"I'm Gerri... from the *Chan... Change... room*," she sobbed.

"You… bought… me lunch," the words escaped through her tattered throat.

"Oh my God," Olga cried out, grabbing Gerri's bloody shoulders and pulling her up into a quick embrace. "Are you alright, honey? Tell me what happened. Who did this awful thing to you?" she demanded, too stunned by the revelation that she knew the victim even to worry about all the spilled bodily fluids.

Gerri's body was covered from head to toe in blood, some dried, some still relatively fresh. Olga had no way of even identifying the individual sources, and no idea if any was contaminated with blood-borne disease. Still, going against all her years of medical training, she bent down and tenderly kissed the girl on her forehead. "You're safe with me now," she gently rocked her patient, instinctively trying to sooth Gerri as if she was comforting a small child.

"Water," the patient managed to croak, her lips almost too cracked to form the puckered motion required for the letter W.

Gingerly laying her back down, Olga reached to the shelf and twisted open a fresh water bottle, popping in a drinking straw before passing it in front of Gerri's lips. "Suck slowly, too much water will only upset your stomach," she warned, ready to pull the bottle away should her instructions be ignored.

Thirst temporarily quenched; Gerri dropped her head back onto the cot. "Thank you," she whispered, eyes beginning to take stock of her surroundings.

"I have to check you for further injuries," Olga explained, beginning with her limbs.

"Nothing's broken. I was walking before I… I saw them," she squeezed her eyes shut against the memories.

"Who are they? Who did this to you?"

"I don't know who they were," Gerri somehow located a fresh cache of tears.

"Gerri," Olga attempted to focus her attention back on the

conversation at hand. "I think it would be best to call 911, and have the paramedics take you to a hospital. Is that alright with you?"

"No," she flatly answered with a painful shake of her head.

"But you need a proper check up by a doctor, not a *once over* by a retired nurse. To be honest, you could have a serious injury that I might miss, and without proper treatment, who knows."

"They'll laugh at me," she coughed to clear another blood clot. "They call me *it,* and when they think I'm unconscious, they bring their friends by to have a look at me."

"Oh Gerri," Olga shook her head, "your attackers can't hurt you here. You're safe and nobody is going to taunt you anymore."

"I was talking about… about the staff… at the hospital," she slowly forced the revelation out in the air.

CHAPTER THIRTY-FOUR

"It's just you're used to winning…
and you're not really a leader until you've lost."

—*The Core, 2003*

Oblivious to his wife's movements as she puttered around the kitchen making him a bowl of tomato soup and a cold pork sandwich, John continued to stare at the two business cards left behind by the supposed FBI agents who had visited just half an hour before.

"You notice anything funny about those guys?" he asked him wife Mae, "like maybe the fact that they didn't show us their badges.

"But you never asked to see their badges."

"But shouldn't they have shown them to us anyway?"

"Maybe. I don't know," she dipped her fork into the pickle jar.

"Well, I got something else," John announced, spreading both cards face side up on top of the kitchen table. "How do you spell investigation?"

"I-N… V-E-S… T-I… G-A… T-I-O-N," Mae proudly announced. "Investigation."

"See, the *FEDERAL BUREAU OF INVESTAGATION* line," John pointed down at the business cards. "Why is there an A? Shouldn't the word Investigations be spelled correctly, like it's spelled on *Criminal Minds* on TV?"

"I think you're right," Mae pushed her glasses up tightly toward the bridge of her nose. "Let me see it again."

Both heads bent down over the cards, they continued to analyze the subtle mistake.

"Now, I'm no English professor," John joked, "But something tells me that real agents from the FBI wouldn't be running around with typos on their business cards."

Picking up one of the cards and holding it up toward the light, Mae squinted at the printed ink. "Sure looks real, but I remember the kind of stuff the guy at the computer store was doing. He could have probably made fake cards, too."

"So, if the cards are fake, and they don't actually work for the FBI, then exactly who *do* they work for?"

Mae shook her head, passed her husband the dummy paper, and turned to shut off the stove. "When'd you figure this out?"

"Not long after they arrived. Why?"

"Cuz you didn't tell them about the boxes in our back closet. Figured you must have had a reason for not sharing, so I just kept my mouth shut."

"I think it's time we opened them up and took a look at just what we're holding, don't you agree?"

"Carmen said she'd be back for the boxes, and to keep them 'til she returned. How can we be sure she's not coming back?"

"It's been what, four, four and a half years? I think it's safe to say they aren't coming back."

"Alright, you get the boxes. I'll close the blinds and lock the door."

With the papers vaguely sorted but far from organized, John and Mae were still dumbfounded. "I really thought we had something here, some kind of clues to their whereabouts, or maybe a reason for their sudden move. But it's just this," John swung his hand to encompass the living room floor. "Just a bunch of Carmen's bingo crap, and copies of Arnold's work schedules."

"There's got to be something else," Mae refused to give up, poking her head back into the empty boxes. "You should have seen the look on Carmen's face when she came banging on our door. She looked petrified. She was scared shitless, like these were the most important papers in the whole damn world. Good God, John, it was three in the morning when she ran over. What in the hell are we missing?"

"We're missing the reason, that's what we're missing. Why in the hell did they run like rabbits in the first place? I can't imagine what kind of shit Arnold got himself into where their only option was to take off for the hills. And how come they didn't take Steven? How come they left him behind to fend for himself?"

As she sat, still thumbing through a collection of used bingo cards, Mae stopped to think for a second. "At first, I really thought it was either Arnold or Carmen sending us the money order to cover Steven's rent, but right now I'm not so sure."

"Why?"

"If my son's home had burned to the ground, no matter how deep I was in hiding, I'd have tried to get some kind of message to him. They didn't. Whoever was paying the trailer rent just stopped paying, and that was all. No money for a hotel room, no gift cards for new clothes. Just nothing. They just stopped paying. That's it. A mother just wouldn't do that."

"Pfffft," John blew air through his lips. "I don't know if Carmen was exactly my idea of the perfect mother to begin with. She kind of raised those kids by proxy, if you know what I mean—always assigning duties before running off to another bingo hall. Do you remember? Arnold and Carmen didn't even go to Steven's graduation?"

"Carmen wasn't the same after Michael died," Mae spoke up in her defense. "She just seemed to wanna escape into the bingo halls, to run away from the memories. It was a really sad time for her."

"Arnold bounced back."

"Arnold never lost any sleep over Michael's death to begin with. I swear," Mae pushed the empty box off her lap, "that man didn't seem to care if those kids lived or died. He never took any responsibility for their upbringing."

"He loved them, just wasn't all that touchy feely about it."

"I wonder how Monica's doing down in Arizona? I'm surprised that she hasn't tried to contact her brother either."

As he began to drop the papers back into one of the empty boxes, John turned back to his wife. "Do you really think they went to Arizona for Monica's wedding, or was that just some kind of ruse? You know—an excuse to run off without raising any suspicions?"

Mae slowly stood up and began helping John repack the papers. "I don't have a clue what to think. But I'm pretty sure that now is the time. We should be handing over these papers to Steven. Maybe he can make some heads or tails out of this mess."

"He was just a boy. What's he gonna know?"

"He's a man now," Mae corrected her husband. "These papers may be his parent's last effects, and he should have them. They're not ours to hang onto indefinitely."

"Fine," John conceded. "Call Steven and I can drop them off tomorrow when I go for my haircut."

"Dr. Marcus, thanks for returning my call so promptly." Doris set down Olga's list of supplies and extensive notes.

"What can I do for you, Doris? I assume you've got another little emergency over there at the shelter."

"We have our fourth *Basher* victim, and I think it's safe to say that he won't be going to the emergency room."

"Same injuries as before?" the doctor began to make notes on his scratch pad.

"Well, he's pre-op and already had breast implants, so we're also looking at fairly deep lacerations and what looks like a detached nipple. At this point, I'm not sure if it's even salvageable. Can you tell me how to establish if the walls of the saline implants have been compromised?"

"That's a problem. There's no simple test. It's just more a case of looking for symptomatic problems."

"Such as?"

"Such as abnormal swelling due to leakage or maybe temperature spikes. Doris, you have to listen to me," he tried to reason with her. "I can't make a definitive list of what to look for, too many of the signs can easily be misread as symptoms stemming from another injury. This patient is going to have to be examined by a professional."

"Can I buy you a weak cup of coffee and a stale donut?"

"You're lucky it's Sunday, or else I'd be up to my ears with my own patients, you know."

"I know. That's why I always light a candle for you at mass."

"Alright, enough sweet talking. Why don't you just tell me what kind of supplies you think you need?"

"Olga said she's going to need a suture kit."

"Olga Heinz?"

"The one and only. You two know each other?"

"Professionally. What's she doing down at your shelter?"

"You've gotta catch up on the gossip, Dr. Marcus. Olga's been put out to pasture by the hospital, and I'm trying to convince her to put her knowledge to good use down here with us."

"Good luck, I heard through the grapevine that she was interested in working on some kind of research project."

"You must be thinking of a different nurse. Research isn't Olga's bag."

"And the *Changeroom* was mine? Things change, Doris. Maybe it's you who's a little behind on the gossip?"

After hanging up his phone, Dr. Clifford looked for some plastic wrap to cover his lunch before heading off downtown. He'd needed this day of rest; he'd had a hell of a week. But even more than he needed to kick back, Dr. Marcus Clifford needed to feel like a doctor again—a healer—not some underground quack who was paid cash to perform the unmentionables and fix other butcher's mistakes.

He reached for the duffle bag he'd long since carried in place of a telltale medical kit, and threw in an additional handful of suture supplies and four vials of prescription antibiotics. Satisfied that he was toting enough basic supplies for his preliminary treatment, Marcus hopped into his car and made his way toward the shelter.

As Martin circled the block looking for a safe place to park his car, Steven's patience level began to wane.

"You've got a security system on here, right?"

"Of course."

"Well, then just pull over and we'll lock her up. You're not going to find a valet anywhere on this block."

Martin sheepishly nodded his head, eased up to the first available parking meter, and shut off his engine. "I don't know if this is really a good idea. Olga always hated the thought of an ambush. How about if Helen and I wait in the car, Steven, and you go inside and see if she's okay?"

"Martin's right," Helen conceded. "If Olga's actually here volunteering her time, she'll be pissed to think that we all drove down to check on her. You know Olga and her privacy issues," she twisted her neck to catch Martin's eye.

"So let's say fifteen minutes," Martin allotted Steven a window of time. "You pop inside, have a look around, and we'll wait to hear from you. Deal?"

Reaching for the handle of the car, Steven stopped cold. "That's Olga's line. She always says *deal* when she wants to make sure I've been paying attention."

"Well, is it a deal?" Martin reiterated.

"Deal," Steven answered as he stepped out of the car and quickly made his way up the shelter's front steps.

"Steven," Doris shouted out the minute she spotted the young man walk by her office door.

"Hello Doris, how are you?"

"Forget me, young man," she smiled ear to ear, "how in the hell are you?"

"I'm going to be just fine," he returned her grin. "But I just stopped by looking for Olga. I've been trying to reach her since I found out I was being released this morning."

"I'm sure she said your release was scheduled for Monday morning."

"Well, I'm a fast healer. So, can you tell me where Olga is?"

While pulling Steven aside to step out of earshot, Doris consciously lowered her voice, and said, "She's been here since yesterday afternoon helping me with two of the shelter's patrons. One who was violently ill and the other had been sexually assaulted."

"Oh, I see," he mumbled a response, not the least bit sure what he was expected to say.

"Would you like to see Olga?"

"Definitely!"

"Then follow me, young man." She led the way down a back hallway toward a closed door.

"Is she inside there?" Steven asked, still confused as to why Olga was hiding out in a broom closet.

"Why don't you just wait outside here and I'll go in and see if everything is okay."

"Sure," Steven nodded, a little unsettled with all the secrecy as he watched Doris disappear behind closed doors.

When she reappeared a second later, she beckoned Steven inside. "We're all clear, you can come in."

It took him a few seconds before he realized that the lump lying on the cot was actually a living and breathing human being. And even then, he wasn't positive until the patient opened her eyes and actually spoke.

"God, I must really look like shit," Gerri tried to laugh, the bruising, and subsequent swelling of her cheeks muffling her voice.

"No… it's just…"

"Steven, what are you doing here?" Olga jumped to her feet. "You're not supposed to be released until Monday morning."

"Change of plans, early parole for good behavior," he joked. "But we were kinda worried when nobody could find you."

"Who's we," Olga turned back toward her patient.

"Dr. Hood, and your neighbor, Helen. They were waiting for you at the house when I got home this afternoon."

She accidentally dropped the blood pressure cuff, and turned toward Steven, her eyes demanding an explanation. "They were in my house?"

"Yes, it kinda freaked me out too, and that's why I came looking for you."

As she shook her head to refocus on her current task, Olga bent down and grabbed the Velcro cuff. "I'm going to be here for a little while longer, so why don't you go home and get some rest. Do you need cab money?"

"No, I have a ride," he answered without offering any further explanation.

"Ouch," Gerri winced as Olga carefully adjusted the cuff around her upper arm. "I'm gonna be sick," the patient suddenly announced, the dry heaves beginning to catch in her throat and throw up her chin.

"Grab me a bucket," Olga ordered Steven, "and a couple of clean towels off the shelf," and before either realized it, they were back at work.

CHAPTER THIRTY-FIVE

"There are worse things than forgetting."

—The Forgotten, 2004

As he watched his daughter inhale the Pasta Alfredo, Ed Greenway was relieved to see that her eating habits had returned to normal. She could pack it away like a trucker, and sometimes her manners were just as refined.

"Pass the parmesan," Camille mumbled through a full mouth of creamy noodles.

"Good eats there, baby girl?"

"Dad, why aren't you having any?" she couldn't help but notice her father had only eaten a large garden salad and a dry dinner roll.

"Shh, just listen," Ed teased. "Can you hear it?"

"Hear what?" Camille laughed.

"The sound of your arteries closing."

"Dad, those aren't my arteries closing, those are your brain cells popping. So why don't you just order another gin?"

"Touché!"

"Too bad Mom couldn't come, she'd love this place with all its tacky jars of pickled peppers, and actual checked tablecloths."

"Your mother had a little last minute shopping before dinner this evening."

Camille leaned back to allow the waitress access to her water glass, and took the opportunity to liberally butter another fresh roll. "She shopping for my birthday present?"

"No, I bought your present last week. As far as I know, it was already delivered on Friday."

"I didn't get anything."

"Sure you did," Ed signaled the waitress and motioned toward his coffee cup. "I ordered you a truck, a cherry-picker truck to be exact."

"Oh," Camille dropped her eyes to her plate, appetite quickly fading. "You're talking about the guy from the accident, aren't you?"

"We were able to work out a private deal through our lawyers," Ed casually announced as the waitress suddenly returned with a carafe of coffee.

"He's not going to sue me?"

Mood suddenly shifted, Ed set both his elbows down on the table and folded his hands in front of his chin. "We were very lucky, Cammy. This could have financially wiped out our entire family. Granted it was also my mistake, having you insured under the company policy, but you jumped in a car and drove under the influence of prescription narcotics. Not even your prescription, I might add!"

"I'm so sorry Dad. I can't say it enough times," her voice began to crack. "I was trying to pretend the abortion never happened, to stay numb, to function without really thinking."

After dropping his hands to take a deep breath, Ed figured he had made his point and it was time to change the mood. "What do you think of the counselor from the hospital?"

"I like him. A little quirky, wears a bow tie and all, but he is all right. He's been helping me with my bad dreams," she announced as the waitress removed her half-eaten dinner plate.

"I didn't know you were having nightmares."

"Nightmare is kind of a strong word. The counselor calls them..." she searched her brain for just the right words. "He calls them *Post Traumatic Flashbacks*—my brain's way of helping me to deal with the specific memories of my attack, and the car accident. Kind of like an overload protector, so I don't freak out."

"He sounds like he knows what he's doing," Ed smiled at his youngest child. "You know your mother and I were devastated to hear that you'd been raped and hadn't told us. We are still having trouble dealing with that," her father painfully admitted.

Camille reached across the table to pluck a dried breadstick out of the glass jar, and nervously nibbled on it. "One day," she promised, "when I'm ready, and I'm convinced that Archie and Joshua won't kill the guy then I'll reveal his identity."

"Maybe he deserves to get his ass kicked," Ed blurted out, his own admission catching him off guard.

"Daddy, I've dealt with this in my own way. I don't need to sic the cops or my brothers on this guy. It's done with."

"What does your counselor have to say about that?"

"That's private," she argued right back, careful not to let her voice betray her sudden anxiety.

"I'm sorry," her father quickly apologized. "It just scares me to think that because he got away with it, he might try it again with another young girl."

"Dad," Camille recovered her wits and sharply lectured her father. "He didn't get away with it. Trust me—it was dealt with, just not through the police."

"If you ever change your mind, I'd stand behind you…"

"I know Daddy, and I'm grateful. But there's actually something else I wanted to talk to you about. I've finally figured out what I want for my birthday."

"Other than a cherry-picker truck?" he teased.

"Yes. I want you and Mom to adopt my half-sister Stacey, and bring her home from Pleasant View to live with us."

After parking his car and grabbing his duffle bag, Marcus took the time to smile at every single person he encountered. For reasons he couldn't quite comprehend, he felt at home inside the shelter's walls. Very few, if any, recognized him from his former position at the University Hospital, and even those who did couldn't have cared less to find out he was now practicing medicine down at the *Changeroom.*

"Doctor Clifford," a lady rushed across the floor to shake his hand. "You still looking for a wife?" she teased with a wink.

"Virginia, you're ten years too young for me, darling. But when you're finally legal, you give me a call, okay?" he winked at the senior citizen.

Marcus politely stepped away to pop his head into Doris's office, and caught a glimpse of her empty chair. He instantly decided just to keep moving through the shelter until he found what he was looking for.

"Marcus," Doris called out to him, her voice barely heard above the din as a trolley of fresh sandwiches and hot soup hit the floor.

He waved his hand to acknowledge her greeting, and quickly stepped out of the way to avoid the stampede clamoring for the freshly prepared lunch.

"Take it easy, Cynthia," Doris turned toward the young girl

frantically shoving bread and meat into her mouth at a much faster rate than her teeth were able to chew.

"Lunch at the plaza?" the doctor teased.

"How about you? Are you hungry?"

"No. I was already eating when you called."

"Well then, let's get to work," Doris began to lead the way.

When he stepped into the shelter's back storage room, the doctor was immediately struck by how organized it suddenly appeared. Wall shelving stacked with clean bedding and folded towels, all the cardboard boxes of supplies had been plainly marked for easy access. A corner sink and the neighboring table appeared almost sterile, and the freshly washed floor gave off the pleasing scent of bleach.

"Olga, I brought you a little help," Doris announced, stepping out of the way to reveal her guest.

"Dr. Clifford, I'm so glad to see you," Olga glowed. "We can sure use a man of your experience here."

The doctor walked straight up to the patient and introduced himself, immediately evaluating the victim's condition. "Vitals?"

"She's stabilized, but severely dehydrated. Right now, my three biggest concerns are the possibilities of internal injuries, the lacerations on her right breast, and of course, the rectal bleeding."

"Gerri, are you a transsexual, or are you in the process of transgender surgery?"

"Transgender," she smiled, shivering under the heavy load of blankets. "As soon as I've saved up enough, I'm going to be castrated—at your clinic. I saw you for my original consultation, but I didn't..." she turned away and tried to clear her throat, "Have the money to make the booking."

"I'm sorry I didn't recognize you," he bluntly stated, "but how about we worry about the present. Do you mind if I examine you?"

"Not at all, Dr. Clifford."

"Alright then, why don't we start at the bottom and work our way up. Doris, if you don't mind keeping watch outside," he started to assign duties. "Nurse Heinz, I'll have you assist me in turning the patient. And…" he stopped the minute Steven popped his head back inside the door.

"Sorry I took so long, but I'm back," Steven announced, closing the door tightly behind his own back.

"Dr. Marcus Clifford," Doris introduced, "I'd like you to meet Steven Whitters. Steven is an orderly down at the University Hospital. He's also Olga's boarder."

"Nice to meet you, Steven," the doctor politely nodded in his direction. "Are you here running an errand?"

"No," he firmly spoke up. "I've volunteered at the shelter in the past, and I'm here to help right now."

"Well then, ladies and gentlemen," the doctor announced, "let's get to work."

All preliminary examinations completed, Doris was called back into the room for the results.

"Gerri," Dr. Clifford pulled a stool up to the edge of her cot. "You're not going to require any stitches in your rectum. The tears have closed sufficiently to lead me to believe they will continue to heal on their own. Unfortunately, I have some major concerns about you right breast."

"What's the matter with it?" both her hands rushed up to protect her bandaged chest.

Sucking in a deep breath, Olga glanced across the room at Doris as the head counselor sadly returned her look. Although both were born as females, and neither had opted for any surgical breast enhancements, they still felt a shared pain of sisterhood with Gerri.

She'd fought so hard to become a woman, and in her mind, her breasts obviously represented that very transformation. Now as she lay on a foldaway cot, in the backroom of a community shelter, her entire sexual identity appeared to be at risk.

After warmly patting Gerri's left shoulder, the doctor pulled his stool in a couple inches closer. "My dear, your right nipple is seventy-five percent detached from your areola, and although I can reattach it with sutures, I'm not convinced it will properly adhere to the surrounding tissue and the result will…"

Waving her hands in the air to stop the conversation, Geri suddenly struggled to sit up and take stock of the situation. "Are you telling me I could lose my nipple?"

"Why don't you let the doctor finish?" Olga calmly suggested.

"As I was saying, since the saline implant in your right breast appears to be leaking fluid through one of your lacerations, I'm sorry to inform you that the implant is going to have to be surgically removed. At that time, the surgeon can properly evaluate the viability of your nipple."

As she broke down, and sobbed into her hands, Gerri fought to digest the flood of information. With her mind whirling, she found herself lashing out at the very professionals risking their careers to help her. "I'm a freak, with a cock and two breasts. Now you tell me you gonna cut off one and leave me lopsided. I can't even begin to imagine what I'm gonna look like."

"Gerri," Doris stepped forward with a box of tissue, "you could always have another transplant."

"Oh sure, cuz I'll find tons of work as a *fluffer* with one tit. I'm so fucked," she began crying, this time inconsolably.

As Doris rushed up to throw her arm around Gerri's shoulder, Dr. Marcus stood up, motioning Olga to step away and join him at the far wall where Steven was quietly standing.

"She needs surgery immediately. Her body is incapable of fighting off the level of contaminants already coursing through her veins, and I'm afraid that with the compromised implant, she might go septic."

"Doctor, you and I both know what will happen if Gerri is left at the hands of the county doctors."

"What will happen?" Steven couldn't help but ask, drawn into the medical facts of her situation.

Olga turned toward Steven, and quietly began to explain, "If Gerri was scheduled for surgery down at the University Hospital, the plastic surgeon would open a small incision at the bottom fold of her breast. He would gently remove the implant, debride the area for foreign contaminants, before packing it in preparation for the eventual replacement of the implant. He'd then reattach the nipple, taking his time to suture it to the best of his abilities with the surrounding areola. After a couple days, when the risk of infection has been reduced, he'd reopen the incision and replace the implant."

"Sounds complicated."

"Not for a plastic surgeon," Dr. Clifford interjected. "Actually, it is a fairly routine procedure since many patients increase the size of their implants over the course of a lifetime."

"Okay then, what's the problem?"

"Here's the problem," Olga crossed her hands at her chest. "At County, it won't be a plastic surgeon. A surgical resident will lop off Gerri's entire breast, including her detached nipple. She'll be left with a horizontal scar measuring roughly three or four inches across her chest in place of her breast. Any future implants will be expensive, and extremely painful, since the remaining skin on her chest would first have to be surgically inflated and stretched over time, before accommodating an implant. In addition, a prosthetic nipple could also be surgically attached, again an expensive procedure, resulting in no tactile sensation at the source."

"I see," Steven nodded, too overwhelmed with the flood of technical information to make any sort of educated comment.

"Nurse Heinz," the doctor turned toward away from Steven, "don't you think it's time to arrange for Gerri's transportation?"

The walk back to the house had helped settle Bert's heavy breakfast, yet as he approached the house, he felt his steps consciously begin to slow.

"You forget something?" Metro turned toward his friend.

"Nah, just thinking," Bert picked up the pace. "When we get home, I'm gonna have a peek upstairs first. If she's awake, you can go up. If she's sleeping, you'll have to come back another time.

Metro silently shook his head in agreement, and continued to tag along.

"I'm home," Bert shouted out the minute he entered the house's back door. "We've got company," he continued to announce in case his wife was still running around in her nightgown and housecoat.

No answer.

"Sit tight," Bert nodded toward a kitchen chair, "I'll go check."

As Metro listened to Bert's footsteps fade as he climbed up the bedroom stairs, he took the opportunity to look around the kitchen. Miranda always had some baking hidden somewhere, and with a little investigation, he was confident he'd find her stash.

No fruitcake in the refrigerator, only crumbs in the breadbox, Metro finally scored in the bottom of the cookie jar. Jacking his coat sleeve up towards his elbow, he reached in and pulled out a handful of raisin oatmeal cookies, instantly popping one into his mouth.

Surprised at the stale texture of the usual *soft chews*, Metro found himself snapping off his next bite. Strolling over to the table to take a seat, he finally noticed the untidy state of the kitchen cupboards.

Miranda never left her dishes undone, no matter how late, or how many were seated at her table. Her house was her pride and joy, and she wouldn't have ever left overflowing ashtrays and a sink of dirty glasses.

"She's still sleeping," Bert announced half way down the stairs. "You want some coffee? I'm gonna make myself a pot."

As Metro watched Bert stumble around the kitchen, he was struck by the fact that his old friend moved like a fish out of water. Bert was not used to fetching for himself, and in the midst of Miranda's domain, it really showed.

"Did she take some sleeping pills? I've heard of people accidentally swallowing too many and sleeping for a week."

After turning around with his eyebrows raised, Bert just shook his head in bewilderment. "You're so full of shit. Where'd you hear that, in some back alley standing around a burning barrel?"

"It's true," Metro began to argue vehemently. "My friend Ruby knows a guy whose wife's brother took a handful and slept for a week. I ain't shitting you Bert, he didn't move. Just laid there like a corpse for nearly a week."

"Who's Ruby?'

"A lady that I know. She works on the corner of seventh, down by the Italian bakery. I could take you there; you could talk to her personally. Wanna do that?"

"No, I don't," Bert threw a fresh measure of coffee grounds right on top of the already used grounds in the drip coffee maker.

"Well, it's true anyhow."

As Burt pulled the last two clean mugs out of the cupboard, he was suddenly struck with an idea. "You take cream in your coffee, don't you?"

"Yeah, but if you're out, I can drink it black," Metro offered, not wanting to offend his host.

He roughly set down a bottle of creamy Irish whiskey, and just silently winked. "Let's kill two birds with one stone," Bert playfully suggested. "Not a lot of cream in the ice box anyway, might as well save it for something else. A little splash of this will work."

With his mouth watering at the mere sight of the sweetened alcohol, Metro just nodded his head in agreement, never the type of man who'd turn down a free drink from a friend, or even an enemy for that matter.

Assigned to dispose of all the soiled towels and the discarded bandaging, Steven made his second trip to the laundry bins at the rear of the building.

"Double snake eyes," one of the kids yelled out as the dice bounced off the wall and rolled across the shelter's floor."

"Pay up," another began shoving his friend. That's six bucks you owe me."

"Yeah, pay up," a smaller version suddenly chirped from the sidelines. "My brother beat you and you gotta pay."

As he stood back watching the dynamics play out, Steven couldn't help but chuckle as the little kid began muscling his older brother's playmates for their payment, hands stretched out as he collected their loose change and dollar bills.

After dropping to the floor with his knees protecting his cache, the kid quickly counted his take while his older brother stood guard.

"You're short fifteen cents," the five year old brazenly announced. "You trying to stick it to us?" The kid immediately jumped up to his feet and began shoving coins into his coat pocket.

"You can't count, you're just a kid," one of the boys leveled back.

"He counts fine," his brother argued in his defense. "He knows numbers better than you ever will."

Ready to step up and intercede should the youngsters decide to duke it out, Steven was glad to see the confrontation come to its own peaceful conclusion when an additional fifteen cents magically appeared. Tragedy averted, the group silently disbanded and headed off in search of other distractions.

Steven walked over to the wall, bent down, and picked up the red dice, casually rattling them back and forth in the palm of his right hand.

"Hey buddy," a young voice called out from behind his back. "You got my dice," he confidently stated. "You gonna give 'em back?"

"Well, if they're yours, why would I keep them?"

"Cuz that's what some people do."

"What's your name, kid?"

Wary of grown men trying to be nice, the kid quickly shot a look over his left shoulder, trying to spot his older brother.

"Well my name is Steven, and I'm a volunteer here at the shelter."

"You work here?"

"Yep, but I work for free. I volunteer, so that means I don't get paid for my time."

Relaxing a little, the kid moved in a foot. "You rich or something, don't need to make money?"

"Hell, you have more money in your pockets than I do," he teased. "But I already have a fulltime job, so I come down here in my spare time, just to lend a hand."

Not letting up, like a dog on a fresh scent, the young boy continued to question him. "What kind of job?"

"I work at a hospital. I'm an orderly, and I help the nurses take care of the sick people."

"Oh, gross. Why ya do that?"

"I like it," Steven answered with a shrug.

"My dad likes construction, but…"

"But what?"

"But he don't work no more. I don't know why."

As he opened his palm to allow the kid to snatch back his dice, Steven tried one last time. "You look like a Chuck. I think I should just call you Chuck. Maybe Chucky, you like Chucky better?"

"David," he laughed before turning to run off toward his big brother.

As he watched the kid run off toward the street, Steven couldn't help but think of his own baby brother, Michael. He died more than ten years ago, and as the time passed, Steven found he thought of him less and less. Maybe it was because no one in his present life had any idea of his past, but that really was no excuse. It was his job to make sure he kept his brother's memory alive—not much different from his responsibility to take care of his baby brother before his death.

Michael would have been seventeen this Christmas and graduating from high school next fall. No doubt, he would have already had his first beer, his first girlfriend, and probably his first job. Well, he would have if he hadn't died, simply because his parents couldn't pay for better medical care.

As he absentmindedly fumbled with the bottle of healing powder still hidden in his coat pocket, Steven suddenly had an idea.

CHAPTER THIRTY-SIX

"And I know what I have to do now. I gotta keep breathing. Because tomorrow the sun will rise. Who knows what the tide will bring?"

—Castaway, 2000

Sitting across the desk from his lawyer, Ed Greenway nervously waited, while the attorney continued to make detailed notes during his phone conversation.

"Thank you," he finally finished and hung up the receiver. "Well Ed, after several attempts, I was finally able to speak to the administrator from Pleasant View, and as you had suspected, the adoption of Stacey is in its final stages."

"Is there anything we can do to stop it?"

"Yes, sure, there are a few different legal avenues at your disposal, but…"

"But what?" Ed reached over and picked up his coffee cup.

"I think it's time you examined your motives. What possible reasons do you and Tammy have for legally blocking this adoption?

Don't you think that as your lawyer, I should be privy to this information?"

"Of course, we trust you with all our legal and family matters. I don't know how we would have handled Camille's lawsuit if you hadn't negotiated that payout."

"Well then, come on Ed, I think it's time you leveled with me. What kind of information did you uncover regarding the interested family?"

"I don't know anything incriminating," he set down his empty cup. "This family might be the next best thing to the Cosby's. I really don't have any inside information."

"Now you're going in circles," the lawyer admitted. "What's this all about?"

"I, well, I mean my family… we wanna adopt Stacey and bring her home."

"So… after all these years… now you've decided that's what you want?'

"Yes, she's part of the family, and it's time she joined us in our home."

Rising from behind his desk, Ed's lawyer pulled open a large mahogany cabinet and removed a two-inch file, carefully setting it down on top of the desk. "Stacey has been on the adoption waiting list since her birth fourteen years ago. With her Down syndrome, she was medically classified as a difficult placement."

"I already know all this," Ed shook his head and threw his hands into the air.

"You placed Stacey in one of the best programs in the state, and finally after years of searching, they've found her a good home. Now what the hell is the matter? You aren't experiencing some warped sense of delayed guilt, are you Ed? Cuz you and Tammy did what you had to for your family. I was there; I remember the circumstances surrounding Stacey's birth. You've done good by her, nobody could have asked for more."

"She is family," he argued back. "She's our kids' half sister. We can't just let her disappear into the woodwork."

Flipping pages until he located the exact paper he was looking for, the lawyer passed it across the desk to his client. "Here are some basic facts about the adoptive parents. I think you should read this. It might help you."

"Help me how?"

"Read it," he strongly urged. "I believe it will help you understand what I've been unable to explain in words."

Ed accepted the paper, and began reading to figure out exactly what his lawyer was alluding to.

PLEASANT VIEW LONG TERM CARE CENTER
Attention: Administrator

Re: Adoption of Stacey Greenway
By Roman and Norma Buller
Dear Sir/Madam:

When my wife Norma and I decided that we were finally ready to start a family, it never occurred to us that we might have waited too long. Happily married in June of 1990, we worked night and day as a team to establish ourselves in the construction business. Many long hours were spent on the road, securing new contracts, and then following through hiring operators and completing the jobs on time.

Before we realized it, we were celebrating our tenth wedding anniversary and we were still childless. Immediately, my wife took a one-year leave of absence from the business and devoted herself to preparing our home for the arrival of our children.

As the months passed, the house was renovated but the baby never came. Norma was thirty-eight, I was forty-five, and it now looked like we'd missed the boat.

Six months stretched into a year, a year into two, and before we realized it, the nursery had been turned into a storage room, and we'd given up all hope of having a child. Is was a truly a sad time in our lives, but there was nothing we could do, so my wife came back to work and we focused all our energies back into our careers.

The first couple of months for Norma were trying times. She was tired and not feeling well, the stress of the long hours took their toll. We had no idea she was actually pregnant until a routine check-up alerted us to the possibility.

Seven months later, our beautiful little daughter Victoria was born. She was so perfect, she was so loved, and we couldn't understand why everyone was so disturbed to find out she had Down syndrome. To us, she was absolutely perfect.

As the time passed and our love grew, my wife and I decided that it would be good idea for Victoria to have a brother or sister, so once again we began our long and difficult journey down the path of fertility clinics and in vitro fertilization.

The doctors have been great, the counselors were extremely supportive, but the truth is that Norma no longer produces viable eggs.

Undaunted in our mission to share our love with a second child, Pleasant View was suggested to us by Victoria's pediatrician.

Originally, we had never set out to adopt a Down's child, but we hadn't ruled it out either. During our very first tour of the care center, we had the pleasure of meeting Stacey.

She warmed to us immediately, as we did to her, and by our third visit, we couldn't wait to bring Victoria along for the two girls to meet. As most people are aware, Down's children are extremely warm and trusting, Stacey is no exception to this rule. But beyond her warmth, there is a genuine intelligence, and what Norma and I believe is free will.

Repeatedly, over the last year, Stacey has made her choice very clear. She wants to come live with us, and we are thrilled at the prospect of legally adopting her into our family.

In retrospect, Norma and I have realized that we did not wait too long, nor did we miss the proverbial boat. We waited just long enough, and at the perfect time, two beautiful young girls have come into our lives.

Yours truly,

Roman and Norma Buller

As he looked up with tears welling in his eyes, Ed realized that somehow his lawyer had managed to slip out of the office undetected. Grateful for the privacy, he gently set the handwritten letter down on top of the file. With his throat swollen with emotion, unable to speak, he walked over to the office window and glanced down at the street, eighteen stories below.

"Sealed glass," his lawyer gently teased upon re-entry, "so please don't try to jump. You'll just break your nose and bleed all over my carpet, and there's no one here to clean up on a Sunday."

After turning and walking straight to the corner wet-bar, Ed poured himself a stiff shot of gin. "Why'd you give me that?" he demanded after downing the shot.

"Well, on paper, your two families have a lot in common. You both run successful businesses—you have positive family values, and marriages that have passed the test of time. You're a loving family man, and most of all, you're always thinking of what's best for your wife and your children. Except on this one occasion."

Ed stopped refilling his glass long enough to turn and glare at his lawyer. "Who do you think that I'm hurting now?"

"You tell me, Ed? What in the world do you and Tammy know about all the hard work and sacrifice that comes with raising a handicapped child? And what in the world would make you want to take something like that on at your age? Hell, you're hitting the prime of your life. Your youngest daughter Camille is off to college in the fall and the business is leveling off. With a little distribution of management, you and Tammy would be free to do some travelling overseas. It just doesn't make sense to me. If you had wanted it fourteen years ago, I would have understood, but now..."

"But now it's just crazy," Ed finished his attorney's sentence. "I guess we're a family looking for some kind of purpose, some kind of glue to hold us all together. Stacey can't be used for that purpose, can she?"

After closing the Stacey Greenway adoption file, the lawyer watched as his client set down his glass and moved away from the bar.

"What will happen if Tammy and I don't oppose this adoption?"

"Then the Buller court petition will be successful, and they will be granted temporary custody of Stacey, pending the ongoing investigations of her living conditions, and personal well being. In short," he continued after a quick breath, "she'll join their family and from what I see, live happily ever after."

Shaking his lawyer's hand goodbye, Ed turned to leave his office.

"One more thing Ed, and please listen carefully to me," his lawyer tried to explain. "There's no guilt, because there's no blame. Stacey does not have to forgive you for any wrong, because in her eyes, there has been no wrong. Your hands are clean Ed, and you have to get on with your life believing that very fact—because if you're going to be any kind of a father, or a husband, you have to let go of any lingering thoughts of *what if?*"

After carrying out the last load of soiled laundry from the shelter's storage room, Steven deposited it all under the plastic lid of the commercial hamper. He spun around to return to the action, and spotted the same two men standing at the rear of the main floor.

"Excuse me Doris," Steven stopped her on the way to the kitchen. "Don't turn around, but do you know the two guys standing by the coffee urn?"

"Actually," she admitted, "they've been here before. They were asking about you, wanting to know about your history with us here at the shelter."

"What are they doing back?" he asked, his heart beginning to pound against the walls of his chest.

"I'm not sure," Doris nodded, "but as head of the shelter, I think it's definitely my job to walk on over and find out. Don't you agree?"

As Steven watched Doris cross the floor, he noticed the two men instantly bristle under the weight of her interrogation. With his eyes darting back and forth between the agent's position and his current task, Steven rushed to finish up with the laundry and return to the makeshift trauma room.

"Steven," Doris called out across the floor. "Can you follow me to my office, please?"

He reluctantly stepped into the confined space already stuffed with the head counselor and the two agents. Steven squeezed himself inside before turning around to close the door.

"Mr. Whitters," the lead agent spoke up, "we seem to have a little situation at hand, and we've come down here to the shelter to speak to you in person."

"I've told you guys a hundred times that I don't know where my parents are, and I promise to call you if they contact me," he repeated as if reading on cue.

"That's not why we're here, Mr. Whitters. Actually, it has been recently brought to our attention that two individuals impersonating FBI agents have also been making the rounds interviewing your friends and neighbors. We believe this most likely has something to do with your parents. Will you speak with us?"

"But I've told you everything I know."

"Yes you have," the senior agent nodded toward his partner. "But now we actually have some information that we'd like to share with you."

Doris gingerly stepped out of her office, and closed the door, affording Steven at least a small measure of privacy. Then she turned and rushed across the shelter's floor, positive that Olga would want to know about Steven's meeting. She burst into the storage room, interrupted the doctor's treatment, and pulled his attending nurse away from their patient.

"Can't this wait?" Olga demanded, annoyed that she'd been summoned away from Gerri's side.

"I think Steven's world might be crashing down around his ears. You might want to go to my office and lend him a helping hand. You're the closest thing he has to a parent, and I think he might really need you right now."

Without waiting for any further details, Olga turned and made a beeline back across the floor. With two quick raps on the frame to announce her presence, she walked straight into the room and found herself in the middle of what she was sure to be a very deep conversation.

"Excuse us, ma'am," one of the agents jumped up from his chair to block her entrance. "This is a private meeting. I'm going to have to ask you to leave the room."

"You can ask," she announced, "but unless Steven wants me to leave, I'm not budging an inch."

The meeting continued as the lead agent reached into his breast pocket and pulled out a stack of autopsy photographs for Steven to identify.

After setting the two Styrofoam cups of soup down on the corner of her desk, Doris turned to face Olga. "Even if you're not hungry, I think you should both try and sip the broth. It's nearly six o'clock, and neither you nor Steven has eaten a bite all day"

"Excuse me," Steven blurted out as he suddenly rose to his feet and stepped toward the door. "I need the bathroom," he muttered, walking as if moving on autopilot.

Doris waited the obligatory thirty seconds to ensure that Steven was out of earshot, plunked down in the empty chair, and reached out to grab her friend's hand. "You look like hell. Is everything all right?"

"His entire family is dead. Murdered," she repeated as if in a trance.

"By who?"

"The agents think it had something to do with his mother's connections to a bingo scam."

"Somebody killed Steven's parents because his mom played too much bingo?"

Olga picked up the cup of soup while taking a moment to organize her thoughts. "It's a lot more complicated than that. It appears that his mother was involved in some sort of organized gambling fraud. These guys, the owners of the satellite bingo company, would tell her which games to play. She'd buy a card and then run to the bathroom and call in her numbers. Then miraculously, when she returned to the floor, her card would be a winner, and she'd drag in the big satellite pot."

Doris nodded her head, beginning to get a clearer picture. "Some of those pots are in the tens of thousands of dollars. You see their advertisements plastered all over town."

"Exactly, and that's why it was profitable to have a shill in the hall, a house player who'd ensure that the money came back to the house. They'd still pay out ninety-nine percent of the small pots, and with their little insurance policy sitting in the crowd, they were confident that the big pot was always coming back home."

Sitting back and watching Olga take a sip of her soup; Doris digested the weight of the information. "But you wouldn't be able to do it in one place for long, people would talk. You'd have to travel, take your show on the road."

"Exactly," Olga confirmed. "That's why the FBI believed the Whitter's packed up and supposedly moved to Arizona."

"You think somebody made them?"

"Don't know, but it sounds logical. Steven told me that they packed up and left without any warning in the middle of the night."

"How did Steven take the news of their deaths?"

Olga stood and suddenly reached across Doris's desk, yanking a tissue out of the cardboard box. "It's hard enough to learn that your parents are both dead, but when their autopsy photos are dropped onto your lap for identification, well… that's a whole other level of hurt."

"That poor boy," Doris turned to look at her office door, wondering what she could possibly say to Steven when he walked back into the room. "What can we do to help him?"

"I don't know," she admitted in total honesty. "A stitch or a bandage won't cure this. Steven has just learned that his parents were wanted criminals on the run from the law. They were most likely murdered when they were deemed no longer useful, and now everyone seems to be focusing their attention on finding his missing sister."

"By everyone, I assume you mean the good guys, and the bad guys?"

"Exactly. Whoever the bad guy turns out to be."

After slowly pushing open the office door, Steven stepped back inside the tight quarters.

"I'm so sorry about your parents," Doris immediately rose to her feet and enveloped her young volunteer in a hug. "I'm not sure what to say except that I'm very sorry for your loss."

"Thank you," he nodded, not trusting his voice with more than a two syllabic reply.

"Why don't you head home," Olga suggested. "We can handle things with Gerri, and I think you could use a little rest."

"Yeah, I think that's a great idea," Doris chimed in. "How about I call you a cab?"

Suddenly feeling dead on his feet, his own stitches beginning to throb, Steven just nodded his head in silent agreement.

With a snifter of brandy at his side, Martin continued to pace up and down the hallways of his house. It had been hours since he'd reluctantly left Steven at the shelter, and still no one was answering Olga's home telephone. Had the woman given up her residence and moved into the shelter with the indigent?

He'd had about all he could take. It was nearly eight o'clock, and he wasn't going to spend the rest of the night pacing the floor. He would give her until nine, and if he didn't have any word, he was going looking for her. His mind was set, and he downed the remaining ounce of brandy as if sealing the deal.

Careful to check Gerri's temperature every thirty minutes, Olga continued to monitor her patient, mindful of the spikes that would immediately spell a massive infection. She'd risen half a degree since the last check, and although the rate was not alarming, no movement at all would have been much preferable.

"I'll stop by first thing in the morning on the way to my clinic," Dr. Clifford announced from the corner of the storage room. "We've done all we can tonight. Hopefully, her common sense will prevail, and in the morning, and we can transfer her to the county hospital."

"Thank you again," Olga walked over to shake her old friend's hand. "You've been quite the life saver here for Doris over the years. I always wondered who supplied her with her emergency supplies, and now I see the face of the angel right before me."

"An angel? No. Just a man who does what little he can. A few vials of antibiotic and a bag of dressings don't qualify me for a set of wings. I've long since given up my place in that line."

"No wings, but a definite halo," she teased, slowly circling the fingers of her right hand over the top of the doctor's head.

"Call me if there are any changes. I think Doris has my home number tattooed on the palm of her right hand," he chuckled to himself.

"I hate to pry, but I was just wondering something."

"Wondering what?" the doctor slipped his arms into his coat.

"Well, I know for a fact that the shelter will be looking for a replacement after Doris's retirement, and I think the position would be a wonderful fit."

"For me?"

"Yes," Olga vigorously nodded her head in agreement.

"Well, from what I understand, the position has already been offered to you."

Crossing her arms at her chest, she silently shook her head side to side. "I'm not ready for this level of responsibility. I'm actually contemplating retirement, not an eighty-hour workweek. And by the way, I'm just a nurse. You're a doctor, much better suited for the position."

"To my knowledge, Doris had no medical training at all and has done marvelous things during her tenure here at the Lilac Tree."

Olga was just about to formulate a reply when suddenly Gerri's upper chest began heaving with convulsions, her body in a full-blown fight against its own infected tissue.

"Hold her down," the doctor yelled, turning to grab his medical supplies already waiting his departure by the door.

"She's lost consciousness," Olga reported, terrified that Gerri would code and they'd be helpless without a crash cart equipped with a mobile defibrillator.

Dr. Clifford yanked the covers off the patient's chest, and searched for a heartbeat, shaking his head as he repositioned his stethoscope. "I'm going to start CPR; you run and call an ambulance."

As Olga fled the room, she ran head first into Martin, nearly bowling the man right off his feet.

CHAPTER THIRTY-SEVEN

"You are not alone. There is hope."

—I am Legend, 2008

After hand washing the remaining wine glasses, Tammy Greenway listened to the family howl as they continued their lively game of *Truth or Dare.*

"My turn, my turn," Camille shouted. "I'm the birthday girl, and I'm going next!"

"Alright," her father interjected, "it's your turn."

"I pick my brother, Archie."

"Truth or dare," the group began to chant, prompting the next victim to pick his fate.

"Truth," he shouted, jumping up from his position on the couch. "Take your best shot, Cammy," he dared her with a tiny shove to her shoulder.

"Well, let's see," she purposely drew out the suspense. "Okay, Archie, why don't you tell everyone here why you hate girls who wear red shoes?"

"Oh, Cammy, come on," he begged. "That's a hundred years ago."

"Truth, truth," the group began to chant in union.

With his eyes darting around the group, and sweat beginning to bead on the skin of his upper lip, Archie blurted out the only two words that might possibly save his butt. "Double dare!"

Camille couldn't believe her luck, and clapped her hands in excitement. Her older brother was willing to take two dares instead of revealing the embarrassing truth surrounding the *red shoes.* It was her lucky day, and she wasn't going to let the opportunity pass her by.

"So, this is your double dare. You have to let me paint your toe nails with bright red nail polish, and…"

"And," Archie smirked; confident that he'd effectively dodged the bullet, "you want to glue some of them little stars on top of the polish?"

"No way. For your second dare, you can't take the polish off for one week," she began to roar, the mere thought of her brother parading around the locker room after lacrosse practice nearly brought her to her knees.

"Hey," Archie yelled back. "That's not fair. All dares have to start and finish tonight. Dad, tell her I'm right."

Ed rose from his coveted spot on the leather recliner, excused himself, and made off like a bandit towards the kitchen, leaving his kids and their guests to battle out their own interpretation of the house rules.

"Dry for me?" Tammy asked motioning her head toward the dishtowel neatly folded on the edge of the counter.

"What's the story with Archie and the red shoes?" he leaned over and whispered into his wife's ear. "It's driving the kids wild. Listen to them bicker."

"I don't know."

"Liar," Ed gently hip checked his wife. "Honey, I can tell you know just by the smile on your face."

"Fifteen minutes?" she bargained.

"Five."

"Ten?" Tammy offered a compromise.

"Fine, I'll brush your hair for ten minutes. Now spill!"

"Well, when Archie was young, I think it was grade three or four, his aunty and uncle were visiting one weekend. Archie woke up in the middle of the night and stumbled into the spare room. It so happens that they were quite passionately making love, and she was wearing a pair of bright red heels."

"Really," Ed's body began to shake with suppressed laughter. "He saw…"

"Yes," she finished his train of thought. "And I guess the memory has kind of turned him off the color red."

"That's hilarious, and kind of sick," he continued to snicker. "How come you never told me?"

"Forgot all about it, I guess."

"Anything else you forgot," he gently chided his wife. "Like maybe you've got a pair of red stilettos hiding up in your closet?"

"No such luck," she gently dried her hands after draining the sink. "But I did want to tell you that I've decided to seek a little therapy. I want to talk to someone about my feelings regarding Stacey. I have a few issues to deal with, and I don't think I'm ready to handle them on my own."

"That's good," Ed turned to pull his wife in toward his chest. "I don't think it would be a bad idea for both of us to get a little help. I know her adoption will finally close that chapter of our lives, but I want to be able to put it to rest properly. No nightmares, no feelings of guilt."

"Mom, Dad, you've gotta help me," Archie begged, his voice at least an octave higher than normal in his agitated state.

"You know the rules," his father teased. "I suggest you suck up the dare and get it over with."

"But I have practice three times next week. What in the hell am I going to do about that?"

"I have one simple word for you, my boy."

Mother and son both waited with baited breath for Ed's solution.

"Socks!"

It was midnight by the time the EMTs had moved Gerri's lifeless body into their rig. After choosing to ride shotgun, Dr. Clifford had climbed into the ambulance, still breathless and more than a little frustrated with his inability to revive his patient.

"I can't believe it," Olga cried into Martin's arms as they stood together on the crowded sidewalk. The milling crowd oblivious to their exchange as the streets buzzed with the death of another *Basher* victim.

"You did everything possible," Martin attempted to comfort her. "She was in rough shape and her refusal of treatment was not your fault."

"It was," Olga argued back, "Gerri believed I would take care of her, and I couldn't. She, she..."

"She succumbed to her injuries," Martin gently interceded through her sobs. "You did what you could with your limited resources. You and I both know there was a good chance she suffered from a multitude of internal injuries."

"Hey lady," a patron of the shelter began to tug on Olga's shirt. "Lady, you gotta help."

Both Martin and Olga turned to look at the face of the young man staring up at them from the edge of the sidewalk.

"Now what?" Olga demanded, her patience worn thin, her energy resources nearly depleted.

"The boss lady is losing it, man. She's freaking out bad. You better check on her," the guy warned before turning and disappearing back into the crowd.

Only sparing a second to glance into each other's eyes, Martin and Olga both turned and ran hand in hand up the shelter's front step.

"It's locked," Martin announced the minute his fingers were unable to budge the handles on the solid wooden doors. "Let's try the back."

Again running through the assembled crowd, they pushed their way past the onlookers and made a beeline for the back of the building.

"Damn, it's locked too," Olga confirmed their fears as the metal doorknob refused to budge an inch between her fingers.

As they stopped to catch their breath, both stood frozen in time as they debated their next move.

Without warning, a recessed emergency door popped open and a darkened figure stepped out into the back alley.

Before either Martin or Olga had a chance to shout out Doris's name and confirm her identity, the figure turned and bolted toward the main street, moving as if fuelled by an indescribable force.

"Follow her," were the only words out of Olga's mouth as she turned to run after her friend.

After pushing and shoving their way back through the crowds, they almost lost sight of their target at least twice, only able to hold onto their position by gluing their eyes to the white stripe bouncing up and down on the jacket's hood.

"Don't lose her," Olga yelled out to Martin as she stumbled along behind, half running and half tripping over the crumbly sidewalk leading down to the edge of the bridge.

"Doris!" Martin shouted for the tenth time, fighting to keep up and not loose Olga in the process. "Hold on, we're just trying to help you!"

His calls did little to persuade Doris to slow down, if in fact, that was whom they were frantically chasing in the first place.

Olga ran straight into Martin's back, and nearly bowled him over right where he stood, as she rounded the corner and came up on the edge of the tree line.

"She went down there." Martin pointed at the darkened path, taking a succession of deep breaths.

Out of wind, unwilling to waste her breath on an answer, Olga pushed past him and began running down the dirt path.

"Olga, where are you going?" Martin yelled; his heart pounding a hundred miles a minute as he frantically searched the blackened path for any signs of her return.

Olga continued to barrel down into the forest, unwilling to lose two friends in one night. Her eyes scrambled to pick up any fragment of the moonlight filtering down through the tangle of overhead branches.

With a frozen container of Olga's homemade chocolate chip cookies tucked under his left arm, and a fresh glass of milk balancing in his right, Steven returned to the living room sofa and gently lowered himself down onto the cushions. He'd actually managed to fall asleep for a couple hours when he'd first returned home, and after being woken by the doorbell, he was starving, his body craving something sweet to combat the exhaustion.

As he flipped through the channels, his eyes wandered back to the boxes that John and Mae had dropped off twenty minute before. They'd offered little by way of explanation, other than to say his mother had left them behind, and now they figured they'd held them long enough. Steven had responded in a kindly fashion, accepting the boxes without revealing the recent confirmation of his parent's death.

He set down the remote, gingerly rose from his position, and walked over to where the boxes sat. "Let's see what we've got," he muttered, flipping open the flaps and pulling out his first handful of papers.

An hour later, the contents finally began to reveal their secrets. His mother had all the original bingo cards that she'd collected after her wins. On the back of each paper card, written in her script, was the date and the amount of the win. Circled below the date was a much smaller figure, written in red ink. He wasn't sure, but since that the number roughly represented ten percent of the cash pot, Steven decided that dollar amount was more than likely her cut of the win.

Carmen Whitter's take was in the tens of thousands, possibly as high as a hundred thousand dollars over an approximate eight-month period. She had been in deep, and the more Steven dug, the more he realized that his parents had probably been murdered to ensure their perpetual silence.

After stuffing the papers back into the boxes, he slowly carried them one by one to his bedroom and shoved them unceremoniously into his closet. The FBI would have to be notified, the evidence turned over for their investigation, but that could wait. Tonight he had the very real, imminent medical emergency of Gerri on his mind. This was someone he could help, someone who had a shot if he interceded, and the musty papers from his dead mother's past would just have to be parked for one more day.

As he sat on his bed and took stock, Steven realized that only half a spice bottle of the dried healing powder lay hidden in Olga's house. More than likely not enough to repair all of the damage inflicted on Gerri's battered body. He needed more, at least enough to fill a large pickle jar. Steven knew what basic supplies he'd have to collect, he just wasn't sure if he'd be able to find enough canisters of fetal tissue in the limited amount of time.

As Doris raced down the path, she stumbled twice, both times nearly impaling herself on the fallen deadwood that lined the hand cut trail. Twenty feet behind her, Olga and Martin were finally able to gain some ground, catching glimpses of the reflective stripe on Doris's hood as she bounded down the hill.

"Hold up, Doris," Olga yelled into the night, her voice weakened by her lack of breath. "We're just trying… trying to help," she croaked.

Another two or three strides down the path's increasing incline, and Doris finally stopped, dropping to her knees, trying to catch her breath.

"Doris," Olga shouted, as she ran straight beside the crouched figure of her friend. "What… what in the hell?" she gasped, her lungs yearning for oxygen as she dropped down onto the soft earth of the dirt path and fought to catch her own breath.

"Damn you both!" Martin cursed the second he reached both women. "What in the hell is going on?" He wheezed, totally unprepared for a midnight jog in his leather-soled dress shoes and tailored wool pants.

Still gasping for breath, Doris finally turned to face Olga. "I got a tip that… that there's going to be another… *Basher Party* tonight and," she gulped another lung full of air. "I just can't allow another innocent victim to be brutally assaulted while I sit at home sipping wine in front of my fireplace."

"That's fine," Martin barked, brushing the twigs and leaves off the shins of his pants. "But what in the hell do you think you're doing, running down here in the middle of the night like some kind of crazed idiot?"

Doris just nodded, still too exhausted to formulate a verbal reply.

"And what in the hell's a *Basher Party*?" Martin suddenly threw out the question, looking to either lady for an answer.

"None of your fucking business, old man," a voice boomed from the side bushes as an assault of bodies rained down on the three would-be rescuers.

When the first clenched fist embedded itself in the unsuspecting muscle of Martin's right side, he instantly dropped to his knees. Without a second to recover his wind or even raise his arms in self-defense, a hail of blows began pummeling his body. "Olga," he screamed, or desperately wanted to, unsure if his voice was actually responding to his commands as the blood began to pour out of his mouth.

As she desperately fought to protect herself from the raining blows, Doris rolled on her side and tucked her knees as close to her chest as possible, burying her face behind the shield of her upper arms.

With her back shoved up against the towering strength of a poplar tree, Olga fought to release herself from the vice-like grip of her attacker as he throttled her with both of his hands firmly clenched around her neck. She kicked at him and flayed her arms, but her limited defense did little to dissuade her attacker as he dropped his right hand from her neck to deliver one quick and decisive lower jab to her right side.

Olga crumbled like a house of cards, gratefully unconscious as the first of several blows from the man's boots landed squarely on her chest and left side of her skull.

As the violent assault continued, Martin recovered his balance long enough to deliver a couple punches of his own. It was his final attempt at self-defense before a brutal whack from a piece of deadfall on the back of his knees sent him crashing face first to the forest floor. This time Martin was not able to recover, and when the fists were replaced with blows from the fallen tree limb, he too faded into unconsciousness.

Doris knew that the second she dropped her hands or her knees, one of the strikes might kill her. So she pulled in tighter, unaware that she was screaming every time a fist connected with the muscles in her upper thighs or lower back.

One attacker was sitting on top of Doris now, raining down his assault as he simultaneously attempted to roller her over and expose her soft belly.

As she continued to struggle, she fought to remain on her side with her head buried in her chest and her face protected by her upper arms. Doris began to choke on the blood rising up in her throat. As she began losing her grip on consciousness, she was suddenly struck by a terrible thought.

She'd forgotten to turn on the shelter's answering machine.

Blowing twenty-five dollars on cab fare wasn't Steven's usual style, but then waiting around for public transit at three in the morning wasn't the answer either. He jumped out near the hospital emergency door, pulled off his coat, and clipped his ID badge onto the material of his uniform, before even entering the building.

As he whisked past the night security with little more than a perfunctory glance, ignoring the treatment floors or the patient wards, Steven reached down and punched the B-3 button on the elevator panel, heading straight to the bowels of the hospital.

After stepping off the elevator, he made his way straight to the biohazard containment room, a small storage area set aside for pick-up of medical waste. Containers of discarded sharps, including needles, blades, and anything else capable of piercing the skin were all pilled neatly along the back wall. Sealed units of amputated limbs or discarded biopsied tissue adorned the right wall of metal shelving. And on the left, were large sealed garbage bins of soiled bandaging and operating sponges. Anything biological or disposable that could not be sterilized for future use was collected and shipped off to a medical incinerator.

As if occupying a place of honor in the center of the room, the nondescript boxes holding the plastic canisters of aborted fetal tissue also awaited their final journey.

Steven turned and closed the door, and began examining the pile, pleasantly surprised to find that the boxes had been timed and dated by each shift before being sent to the basement storage. Obviously choosing the most recent cases from the night's last shift, Steven lifted a top box off the pile and flipped open the cardboard flaps.

"Twelve," he mumbled, confirming a dozen canisters of fresh tissue. Unfortunately not refrigerated, he was still confident that none of the canisters were more than eight to ten hours old and would be fine, as long as he dehydrated them as soon as possible. He closed the lid, hoisted up the heavy box, and turned toward the door. Steven suddenly stopped to debate whether or not he'd be able to carry the heavy load all the way out the hospital's doors, and gratefully had a burst of inspiration.

After setting the box back on the floor, he ran out into the hall and grabbed a pushcart, opting to load the canisters before returning to the elevator.

As the elevator rose two floors to the cafeteria, Steven rolled his cart out into the hallway and headed straight toward the rear kitchen. He'd reasoned that his best chance of leaving with the box was going to be through one of the back entrances, so he continued with his plan. The morgue was definitely out of the question, heavily monitored, complete with video cameras and sign-in sheets. Shipping and receiving was even worse with manned security personnel checking any and all freight, matching it to their master dossier. His last option and best chance was probably the cafeteria.

"Hey buddy," Steven called out to one of the staff cleaning the staff dining room. "I've got a box of rotten food from the fridge on the maternity ward. Where you want me to dump it?"

"Give it here, I'll take it," the guy shook his head, annoyed that he was being distracted from his job.

"Actually, some of this shit was leaking. If I lift it off the cart, the box will probably split open and rotten yogurt will run all over your floors."

"Dumpsters out back, past the dishwashers. Door locks itself, so unless you prop it open, you'll have to walk all the way around to emergency to get in. Got it?"

"Got it," Steven nodded, passing through the empty kitchen as he wheeled the twelve canisters right out the hospital's back door.

CHAPTER THIRTY-EIGHT

"Because I believe that God, whomever you hold that to be, hears all prayers, even if sometimes the answer is no."

—Deep Impact, 1998

Metro Bobinsky needed to urinate so badly that he was actually afraid his bladder might burst open from the pressure. He had been passed out on the couch in Bert's living room after a long day of heavy drinking, when he was jarred awake by the crippling pains.

He half rolled and half crawled off the couch, and made his way in the darkness, staggering toward the staircase. If memory served him well, there would be a bathroom at the top of the stairs to the left of the master bedroom, and by his calculations, it was his best chance of not soiling Miranda's wall-to-wall carpeting.

With his bladder empty, accident averted, Metro emerged from the washroom and took a second to take stock of his surroundings. He could hear Bert snoring like a locomotive off in the spare room while some streams of light snuck out from under the door in the master bedroom.

"Miranda?" he called out in a whisper, wondering if she had been inadvertently startled by his lumbering footsteps. "Did I wake you?" he gently called again, reaching for the bedroom's doorknob.

Metro strained to pick up any verbal reply, and shook his head, unable to focus with the intermittent ringing in his eardrums brought on by his own high blood pressure. Suddenly, he opted to peek discreetly inside the bedroom—his sense of smell was the first to be assaulted.

"Miranda?" Metro called out again, this time his voice taking on a more urgent tone as the fingers of his right hand rushed up to shield his nose from the overwhelming stench.

In a pool of soiled bedding, in the center of the bed, lay a woman's naked body. His brain recognized that it was Miranda's face, yet his mind was having difficulty assimilating the condition in which she lay. Smears of fecal matter, and what appeared to be dried blood, ran up and down the length of her thighs and abdomen. Days of urinating right where she lay had discolored the cream-colored sheets and the matching comforter, the outer rings already drying into deep yellowy stains, those closest to her body still dark with moisture.

Continuing to mutter Miranda's name, Metro forced himself to move in closer, actually bending over the bed to tentatively reach out and touch her right arm. Her skin was cool to the touch, but not ice cold. Having stumbled over more than one dead body in his life, she just didn't have that telltale grayish color. Miranda's skin was actually darker than usual, as if tanned after a weekend of sunning at the beach.

As he held his breath and leaned in yet closer, Metro tried unsuccessfully to catch her eyes. The tattered bandages from Miranda's previous facial burns had peeled upward, effectively hiding the upper portion of her face. He forced himself to reach across her head and lift the soiled gauze off her eyelids, and Metro's breath caught in his throat when Miranda's pale blue eyes just stared back at him.

"What's the matter?" he demanded, his stomach churning in response to the horrific sight.

Miranda did the only thing she could do—she blinked, and blinked, and blinked.

Metro responded by doing the one thing he shouldn't have done. He turned and ran down the hall, repeatedly shouting out Bert's name.

As the early morning sunshine began to crest over the towering spruce trees, Martin was still struggling to stop the bleeding from the deep lacerations criss-crossing Olga's skull. Already stripped of his shirt and tie, Martin had long since shredded the cotton into strips and done his best to bandage her head. It was not an easy task, considering that any movement across the ground came with bone-jarring stabs of pain, as he was forced to drag his broken leg behind him.

"Doris," he called out for the hundredth time, still deeply bothered by his inability to raise her from unconsciousness. She was breathing, with no apparent lacerations or broken limbs, yet she was obviously suffering from fairly serious internal injuries. Her abdomen was distended, obviously filling with blood, and unless he was able to summon some help, her chances of survival were quickly fading.

"My head," Olga moaned, her right hand continuing to clutch the tattered cartilage barely connecting the tissue of her ear to the right side of her head. As the attackers had dragged her kicking and screaming from the forest edge, Olga had bounced over piles of dead wood, the brittle limbs ripping and tearing her skull and any other soft tissue they encountered.

"You're going to be fine," Martin attempted to soothe her, his voice easily betraying his uncertainty.

He felt dizzy, and extremely disorientated, from what he assumed to be his own concussion. His broken fibula protruding not only through his skin, but also through the wool fabric of his pants, was beginning to worry him. Since he had no material or bandaging left for any sort of a splint, Martin pondered whether his own blood loss would soon render him unconscious. It was highly possible that they'd succumb either to their injuries or to the elements, not more than a hundred feet from the edge of the city. They were just five minutes from the edge of the Westside Bridge, and although they'd all been dragged off the path and left to die in the underbrush, Martin still prayed that a possible rescue was only minutes away.

Unable to summon help himself, he needed to alert some bystander to their plight. He'd lost his phone, and was nearing the point of physical exhaustion. The only thought that crossed his mind was some sort of signal—maybe a fire, something to bring the authorities down the path within shouting range.

"How, how, how?" Martin chanted to himself. Forget the fact that a small, uncontained fire in the middle of the forest could easily escalate into a roaring brushfire and burn all three of them alive. He just couldn't allow himself to dwell on those negative details. Martin just concentrated on his options for making any kind of spark, and at the moment, they all looked extremely dim.

As he stumbled into the darkness of the spare room, Metro

scrambled to find the light switch, finally locating the wall plate and illuminating the room.

"Leave me alone," Bert groaned, rolling over to hide his face as he slept on top of the bed's covers.

"It's Miranda, Bert," Metro shouted. "Get up man. There's something really wrong with your wife."

"Leave her sleep," he growled. "We had a wild night," he reluctantly rolled back, rubbing his eyes in a futile attempt to clear his vision. "Woman probably needs a little extra sleep, is all."

"No," Metro argued, reaching down to yank his buddy up into a sitting position. "Listen to me. She's wet the bed, and there's blood! You gotta call 911!"

"I might… I might have been a little rough," Bert groaned, pulling himself to his feet and staggering to the bathroom. "Hate it when she pretends to be sleeping," he continued to whine from behind the closed door. "You gonna make some coffee?"

Metro wasn't listening; he was back at Miranda's side dialing 911—the first thing he'd done right in years.

Just minutes before the ambulance and fire truck had arrived; Bert had finally realized that he too was covered in blood and feces. Disgusted with his own appearance, Bert stepped straight into the shower. He was still washing his body when the police arrived. By the time he'd wrapped a terry housecoat around his chest and cinched the belt at his waist, the authorities were pounding on his bathroom door.

Moments later, Bert found himself sequestered in the spare room as the paramedics fought to stabilize his severely dehydrated wife.

Downstairs in the kitchen, Metro sucked heavily on a cigarette he'd found on the counter, answering as many of the officer's questions as he was able. By the time they turned their attention to the husband, they'd already established a fairly accurate picture of what had taken place over the weekend.

"You just called us in the nick of time," one of the officers reiterated. "A human body can only exist roughly three days without any form of re-hydration, and from what we've seen; our victim was already near death."

"But is Miranda going to be okay?" Metro asked for the tenth time.

"She appears to be suffering from some form of paralysis, so I wouldn't assume to make any predictions. Do you know what happened? Did she have a fall? Do you possibly know how she sustained the burns to her face?"

Metro began to unload, sharing every scrap of information he could muster. Beginning with the boiling pudding, and ending with Bert's admission to a night of wild sex. Point by point, he attempted to clear his conscience.

By the time the paramedics had hooked Miranda to an IV, stabilized her neck and entire body on the wooden backboard, she already looked a little better. Cocooned in clean white sheets and cotton blankets, the pink was slowly returning to her cheeks, as were the tears. Once again flowing freely from her eyes, she proved to be alive and cognitive of her surroundings. Blinking once for yes, and twice for no, under the instructions of the paramedics, she let them know she was ready to be moved down the stairs and out of her *Little Shop of Horrors*.

Transported down the stairs, past the living room couch and kitchen table, Miranda managed to grab quick glimpses of her surroundings. She honestly feared that she would die in that upstairs bedroom, left to starve to death, or even choke on her own spittle. It was a reality that almost came to fruition when Bert had raped her lifeless body and then nearly passed out on top of her with his entire weight bearing down on her already weakened chest.

But this morning she was going to the hospital—this Miranda knew. Hopefully, she'd never have to see his disgusting face again.

As soon as the ambulance attendants finished loading their patient into the back of their ambulance, Bert was unceremoniously dragged kicking and screaming from the house. Instead of clean blankets and tender words, he was cuffed and pushed down into the back seat of a police cruiser. His nightmare had just now begun.

With sweat pouring off his face, and blood still seeping from his wounds, Martin continued to drag himself over the rough terrain, fighting to move across the remaining six feet to Doris's side. She was still unconscious, with the signs of petechial hemorrhaging becoming more apparent in the soft tissue surrounding her eyes.

"I need to check your pockets, darling," he whispered, hoping to find anything that might assist him in his quest for fire.

"Martin," Olga groaned, her hands struggling to remove that makeshift bandages wrapped horizontally around her skull. "I can't see."

"Hang on, I'll be right there," Martin called out, taking one last second to check the remaining pockets in Doris's tracksuit carefully.

"What happened? Who… who attacked me?" she mumbled.

As he turned his remaining energy to the next immediate task, Martin gritted his teeth and began dragging himself toward Olga. His wool pants were already ripped at his left hip where the rocks and sticks had pierced his skin. With every inch of progress, he further managed to tear his pant leg and shred the tender skin.

"I need to start a fire," he explained, almost as if speaking aloud helped to keep him focused. "Do you have any matches, a lighter, something?"

Suddenly, Olga's hands stopped fidgeting with the bandaging, as she froze, motionless.

"What?" Martin demanded, panting through his gritted teeth.

"I… I think I hear someone coming through the forest," she gingerly explained, the left side of her face lying in the soft dirt at the edge of the path.

Martin realized that it could be their attackers, so his first instinct was to lay motionless, absolutely silent.

"Help us," Olga weakly pleaded.

Suddenly, Martin also began to yell at the top of his lungs. He reasoned that if the attackers had come back to finish them off, they were already dead, unable to run and hide from their position on the path. But if it was an innocent hiker, he needed to get their attention and draw them to where they lay.

"Hello," some girl's voice answered back.

"We need help. We've been hurt," Martin shouted.

As the group of early morning joggers happened upon them, Martin dropped his head down into his hands and suddenly began sobbing with relief.

After rising from his bed to shut the ringer off his alarm clock, Steven stumbled off toward the kitchen to check on his latest batch. Every sixty minutes throughout the night, he'd moved the trays, emptying the dried chips into a bowl and refilling the trays with fresh liquid tissue.

He was exhausted, and Olga's kitchen looked like a war zone. Whenever he had an accident, he had used paper towels to wipe up the mess. The kitchen's garbage had long since over flowed with bloody paper, so Steven had just resigned himself to drop everything else in a pile.

By the time Steven had finished reducing the last batch to a coarse powder with the mortar and pestle, he'd miraculously managed to fill one of Olga's sterilized fruit sealers with the combined contents of four different containers.

He tightly secured the metal lid, and looked across the kitchen, realizing that it was already six o'clock in the morning. As he suddenly reasoned that he'd better call the hospital if he wasn't going to show up for his first shift back at work, Steven rationalized that now would not be an opportune time to lose his job.

Dialing from memory, Steven waited while the operator transferred his call to personnel.

"Hello, you've reached the personnel office. Sorry no one is available to answer your call. Our regular office hours are seven a.m. to four-thirty p.m., Monday through Friday. Eight-thirty a.m. to three p.m. on Saturday and..."

Steven hung up the phone. It was too early to call. He knew that there had to be another way to register in if you woke up sick with some kind of virus, but having never risen too ill to make a shift, he was unfamiliar with the procedure.

He decided that his best bet was to stop by in person, so Steven ran to the shower and quickly rinsed off his body, dragging a disposable razor over his face while standing right under the hot spray. After throwing on a uniform, the only clean outfit he could find, Steven was ready for a quick trip to the hospital to cancel his shifts.

He arrived just as the night's cleaning staff was finishing the main lobby. Steven sidestepped the barrage of rolling carts, and made his way to the far bank of elevators.

"Was it a car accident?" one of the nurses turned to ask another.

"I don't think so," she answered with a shake of her head. "From what I heard down in Emergency, Dr. Hood was jumped somewhere near the Westside Bridge."

Steven stopped breathing, spinning on his heels to address the two young women.

"Dr. Hood was attacked? Is he all right? What happened? Was he alone? Was he stabbed?"

Before the startled nurses could even formulate an answer, Steven turned and ran straight for the basement stairs, making his way directly toward the underground tunnel. Running full speed, he raced down the concrete pathway in a direct beeline for the emergency room.

"Dr. Hood," he shouted at the receptionist. "He's here in emergency?"

Glancing first at Steven as she instantly recognized the hospital's staff uniform, the woman took a deep breath before motioning for him to lean in a little closer.

"Dr. Hood's in orthopedics with a compound fracture waiting for surgery, but Nurse Heinz and…" the receptionist dropped her face to read her own papers in an attempt to recall a name, "and Doris McDougall are still both in surgery."

"Status?" he demanded, working hard to control the hysteria threatening to overtake him.

"Well," she continued to whisper, actually taking the time to raise her right hand up to her mouth in an attempt to shield her words. "The doctor is going to be fine, but I hear the two women are in pretty rough shape. Internal injuries, broken bones, and all types of lacerations," she nodded after giving up the information.

"Can I see Olga, Nurse Heinz?"

"She's in surgery," the lady repeated for the second time. "You know you can't go in there."

Steven's head turned toward the swinging doors concealing the hallway that led directly to the emergency room operating theaters.

"Are you family?"

"No, but…"

"Hey," the receptionist suddenly stopped him in mid explanation. "Are you Steven Whitters the orderly?"

"Yes I am," he fumbled in his pocket to produce the identification badge that should have been already pinned to his uniform.

"I've been trying to reach you. Nurse Heinz kept mumbling your name before surgery, so when I looked you up in our staff directory, I…"

"That's an old number," he cut the woman off.

"You should always update your personnel file in case of emergency. Look what happened today."

Not the least bit interested in a lecture, Steven turned and walked straight through the swinging doors.

As the surgeon and anesthesiologist reluctantly stepped out of the first theater, Steven caught a quick glimpse of some masked person pulling the cotton sheet over the head of the patient.

"Was that Olga?" he blurted out to the doctors. "Who just died?"

As they snapped off their gloves, both took turns shoving them into the hallway receptacle.

"Patient's name was McDougall," one of the men reported. "Heinz is in number two."

"Doris McDougall?"

Reaching for the chart hanging outside the operating theater, the doctor flipped open the metal cover and scanned the information. "Yes. Her first name was Doris. Did you know this woman? Was she family?"

"She was the director of the Lilac Tree Shelter," Steven flatly stated.

"I'm going in for a consult on Heinz," the anesthesiologist announced, stepping away to grab a clean gown and facemask. "Barry's having a hard time with her skull fractures. Going to see if

I can help," he offered before disappearing behind the doors of the second operating theater.

As the surgeon walked off, making notes in the chart, Steven stepped back until he met the solid resistance of the hallway wall. As he leaned back heavily against the support, he fought to digest all the news.

CHAPTER THIRTY-NINE

"...for your glory walks hand in hand with your doom."

—Troy, 2004

Martin struggled to reach the nurse's call button, and rang it for the fifth time since returning from his trip to orthopedics.

"Yes doctor," the nurse rushed into his private room.

"I'm still waiting for any news from emergency. Has anybody called up with any kind of report?" he demanded, frustrated with his inability to move.

"No doctor, still no report," she shook her head. "But I can check again for you."

"No need," the surgeon reported as he entered the doctor's room. "Thank you, nurse," he politely dismissed the woman.

After dragging a chair to the side of Martin's bed, the surgeon dropped down into the padded vinyl seat. "We did all we could for

Doris McDougall, but when we opened her up to stop the abdominal bleeding, I was shocked."

"What'd you find?" Martin demanded.

"A large ulcerated neoplasm arising from gastric mucosa, all extending upward to the gastro-esophageal junction."

"Doris had stomach cancer," Martin reiterated aloud. "How advanced?"

"Stage three for sure, possibly four. The autopsy will be more definitive."

"Do you think she knew? Any signs of a recent endoscopy?"

"Nothing recent, but again without her history, I can't be sure. We both know how ulcerated gastric carcinomas can manifest symptoms similar to those of a benign peptic ulcer."

"True," Martin reluctantly nodded his head in agreement. "She might have misread the iron deficiency as anemia, and the vague upper abdominal discomfort as an ulcer. Doris was in the process of retiring her position of shelter director, so I think it's safe to say that she was experiencing some form of discomfort whether or not her condition had been diagnosed."

"We did all we could Martin, but she was basically DOA."

"How about Olga? Is she out of surgery yet?" he continued, forty years of experience having taught him to concentrate his energies on the living.

"No, that's actually why I stopped by," the doctor rose from his chair and walked over toward the window in an attempt to organize his thoughts. "Underneath the fairly extensive tissue lacerations, we found that Olga has multiple skull fractures, inflicted by blunt force trauma."

"How bad?"

"Well, her primary brain injury is in the occipital lobe, the location of the original blow. However, her secondary injuries in the temporal and frontal lobes are just as..."

"Steven," Martin announced the minute the young man burst into his hospital room.

"I can't find Olga," Steven muttered, his eyes betraying the sense of loss beginning to consume his entire being.

"She's been moved upstairs from emergency," the surgeon interjected. "I was just explaining everything to Dr. Hood," he stated, unwilling to continue discussing his patient's status with the orderly still standing in the room.

"This young man is Olga's boarder, and close friend," Martin explained. "Please continue, doctor."

"Alright," the surgeon conceded, motioning for Steven to take his seat before the kid crumbled to the floor right in front of his eyes. "The four discernible fractures in Olga's skull are already showing pinpoint hemorrhages caused by disruption of the small intra-cerebral blood vessels."

Steven looked to Martin for an explanation in plain English.

"After being struck in the back of the head by some sort of weapon, Olga started bleeding in her brain. The surgeons need to relieve the pressure before there is any resulting brain damage."

"Yes, that's it in a nut shell," the surgeon agreed.

Turning back to his old colleague, Martin had one more important question. "What's the location of the bleeding? Is it an epidural, a subdural, or a subarachnoid hemorrhage?"

"Yes," the doctor sadly nodded his head, realizing that Martin would now understand the precarious nature of Olga's injuries.

"What is it?" Steven demanded, terrified by their silence as he jumped to his feet to demand an answer.

Reaching out to grab the young man's hand as he stood at the edge of the hospital bed, Martin tightly squeezed Steven's fingers for support. "She's bleeding all throughout her brain. Olga's fighting for her life."

Steven sat with Martin for hours, waiting for any further news of Olga's condition when he suddenly remembered the dehydrator still running on the kitchen cupboard.

"I've gotta go," he announced. "I have to check on something at home. I'll be back as soon as I can," he promised.

Martin shook the boy's hand and promised to have a nurse leave a message on the house phone if anything should drastically change within the next hour.

Back on the bus, Steven watched in silence as the streets buzzed by his window. The sidewalks were filled with people in varying degrees of health. Joggers running in the park at their physical peak, junkies in the back alley shooting up as they courted death with each new fix. Realistically, the average man or woman existed somewhere in the middle, and Steven was totally unprepared for Olga to slip into the latter category. He had an alternate solution, and within the flash of a microsecond, he decided that it was the only viable option.

Jamming his key into the house's front door, Steven was instantly assaulted with the odor of burning flesh. The tissue in the dehydrator trays was crisp; the crumbly pieces a dark, blackish color. The heavy stench of burnt tissue hung heavy in the air, and Steven choked in response to the smell, grateful that the home's smoke alarms hadn't begun to wail.

After pulling the plug on the electric machine, he yanked open the kitchen window, not bothering to hang around longer than necessary to air out the house. Steven grabbed the jar of previously dehydrated tissue, and wrapped the glass in a kitchen towel, gingerly placing it in the bottom of his duffle bag. As he turned to leave the house, he slammed the door shut behind him and ran off back toward the bus stop.

By the time he had returned to the hospital, two hours had elapsed, and Martin's hospital room was totally empty.

"Where's Dr. Hood?" he demanded at the nurse's station, unconcerned with the phone call the nurse was presently engaged in.

"I'll be right with you," she mouthed, continuing to record information in a file.

"Now," Steven demanded, reaching down over the counter to disconnect her line. "This is an emergency!" he shouted. "Where is Dr. Hood?"

"ICU," the nurse hissed, shooting him a dirty look as she hurriedly punched the number back into her phone.

Steven raced down the corridor, to the Intensive Care Unit, imagining the worse with each step.

"When will the doctor be able to speak to us?" one of the police officers insistently pestered the duty nurse. "Looks like we have two homicides on our hands, and we've yet to interview the only survivor."

"I'll check again with Dr. Hood," the nurse responded, stepping around her desk and making her way toward a set of VIP rooms.

After quickly stuffing his duffle bag and jacket into the bottom drawer of the unit's dressing cart, Steven wheeled his way past the assembled crowd and quickly picked up the path of the nurse. As she disappeared into a patient room, Steven stopped in his tracks and debated his next move. Seconds before reaching a decision, the nurse reappeared, flustered and obviously wishing she'd been scheduled to any other unit than intensive care.

"Excuse me sir," she addressed the police officers. "Dr. Hood is saying his goodbyes to Olga Heinz, and asks not to be disturbed. He asked that I take your cards, and he'll have the hospital call you as soon as he returns to his room."

"I guess that'll be fine," one of the detectives replied, digging in his coat for a card.

As the officers moved down the hall, Steven gently pushed open the door with his left hand, steering the cart inside with his right.

"Steven," Martin gasped as he fought to speak through the veil of his own tears. "We've lost her."

Steven abandoned the cart and rushed up to the bedside to stare down at Olga's form, her face barely visible behind the inches of gauze bandaging swaddling her entire head. "What happened?" he whispered.

"She stroked out," the doctor tried to explain in the simplest of terms.

"She's breathing," Steven argued, pointing to the blankets as they gently rose and fell on Olga's chest.

"She's brain dead," the doctor admitted as if announcing a personal defeat. "They're allowing me to say goodbye before they disconnect her life support."

Steven was unable to digest the information. His mind struggled to get a grip on the reality of the situation. "Then operate again! Fix her!" he demanded, his voice raising several decibels as he fought to find a solution. "You're a doctor, so do something!"

"I can't," Martin began to sob from the confines of his wheel chair. "There's nothing we… we can do."

"Yes there is," Steven muttered under his breath. "I can help."

Raising his face from his own hands, Martin wiped his eyes as he tried to understand Steven's point. "What do you mean?"

Steven returned to the dressing cart and grabbed his duffle bag, pulling out the sealed jar and placing it gently in Martin's lap. "I know you love her, and I think you'd want her to have any chance at all. Right?"

Armed with strict instructions not to intervene on their final moments of closure, the hospital staff placed a rarely used *Do Not Disturb* sign on the VIP door and kept their distance. Inside, Steven and Martin prepared to play God.

"Careful," Martin instructed Steven for the tenth time. "You have to cut the gauze without catching the padding beneath."

"I'm doing it," Steven barked back, the sweat beginning to dampen his forehead as he dropped another swatch of bloody dressing down onto the floor.

"Now slip your left hand under her neck and gently turn Olga's head to the right," he continued to instruct his student, mindful that their best intentions were probably going to land them both in jail. "Be careful with her right ear. It was reattached in surgery."

"There's so much padding," Steven moaned, having finally removed the last of the gauze.

"Now, when you slowly remove the padding, her head will be totally exposed, and then…" Martin stalled, the absurdity of the situation starting to sink in.

"Then I'll cover her head with the healing powder," Steven announced, picking up where Martin left off. "Then you can tell me how to re-bandage her," he confidentially reassured the doctor. "We have a whole cart full of supplies at our disposal."

Martin nodded as Steven began peeling off the padding, exposing Olga's shaved head and the intricate maze of dark black stitching. Her head was grotesquely swollen and terribly bruised—her face nearly unrecognizable—her appearance almost scaring Steven senseless. All he could fixate on was a childhood picture of Frankenstein's evil monster, rising off his stone slab to chase the terrified villagers.

"She may begin to bleed slightly from the incisions. That's normal, and to be expected," Martin announced, head bowed as he continued to monitor Olga's ever-weakening heartbeat through the stethoscope positioned on her chest.

As he picked up the jar, Steven suddenly felt stumped. How in the hell was he going to make the healing powder stick to her head? It wasn't at all like sprinkling dried powder on a flat surface and then wrapping the wound in a dressing. Suddenly the spherical shape of Olga's skull began to present an unforeseen problem.

"What's the matter," Martin asked, noticing Steven's reluctance to continue.

"How am I going to make it stick to the back and sides?"

"Can you make it into a paste and spread it on?"

Debating his choice, Steven suddenly nodded his head in agreement. "I guess so; it's going to get wet when it soaks past the stitches anyway."

Forty-five minutes later, Olga's skull was totally covered in reddish paste and completely re-bandaged, the resulting dressing not very dissimilar from the original.

"How long?" Martin asked, haunted by a fleeting image—he saw himself sitting at an empty metal desk behind rusted metal bars in some dingy, underground prison cell.

"Overnight, I think," Steven mused, not exactly sure from their limited trials.

"Then we'll wait," Martin announced as Steven absentmindedly wiped the droplets of paste off the hospital sheets before turning to stuff the discarded bandaging and empty jar back into his duffle bag.

EPILOGUE

"I'd tell you to go to hell, but I think you're already there."

—Lord of War, 2005

As they sat side by side, they continued to wait to see the doctor. Since they had arrived without an appointment, Paul Harder was lucky they'd even agreed to perform his girlfriend's abortion on the same day.

"I don't feel that well, maybe I need to go home and just lie down," she whispered into Paul's ear.

"Look!" he barked. "I took the afternoon off work to get this done, and I'm not leaving here today until you've seen the god damn doctor!"

"I'm sorry," the young girl began to sniffle, digging in her purse for a handful of damp tissues.

"Well, then just try and get a grip on yourself," he flatly stated before rising from his seat and strolling over to the coffee machine. After filling a cup with two cubes of sugar and a teaspoon of powdered whitener, Paul Harder casually flipped open his phone, and checked the screen for any messages.

"Jane Brown," Tony read off the papers on his clipboard after reappearing in the waiting room. "Jane Brown," he repeated one last time for clarity.

"That's you," Paul sharply announced, rushing over to his girlfriend's side before roughly yanking her upwards into a standing position.

"Jane Brown?" she questioned him in a whisper.

"Jane Brown," he confirmed, propelling her toward the waiting figure at the back of the room.

"Are you coming with me?" she spun on her heels, terrified at whatever may be waiting for her behind the closed doors.

"Your call, man." Tony shook his head side-to-side, bored with the tears and dramatics common with many of the waiting patients.

As he reluctantly followed his pregnant girlfriend into the back halls, Paul Harder grabbed a small stool in the corner of the room while Tony dropped a paper gown and a thin cotton blanket on the edge of the examination table.

"Strip down naked, put this on, and lay back on the table with your feet in the stirrups. The doctor will be right in. He turned to shoot Paul a glance, and stopped to offer another few words of parting advice. "Stay out of the way, and if you think you're gonna faint, get the hell out of the room. If I have to pick you up and wet-nurse your ass, it's an extra fifty bucks! Got it?"

"As long as you don't ask me to get a red blanket," Paul nervously chuckled.

"A red blanket? What the fuck you talking 'bout, red blanket?"

"Just a little private joke, don't pay any attention to me."

"Whatever, man." Tony shook his head before leaving the room.

Less than a minute later, the doctor suddenly appeared at the door. "Hello, I'm Dr. Clifford. I'll be performing the termination of your pregnancy here at the *Changeroom*," he introduced himself with the most fatherly of tones. "I see you haven't had a chance to undress yet, so I'll just get my instruments ready while you slip into the gown," he purposely managed to meet the young woman's eyes.

As he stepped up to the sink to scrub his hands, the doctor took a second to glance down the counter at the girl's handwritten form. Her boyfriend had paid for the cheapest procedure possible. No anesthetic, only a single dose of oral antibiotics after completion, this guy wasn't wasting any of his hard-earned cash on the young woman's comfort. How the doctor desperately prayed she wasn't a screamer; they always gave him such a headache. Maybe the pretty little thing had a high tolerance for pain. He hoped. But then again, it didn't really matter, he was just paid to perform the procedure and get the patient back out the door. *Treat 'em and Street 'em,* an unwritten rule of clinic care around the world.

"So are you ready, dear?" he turned and smiled , snapping on his rubber gloves seconds before dragging the wheeled tray toward the trembling young woman.

Bert balanced the plastic tray on the edge of his knees, and scrambled to inhale his lunch in the allotted ten minutes. The plastic cutlery did little to assist his efforts, and after only two swipes at the Salisbury steak, he'd inadvertently managed to snap the plastic knife in two. He angrily threw both pieces down on his tray, picked up the fork in his right hand, and began shoveling the cold egg noodles into his mouth. Chewing as quickly as possible, he picked up the gravy-soaked piece of meat with his left, and began tearing off bite-sized pieces with his teeth.

"One bread for your pudding?" a voice called out from the upper bunk.

"No way," Bert answered back. "Two breads with butter."

"Fine," the young inmate relented, passing down both his slices of white bread with the two tabs of margarine in exchange for a half cup of chocolate pudding.

After coming down cold turkey off crystal methamphetamine, the kid's body was deep in the throes of a glucose craving, and if he wasn't puking out his guts all over the cell floor, he was begging for extra food. He'd trade anything he had for a dose of sugar in any form—so two pieces of bread actually seemed a small price for a disposable Styrofoam cup of instant pudding.

Bert wrapped his extra bread snack in clean toilet paper, rose from his lower bunk, and took the three steps to his cell door. Lunch was over, and it was time to return his tray. Forced to stand in line as the guards counted to make sure all plates and plastic cutlery were accounted for, Bert's eyes never left the stain patterns on the concrete floor.

This was Bert's life now, and it would follow this exact pattern for the remainder of his days, as would Miranda's.

"Mom, Dad, we've got another letter from the Bullers," Camille shouted as she raced into the house.

"Did Stacey make the track team?" Ed patiently waited for his daughter to tear open the letter.

"She did, and they'll be posting some pictures on their website with a link to the Special Olympics Foundation."

"If she ever makes the Olympic Team, I'm going to see her run," Camille solemnly vowed.

"We all will," Tammy enthusiastically agreed. "Now pass the letter over here. I want to read it myself."

"How about something different? Even I'm getting a little tired of looking at this poster," the nurse cheerfully announced to her patient. "I brought a few different ones for you to choose from. Do you like this?" she held up a glossy print of a tropical rainforest.

Blinking her response of no, Miranda waited for the next poster to be unveiled.

"Me neither," she nodded her head in agreement. "Let me show you one of my favorites," the nurse quickly snapped her wrists to unroll the large print. "It's not the usual *calm the nerves* kind of picture we'd hang here on a hospital wall, but it just kind of spoke to me. What do you think?"

Miranda's eyes scanned the photograph from top to bottom, soaking in the rich colors of the New York Street.

"I loved it the minute I spotted it. Look at all the faces," she pointed out a few of the men and women caught on film. "They all have such different expressions, everyone rushing off in one direction or another."

Blinking a repeated reply of yes, Miranda watched as the print was taped up on the wall at the foot of her bed.

"You excited about your therapy?" the nurse turned to brush her patient's hair gently. "I heard the doctor say you were going to start working at strengthening your breathing so in the not too distant future, you might be able to operate an alphabetized breath-board for communication.

Miranda blinked the word *yes* a second time, utilizing fifty percent of her present vocabulary.

Packing up the last of his belongings, Steven marked all the boxes with his full name. The real estate agent would be showing the property to a handful of potential buyers this evening, and he'd promised to be moved out before they walked through the house.

"These too?" the movers asked.

"No, they're mine," Steven walked over to the small pile. "Don't load anything with my name on it," he pointed to the few scattered boxes with felt marker emblazed on the top.

Tired of watching the three hired men stuff all of Olga's furniture into their moving truck, he made his way to the back bedroom to check his closet one last time.

"Steven, you back there?" a man's voice echoed through the empty house.

"I'll be right out," he called back, stepping out of his bedroom before closing the door for the last time.

"All your boxes marked, son?" John asked, casually swinging open the fridge in the slight hope there'd be a forgotten can of soda hiding somewhere along the back wall.

"All marked," he forced himself to nod and smile. "It's real nice of you and Mae to hang on to my stuff down at the trailer park while I'm gone."

"It's the least we can do. Besides, Mae would tan my hide if she figured you'd paid good money to store your boxes in someone else's garage."

With three trips to John's car, all of Steven's belongs were safely stowed.

"Any idea how long you're gonna be?" John asked, casually leaning on the *For Sale* sign.

"Best I can promise is to call now and then. I don't know exactly where I'm gonna look, but I'm gonna start in Arizona, and I'm gonna hit every bingo hall 'til someone recognizes a picture of my mom. And then maybe, I'll find some information about Monica."

"You think your sister is still alive?" John couldn't help but ask.

"I'm not sure, but I have to find out," Steven stepped forward to shake his hand.

John ignored the boy's motion, and instead threw his arms around his shoulders and embraced him in a big old bear hug. "Mae said to remind you that you can come back and stay with us whenever you're done with your searching," John passed along the message.

Steven nodded his thanks, standing back to wave goodbye as his old neighbor slowly pulled away from the front curb. Then, without turning back to face the empty house, he picked his duffle bag up off the front lawn and began slowly making his own way down the street.

After carefully arranging the teacups and saucers near the plate of tea biscuits, Martin checked his tray one last time. Confident that he hadn't forgotten anything, he began making his way up to the second story.

"Knock, knock," he gently called out. "I've brought tea."

"Cuuu… mmm," a mumbled voice struggled to answer.

"Earl Grey, Helen's favorite," Martin reminded Olga. "I thought that since she was stopping by for a visit, we'd honor her."

"That's nice," Olga replied, her words phonetically sounding more like *thasss… lice.*

Momentarily caught off guard by the chiming of his doorbell, Martin excused himself to answer the front door.

He welcomed Olga's old neighbor into his house, and graciously thanked Helen for taking the time to visit, before ushering her up the curved staircase.

"How's she been?" she asked as they slowly made the climb.

"Well," Martin stopped and turned halfway up the stairs, "it's time for another procedure, and you know how she hates those."

"And if you didn't remove them?"

"I'm not sure long term what the results would be, but short term, within a month, she wouldn't be able to sleep comfortably, or even balance the weight of her head. I'd be forced to mount her skull in halo traction just to support its growing weight."

"Do you need me to assist?" Helen offered her services.

"Thank you. I appreciate that," Martin solemnly nodded his head. "So how about tea, I've already served the tray?"

They continued their remaining steps in silence, Helen the first to step into Olga's bedroom.

It had been only a week and a half since her last visit, but the fleshy protrusions jutting out from every angle of Olga's head had at least doubled in size. The first and foremost adorning the right frontal lobe now appeared to be the size of a child's fist, knotted and bumpy, as if filled with rocks or marbles. An odd strand of reddish brown hair hung off the sides of the protrusion, and every time Olga pivoted her neck, the hairs swished back and forth across her line of sight.

"Hello Olga," Helen cheerfully greeted her. "I've come for tea."

"Helll… lllooo," she slowly returned the greeting.

"You have a chance to catch some TV last night? They were making spicy vegetarian lasagna on some cooking show, and I couldn't help but think of you."

"Nee… nee… neess mee… meettt," Olga reminded her friend as Martin quickly stepped forward to tuck a napkin in at Olga's collar while discreetly wiping the drool running down the front of her chin.

"Yes, it needs meat," Martin lovingly clarified her last statement.

As Helen reached forward to pour the tea, she almost jumped out of her chair when one of the longer tissue masses jutting out from behind Olga's right ear began to twitch up and down.

"It appears to have developed some form of rudimentary joint," Martin took a deep breath and unconsciously rubbed his forehead. "Now you see why I want to surgically remove them all again as soon as possible."

Watching Olga painfully lean her head back on the padded chair, Helen realized for the first time just how much pressure the added weight of the multiple growths might actually bear down on her weakened neck muscles.

"Teeee," Olga still managed to request from her semi-reclined position.

To respond to her wish, as he'd done since the day he'd signed her out of the hospital into his own care, Martin stepped forward, inserted a plastic straw into the lukewarm liquid, and raised the cup to Olga's lips.

"As far as I can tell, the growths are still confined and not spreading," the retired doctor announced upon returning to his own chair. "They all seem to originate and protrude from the surgical incisions in her skull and right ear."

"Skkk... kullll. Skkk... kullll" Olga repeated in her monotone voice as if amused with the very sound of the word.

"And her speech? Do you notice any improvement?" Helen inquired, forcing herself to sip the tea as her stomach continued to churn.

"No measurable change, however, her agitation levels have been measurably lower. It seemed to help considerably when I removed the wall and dresser mirrors, and covered the glass windowpanes with dark shades. Without any distinguishable reflections, she appears much more subdued and content with her surroundings."

"Teee..." Olga called out again, exerting all her expendable energy to turn her head and focus on their guest.

"Let me," Helen offered, rising from her chair and reaching for Olga's cup. "You look exhausted Martin. When's the last time you slept a solid five or six hours?"

As if oblivious to Helen's well-meaning question, Martin continued with his train of thought. "Without the need for any tranquilization, I've also found that Olga hasn't been as bothered by the repeated bowel problems she was plagued with last week," he stated matter of factly, as if discussing a patient's medical chart, not the condition of his beloved fiancé.

"Any new theories on the origin of the growths?" Helen casually threw the question out.

"Well, I've established that Steven had used a multitude of unidentified tissue donors, possibly as high as a half a dozen in his last batch of healing powder. It seems that the combination of donors is somehow toxic, and the manifestation of protruding tissue growth is spurred on by the mingling of the regenerative powder in her open wounds."

"Still nothing really new," Helen nodded her head, deciding to try her luck with one of the delicate tea biscuits her host had served.

"Not exactly true," Martin chirped up. "Regarding Olga's mental state, I'm quite sure the diminished capacity can be connected to the rejuvenation of her brain tissue. As the tissue healed at an extremely accelerated rate, the new growth has somehow altered her neural pathways. Unfortunately, I can't be sure without proper testing, and you know the hospital's policy."

"You don't exist," Helen recited the company line.

"So here we are," Martin slowly stood up for the hundredth time that day and moved across the floor to untie the napkin hanging down from Olga's neck. "We spend a lot of our time watching television. She really loves cooking shows," Martin peered off toward the darkened window. "But anything longer than a half hour and her interest wanes."

"Well, I guess it's time I said my goodbyes," Helen announced, rising to her feet. Reaching toward the heavily padded chair, she gently lifted Olga's left hand off the armrest, lovingly stroking her fingers in a gesture of compassion. She suddenly noticed that Martin had added a simple gold wedding band behind the beautiful diamond engagement ring she'd been wearing since leaving the hospital. Doris raised her face toward Martin in anticipation of the forthcoming explanation.

"She'd never be comfortable living in sin," Martin teased, "So last Sunday I read out a set of wedding vows from the Bible, and we took each other in marriage," he gently explained.

"God bless you both," Helen offered before turning to leave. "Call me when you want to set up the next procedure."

"I will." Martin escorted his guest down the stairs to the front door. He squinted at the late afternoon sunshine since it seemed to burn his sensitive eyes, and blindly waved goodbye before closing and then locking the door on the outside world.

The End

If you have enjoyed reading THE HEALING POWDER by Lynne Martin, I'm confident you will also enjoy her other two novels CURES FOR CASH, and READY, SET, ACTION!

Disgraced physician and social pariah Dr. Marcus Clifford has resigned himself to continuing on with the legacy of his family's underground medical clinic. Unexpectedly willed to him upon his uncle's death, *The Changeroom* was an unwanted gift that not only cost him his marriage, but his prominent medical career. Now destined to complete his life's work in the bowels of society, Dr. Clifford treats the uninsured and the downtrodden of his neighbourhood. (This is Adult Fiction with some graphic sexual content and descriptive medical procedures.)

In this raw, gritty tale that exposes a dark and realistic glimpse into the porn industry, only time will tell if Julia Giovanni, a headstrong entrepreneur, can rescue her company---and all those she loves---before it is too late. An extremely graphic look into the lives of pornographers, their clientele, and the prevalent drug use surrounding the industry. (This is Adult Fiction with some graphic sexual content and illegal drug use.)

Lynne Martin is an avid movie collector, an animal lover, and a staunch supporter of sexual education. She currently resides in Alberta, Canada, with her husband and their large extended family.

To learn more about LYNNE MARTIN, or to leave her a personal message, she can be reached through her website and blog @ www.lynnemartinbooks.com

CPSIA information can be obtained at www.ICGtesting.com
Printed in the USA
LVOW090009270612

287768LV00001B/21/P

9 781475 923117